The Disappearance of Lilya Bekirova

The Disappearance of Lilya Bekirova

A Novel of the Supernatural

Michelle D. Dixon

iUniverse, Inc.
New York Lincoln Shanghai

The Disappearance of Lilya Bekirova
A Novel of the Supernatural

Copyright © 2007 by Michelle D. Dixon

All rights reserved. No part of this book may be used or reproduced by any means, graphic, electronic, or mechanical, including photocopying, recording, taping or by any information storage retrieval system without the written permission of the publisher except in the case of brief quotations embodied in critical articles and reviews.

iUniverse books may be ordered through booksellers or by contacting:

iUniverse
2021 Pine Lake Road, Suite 100
Lincoln, NE 68512
www.iuniverse.com
1-800-Authors (1-800-288-4677)

This is a work of fiction. All of the characters, names, incidents, organizations, and dialogue in this novel are either the products of the author's imagination or are used fictitiously.

ISBN: 978-0-595-42549-5 (pbk)
ISBN: 978-0-595-86877-3 (ebk)

Printed in the United States of America

For Jonathan

Acknowledgments

I am indebted to my first and best critical readers, without whose editorial insight I would never have shown this novel to anyone else. I am in awe of my husband Jonathan's analytical, logical mind, specifically his ability to pick up on the slightest inconsistency or lack of clarity. The red chicken-scratch of his editorial commentary has—in addition to causing me some trepidation—made a tremendous positive difference to this novel. My gratitude goes also to Rowan McAuley, a talented writer and dear friend whose psychological insight and literary savvy guided me in rounding out my characters.

Thanks are also due to Christine Cohen at the Virginia Kidd Agency for her editorial insight into this novel, and to Nanci McCloskey at Virginia Kidd, who was the first person in the publishing industry to give me the confidence to pursue my writing career. Finally, the consultants and editors at iUniverse have impressed me with their professionalism and the quality of their services, and I am grateful for their help.

Over the years friends and family have quietly and resolutely believed in my future as a novelist in the face of the seeming inertia of my career, and to them, collectively, I must express my gratitude. In particular, my parents, Babette and David Broussard, have always taken for granted that I would publish my books—they saw inevitable success where I saw only interminable delay! Thank you also to the "dreamgirls," my fellow explorers in the shadow realm of the psyche: Jan Scott, our fearless High Priestess, and Jannah Morgan Brown, Anne Marcellino, and Renée Murphy. Together we have learned how the mystical coexists with the mundane, and my novel is richer for it. They may have seen signs and omens of my publishing success, but in the end, their friendship was all I needed to believe in myself.

People often say that one of the hardest aspects of being a writer is the isolation—working away in solitude for hours on end. As the full-time mother of two small, active children, I cannot imagine anything I crave more than the quietude of being utterly alone with my thoughts! Far more difficult for me is that writing is always a vocation but not necessarily a career: there is no guarantee of income, no structure for promotion or career advancement, and no regular feedback on one's performance. Without the unwavering support of my husband—financial, emotional, and practical—I simply could not go on writing despite the immense satisfaction of seeing my creations come to life on the page. Thus to you, Jonathan, I must express my final and biggest *thank you*.

1

The day my mother died I thought I saw Victor Tehusa in our garden. He stood next to the wisteria that ran along the fence separating our backyards, in a cloud of pink blossoms, two brightly colored butterflies circling his head. It was a typical sight. Victor was, he once told me, "the caller of butterflies," and he did seem to have some kind of aura that drew them to him. If it were the right season he could just hold up his hands, smile into the sky, and butterflies would come to him as if he wore nectar. They would land, two and three at a time on his fingertips and forearms.

That day I thought I saw him when I pulled into our driveway, but Victor Tehusa had died five years earlier and I do not believe in ghosts or anything else otherworldly.

Fact must be separated from fabrication, objective truth from illusion. My childhood violin teacher, Patrice, said that the greatest lesson to be learned from Yehudi Menuhin, lest I be tempted into fanciful flights by his performance of Bartók's Solo Sonata, was *technical mastery*. I had not yet heard Menuhin play—I had no interest in the violin at all. When I was eight, my mother had hired Patrice to instill in me a precocious talent in music. After having been his pupil for two months I could already repeat his homilies verbatim. "Talent is following the rules with absolute precision," he would say, as if music were calculus and musicians mathematicians. "A musician's brilliance is the ability to apply established principles in a previously untried way." Untried? As in extra-fast allegro or super-slow adagio? It seemed that he did not believe in the Muses, only cold, hard dedication. I asked him once if his theories held true for the creators of music, composers. He did not respond. If memory serves, he shrugged and pouted.

So before I ever picked up the bow, I was made to practice, over and over again, by singing a page of musical notes as he rapped out time, until my fingers found the correct spot on the violin, pressing against the strings, my eyes closed. I could wax my bow, tighten it to perfect tautness, and tune my instrument before I ever played a single note. And when I finally drew the bow across the strings to make a mighty, rusty squeak, I knew within seconds what I had done wrong and proceeded within minutes to produce a smooth, resonant E major, followed by the beginnings of the William Tell Overture. That's right. As in *The Lone Ranger*.

It might have seemed to anyone else that I had talent. To Patrice I was only a reverential pupil.

I almost adopted his view of talent, until I discovered my mother's recording of Menuhin playing Beethoven's Violin Concerto. No amount of dedication could make music such as his. Not just any person could coax an instrument into creating magic. Menuhin could bring the dead to life with his playing. The fact was, he had a talent that no amount of practice could instill in me.

Fact must be distinguished from illusion. Patrice and my mother did nicely illustrate how merrily illusion can go around masquerading as reality.

Illusion: Patrice was utterly dedicated to my musical development.

Fact: Patrice had lustful designs on my mother.

Reality check: 4:00 PM. I was supposed to be at my best friend Elisa's after school, but we had decided to come to my house instead, because I had a cabbage patch doll and Elisa didn't. The doll was crucial to our play.

We passed my mother's room on the way to mine. I heard squeaking, so I paused. The door was cracked open. I had a view of the fireplace, and the mirror above it. In the mirror was a reflection of the four posters of my mother's bed. They were moving, kind of like a string that had been plucked—quivering, just a bit.

My eyes strained to see the action properly, but my brain had no trouble recognizing what I was seeing. I knew what was happening. I had seen this kind of thing before. Still, I was only eight. I hoped that one day my mother would turn into June from *Leave it to Beaver*.

I saw a head full of dark, curly hair; it bounced up into view, down out of view, up, down. I stared at the mirror, mesmerized by the head's appearance and disappearance. Elisa, who was behind me, came to my side, put a hand on my shoulder, and innocently whispered, "Catherine, does your mother jump on her bed?" Then she giggled. No one heard her. The four-poster movement did not cease. I poked my head around the door. I had a terrible compulsion to know who was with my mother. I saw her arms, pink, her long legs the same, all four limbs wrapped around a back, her head buried in a shoulder. I could not see his face, but I recognized his voice. Patrice, my instructor in understanding talent, groaned, "Oh what a talented woman you are, Susan."

"Yuck," I thought. Talent, huh? This was hardly applying established principles in a previously untried way. My mother had applied them in this sitting-up way, in the on-the-stomach way, in the on-the-side way, in the up-against-the-washing-machine way and in God-knows-how-many-other ways.

Figured that he was after her. Men always were. She'd have slept with any of them. Well, not everyone, but a damned whole lot of them.

Elisa had just peeped around my peeping head. She squealed. I thought, "No doubt she's from a normal family and her mother doesn't have sex." That's what I thought normal was.

"Patrice," I whispered, too late, for Elisa's squeal had drawn attention—the bed and its occupants had gone silent. I took Elisa's hand and we tiptoed a few steps away; then, when the sounds resumed, we took off down the hall, into safety.

I had learned not to interrupt. My mother could be wrathful when she was interrupted.

My grandmother, or as my mother and I have always called her, Natasha—let herself in the front door, just as Elisa and I burst into the living room, panting from our mad dash.

"What is the rush?" Natasha asked. "Why are you both blushing?"

"Patrice!" Elisa gasped.

"That bastard!" I added (my mother's favorite expletive).

"Catherine!" Natasha reprimanded.

"Why are you here?" I asked her. She had the key but almost never let herself in.

"I left my book here yesterday. I called and there was no answer, so I just came to get it."

Just then my mother screamed.

Natasha jumped, just slightly. Then, "Oh! Oh. I see," she said.

We stood, Elisa, Natasha, and I, frozen to the spot. I was uncomfortable.

"She is with Patrice," I explained, and something went *thump*, like someone was hitting the wall. Then it became louder. The bedposts against the wall? Patrice's head? The thumping was quite rhythmic. I could see half notes one after the other, could hear the trombone's sonorous groan and the off-key violin's faint wail.

"He is my violin teacher," I said. "He knows all about talent."

Natasha replied, "Your mother always was a patron of the arts."

It was true; she was a patron of the arts. Not because she went to New York to hear the symphony and to see plays, or because she organized local productions of Shakespeare, or because she helped fundraise to bring the youngest Bulgarian opera singer of his time to the suburbs. She was a patron of the arts because she was a patron of artists. Arty types really turned her on. She loved to be involved with young, undiscovered talent, men with great skill and short resumes, men who had an air of desperation. She loved introducing them to the players, pouring their champagne at their first exhibition, sending them flowers onstage at their first big concert, making them Irish coffee in the morning after a late night out. And when their desperation turned to hope, and their feet left the ground to climb ladders, my mother told them to fly away and not come back, and she did it with a smile.

Radomil Davidoff, the Bulgarian opera singer, was her beau of one whole year. Patrice lasted a month, after which he stopped instructing me as well. He had lust, but not for his own artistic success—which just didn't do it for her, even if it did put a slightly bigger than hairline crack in one of the bed's posts. I asked my mother if Patrice had done it. She said yes, and then explained a few things. She must have thought I was finally old enough for the truth, even though I'd caught her having sex more than a few times and knew that she was a seductress. I just hadn't known what her motivation was. She told me that day how she liked to help young artists but only if they wanted to help themselves, and that Patrice simply did not have the ambition, though he had talent—at which point she blushed. I had also read my mother's copy of *The Joy of Sex* by this time so I understood that skill played an important role in sexual encounters. I put two and two together and understood that my mother enjoyed sex with ambitious, promising young artists (although I didn't understand any more than that for some years). I don't know why my mother felt it necessary to confess even more to me about her artistic promiscuity, but she must have. Patrice was not the only one creating illusions. Illusion, it turns out, had almost bamboozled me again.

Fact: My mother never really cared that I learn to play the violin. She had hired Patrice in the first place because when she met him at a party (of their mutual painter friend who had five years earlier been unknown—before he had had sex with my mother), he told her he was only teaching music until his career took off.

You can bet this whole business of discerning fact from fancy was imprinted onto my subconscious. My mother's revelations did influence me to watch people like a detective, of course, but then again my search for objectivity surfaces in most everything I do. That is to say, I have always been analytical, and if the illusion of music-making that disguised Patrice and my mother's merrymaking had any influence at all, it was to make me aware of how an onlooker can so easily fall prey to believing what she sees.

I was a very serious student, a bit overzealous perhaps; I was never the teacher's pet so much as the good student who always had a hand in the air. I always wrote too much by way of explanation, be it analyzing literature or drawing conclusions about a scientific experiment. It was a natural progression to tertiary study. That I furthered my studies in history was more coincidence than progression. True, my academic proclivities were more in the way of reading and writing than experimentation, but the more decisive factor was that when I was a sophomore in college I had a particularly good history professor who brought the past to life.

Now, many years later, with a bachelor's and two master's degrees to my name, I am finally writing my thesis, "Decisive Battles of the Twentieth Century: Truth versus Propaganda." It concerns how so-called "decisive" battles are remembered by history. Are they decisive, in retrospect, because their tangible military effects changed the course of a war, or because they were made into symbols for the purpose of propaganda? I have been accused of treading on hallowed cultural ground, which is often the case, but I owe no apologies. I am searching for truth.

Disentangling fact from fiction has, more or less, become the sole occupation of my day-to-day life. It is essentially the only career I have. It is satisfying to have honed my skills for detecting the signs of deception and illusion, and I usually enjoy it—although, truth be told, I've become bored with my thesis. Actually, I don't really know anymore why I wanted to have a PhD in the first place. I should keeping working toward it, seeing as I've come this far, but I can't seem to get any work done.

Still, there are things that cry out for an explanation. Things that do not belong in my thesis. Normally I wouldn't have time for outside interests, but it seems that lately I have nothing but time. Procrastination will do that—make time when there isn't any.

Fact: There were fifty-three surviving men in the 21st U.S. Airborne Division of the United States Army on August 10, 1944. A week earlier there had been five hundred and sixty-five men. Some had been shot down over the Pacific; others, who parachuted out alive, were killed upon landing; many were later classified as missing in action. One day, during a sortie into enemy airspace, all fifty-three surviving men and their aircraft disappeared without a trace. Various eyewitnesses claimed to have seen the aircraft fade into thin air. Neither the aircraft nor the men of the 21st Airborne have ever been found.

Illusion: The men and planes of the 21st Airborne disappeared into another dimension, into a distortion in the space-time continuum. They are in the past or the future, or on another planet, or in some other kind of reality.

Fact: All living things have electromagnetic fields, including humans. The Earth has an electromagnetic field of roughly seven hertz. Different locations have slightly varying measurements. Scientists refer to some places with particularly high or low electromagnetic radiation as "geophysical anomalies." During certain types of weather the electromagnetic field alters, such as during a thunderstorm, or just before an earthquake. There is speculation that animals can sense shifts in electromagnetic frequency—variations might be uncomfortable for them, or perhaps they simply know that a change signifies natural disaster. The ability of animals to sense a shift in the electromagnetic field might explain why they often behave erratically just prior to climatic or seismic events. Various unexplained events have been reported as happening in places rumored to have electromagnetic distortions, but precise measurements of hertz in those areas, and convincing descriptions of those events, have not been documented by the scientific establishment.

Illusion: In places of unusually high or low electromagnetic energy, supernatural events are more common. Time travel is possible in these places, as is travel to other locations and dimensions.

I once asked my advisor, Dr. Upshaw, if he had heard of the disappearance of the 21st Airborne. He said he had not. That annoyed me—I'd come across references to it more than once and Dr. Upshaw was supposed to be an expert in military strategy of the two world wars. He said people just disappeared during war sometimes, that war is chaos.

Life is chaos, but when fifty-three people disappear into thin air you'd think there would be some kind of convincing explanation, if not physical evidence. I was a bit grumpy with Dr. Upshaw for the rest of our meeting that day.

The next time we met he asked me if I was depressed. This was before there was any reason to be, when my mother was bouncing from one gallery to the next to see Eduardo one day and Laurent the next, when I had a boyfriend, when I had written three chapters in six months and seemed to be on a roll. I told him that I was just like that, that I was not the bubbly type. It was the closest we ever got to a personal conversation.

Fact: My mother was irritatingly cheerful. She always had a smile on her face. Nothing seemed to upset her much. Her oncologist even took me aside one day at the hospital and asked me if she was in denial. He said that she was the most cheerful dying person he'd ever seen. I told him she was just like that. At the funeral he said a few words about it. "Susan has become my inspiration," he said, or some such thing.

I have been avoiding a particular spot in my backyard. It is roughly between the wisteria and the oak tree, and you have to go through it to get to the pond. There is nothing there, just grass like everywhere else, but it feels strange to me. I get lightheaded when I'm there. I have found five dead birds there in the past year. Two times I have seen lightning strike the ground there during thunderstorms.

I have had the same feeling elsewhere. At summer camp when I was ten, we went canoeing on the lake. There was one area of the lake, near a bank, under some trees, and whenever we paddled toward the area I would get chills up and down my arms and legs. We had no reason to go near there—we never paddled around with a particular destination in mind. It's just that a few times when the other girls in my canoe headed in that direction, I couldn't explain why I wanted them to turn around, so I would just say with sudden enthusiasm, "Look! Over there! I saw a deer! Let's go that way!"—and we would, but not before, on two occasions, we had gotten too close, so close that my hair stood up on end. On one of those occasions I saw a dead fox half in and half out the water, as if tethered to the bank on purpose, just so I, and I alone, could see it.

And there was another place, near Paris. I was there with my mother at the funeral of a musician friend when I was sixteen. After the burial service we drove to a country house where we held a wake. It was a loud, happy affair, with vast quantities of wine, numerous speeches, and much dancing everywhere—except, I noticed, around the gazebo behind house. For some reason, the gazebo appeared to be invisibly cordoned off, despite the table inside laden with wine and hors d'oeuvres. I watched guests walk right up to the gazebo, see the table and its untouched offerings, and then wander away for no discernible reason. I was curious, so I dashed inside to take some Camembert and grapes, ignoring as I did so the rush of goosebumps and an onset of dizziness. When I stumbled out, hand to forehead, vision swimming, an elderly gentleman took my arm and asked me if I was okay—"Ça va?" he inquired.

I told him, in English, that I was fine.

He regarded me with a look of bewilderment. I think he was drunk; I also think he didn't believe that I was okay but instead must be overwrought with sorrow. He said, in heavily accented English, "Do not worry about François" (the deceased musician). "His world is better than ours. He," the old man pointed toward the sky, "has transcended."

"That," I thought, "is bullshit. He is dead, food for the worms, memories for the rest of us."

I haven't yet gotten to the bottom of the disappearing soldiers. It's become something of a hobby, trying to find more information about what happened. My theory is that there might be some instability in the electromagnetic field that causes dizziness and affects magnetic mechanisms such as compasses, both of which could have made the pilots of the 21st Airborne crash into the sea. I have found a few scientific papers describing the possible effects of electromagnetic fields. In contrast, I have found nothing to add to my thesis for over a year. Technically it was due two years ago.

I haven't spoken to my advisor in exactly six months. The last time he called, he said that he was very sorry to hear about my mother's illness and that I should submit a leave of absence and apply for an extension, which I did.

He is under the illusion that I just need some time off, that I will one day finish.

Fact: Yehudi Menuhin lost his touch. In his fourth decade, a time when most musicians achieve their peak performances, his magic began to wane. He wrote in his memoirs of his decline: "Intuition was no longer to be relied on; the intellect would have to replace it."

Fact: My mother died exactly two months ago Friday. Her ashes have been dispersed in two places: in Venice, in the canals—God knows why, probably some artistic connection—and in our backyard. I was supposed to sprinkle her ashes into the pond myself, but I asked Natasha to do it instead. My cat refuses to go in the area between the wisteria and the oak tree, even when I put her food there and she hasn't eaten in two days, so I don't see why I should go there either.

Illusion: Time will heal all wounds. Dead people "transcend." Victor Tehusa was standing in the garden on the day my mother died.

2

Should a natural disaster occur I am capable of getting myself, my cat, and my dearest possessions to safety at a moment's notice. I have never personally experienced a natural disaster, for which reason I freely admit that I am being paranoid (that is, I admit this to myself; no one else knows about my fear). In the wee hours of the morning when I lie in bed, unable to sleep, I can almost hear the whine of a tornado rushing toward my home, or feel the floorboards quake as fault lines shift. Speculation turns to panic as in my imagination I pack and repack, never finding the right things, or the right bags to put them in, always discovering forgotten valuables in closets but not being able to squeeze them into my overfull bags. In the midst of my frenzy I watch, horrified, as my car spins into the air or my neighbor's house is swallowed up by the earth. The worst part is that I have forgotten the most important thing, though for the life of me I can't remember what that thing is.

As a result of this anxiety I have devised an escape plan. The carry box for my cat Pinky is always next to the front door; conveniently, she sometimes sleeps in it. My suitcases and bags are all stored in the front closet with the coats. In one bag I keep my most valuable possessions: the family photo album (one of several, but the one I've chosen covers the most years, and I've put my favorites in it), some jewelry, my grandfather's watch and chain, and a stone I found on the beach in Yugoslavia when I was seventeen. In another bag I keep practical items: a first-aid kit, cans of cat food, cans of food for me (replaced regularly to keep fresh), a can opener, a mini-picnic kit that comes with plates and cutlery, two large bottles of water, a flashlight, a blanket, two pairs of underwear and socks, and pens and a notebook. I know exactly which additional items I would take with me in a hurry (such as a good novel, or a box of chocolate), the precise whereabouts of each item, and the order in which I would traverse the rooms of my house gathering them.

I blame my anxiety and the obsessive planning that comes with it on insomnia, but I feel that I am managing well—after all, I *am* fully prepared to escape with my most vital worldly goods. That consoles me, and once I am consoled, eventually I fall asleep.

I wonder if I am eccentric, and if so, if this is a recent development. I don't remember always being like this. It must be the years of academia. I once met an astrologer at a dinner party who spoke of a client whose life took place in one institution after another. She said, among other things, that institutional structures imprint the subconscious mind as much as they influence the external environment, that one can become dependent on the routine and values of an institution and cease to function normally outside it. From her descriptions I assumed she was referring to mental hospitals, and I asked an innocent question. But no, she clarified, she meant academic institutions—and this woman, this disconcertingly articulate woman dressed like a nun, asked me if it sounded familiar.

"You mean mental hospitals?" I joked. "Or universities?"

She was the only nonacademic in the room. I could not believe that she could silence a table full of academics. Everyone looked at me; they were humorless.

I said, "There are similarities, I guess."

Frida, a German psychologist (who, I found out later, had invited the astrologer), made a joke about those similarities. We all laughed. Edgar, my then-boyfriend, who was planning on leaving academia for good, laughed loudest. But I was far from amused. I felt like some visible evidence of my mental state had singled me out, and I spent the rest of the evening trying to figure out what it was.

So my mind is fixated, a victim of its own inertia—inertia, I surmise, born of boredom and melancholy. I don't like to think it's grief, but probably it is. More evidence of my possible eccentricity: I am not doing anything the least bit useful. My thesis has finished its slow journey to obscurity and is off the hard drive, having migrated to a floppy disk now wedged somewhere in the back of my desk drawer. I wonder if my interest in finding truth in the face of deception has been misdirected all along—that this intellectual preoccupation is merely the way I think, and cannot possibly form the basis of an academic career. I wonder if I have ever really been interested in history.

I have this feeling, lately intensifying, that I have completely missed the point of my own life, and that feeling is accompanied by mild despair—what if there is no point?

At least I have something to do that is free of professional expectation, a hobby I never intend to make a vocation. For the past week and a half I have been searching the Internet for information on fault lines in the Pacific Ocean, and before that, on fault lines in general. I began this research a year and a half ago, but in the past six months it has become all-consuming. On top of my desk next to my computer is a small stack of manila folders, which are filled with articles on electromagnetism, earthquakes, and supposed supernatural phenomena. When I am being my more rational self it strikes me that perhaps this is all madness, yet I carry on. It intrigues me. And it gets me through most days without a thought about anything else.

I should—although of course I don't—look forward to my weekly visits with Natasha, at the very least because I get out of the house for the afternoon (and I'm not counting when I swap my desk at home for one in the library). The hour-long drive to Natasha's retirement village is invariably therapeutic, particularly in the spring, when everything is green and flowering, or autumn, when the trees are red and gold. Now it is August and the grass is brittle and brown. I drive past pastures and grazing cattle, winding up and down hills, passing an abandoned farmhouse or two, a ramshackle shed with a car decaying out front, bucolic scenery far removed from my suburban life. I often wonder what this land would have looked like before highways and billboards. Inhospitable is my guess. It is best experienced like this: the open windows letting in the smell of warm, dry earth, the scenery passing by at seventy miles an hour, seen but not inhabited.

After the turnoff to Crest Hill Road, at the end of which is Crest Hill Retirement Village, the road is narrower, the pavement older and bumpier. There are barbed wire fences on either side, cows grazing behind them, some horses further along. Natasha lives two hours and a world away from New York City. Within a ten-mile radius there are only gas stations, fast-food restaurants, pasture and a sky full of visible stars. From Crest Hill Road you have to go twenty-five miles to a sit-down restaurant, the closest of which is Denny's. The "villagers" (as Natasha calls them) are taken there on the occasional field trip, large groups of death-defying old people who order pancakes and hamburgers which they wash down with coffee, PeptoBismol and their blood pressure tablets. Natasha refuses to go along. She says she would prefer visiting the Crest Hill Stables down the road, where you can go horseback riding for ten dollars an hour, but she claims a lack of stamina. This is true enough, but I suspect she'd rather fall off a horse than suffer the company of her fellow villagers.

Other than disliking, to a person, all of the people who live there, Natasha has few other complaints about her place of residence. The Crest Hill Retirement Village is comfortable enough. The five-story building curves around the circular driveway, a wing extending from each side. As you approach you can see through the glass doors to the receptionist. As if the place were a holiday resort, all the rooms have small balconies in the back, overlooking a swimming pool that is open from Memorial Day to Labor Day. Natasha complains that all summer long you can hear the sound of splashing and smell the suntan oil wafting up from below. She never understood why my mother loved to sit in the backyard in her string bikini; she understands even less why old people with their wrinkly, spotted skin (her words) should enjoy it, too. She believes sunbathing is vulgar. For fun she sometimes sprays the offending tanners with her hose while watering the plants on her balcony. I don't think Natasha is particularly liked by her fellow residents, and I think that is the one thing she likes about them.

What I don't like about Crest Hill is, first, the smell (high school cafeteria), and, second, the Musak—inevitably a rendition of something by Michael Jackson. Finally, along the fourth-floor corridor toward Natasha's door, there is the artwork. Prints of quiet landscapes, the occasional still life with a dead animal, and *several* of Monet's famed Haystack series. Five or six pictures of a pile of hay, identical but for the colors and mood. Apparently Monet painted more than twenty of these haystacks, a supposedly brilliant study of light and atmosphere. Personally, I think being confronted by such lifeless images is the equivalent of a cocktail of sedatives and beta blockers. The haystacks could induce a coma if looked at for too long—and in a retirement home? Is it the intention of the administration that its charges be led down this corridor to an early death? My grandmother has lived here for a year and a half and I visit her weekly. There hasn't been a time when I have not imagined inserting a tape of Led Zeppelin into the lobby sound system, lighting incense at the front desk, and replacing the artwork with something by Robert Mapplethorpe—anything would do as long as it included large penises. Each time I visit, my imaginary act of rebellion livens me up just in time to deal with Natasha, which is a good thing. She demands a certain amount of energy.

Today her door is open so I walk in. The first thing I do is relocate her Peace Lily to the far corner of the living room, near the sliding glass door but out of the light. "A lily will not thrive in direct sunlight," I remind her. I look around but Natasha is nowhere to be seen.

"Here I am," she says; I turn to find her on hands and knees just behind the opened door. She is clutching a towel and seems surprised to see me.

"I almost bumped into you!" I exclaim, shutting the door behind us. She scoots forward and stuffs the towel into the crack beneath the door.

"Just a precaution," she replies. "Can you help me up? Getting up is not so easy as getting down."

I lift her slight frame upright as if she were a doll. She asks me to open the window for her, then offers me a hot drink. I decline by reminding her that it is already 85 degrees outside; she should be drinking iced coffee.

"Oh no," she responds, wagging her finger as she walks toward the kitchen, "I always have coffee or tea. Anyway, with this air conditioning you'd never know it was summer. Except for that racket out there—" referring to the splashing outside. The heat begins to seep into her apartment along with the noise. I am guessing she asked me to open the window so that she could smoke.

She puts the kettle on and motions me toward the table just outside of the kitchen. A long dining table and a wall-to-wall cabinet with shelves and drawers serves to mark this side of the room as the dining room. The arrangement of couches and an armchair separates it from the living room a few feet away. I wait for her to sit down, but she doesn't.

"We'll just wait for it to boil and then we'll have lunch," she says, clasping her hands before her on the table. She is bright and alert today. She pats her pocket on the front of her shirt, then her skirt pocket. Her eyes widen and she reaches behind her ear to withdraw a cigarette. "I was just going to have one of these when you came in," she says.

I take the matches off the table and light her cigarette. I long ago gave up trying to advise her on her health, and now it seems hardly fair to deny her anything at all.

Natasha became old suddenly. It happened not when she broke her hip and had to move in with Susan and me a year and a half ago (thankfully for only six months), or when her daughter lost her battle with cancer in June, two months ago, but just last week, for no apparent reason. Her hair lightened two shades of white and her skin became a pale yellow. Deep, fleshy lines have for many years now encroached upon her eyes, which have finally been reduced to tiny slits. Spectacles for the legally blind magnify them to near-normal size; only when she took her glasses off for a clean last week did I notice how, squinting out at me, were eyes that should belong to a mole caught in daylight.

I imagine this latest acceleration in aging will not diminish her character in the least—nothing else has. She is as willful and stubborn as she has been my entire life. She refuses to quit smoking, each day managing to get through nearly a pack of cigarettes. She fears neither death nor disease. Why should she not smoke when, after all, her daughter died of breast cancer and not lung cancer although she, too, had been a smoker her entire life? And somehow, despite how crotchety she can be, Natasha manages to bewitch others into doing her bidding. Never mind the fact that smoking is against the home's regulations; Marie, the nurse who checks in on her, chooses to look the other way. Most recently, after the smoke detector in Natasha's room sent its shrieks screaming down the hallway, resulting in irate neighbors and threats of increased surveillance (and, as I found out, the first contact with her peers that she had had for nearly eight months), Marie showed her how to disable it, with the admonition that she be sure to turn it back on after each smoking session. Natasha agreed. My only explanation for Marie's complicity is that she knows my grandmother will do as she likes regardless of the consequences, and would likely make herself a nuisance if caught.

Today Natasha is wearing a sequined purple top and black pants. Her lipstick is a bright red, applied slightly outside her lip lines, and her face is powdered so much that there is a distinct beige line running from chin to ear. I feel, as usual, slightly awkward in my khaki shorts and t-shirt, as if I have dropped by a Las Vegas show on my way to go camping. Each time she inhales the smoke a bit more lipstick is transferred from her lips to the cigarette, so that by her second cigarette her lips are only red around the outside. Her white hair hangs scraggly and loose about her face; her fingers clink from her many gold rings. I sometimes wonder if her eyesight is failing her or if she is revealing a sense of humor. She sets the table, oblivious to my stare.

I have always believed that her eccentricities reflect her Russian origins. I don't know anything about Russians—then again, I don't know much about Natasha. I know that her father was a military officer posted with his family to the Ukraine just before the Second World War, that he was killed early on, and that somehow her mother managed to get her out of the Soviet Union once the war ended. She came to America via Germany and France; of her lost childhood in Russia I know nothing. However, I have ideas about her tragic Russian soul; I have read *Anna Karenina*, *The Brothers Karamazov*, and the emotionally charged poetry of Anna Akhmatova. I have drawn on these to form my impressions and explain Natasha. She is ordinary in every explicable way, so I have decided that in every inexplicable way she is Russian.

She puffs away at her cigarette and folds the napkins. The room is rapidly becoming too warm for comfort and I am ready to close the window. I hover next to it, waiting for her to finish smoking.

"How is Edgar?" she asks, out of the blue. Normally she does not ask me about myself.

"Who? Oh, yeah. We split up some time ago."

"You broke up? I hadn't heard. He was such a nice man."

"We didn't have much in common."

"No?"

"No."

She puts out her cigarette and turns on a fan. The room reeks of smoke so overwhelmingly that the fan doesn't really help. At last, she closes the window.

"Anyway," she says, "I don't want to talk about Edgar, I was just asking."

Good. There was nothing more tedious than discussing my ex-boyfriend Edgar, *homo erectus*, except actually being with him (unless we were having sex).

Natasha goes into the kitchen. She is not really a good cook, and I wonder what it is she has made for us today. Luckily, it is sandwiches, make-your-own style. She brings out plates and knives, a bag of sliced bread, a package of Muenster cheese, a jar of mayonnaise, and deli-style meat.

"Are you lonely, Catherine?" Natasha asks when she is finished setting the table.

"You're talking about Edgar, now, aren't you?"

"Well, I suppose I do have a desire for you to not be alone."

"Being on your own isn't bad," I tell her, "It's being alone when you're with someone that's bad." I catch her eye. She smiles at me. There; now that we've talked about Edgar, that should satisfy her curiosity.

But no, she is feisty today, I can see it coming. One eyebrow raised, mouth a thin, smug line. Disapproval. Natasha is good at conveying her disapproval.

"Sometimes a man and a woman have more in common than they might at first think. I am not saying you and Edgar did. But you do have very high expectations, Catherine."

She often accuses me of having high expectations. Normally I feel the heat coming off me—it really gets to me, the idea that high expectations explain my love life better than the sheer mediocrity of the men I meet. But recent events have mellowed me somewhat, or perhaps just sapped my energy. I say, sternly, "It would never have worked out. We just weren't compatible."

"You only gave it a few months, didn't you?"

"Ten. Long enough."

"Well, I still say there are some things you can't know for sure, Catherine, especially when it comes to relationships."

"And how long does one wait, Natasha? Should I just settle for anyone?" The interminable boredom of Edgar was hazardous to my emotional health. Does she want me to die trying?

"I'm just saying, you never know how things could change in the long run."

I'm not planning on answering her. She is worried about my being alone, that's all. Then it dawns on me: Alone like my mother. It's tricky, this business of deciphering human motivation. I see Natasha in a different light, for a moment, as if her thoughts are crawling across her forehead like a newsflash at the bottom of a television screen. *Alert! I do not want my granddaughter to end up fifty and alone like my daughter. I don't care if her boyfriends are dull and lacking intelligence;, they are warm-blooded mammals who can be legally, inextricably bound to her by marriage.*

Natasha brings over a bowl of Fritos. She holds up the vase she had placed in the center of the table. Yellow lilies with speckled petals. "I suppose you have an idea where these should go?" she asks.

"They're fine on the table," I tell her, "but better on the bookshelf."

We exchange a look. She moves the flowers to the bookshelf.

"You're sure?"

"Some things I do know," I tell her.

"You and my plants," she mutters. She makes me a sandwich and we talk about the weather. I forget about Edgar. He is forgettable.

Certainty feels like a stone at the bottom of your stomach. It's as tangible and reliable as the five senses.

I don't know how I know the lilies would live an extra three to four days on the bookshelf, but I do. I know this sort of fact like I know whether it's raining when I look outside, like I know an ambulance is coming when I hear the siren. Like I know a man is lying when he looks in your eyes and says, "I love you."

3

Not that Edgar thought he was putting one past me when he said it; we both knew it was a little game we played, the "healthy relationship game"—meaning the relationship progressed from dating to exclusivity, to love, to long-term commitment. I didn't care if he loved me anyway. I didn't love him. It's such a shame, though, that our emotional connection was so shallow we could see the bottom when we were at our very deepest.

I can hardly remember what we did for the ten months we were together, other than have sex. When I think of Edgar now I recall how he picked his nose on our second date, and from then on. There always seemed to be some intractable bit of snot in some difficult to reach corner of his nasal passage, but he was good in bed, so I passed him the tissues without comment.

A typical evening with him went something like this:

I get to Edgar's apartment just after five.

"Hungry?" he asks.

I say, "Not yet."

We make out, progress to foreplay, have sex. He's on top. It's fast and invigorating.

"Hungry?" he asks again. Now I'm hungry.

"Pizza?" he suggests. (Or Chinese, or Mexican. Edgar used a form of shorthand with me—I think it was so that he could dedicate all neurons to his penis).

We order pizza, or Chinese, or whatever. In the process of waiting we've discovered our naked bodies in contact, so we have no choice. We are compelled to fornicate, again. This time I am on top.

We eat. Watch a bit of TV. Edgar does not burp or fart, and I appreciate that about him. He has an arm casually across my shoulder; he reads some of that day's newspaper during the commercials. At some point he asks me how my day has gone, and I ask him about his, and it's always the same. I moan and he raves on and on. He is thrilled with his job. Having recently finished a PhD in anthropology, Edgar has become a real estate agent.

Then off to bed. Candles are lit. His fingers, cleansed of pizza, work their magic. We are spoons; he nuzzles my ears, kisses my neck, he stays behind me, one hand on my breasts. We are full and tired, and everything happens slowly. This is the closest we come to making love.

This scene repeats itself, four to five times a week, month after month. In the mornings I am up by dawn and have begun perusing the notes I've brought with me (the previous day's work), leaving Edgar to sleep until eight. Before he goes to work we have coffee together and he picks his nose.

Our relationship ended at my mother's funeral, the day we buried an empty casket while her ashes, the half that hadn't already been flown to Italy, sat at home awaiting their domestic dispersal. There was no obvious reason for my ending Edgar's and my relationship, just as there was no obvious reason for our having had one in the first place. It was one long, lustful siesta, and in the end I just woke up.

The day of the funeral started out bad, then got weird. Or maybe it started out weird, too. I remember, first of all, staring at the casket. The *empty* casket, the excuse for a ceremony and a tombstone and, of course, a party, all according to my mother's plan. The casket was so polished that it had the clarity of a mirror. I could see my face, which sort of disturbed me. "Blah," I thought. "That's how I look. Washed out, pathetic." I could hear my mother tease me for being so self-pitying. I could hear her voice: *Yep, that's right kiddo! You're the one who's got to go on living.*

I hated it all. The blur of mourners, the insistent condolences and the oppressive heat of summertime induced in me a light nausea. I weaved in and out among the gravestones, praying that no one else would press his sweaty hand into mine and tell me he wished me well, how so very sorry he was. No one seemed deterred by the heat apart from myself, and I looked to be the only one who sought out shade. There were no trees in the cemetery. It was depressing, really, the thought that in this big, green expanse there were no roots to be found, that nothing would ever come up. All that space was focused on what you couldn't see, row after row of relatives, friends, neighbors, strangers all in their own private boxes. It all seemed wrong to me. Don't most people hope to ascend heavenward in death? Shouldn't there be trees and bushes and flowers?

Three old women milling around nearby lamented the fact that they had been to so many funerals in the last few years, though I was sure I detected the briefest sparkle in their eyes despite their deeply-lined and concerned faces. I had no idea if they were here for my mother or someone else. They mopped the sweat off their foreheads, voicing a longing for shade, but made no move toward the rest of the crowd. There was a marquee near the open grave, and so I headed that way, to where the minister waited on the mourners for the internment. I nearly walked straight into a man standing apart from the others in a starched white dress shirt with navy pants. For a second I gave a start, thinking he was Patrice, my old violin instructor, then saw that clearly he wasn't. This man was quite a bit older. He stood perfectly straight and still, oddly detached from the event unfolding around him. He wore dark sunglasses and a frown, as if he were not upset, but curious. He shuffled out of my way as I apologized, not meeting my eyes, for which I was grateful. I felt a sudden empathy for him. He looked as out of place as I felt. "He's probably a musician," I thought; there were quite a few in attendance, most of whom recognized me although I no longer recognized them, most of them eager to reminisce with me about my mother.

What would she think of all this, I wondered? I recalled her lying in bed looking like a beached octopus, tubes protruding in every direction. The minister visited her a few times (he was an old family friend—none of us attended church). She told him not to so much as frown during her funeral service. "Tell them that I want no tears on my behalf! Do I make myself clear?" So adamant that no one mourn unduly, that we all be as happy as she had always been—she was, as ever, at her most unpleasant when she insisted that others recognize the beauty, joy, or peace that formed her world.

I wiped the sweat off my face with a tissue from my purse and sat down, relieved to have made it to my seat without another encounter. Across the marquee, among the many empty chairs, Natasha sat on her own. Not acknowledging me except to stand, she approached, eyes downward, and sat beside me. Her hand rested immobile on my shoulder, until, in one fluid movement she removed the hand from my shoulder, leant over, took my hand in hers and pressed a small cool object into it. She whispered into my ear. "Do you know I never really told your mother about what my life was like before I came to this country? This is my sole memento from that time. Don't lose it." Her hand now held my own firmly. She closed my hand into a fist and held it shut. She made a sound like a hiccup, which I understood to be her attempt at stifling a tear. She wiped her eyes with her free hand.

A bell rang in the distance—a church bell—and simultaneously a car horn honked. They startled me. The heat was beginning to tire me; my eyelids were heavy. "At a time like this?" I thought, but I couldn't escape my own drowsiness. Natasha squeezed my knuckles, which ached from the pressure. Her admission was strange, but I was too drowsy to process it. I squirmed in my chair. She let go of my hand. I forgot about the small object pressed tightly into my fist. My grandmother began to cry. She began softly, then she coughed, cleared her throat, and turned to face me.

Suddenly I realized that Natasha was going to tell me something important. Blinking myself awake, I felt nervous. A family secret? A long-hidden regret? Something from her past she could only mention now that my mother had died?

I thought about possible clues as memories surfaced: of when I was a very young girl stumbling upon Natasha in some corner chair, catching her as she stared out of the window with a hot cup of tea clutched in both hands. Her lonely tea-drinking always seemed an act accompanied by the direst and most contemplative of moods. I learned to enter rooms cautiously and silently at her house, for I could not bring myself to risk disturbing what seemed the most intimate sadness radiating from her dark, viscous pupils—at times they would seem to fill up with tears, but it was only an illusion. She looked like one of those heroines from a period movie, suppressing profound emotional turmoil behind a stoic Victorian veneer. Could it be that she was about to tell me something of what had been going on in those quiet moments?

"Tell me about your life before," I said. "I would like to know."

Natasha looked away, her eyes glazed over.

"I have decided that I will," she said. And then the minister tapped the microphone with his finger and cleared his throat. Something hit the ground with a click. I bent over to find a small silver coin inscribed with the year 1921 and indecipherable writing.

Of course Edgar appeared at this critical moment, and it was a universal law that nothing profound could take place in his vicinity. There he was, having walked right across the cemetery in the heat, with not a trace of sweat on his perfect brow, smelling of Polo aftershave. He wore an Armani suit without the jacket and there was not a wrinkle to be seen—he was as fresh as if he'd just walked out of the air-conditioned store where he bought it (with what money I had no idea). Natasha got up and moved a few seats away without a backwards glance.

"You look beautiful," he told me. He sat down next to me.

Was that the most useful thing he could say at this particular moment?

Edgar's eyes were so clear I could see myself in them, and the impression I had was not much better than it had been looking onto the casket. I was not in the mood for him right now.

"Did you come with your grandmother?" he asked.

I nodded.

"Tell her I'll drive you home," he said.

"You're quite the bright-eyed and bushy-tailed boy today," I observed. "Coffee went down well?"

He could not restrain the grin that instantly materialized on his face. "Oh, darling, I've got fantastic news. I'll tell you about it later. It's your day now."

He patted my hand.

My day? Was he on another planet? For the first time ever his aftershave did not make me think of how the ceiling looked from the two-seater couch in the sunroom.

"This is a funeral, Edgar."

"I'm so sorry, Cat."

"About what?"

"Huh?" he asked.

"Why are you sorry? I'm just pointing out that your exuberance is wearing."

"That's why I'm sorry. Sorry." He took a breath. "About your mother, too, I mean."

He sounded suitably sorry. The minister looked like he was about to speak into the microphone. The seats began to fill up. Edgar took my hand and began to caress my palm with his forefinger.

After a few minutes he leaned over and said to me, "Order in tonight?"

Meanwhile I had been trying not to look at him too closely, for fear I would lose my way, I would succumb and be seduced. I was enjoying my irritation. Was he really thinking about dinner? Or about what came before and after dinner? Was this an attempt to take my mind off things, or was he just dumb?

I snapped.

"I don't think we'll be ordering in anymore," I said. And then on a whim, "This is goodbye, Edgar."

Cold and cruel, perhaps, but I didn't want to play games anymore. It took Edgar several minutes to figure out what I was saying—I didn't help him out any—then he left graciously. My only regret that day is that I did not wait until after we'd ordered in. I mean, why *not* get some pleasure out of the day?

I had been too abrupt with Edgar, and I didn't sleep well that night. Fortunately, he called me the next day and we got back together. When we broke up two weeks later, it was mutual. We kindly ended our relationship over our morning cup of coffee.

4

The coin that Natasha pressed into my hand has for weeks lain on my desk, next to my pile of folders. I do not look at it, though I find its presence reassuring. My hand slides across it to retrieve papers, or rests on it when I am reading something on the computer screen. I keep meaning to bring it back to her and ask her where it's from and why she handed it to me, ask her again what her life was like before, but I don't. For the same reason, probably, that I don't do much else either, like leave the computer to watch television, or leave the house to see a movie, or just leave the house. I assume the moment has passed.

I live in my mother's house. Our house. The house we shared for the better part of my life, and the one to which I returned, after college dormitories and low-rent apartments, in order to help her through the worst of her treatment. I do not like it. I am not comfortable in the room that has become my office, nor the cozy kitchen, nor the colorful living room, nor the huge, luxurious bathrooms. It is a house anyone would love to own, especially someone with good taste who relishes comfort above all else, and on that level, I couldn't think of a better place to live. Yet most of the time I hide in the office and almost believe that I am elsewhere, in a stuffy one-room apartment, crowded in with my folders, the thoughts they contain and the thoughts they make me have. Thoughts not about me or my life.

The rest of the house is distracting. I wish the part of me that grew up here and then came back would just go away. Forever. Here I revert to the passive me, the one created by my mother—it's hard to even remember the individual who existed out there, in the wider world. My mother's inspiration, not mine, breathed life into this house. It was all hers, her creation, a reflection of her personality, a glimpse of her artistry. The story of her life is told by the artwork that lines the walls, by the collections of books on music, on painting, on architecture, by the knick-knacks frozen in time on shelves—whimsical figurines of a pig and a fat lady behind glass-fronted Scandinavian shelving units, next to genuine African sculptures and framed black-and-white photographs of famous musicians. By an arrangement of silk lilies in an oriental vase. She had a penchant for dried and fake flowers and, secretly, rose patterns; girliness went hand in hand with sophistication. These possessions *are* Susan, the entirety of what is left of her. In some corners, in some peculiar places where I cannot shake off her memory, I feel that I am glimpsing her soul.

The house of my early youth is a ghost within the skeleton of this new home, remodeled during my first year of college. Though the older version was not as spacious and full of light as this one, nor nearly as posh, it was full of memories that confer a quiet resonance upon certain areas even now. I swear I have glimpsed the old yellow linoleum of the phantom kitchen from the corner of my eye. One memory among all others seems to permeate that space: an elementary school night when the electricity went out during a storm in the dead of winter. My mother and I sat around the table playing cards, reading books and magazine articles aloud, and telling jokes with the gas oven on high, wide open. There is an ever-present smell in the kitchen that has not diminished with time, either, a combination of cinnamon, freshly toasted bread, and the slim branches of lavender my mother placed in vases on the table and countertops in the springtime.

There are other nostalgic places in the house, but for the most part the past cannot penetrate the present and its bland, dusty smell of illness. There was not one moment my mother lived in this renovated house that disease had not already colonized her body, at first surreptitiously so as not to arouse her suspicion until one day, she fell—quite suddenly and seriously—ill. Her illness made me a prisoner of this house. Over a three year period I spent the longest time here that I had since I left home for college. After a second remission ended as quickly as it had begun, we began the prolonged process of awaiting death.

I could sell this house and move on now, but for laziness combined with a lack of incentive. Princeton is close enough for me to commute to, in order to do research or meet with my advisor—not that I do the latter anymore. Also, I have so few expenses. Musical men had paid bits of the mortgage here and there; musical men had bought her cars; musical men had lent her money when she needed it; and, it turns out, two particular musical men had competent stockbrokers who helped her invest her money wisely. So my mother, who couldn't plan a day ahead much less years, had quite unintentionally ensured that my grandmother and I were left with all that we'd need.

Since the house became legally mine, I have changed nothing except the office, which I created out of the spare room. When I have some free time I intend to put a bed back in it and abandon the sofabed, the guestroom, and my old bedroom, where I sleep by rotation. But that would denote a permanence I have so far managed to avoid.

I am not the only one who avoids this house. My mother's friends have stopped coming around, though I suppose they have no reason to visit me anymore—no doubt they only did so out of loyalty to my mother in the first place. Natasha, of everyone, has the most obvious reason not to return. Unfortunately, the time when she lived with us for six months—between breaking her hip and moving into her retirement village—coincided with one of the worst stages of my mother's illness. The discomfort of those two women living together for the first time in decades was infecting. We all tiptoed around one another, with the result that we were only face to face when we had to bring my mother into the hospital. Then I nodded away as my optimist mother discussed normal life (as if she had one), as Natasha made acerbic comments to the doctors and said not much at all to her daughter. The only conversation I remember that wasn't about what one or the other wanted for dinner or lunch was when Natasha said, "Susan, look at you. You're in pain. Do you want me to get that doctor to give you more painkillers?"

My mother said, "It reminds me that I am alive." Natasha sneered; my mother took her hand and said, "Will *you* ever be happy, Natasha? And you, Catherine, darling?" I don't remember many more words passing between them; as for me and my mother, we never seemed to talk much anyway.

Two weeks after the funeral, when Natasha came over for the reading of the will, she climbed the steps with visible reluctance, as if she half expected to come in and find my mother lying in wait for her with something cheerful to say. She paused in the doorway, looked up toward the top of the door frame and announced, "Okay, now, I'm coming in." Maybe she was talking to me, but it was almost as if she were hoping the door frame would collapse on her and save her the experience of entering the house. Before she finally stepped inside she said, "I don't think I'll come back here. Catherine, you can visit me from now on."

Despite my general lack of enthusiasm for just about everything, once I'm in her apartment I really do enjoy visiting Natasha. We have never been particularly close, by which I mean there is a certain sobriety that has always characterized our relationship. Compared to being with my mother, where passion, in all its platonic forms, typified most interaction, being with Natasha is like being in a Norman Rockwell painting of middle-American normality. Well, sort of.

When I was growing up, Natasha lived down the road, and had a key to our house. She visited regularly, though on appointed days: Tuesdays, Thursdays—when my mother's special committees held late meetings—and Sundays, when she came for dinner with my grandfather. Natasha was never so much there to look after me, or play with me, as to be an adult presence on the watch for my needs. I had few. I played happily on my own, but always in her proximity. When I discovered literature, perhaps around age seven, I recall Natasha reading in one armchair, me reading in the other, side by side. I do not recall that we conversed all that much. She made me snacks, sometimes dinner; she asked me what I was reading, and whether I enjoyed it as much as the previous novel I'd read. On Sundays we played board games with my mother after dinner while my grandfather smoked cigars outside. The games were a living demonstration of how we differed: Susan was impetuous and announced her every move; I was cool, calm, and strategic; Natasha kept a moody silence then surprised us with sudden, winning choices.

I found Natasha easier to be with than my mother, who said whatever she thought, whether or not I wanted to hear it. Susan was fire while Natasha was all water, deep, dark and silent. Even though Natasha's moods were, when I was a child, slightly off-putting, she nonetheless intrigued me. In some way I took comfort from her nearness.

We are now, as always, comfortable in each other's company; however, since my mother's funeral, there is an edge to my visit. I expect, at some point, she will tell me something important about her past.

My expectation stems as much from what she said at the funeral as from the fact of the death itself. Now that my mother is gone, I find myself drawn to know Natasha as Natasha, instead of as my grandmother. I can no longer think of her merely in terms of my familial relations: that she came over because of my mother's work obligations, that her presence at Sunday dinners was a family tradition. I have to contend with her as an individual now.

Today Natasha sits across from me at the table in the dining room explaining how her interest in watercolors began when my mother was just a toddler. My grandfather worked long hours then. He was rarely home, and she had few friends. Even after many years, this country was so new and unimaginable to her that she had to get the colors right just to put everything else in order. My mother has some of her early pictures on the walls at home. The colors are so pale, the details so muted, that there is the sense she did not fully live in her new world.

"Who is this woman, then?" I ask myself. I thought I had some idea of who she was, but I now suspect she was just a figure I took for granted in my childhood landscape, a character whom I never went to any length to interpret. I realize I have no notion of her at all—and I stare at her as if she is nude, judging her black eyeliner and ruby lips. I see only the surface, the brashness concealing the deep well that is Natasha. Only my emotions give me any clue of what lies beneath, and I feel a certain comfort, an intuition or delusion that in fact, I know exactly what is there.

It has been years since she has indulged herself in her artwork, Natasha admits, more than a decade since she has picked up a paintbrush, until a few months ago. Today she is working on a landscape, beginning to paint a tree. She demonstrates, brush in hand, how she is able, with a series of long strokes, to paint all that the tree calls forth from her memory. She paints with concentrated ease; it is this controlled movement that an artist must perfect, she says. Over the next hour I watch as she fills in the dark green leaves and deep blue sky, and the crevice-filled contrasts of rocky white mountain slopes that she says were once her home.

She as much as admits that, whereas before she sought in her painting to come to terms with her present—Northeastern pines and New England autumns—now she uses it to recreate her past.

"That," she says, indicating with her brush a bright spot of yellow flowers, "is what I would pass coming from school in the late spring and early summer, when they were so many, you cannot imagine!"

Then Natasha says to me, "I have been working on a portrait of your mother."

"Really?"

I don't particularly want to see it, truth be told.

She pushes her unfinished landscape to the side and gives it an affectionate glance. Turning her back to me, she walks to her cabinet, opens one of the doors and takes out a black portfolio. She lays it on the table.

"Well, I must admit that it has been a good three months since I began it."

She opens it to the face of my mother, devoid of hair, her eyes protuding ominously in their dark tones. I am shocked for a moment and cannot believe my grandmother would paint my mother as she would least wish to be remembered—in the midst of chemotherapy, half-alive. I shift uncomfortably in my seat.

"Natasha ..." I say, but I don't know how to continue. We exchange looks. Hers is quizzical. Embarrassed, I look at the picture once more, hoping to find something positive to say. All of a sudden I realize I am the one at fault. It is obviously incomplete. She has painted my mother's bare features, has left the hair for last, shaded in only primary tones.

She explains, "I am using this picture." She pulls a small photograph out of the portfolio.

My mother looks out from beneath a large straw hat. She is grinning, standing in front of the ivy-covered brick wall in her garden. I remember this day. Her cancer was in retreat. A second chance, we thought, though for my mother every day was another chance, and it had been that way as long as I could remember. My mother's inner peace was incomprehensible to me. She was the kind of person who gave money to the homeless, handed out five- and ten-dollar bills even while maintaining that the world was full of so much good. She knew of no injustice that would last, because she refused to believe people were inherently bad. One day we would all come to our senses.

The picture makes me angry. I still do not understand how she could believe that her circumstances held so much meaning for her soul, as if pain were exceptional, not an inescapable part of life. It was her saving grace at the end, but it did nothing for me. Nor for Natasha, who declared to me in the hospital waiting room one day, shaking her head angrily, "Susan is a New Age nut! Sometimes, I hate to say it, but I wish she would just suffer in silence!"

I agreed about the silence. She was not silent; with Susan life was never silent. Whether at home or at the hospital there were the ceaseless sounds of television shows or visiting quartets (not to be avoided when you have as many musical friends as did my mother), or my mother's divulgences, which passed for conversation between us: how happy she was to have been able to watch me grow to adulthood, how lucky she was to have had such a fulfilling life and to have seen so many beautiful things. Natasha grew exasperated, no doubt, but I also saw her disappointment. Maybe I was projecting, but I could well imagine that, like me, Natasha was wondering how this woman could be her own flesh and blood. With my mother's passing I felt I'd lost a connection that never was, a relationship we had therefore taken for granted, and it would not surprise me if Natasha felt the same way.

I wish I saw something else in the photo, such as just another beautiful woman in a hat. I wonder if Natasha sees what I see. She cocks her head to one side, her gaze passes over it and then me, and she says, "I like the painting so far." She holds up the painting and scrutinizes it.

"You should hang your paintings in the halls," I tell her, "to replace what's there now. Even better, paint something rude, just to get the fogies all flustered."

"That's an excellent idea! Why didn't I think of it?"

"Because at heart you are a kind, neighborly woman," I say.

She puts the photo and the painting away, and I go to make lunch.

I tell Natasha that I should get going, that I am anxious to do some reading before dinner.

She says nothing as I get up and start clearing the table. Then: "I gave you a coin two months ago from Crimea. It was issued in the same year I was born. I presume you still have it?"

"Yes."

"Good. Before you go, I'll make us tea, and you can read this." She takes a newspaper out of the drawer in the cabinet where she keeps her drawing paper and leaves it on the table.

I have no sense that this is anything important; in fact, my mind has already wandered to the articles that await me at home. I pick up the newspaper. "Crimean Tatars Reclaim Homeland."

The piece recounts how a small Muslim ethnic group, the Crimean Tatars, are returning to their native land of Crimea in present-day Ukraine after fifty years in exile. They were one of several ethnic groups deported by Stalin to Central Asia and Siberia during the Second World War. Now that the Soviet Union has collapsed, tens of thousands of Crimean Tatars are resettling their land.

Natasha returns, empty-handed.

"Interesting," I say. "Had you heard of them before? I mean, before you came to America."

This news sounds vaguely familiar, but I can't place it. I wonder what it is like for Natasha to hear about all these changes in the empire that was once her home.

"I used to live in Crimea," she says. "My very best friend was a Crimean Tatar girl named Lilya, and she and her entire family were deported."

With that she turns and goes back into the kitchen. For some reason I feel my breathing quicken and my chest tighten. Was I supposed to know that? I have the sense that I *should* know Natasha better—if not her emotional, psychological self, then at the very least the bare facts of her life. I feel as if I have overlooked, carelessly, something fundamental—yet, strangely, I do not experience shock. Rather, it is as if we have made a smooth, effortless quantum leap to a new level of intimacy. A sudden, reassuring comfort floods my being, the same physical release I feel upon settling into my plush couch after a day at the desk.

I can recall nothing about Crimea in relation to Natasha. I stare at the photo next to the text. There is a woman my grandmother's age, head swathed in a scarf, the flesh of her face thin and crinkled, staring into a field filled with tents. I sit and wait for Natasha, hands folded in my lap like a child waiting for her teacher. Still, I think, she will explain while I have a cup of tea, and shortly I will go.

When Natasha returns she sits down across from me with a cup of tea and places a teapot on the table. She passes me a cup and saucer. I wait for her to explain herself. I don't know what I expect her to say, but certainly not the words, "I was born in the year of the Rooster, 1921. The same year as that coin I gave you. The same year Lilya was born."

Since when does Natasha know about the Chinese zodiac? Her reference to it, along with her tone of voice, catches me off guard. I realize that I am probably not leaving just yet.

"The Rooster is supposed to be the most misunderstood of all the signs of the Chinese horoscope," she says. She takes a sip of her tea. She drinks slowly and smacks her lips.

"I'm going to tell you the story," she says, "of my friend Lilya Bekirova, and Refat Chobanov, and myself. I still don't know how this story ends."

The weepiness from my mother's funeral is no more; Natasha is eager, as if suddenly it is so natural to be opening up to someone after all these years. As if she had merely put this chapter of her past away like wine that needed aging.

"Why now?" I ask her.

"I am old and ready to live out the rest of my life free of memory. Its joys and burdens, its terrible weight.

"Freedom," she says, just before she begins her story, "is living in the present."

It sounds like wisdom, but I'm not so sure.

5

Crimea, Natasha begins, possesses a striking landscape; in her memory it is fantastical.

"Here," she says, opening a book with an illustration of Europe. She points to a diamond-shaped peninsula jutting out into the Black Sea. "It was taken over by Russians under Catherine the Great. Before that it was at the crossroads of ancient civilization. There were all kinds of ancient peoples who settled there, I can't even name them all—you should see the ruins of the fortresses, there are so many. There were Goths, and Turks, there were Greeks, and Venetians, and Genghis Khan's Golden Horde. The Crimean Tatars descend from all these peoples. They had their own kingdom, the Crimean Tatar Khanate, from the fourteenth century. If you went you could still see the Khan's palace at Bakçhisaray."

She closes the book.

"I assume you know your history. Do you remember the war-time conference in Yalta, at the Livadia Palace during the Second World War?"

"I studied it, yes."

"Well, that's all most people know about Crimea. You see, the tsars all had summer homes there, like the Livadia Palace, and so did the Soviet leaders after them, because Crimea is such a beautiful place and has such a nice climate. Of course, in the mountains the winters are cold and there is snow, but on the coast the winters are mild, and the summers are hot. The sea is deep blue and shallow. In my day everybody went to Crimea in the summer to bathe in the sea. Many workers' unions had resorts for their employees and their families."

Natasha opens the book to another page. Now I see that the writing is Cyrillic, the pages old and worn, the photographs black-and-white. I ask her where she found the book.

"Like many of my old books, from the city, from émigré friends who have friends, who bring them over. There are bookstores filled with such books in New York."

"Do you still read in Russian?"

"Of course," she says, with the slightest tone of indignation. "All my life."

Now that I think about it, I do remember the long, waist-high bookshelves that ran the length of her living room, whole sections of them filled with book jackets covered in the indecipherable writing I now know to be Russian. At the time I did not register their significance. Now, I stare at a black-and-white photo of a cliff top, the background view of the sea. I try hard to imagine Natasha there, standing against that wild backdrop, the words of text a living language filling the air around her.

"It looks like Greece," I say.

Natasha is thoughtful for a long moment. I stare at the photograph in the book. She turns the page to another photo, this time small, of an old woman in traditional dress. As there is no color I cannot glean much from the photo—the woman looks Caucasian, her hair blond. Her dress is long and full and she carries a basket. She could be a Russian peasant.

"The Crimean Tatars are not dark-skinned?" I ask. I assume they would look Turkish.

"Their ancestors are so many," Natasha says. "Some are dark, some are Asian, some are white. It depends on where in the Crimea they are from. They are all Muslim." She looks up, thoughtful, then smiles, "There is so much I could say. They made delicious foods, like çiborek—fried meat pies. They are very polite and extremely hospitable. But that's all beside the point."

"When were you there?" I ask her.

"I moved there in June, 1937," she says. "My father was posted there. He was an officer in the army. We had lived there once before when I was very small, though I don't remember it. My mother was a schoolteacher then, teaching Russian to Crimean Tatar children. Apparently an old Tatar woman looked after me sometimes. I still know many words, but I'm afraid I've forgotten how to put a sentence together. It makes me sad, you know. Lilya was such a good friend, and I can't even remember how she spoke."

I am waiting for her to continue, grasping at my imprecise knowledge of Russian history to put in context what was happening in the world at the time my grandmother moved to Crimea.

"You were there during the worst of Stalinist repression, weren't you?" I ask.

"Yes. Which brings me to what happened."

"To you?"

"I'll tell you about me later. I mean what happened to the Crimean Tatars."

"You mean the deportation?"

"Precisely."

"But that was years after you moved there, wasn't it? It was in the article."

"Do you think you've learned all there is to know, then?" she asks.

"No, not at all," I say. "I just—can't I hear the full story of your life, or at least about the time you spent in Crimea before the war?"

"Oh, I see." She cracks a smile. "Don't be impatient!" Then her face loses all trace of jollity and she says, "It was a turning point."

"The deportation?"

"Of course. I mean, for everyone. But what I am trying to say is that there are some things ... that change the meaning of even one's very beginnings. The fact that Lilya Bekirova was going to be deported, along with all the other Crimean Tatars in Crimea, meant that from the moment she was born she wasn't just Lilya of Crimea. Her whole life, her whole being was part of that event ..."

"I don't know about that," I interject. "Are you saying she was destined—"

"I'm sure you don't believe in such things—but let me put it this way—a Crimean Tatar girl of her generation would never have left Crimea, and so unless she died young, she would have been deported. There was no other destiny for her.

"Back to history." Natasha takes a deep breath, and holds her hand up to silence any further questions. "Stalin did not like any minorities. He was a totalitarian madman. Ethnic identity was considered a threat to the Soviet state. Now, before the deportation, more than twenty percent of Crimea's population was Crimean Tatar, which is not insignificant. So, in the late thirties the Tatars' political, cultural, and religious leaders were deported or shot. The Soviets wanted to erase the Tatars' ethnic identity in Crimea, in order to create a nation of ..." With care she pronounces the words, "Obedient Soviet citizens."

My grandmother has never spoken like this to me. She has never done much in the way of recounting. Natasha is observant and pithy, not prone to giving lengthy explanations. She is the one who taught me how to use an encyclopedia, the one in whose company I enjoyed silence as we sat together, each with a book on our laps. Not to mention the sensible one. I have never even heard her use the word "destiny."

"During the Second World War, Stalin ordered several ethnic groups—hundreds of thousands of people—to be deported from their native lands to faraway Soviet regions on the flimsiest of reasons. They believed that moving people away from their homeland would ... what is the word? Sever their ethnic ties and identity. They were very wrong, of course, which explains many of the problems in the former Soviet Union today.

"As you know, during the war the Nazis occupied Crimea. You know the rest from the article I showed you. Perhaps you have also come across this in your studies? Stalin accused the Crimean Tatars of collaborating with the Germans, which wasn't true. He ordered that the Crimean Tatars be deported. So, one May night, Soviet militia rounded up all two hundred and fifty thousand Crimean Tatar residents in Crimea and packed them into trains. It took weeks to move them to Central Asia. They were not fed or cared for. Almost half died during the journey. They fell ill, or starved to death."

Natasha withers and her face goes dark, yet her voice is controlled, fierce. I can hear her anger, and also her sadness.

"Lilya Bekirova and Refat Chubarov were among those deported," she says quietly, "I can't even imagine how to tell you all this. I guess I just have to talk."

She speaks fast, eyes aflame, the lipstick worn off her dry, cracked lips.

Natasha says history is always personal, and facts make no sense without memory. She explains, though, that memories can be a tangled mess. These jumbled recollections can intrude where they are not welcome, interrupt a settled life. Some such memories are best forgotten. Others, however, must be cultivated like good manners. They must be told like a story. Like that of Lilya, Refat, and Natasha.

She says she will begin the story with Lilya Bekirova, who like Natasha was born in 1921, in the year of the Rooster, to a people soon to be uprooted. It was the same year that Crimea became its own autonomous Crimean Tatar republic within Ukraine—when it gained some measure of approval for its ethnic culture. The time of celebration was short-lived, for famine followed during the Soviet collectivization of agriculture. The Crimean Tatars were a largely agricultural people, so many of them perished. Yet Lilya's youthful optimism obscured, to her eyes, the adversity suffered by her people. She did not anticipate that politics could bring even more trauma. Lilya was slow to grow out of her naïveté, and only after the deportation did she permanently abandon it.

My grandmother thus skips ahead to 1944: In May of that year Lilya was not yet married, and for that reason still lived at home. Her mother and father had spent years scouting for suitors far and wide while Lilya resisted their every attempt. Then, at last, on the eve of war, unfathomably, she accepted a proposal and became engaged, though she and the young man in question agreed to wait until after the war to wed.

The army sent Lilya's young man straight to the front, and her parents justifiably feared he would die before they could marry. They feared that they'd never find anyone else for her and Lilya would grow old alone. War is a time of fervent prayers, and Lilya's parents, her mother especially, prayed fervently every day that Lilya's fiancé would come home, and if not, that she would marry someone else in time to bear children. But most parents know half-truths at best when it concerns the hearts of their children, and such was the case here. Lilya's parents did not know the most important truth: she had no desire to marry her fiancé, and intended to extricate herself from the relationship one way or another. Lilya could not see herself living the life of a common householder.

To those closest to her (her parents, her brothers), she seemed a young woman not grounded in this world: too intelligent and too intellectually curious. She lacked the meekness of opinion that is expected in public and appreciated in private. But no one knew Lilya truly, for she hid herself well.

The real reason for her aversion to marriage had not so much to do with her intellectual fantasies, Natasha tells me. She gives me a slow, mysterious smile, and says, "Lilya doubted the world as it appeared to exist, and she doubted her preordained place in it."

It seems that Lilya believed an unseen world existed in which divinity was hidden among the details of mundane life. She was not religious; she was spiritual, though it was not a word she knew (her family was Muslim, non-observant, and in any case her country forbade religious practice). Lilya was aware of the supernatural before she knew the concept existed as something separate from life's accepted phenomena. She had seen nature spirits as a child, had watched shooting stars fall to earth, and in all this and more she saw a metaphysical significance that her authorities (be they her elders or her books) failed to explain. If only she listened, watched, and waited, she believed, she might understand something of life's meaning. Of these thoughts, she told no one but her best friend, Natasha.

My grandmother is gaining momentum and her cheeks are flushed. She hardly pauses for breath as she recounts how on May 18, 1944, exactly twenty-two years and seven months after Lilya's birth, soldiers and police came under the canopy of night, banging on doors, telling the villagers to leave now, to gather themselves together, quickly, for the trains stood waiting in the station. They were traitors to their Motherland, read the decree, Nazi collaborators, the worst crime imaginable; to cry out that your brother, your son, your husband was fighting for the Red Partisans would have fallen on the deaf ears of those who had time only for considerations of duty. Please refer to State Defense Committee Decree No. 5859ss issued on May 11, 1944 by the Kremlin: the traitors must be banished from the territory of the Crimea, and so must gather their things and leave.

On that dreadful night just before the men burst in the door—as Lilya's mother later confessed to her daughter on the train, which Lilya later told someone else, who told someone else, who eventually told Natasha—Lilya's mother was, just then, dreaming of Lilya married to a young man who had survived. It was a yearning for continuity; Lilya's marriage would mark the progression of time. The other three children, all boys, the youngest of whom had just started school, were at that moment sleeping peacefully in their one small, crowded bedroom. Other details of Lilya's ordeal did eventually reach Natasha, too: Lilya had just fallen deeply asleep. A handwritten copy of three poems by Cemil Kermencikli was hidden beneath her pillow, and the last verse she had read resounded faintly in her mind, a steady refrain against the clutter of her dreams.

At three o'clock in the morning, Soviet army and security forces forced them from their homes. They were made to march down hills and through puddles, to trample flowers and grass, with guns pointed at them all the while. Herded like cattle to an open field, they joined others who sat or stood on the dewy grass, surrounded by soldiers. No one told them their final destination. They all stood in their nightclothes waiting for their names to be called out. At five AM they were loaded into trucks to be taken somewhere, perhaps to their death.

At an empty train station, soldiers shoved them into cattle cars where they waited, motionless, until several hours later the trains finally departed. The cars were packed so tightly that few could sit, much less breathe, freely. The air was warm then, and filled only with the crisp odor of fear, though after a twenty-five day journey the smells would be infinitely more horrible. Another country, another leader, another destiny might have prevented the deportation. But in that place, at that time, it was too late.

The deportation, Natasha tells me, was the first turning point in Lilya's life. The second turning point occurred nine months later, when she went for a walk in the desert hills of Uzbekistan and was never heard from again.

6

Composure does not suit Natasha, so I am more at ease when on our next visit she appears at her door with uncombed hair, eyes red, still in a bathrobe.

"I've got ahead of myself," she says, rummaging around under her couch cushions and cursing under her breath, all to find a cigarette, which she finally does. "I dropped it." She lights her cigarette, hand trembling.

"I had to start somewhere. I dislike having to explain certain things, but I had to start with the worst thing that happened to Lilya, because it was the event that determined who she was. Had she not ended up in Uzbekistan, who knows what would have happened?"

"What do you mean?" I ask. "Do you mean ... what you said ... you said she disappeared ..." I don't know what to make of the cryptic ending she left me with on our previous visit.

"Yes." She sucks on her cigarette. "It has stirred me up, talking about things I haven't talked about to anyone in this country. Not even your grandfather."

It is true—I've never seen her like this, not just disheveled, but in a state of real distress. She was less distraught at my mother's funeral. I am speechless.

"Let me put your mind at rest. I am not crazy. I am not nostalgic. I have no regrets—in general. Look—" she points to her cigarette, "I am not sensible. Why waste time being sensible, of all things?"

"What are you then?" I ask.

"I am a woman getting to the point," she says, "in the most comprehensible way. There were three people involved—and I have to piece it all together, to make sense of it. Of what happened to me, of what happened to Lilya. Of course it is subjective, which may not appeal to you, my dear, with all those facts floating around in that academic head of yours ... You need a good story."

She sweeps up an envelope from the table. I see that it is addressed to Natasha Matveeva.

"From Refat. I was in love with him."

I say nothing. The face of my grandfather appears and disappears in my mind's eye. In love?

"Did you hear me?" she asks me. "You heard me, didn't you?"

I wonder if I have the right to speak today. I can't seem to think of anything to say.

"Do I look shocked?" I ask.

"You're hiding it well, my dear. This is my point." She taps the envelope. "Refat has returned."

"Who is Refat?"

"You'll soon find out."

"When did this happen?"

"Nothing happened, if you mean a love affair. And it happened long ago, before I became a woman."

Now what does that mean? Does she merely want to get this off her chest—some pubescent affair of the heart? I can't possibly ask her these things, so I wait for her to say something normal, less shocking, something that resembles casual conversation. That, I can handle.

I realize that I'm still standing, so I sit down. Natasha sits on the couch across from me.

She puts out her cigarette. She is not wearing lipstick and her lips are leached of color. Her eyebrows have begun to wear thin. She lowers her eyes and scrunches her bathrobe in at the neckline. For the first time in her company I do not feel underdressed.

She looks right at me. "I have no one to talk with, Catherine."

I catch my breath. It is so unexpected a confession, but so simple, so obvious. Her husband is dead, as are her friends, at least the ones who have not moved away to be with their children. It seems so unfathomable that, after a lifetime of companionship, a lifetime of company parties and picnics and dinners out with friends, she should end up alone.

She appears resigned. Then, unexpectedly, she chokes up. I grab a tissue and hand it to her. Then I start to cry, too. I don't have anyone to talk with either. I silently curse this saccharine moment; it suits neither of us. Anyway, we have each other.

"I don't know what to do," she says. She sniffs and wipes her eyes with the tissue.

"You're talking to me. I mean, maybe it's not ideal, maybe you wish you could share this with someone else …"

"Don't be ridiculous! Who with? Hush. We are stuck with one another. Listen. Lilya has been on my mind, day and night. After the deportation we lost touch, and that was that. But through mutual acquaintances, friends of friends and so on, I heard that she had disappeared. It was quite newsworthy at the time, apparently, and word traveled. I thought—others thought—she had been taken to a prison camp. Awful, just awful, but I dealt with it. It happened back then; you never knew who was considered politically subversive. But then, I got this letter from Refat—"

"When you say she disappeared, you mean ...?"

"I mean poof! Seemingly into thin air. I didn't know until Refat wrote me and told me that she'd really just disappeared, not a single clue as to where or how—listen: he wrote me years ago, out of the blue, after forty-something years of nothing, no contact whatsoever, can you imagine? He tracked me down after all that time! I wrote him back and thought that was it, but he wrote a few more times. Then, not long ago, I began to dream of Lilya, and suddenly Refat wrote me again. Only now he is in the city, raising money for a non-profit organization, to fund housing and medical care and so on for Crimean Tatars. He says he has some information for me about Lilya, what might have really happened. I can't imagine what it could be. Anyway, I want to tell you about it all. I have never told anyone. I guess it's not the kind of thing you mention at a dinner party over cocktails. Who knows a single thing about Crimea? Who really cares?"

"I do."

"Yes, I know. You are a sweet girl. Like Lilya. Did I mention Refat wants to see me, after all this time? What in the world could be the point of that?"

"Do you still love him, Natasha?" I ask, before I have a chance to stop myself.

She reaches for a cup on the table, sighing as she sees that it's empty. She takes it to the kitchen and returns, a moment later, with a full cup. "I've made some coffee. This is for you. I don't want any."

I thank her and ask if I can have something to eat. Better that I let her take the lead in this conversation. Anyway, I am starving, and she is not, apparently, intending to lunch with me any time soon.

"I have made some sandwiches. Take one from the kitchen counter. Just don't get any crumbs on the floor—I've just vacuumed. Listen while you eat, though. I have to start telling the story now, while it's weighing on my mind.

"Lilya remembered vividly the day she found out we were to meet, though she didn't tell me about it until many years had passed. She said that in hindsight she could see that day was the beginning of the end of her innocence. I only ever remember her as innocent."

I do wonder why Natasha is still telling me about Lilya's life and not her own. I am soon so drawn into Lilya's world, however, that it no longer occurs to me to ask if, or how, my grandmother will ever speak of herself.

7

June 1937

Of course, there was a time when Lilya was young and did not yet fully share her peoples' apprehension that yet another tragedy would befall them. On this day, in June of 1937, the world was particularly good for her. It was her brother Yusuf's seventh birthday and as their mother prepared in the kitchen for the celebration, he sat in the corner of the adjoining room on the cool wooden floor playing with a puzzle. It was a gigantic puzzle of four workers holding a red flag, with modern high-rise buildings in the background—a special birthday gift that his father had procured from a colleague who had gone to Moscow on business. It was complicated, with hundreds of pieces, but Yusuf worked at it with undaunted determination. He took each piece in his hands, analyzing it carefully before looking for its place on the floor. He had just enough light to work from the sun, which shone in great, wide rays through the open back door, warming his ankles and illuminating the puzzle. His torso was hidden from sight in the shadowy corner. He sensibly stayed out of the noonday sun.

His mother, Ayshe, was preparing their celebratory feast of köbete, baked meat turnovers filled with minced beef and rice; çiborek, fried beef and onion turnovers; an assortment of fresh and pickled vegetables—onions, eggplants, cabbage; and for desert Yusuf's favorite pastries, Russian-style pirozhki, some filled with apple, others with sweetened cheese. The sweet, rich smells of frying meat, garlic and onion suffused the house, and the smoke rising from the stove crept into fabric and wallpaper, clothing and hair, where it would remain for days until the rain and wind came and cleaned the air in the rooms of their cottage.

It was a hot day, and the sun shone directly into the kitchen where Ayshe and Lilya stood kneading the dough for the fried bread. The heat of the oven was overpowering, and perspiration gave a luminous sheen to their faces and necks, burnt brown from working in the sun. Ayshe paused for a moment, wiping her brow and sighing audibly. Suddenly a cool breeze entered the kitchen through the windows and brought with it a moment of relief. Lilya inhaled deeply to take in the scents of the kitchen and the pungent, sweet aroma of the wilting yellow crocuses that grew untamed in the rocky crevices on the hill behind their house.

Her face relaxed as she leant against the table. Every few minutes Ayshe or Lilya went into the main room to check on Yusuf. He barely noticed them, so engrossed was he in the challenge of his newest plaything. He had such a look of concentration on his face that Ayshe told her daughter, "See how focused he is? He is seven going on twenty."

To which Lilya replied, "And already the most ambitious of us all."

"You're not counting yourself, then?" Ayshe asked her daughter.

Lilya demurred, "I'll not count my ambitions, isn't that proper?"

Ayshe took a hand towel off the counter and wiped her daughter's brow. "Will you run an errand for me down to the stalls?"

"I'll just finish folding these turnovers."

Mother and daughter fell silent. Just then Yusuf mooed in perfect imitation of the sun-weary bovine wandering the nearby hills, and they laughed.

Lilya was relieved to hear him betray his age. Children grew up quickly in those parts, in those days. If it was not famine, or the reality of discrimination against the Crimean Tatars, it was something else, such as the responsibility of outdoor work; sometimes the entire summer holiday was spent helping in the fields or in the garden, though the Bekirov children were lucky in that regard. They had only a small garden, as it was not the sole source of their livelihood, and with several pairs of hands the work was accomplished quickly.

Lilya's parents often bemoaned the fact that Yusuf, Lilya's older brother Ayder, and her baby brother Fevzi were growing up so quickly. Already, as they saw it, they would soon lose Lilya—a whole village of boys to choose from meant she would marry and leave home. Lilya's parents desired a good match for her, but, as they told her, the sounds of the children playing in their small cottage, their squeals of laughter, their constant chattering, and of course their sibling squabbles, were what gave life to their home; it was no small sadness that it would not last forever. Yusuf, especially, was already too grown up at seven, Ayshe thought, though Ayder could draw him out, if not playfully then with fraternal spite, which would end in laughter, if not immediately, then within the day. Just the other day Ayder had stolen some toy of Yusuf's just to rouse him from one of his meditative states. He stood before his younger brother holding up the toy and egged him on until soon they were chasing each other in circles in the great room and then outside. Yusuf eventually collapsed in tears, so Ayshe had been forced to intervene. As usual she punished them to silent companionship on the sofa, where soon they were giggling at the silly faces they made at one another.

The youngest of Lilya's three brothers, Fevzi, was just ten months old. Just a few days ago at the market, much to Ayshe's dismay, he took his first steps. "Next thing you know," she announced at the time, "he'll start talking, then he'll be demanding things—one more voice to add to their orchestra!" Lilya doubted it: he was one of those unusual babies who rarely cried and smiled often. She was certain his easygoing temperament would remain when he began to speak, but Ayshe said she knew better.

By any account theirs was a happy family, unnaturally blessed with material and spiritual sustenance, exceptionally immune, it seemed, to troubles of any sort. Lilya lived almost exclusively in the present, of course, and they were having a good summer that year, one of many in a row, and truly a lightness of being prevailed—the sense that in the peace and quiet of a land so beautiful, in a house full of the exuberance of youth, very little could go wrong. Maybe there was something brewing beneath the surface, but as far as Lilya was concerned, it was nothing but a shadow that crossed over Father's eyes, an occasional darkening of his expression and a mood he seemed to share with his compatriots when they met late at night in the kitchen. At such times the men mused and moped, complained and fretted. Occasionally they raised their voices. Lately they kept them quiet. But that was men's business; Lilya thought it was as much in their nature to brood together as to celebrate together.

Of course Lilya had heard rumors about important people, the intelligentsia, university department chairs and theater directors being removed from their posts by the Soviets and sent to prison camps, even shot. She had heard such stories for as long as she could remember. But it was all somehow like static in the background that did not form part of her daily existence. Hers was a fortunate village. During the famine of '32–'33 which followed the beginning of the Soviet collectivization of agriculture, relatively few of their people had perished, and no one Lilya knew personally, so she could not imagine that misfortune could suddenly reach them now. (She did not know yet that her favorite uncle, Uncle Mahmedi, her father's youngest brother, was even now languishing in a prison camp in Siberia on accusations of being a Kulak. She was only seven when he disappeared and her parents told her only that he had moved.) Even when she heard her classmates whisper, when she heard her father speaking to her mother in hushed tones at night when they thought the children were all asleep—and those few times she overheard one of her father's circle referring to an incident of the police abusing their power—she filed such instances away in her mind under the heading "Things Not to Be Bothered By."

Anyway, Lilya had her own life and her own involvements—that is, distractions. She was a good student, earning the highest possible marks in Crimean Tatar literature and translation between Russian and Crimean Tatar. She even did well in mathematics and the sciences, although that was not where her passions lay. She could read Crimean Tatar both in the Arabic script, which she had learned when she first began to read, and the Latin script, which officially replaced the Arabic script when she was about seven. She remembered the day well; like many, she was pleased, but not by the simplification of the alphabet. Rather, she saw it as an enjoyable challenge to her translation skills. She loved reading the books and magazines that lined their bookshelves at home, especially the ones written in the Arabic script, and then immediately reading something else in Latin script. The language was the same, yet the process of interpreting two sets of symbols revealed mysterious differences. She felt herself privy to a special skill of deciphering that was lost to others, like having a window into unknown universes, or, better yet, like seeing things that were invisible to others. In the past two years she had begun teaching herself English with some old texts that she received from a neighbor whose son taught English at the university in Akmescit, or Simferopol as it was also known. They were old books that had a funny smell, a bit like dried leaves or vinegar. The pages were yellowed and brittle and the ragged cover was slowly losing its blue color. Still, she was beside herself learning a foreign language, the language of the English who drank tea and went for afternoon strolls with fancy parasols in elaborately pruned gardens. She did not particularly have a real ambition to travel abroad; it was enough for her that she be able to decode what others could not. Perhaps, someday, she would be able to go abroad, just to practice speaking another language. Not for too long, though. Lilya could not imagine anyplace in the world from which she would not return to the mountain home in her native Crimea.

Little was for sale today, but Lilya did as instructed, and got what she could find: onions and flour. She took her time returning home and stopped short of the bend leading around the market stalls and up the hillside. She caught her breath to gaze at the burst of tiny purple flowers atop tall, lavender stalks that had recently appeared in the woods along the hillside. The landscape never failed to induce in her a deep longing to stand outside of time and watch the seasons change, to witness the rocks and hills go bare of flowers and the snow flurry through the air, and then to see the tiny green shoots reappear. She hurried over to a rock and grabbed a handful of fiery orange crocuses. They would look lovely scattered across the table for her brother's birthday feast.

"Lilya!" came a voice from behind, and she turned. "I've come to ask a favor!"

Elmira Mamut took dusty strides toward Lilya. The older woman perspired and smelled of fieldwork. She placed a basket full of potatoes on the ground before her and grunted as she resumed standing. She gave a polite smile and added by way of greeting, "You are on your way home now, I see?"

Lilya looked up the hill that led to her house and to the bunch of flowers in her hand. She suspected she would be asked to change her course, and was grateful that she had good reason not to. Elmira Mamut demanded a certain degree of attention that came only with concentrated effort.

"Yes, today is Yusuf's birthday, we are having a celebration."

The older woman looked thoughtful for a moment and then said, "He is seven, correct?" She brushed a strand of thick, black hair from her face, leaving in its stead a brown smudge. Her sister was the local midwife, so Elmira tended to remember local births. More importantly, she filled her mind with others' details, collecting facts and gossip with a vigor which, it seemed to Lilya, far exceeded that with which she toiled after her seven children, two cows, several sheep, and husband. Unfortunately, Lilya's father had been helping her husband erect a new fence to keep wild animals out of their bordering properties, so, in return, Elmira was forever making herself 'useful' to Lilya's family.

"Yes, he is," nodded Lilya. She looked up the hill again, making every effort to disguise her very mild impatience.

"Well, perhaps not today then, but I would like to introduce you to someone. Her name is Natasha. You remember the schoolteacher you had when you were small? Mira Vladimirovna Matveeva?" She spoke without taking breaths. "The Russian. Her husband is an army officer, so they have been living in Leningrad for the past ten years—but never mind. They have returned. She has a daughter your age. Do you remember, perhaps, young Natasha? She lived here as a young child, until age five, that is. Her family lived not in this village, but to the east. You probably did not meet her."

Lilya had not, although she thought that in truth, Elmira Mamut did not really care either way.

"Well, Natasha's father is stationed here now. They live up the hill from my house, in the house my father lived in before he died, you remember visiting? It has been empty for a year now, thank goodness, though I don't suppose army people would care if a family lived there already. Anyway, I have already spoken to Mira Vladimirovna and she is expecting you to visit."

"No," Lilya thought, "I have no memory of visiting Elmira Mamut's infirm father," but, she wondered, more importantly, how had this decision to visit Natasha been made without her input? She sighed. She knew that her opinions were irrelevant in this conversation, so she hid her annoyance behind politeness.

"I would like to meet Natasha. When did you say I would come?"

"You can drop in tomorrow, then, at Mira Vladimirovna's, after midday? Natasha will be attending school with you." She seemed unable to contain her excitement, and added, "She can help you with Russian. You can teach her Crimean Tatar. When she says a few words in Tatar it is as if she has a mouthful of overripe fruit." She eyed Lilya with hesitation, as if wondering what would be her reaction, or as if she were assessing whether the girl had comprehended the significance of the facts laid before her. Lilya thought this favor was not devoid of self-interest.

"I wonder what Leningrad is like. I have heard that it is so full of culture!" Elmira Mamut beamed and looked into the sky. So that was it, Lilya thought. Leningrad was as far from the Mamut matriarch as China, and from her perspective, no doubt equally exotic. There would be information to mine through Lilya's acquaintance with Natasha.

Lilya felt a twinge of jealousy for a girl her own age who was so cosmopolitan. She realized then that Elmira Mamut had probably suggested to Mira Matveeva that Lilya and Natasha meet. Elmira Mamut's nephew was Lilya's schoolteacher, and he must have told his aunt that Lilya spoke Russian well, enlivening her private, fervent hope to unearth gossip about her new neighbors. She no doubt expected Lilya to divulge whatever she found out, as neighbors do.

Lilya toyed with her flower stems, breaking off bits and pieces, and like her neighbor, wondered what Leningrad was like, but more so what Natasha would be like. It had been a lifetime since she had a female friend, a real companion—since age four, to be exact—and she could not remember it. Her mother was her only source of information on the topic. Ayshe often recounted how Lilya did not leave Pera's side until the day Pera fell ill with tuberculosis, and when they were banned from playing together, it was to young Lilya as if Pera had already died. When she finally did, it seemed a silly thing to be upset about. She had lost Pera already, and she told her mother so. Afterwards, friendship seemed somehow more elusive. She had several cousins, not to mention classmates, plenty of peers with whom to forge friendships, but they were all strangers to her.

Elmira Mamut said, "You can go tomorrow?"

"Oh yes," Lilya said.

No one she knew felt familiar to her in the way that friends do; it was as if other people her age inhabited a different world. Perhaps one who had in fact lived in another world would at last be a friend? In any case she considered herself quite content to wander these hills on her own, to help her family and do her school work, to live in her imagination.

Mrs. Mamut was unduly pleased.

"Thank you, thank you! Lilya, dear, and a happy birthday to little Yusuf from me. I must go home to my children." She picked up her basket, heaved it into the curve of her hip, and lumbered away. Lilya put the encounter out of her mind. She climbed upward. The sun stung her eyes as she made the ascent home.

Lilya entered the back garden to find her mother standing with a glass of water pressed to her forehead, peering around the rocks that formed a barrier on one side of the house, into the brambled bushes.

Lilya stepped out from behind her, breathless from the walk up, holding out the orange flowers for her mother to see. "To go on the table?"

Her mother did not tear her eyes away from the bushes and she took her daughter's arm, grasping it firmly, pointing her chin in the direction of the bushes. She whispered, "Shhh, look over there, what do you suppose ... could it be a rabbit?"

Lilya knew her mother well. Ayshe no doubt hoped it were some beast she could quickly skin and cook for their midday meal. She was forever complaining that there just was not as much food as she was used to in the stalls, and that the food from their home garden barely lasted half the winter. True, Lilya knew, but they always got by.

The bush shook. It appeared to be an even larger animal than her mother had first thought; it was thrashing about, as if with prey of its own. A low growl emanated from the clump of bushes. Suddenly, Lilya noticed that bits of leaves were being tossed into the air and saw her mother step back toward the safety of their house. Lilya was not the least bit perturbed, only curious. She looked up the hill to where she could just make out a stray sheep belonging to their neighbor, and she suspected her mother already feared for the creature's life. Lilya cracked a smile when she caught her mother squinting toward the bush, on the verge of panic.

She laughed, calling out, "Tin-Tin! Hey, you!" The bushes went still and from behind them a fully-grown puppy emerged looking abashed, its gray mutt-face covered in dirt. Tin-Tin released two yelp-like barks, and Lilya knelt down, beckoning him to her.

"Oh, my! I didn't know what it was! I had such a fright. Naughty dog, scaring me so!"

Lilya gave her mother a weary look, and Ayshe frowned in return. Lilya was more patient with her mother than another girl her age might have been, but she knew how much Ayshe disliked the unexpected.

"Mother, you are so silly! Look at him, it's just little Tin-Tin."

"He is not little, Lilya," Ayshe said. She sounded frustrated.

"He is a puppy, mother, honestly! You are frightened by anything."

"Well, *that* is certainly not true. I had good reason, a noise like he was making, and out of view. Why, I didn't know!"

Lilya was kneeling down, petting the overactive puppy. Tin-Tin licked Lilya's arms, neck, and reached up to her salty face until she gently guided him back to her arms. She stood and he jumped eagerly onto her, his paws resting on her midriff. "Oh, Tin-Tin!" She pushed him to the ground. Her mother sighed in disapproval.

"Lilya, please take him back to the Mamuts. For goodness sake, he should not be roaming around here!" she insisted.

"He is a dog—where else is he to roam?" replied Lilya. She had spent most of her pre-teenage years begging for a puppy of her own, only to be met with procrastination and finally an exasperated refusal from her mother, who had a passionate fear of germs. She had explained it to Lilya as bearing some relation to the bedpans she had been responsible for emptying when Ayshe's mother gave birth to Lilya's youngest uncle. How bedpans had turned her mother off animals for life Lilya could not fathom, but she could not try her mother's patience past a certain clearly defined limit, so she had sulked for a few days and then took to befriending other pets in the village. Tin-Tin was only a recent addition, but he was already as much her own as her neighbor's, for all the time he spent in their garden.

"Very well," Lilya said and then handed her mother the flowers, the onions, and the small bag of flour. Her mother took them indoors to continue preparations for the party. The guests would be arriving in two hours.

Yusuf had just turned up to watch the goings-on, and saw at once that his sister was playing with Tin-Tin. He rushed outside as his mother came in and she called after him, "Go with your sister to the Mamuts, then, to take the dog back." He had already wrapped his arms around Tin-Tin, who seemed even happier than the boy at their meeting.

Just then Enver shouted, "I am home!" Ayshe went to greet him at the door. Lilya said hello as she ran past him into the room she shared with her baby brother Fevzi. She never left home without kissing him goodbye. He was lying on her bed surrounded by pillows to cushion a potential fall. Her sleeping cherub. She stroked his cheek and planted a kiss on his hot little head. She could hear their father grumbling in the next room about the scarcity of meat, about the fact that the villagers had access to hardly any of their own produce, about the meaningless figures he had spent all week working on at the local government administration where he had a minor position. Lilya barely took in his words. She stroked Fevzi's cheek. To have a child like him was the only reason she could ever contemplate marriage.

Then Lilya heard her father say the word "Natasha."

"Same age as Lilya. It is unavoidable they will meet. But her father," Enver told Ayshe, lowering his voice a notch, "is an officer. A good man, but Soviet no less. His conscience is subservient to his title. Something is afoot, or why would he be sent here? I heard today that our great writer Cemil Kermencikli was arrested and deported because he dared write about his love for his homeland. Lilya is lucky to have studied for so long her native language in school, because within the next month there will be no trace of it. Can you see why it worries me, this army man? Lilya may see Natasha—we will not be rude—but the Matveevs are dangerous, make no mistake."

Lilya could not believe what she'd overheard. Kermencikli arrested? Could it be true? Natasha's parents, dangerous? She held her breath, and stepped away from her sleeping brother lest she wake him up. And then for a quick, bright moment Lilya experienced an impatience bordering on joy—she *had* to meet this Russian girl now. What could be more exciting than danger? Then, just as suddenly, her mood turned. What was she thinking? What was happening—what was that about the Crimean Tatar language disappearing? What did that mean? Who would ensure the children knew their native songs and writing? Lilya slipped out of the bedroom when her father stopped talking. He saw her and smiled, but she did not stop to chat. She could not bear to hear any more bad news.

"I'll be right back," she told him as she ran past him to join Yusuf, who was already walking Tin-Tin out of their backyard. She ran so that Yusuf and Tin-Tin would have to chase her, so that she could feel the air on her face and not hear her heart pounding.

8

That evening, when I finally arrive home, I go to stand in the backyard, hoping the fresh air will shake Lilya from my thoughts. How has Natasha managed to recount this part of Lilya's life so vividly, as if she were there, inside her head? My attempts to reground myself fail: instead of roses and wisteria I see the orange crocuses I imagine Lilya picked; I think I hear a sound in the bushes and imagine it is Tin-Tin. The scenes Natasha described cling to me, they are here, everywhere, and I begin to feel claustrophobic. I want to cleanse myself of these memories. It is not that they are unpleasant—on the contrary, they are too enticing. I have work to do. I must get back to the computer. But first I have to shower. I attempt to wash the smell of Lilya's world out of my hair, the birthday feast and the flowers and the dog. Her life should not be so interesting, should not seem more meaningful than my own. I should be getting on with my life instead of thinking about hers. No matter that I'm collecting information to no end. I mean (I am working myself up), here I am, not writing a book, not earning a degree, merely trying to understand how a plane could disappear into thin air—God only knows why.

The truth is, I am obsessive.

I drop the soap on my toe and cry out loudly, "Goddammit, I'm completely useless!"

I go to my office, where, wrapped in a towel, dripping wet, I pace. I make circles in front of my computer. There are only a few feet from the desk to the far wall, but no mind. I am possessed. What am I doing with my life? Why do I care so much about a plane from decades ago? At last, face to face with my own uselessness, I have forgotten Lilya.

I take my folders and throw them on the floor one by one, enjoying the smack they make upon landing. Papers come flying out. A map of Earth with different colors identifying areas of unusual electromagnetic energy. A list of places where disappearances have been recorded.

I take the Crimean coin and hold it. Then I throw it down, too. It lands on the map. Right on my state. Which is shaded blue, but I forget why. I look out of the window to see someone standing in the neighboring yard, trimming the wisteria. It must be some gardener, hired to maintain Victor's backyard; maybe his family wishes to sell his house, finally, since it has stood vacant for years. When I look again no one is there, which is just as well since I am only wearing a towel. I make myself a cup of tea and return to my office where I turn on the computer. Then two things that never happen to me happen at once: the light blinks on my answering machine indicating a waiting message, and the doorbell rings.

"Just a minute!" I call out, forgetting the answering machine. I have not yet put on my clothes, and grab the bathrobe that lives permanently on my desk chair.

There is a man standing outside holding a package.

"Delivery for Victor Tehusa," he says.

"Wrong house," I say. "And he's dead."

"This isn't your address?" he asks. I look at the padded envelope he holds out. It bears my address.

"But he lived next door," I say.

"Your address is the one I've got down, so can you just sign for it, give it to his relatives or whatever?"

I am suspicious, but I am a woman living alone, standing naked inside my bathrobe facing an obviously irritable delivery guy, so I do not particularly want to continue this conversation. I sign for it; I'm sure that one of these days someone will show up next door and I can give the package to them. Maybe the gardener I saw earlier is back, and I can run out and hand it over. I go to the kitchen window to look for him. There is nobody there. So I leave the package near the front door in the basket where I keep unread mail indefinitely. I have an aversion to bills, and ignore them until they are well overdue.

I return to my desk and retrieve the message from my answering machine. It is Elisa, my best friend from elementary and high school, whom I haven't heard from in eleven years.

First Victor, then Elisa. As soon as I have let go of Natasha's past, have settled my mind, have relaxed and focused on the present, my own past intrudes. I have lost touch with all of my friends from university. I stopped returning phone calls after I took a leave of absence. I am, for all practical purposes, friendless, and today of all days I am not in the mood to change that.

Her message: "Catherine, it's Elisa, Elisa Stein. Gosh, it's been a long time since we've spoken, hasn't it? I hope you're doing okay. I just found out about Susan. I'm so sorry, Catherine. I'd love to see you. I live in the city, but my boyfriend just got a job not far from home, so I'm home a lot. Let's get together.

What do you think? I was just thinking about when we went to Yugoslavia. What a strange time. Anyway. Call me."

She left three numbers: hers, her parents, her boyfriend's. I write them all down on a piece of paper which I put on the back right-hand corner of my desk. I take the coin from the floor and place it on top. Some other time.

Elisa Stein was my best friend from the first grade straight through high school. We met at a neighborhood park dominated by a large wooden structure that was fitted with every type of climbing and swinging equipment known to man. But it had only one tire swing, and Elisa and I arrived at it simultaneously.

Remembering this earliest part of my life is like peering at my reflection in a steamed-up mirror, but I do recall that day, perhaps because I had just begun elementary school and knew no one my age except for a little boy who always seemed to be either climbing trees or throwing balls—not my idea of a friend. I was looking for something else, and found Elisa by pure coincidence.

"I think you were here first," I told her. She was so small and slight, I might have missed her had we not almost collided. She looked out at me from under her long, dark lashes like a frightened animal. I was struck by how pretty she was. Her face was like a wax doll's. I remember wondering if she was real inside, wanting to reach out and touch her to see for myself.

"Go ahead," I said, feeling like she needed my encouragement.

She flashed me a gap-filled grin and jumped on, holding the rope above the tire as she climbed onto it and slid through the hole effortlessly. I waited patiently for her to finish, taking in her black French-braided hair that pulled at her forehead so tautly, the polished ivory of her skin. When she finished I rushed up and took my turn, informing her that I would not be long should she wish to go again.

It turned out that we went to the same elementary school, but were in different classes. This meant that we never saw each other in school except when lined up for the cafeteria, or on our way to the playground. But it also meant that being friends with Elisa was special, nourished as it was on separation. Class days filled with speculation, the building of anticipation. We walked to our bus stop together after school, a mere five minutes of breathless talk, and on weekends we played at each other's homes. I felt my experiment in selflessness on the playground had set a precedent, which I nurtured the more I got to know her. She was as insubstantial as water; I had to capture her or she would slip through my fingers. One had only to look at her doll-like features, the big, deep-set brown eyes, to see that she needed looking after.

I was projecting, no doubt—I needed more looking after than she did. She had wonderful parents, both doctors, and plenty of self-worth. Her mother called me Cathy despite Elisa's constant corrections, but I minded not a bit because she always invited me for dinner, and the Steins always served desert, a thing my mother reserved only for special occasions. Also, Elisa's mother was always saying to me, "You are such a delightful little girl," and to her husband, "Jacob, isn't Cathy smart? A real brain." He was always nodding in agreement and winking at me.

I especially loved playing checkers with Elisa's father. He even looked like a father, with a face that was always unshaven and lived in, the kind of face that invited a daughter's confidences and conveyed a sort of constant, anticipatory concern. He was the gentlest of men; his delicate hands tapered into long, white fingers webbed with the delicate glow of healing. When he played checkers, I had a front-row view of his hands. I gazed at them endlessly, imagining how he used them to tend to the sick, but I still managed to win almost as much as he did, for which he praised me generously. Sometimes, only rarely, I would feign illness in his presence so that he would bend down around me and clasp his hand over my forehead, peer into my eyes and look at my tongue. Once, I was actually sick; both Elisa and I had caught the flu. He confined us both to bed and brought us orange juice and chicken soup. My mother had to be in the city that day—Elisa's mother was on-call that afternoon and he was not, so for a glorious five hours we were cared for by Dr. Stein. He hovered over us, read us stories, and said more than once, "My poor girls." It is one of my favorite childhood memories.

By third grade Elisa and I were in the same class; by high school we were inseparable, even though Elisa was becoming popular and I wasn't. She was so loyal. I suppose she had a lot to contend with, back then, when looks were crucial and popularity alluring. She was beautiful and I was not, though I never thought of myself in those terms. In the eighth grade, after Elisa's mother had just done my hair in a tight French braid like hers, she told me, "You are becoming so pretty, Catherine!" It had never occurred to me that I had not been pretty already; in fact, it had never occurred to me how I looked at all. Elisa's mother held a mirror before me to show me my hair and I thought, at that moment, that I was nondescript but certainly presentable. I was oblivious to the truth—that I was a fashion nightmare, as evidenced by my overalls and tie-dyed t-shirts. My mother told me I was going through a bad fashion phase but did not give me a complex about it. After Elisa's mother braided my hair, I vowed never to wear brown again. That was my idea of fashion. Within the year, I realized I was the opposite of trendy, and that I didn't have the looks to be trendy in the first place.

Actually, I was sort of pretty from age fifteen to seventeen, then grew out of it, if that is possible, never to see any thing like it in the mirror again until I was in my early twenties. The years from seventeen to twenty-two constituted a terrible time to be not very pretty—most of it I was an undergraduate—and to make matters worse, out of nowhere came an extra layer of fat that put me on the chubby side of full-figured. I had breasts, at least.

By her mid-teens Elisa, always lithe, had gained the substance she had lacked as a child, but it merely made her impossibly real. With delicate long arms and legs and wavy black hair that fell just beyond her shoulders, she was slim, yet curvy at the same time; her breasts were small, but obvious, her stomach had a caved-in look in contrast, and her hips—bony as they were—were wide enough to set off her tiny waist. Elisa never grew out of her looks, as far as I know. By the age of fifteen she was stunning, and still my best friend.

There was nothing particularly interesting or unusual about our friendship other than the fact that, as a result of her looks, she was never without a date and I never had one. She had to put up with my eccentric mother, and I had to put up with her raving on about boyfriends and the occasional sleepover with popular girls to which I was not invited. But for the most part we were inseparable, until almost the end of high school.

When we were seventeen my mother and I took Elisa to Yugoslavia during a summer holiday. We all stayed with my mother's then-boyfriend, Roman, in a rented cottage on a little island off the Adriatic Sea in Croatia. In the evenings, while Roman and my mother were otherwise occupied, Elisa and I sat on the beach and talked, drank, and smoked (I smoked from age fifteen to seventeen, nearly a pack a day; it was my only real act of rebellion). We met some other vacationers from Yugoslavia, Italy, and France, mostly boys with whom we flirted in pidgin English as we listened to strange European pop music and giggled a lot. Once we went skinny dipping. We always had something to do and someone to do it with, but on one particular evening we sat on the beach alone. For some reason there was no one around that night to hang out with, and as a result the conversation got as deep as conversations got at that time in my life. Elisa sobbed over her ex-boyfriend—she'd just been dumped, only she hadn't had the time to really process it, apparently. I griped about my lack of boyfriends and my age-old virginity. We were drunk by the time our bottle of champagne was half-empty, when Elisa wandered away.

I quelled my jittery nerves—nothing wrong with a drunken wander, we'd done it at home many times before. I followed Elisa; she moved faster than I did.

First she went toward the beach, then she made a sudden turn onto a dirt lane, and on down the road. There were trees ahead; it was hilly. I saw her dip down into a valley, then up to the foot of a hill, and I went cold.

"Let's go back," I said. She didn't look back.

"Don't go there!" I called out, when she began climbing the hill.

"Stop being so sober, Cat."

"Stop!" I shouted, as she kept climbing.

"What's your problem?" She zigzagged, stumbling, higher and higher. "Are you afraid someone might see us?" She started to giggle, one hand clutching the half-empty bottle, the other crashing to the ground now and then to catch her fall.

"I just don't want to go up there. Let's stay down here."

"But the view! Look, I bet we can see the house! I can see little flashing lights. And look at the stars, Cat."

"I don't want to see the house, and I can see the stars from down here, Elisa. Please?" I stood at the bottom of the hill, holding on to myself to keep from falling. I felt nauseous every time I looked up. It wasn't that high, maybe a couple hundred feet, and it wasn't a steep slope. But she was already at the top, dancing around on it, gesticulating for me to come, the champagne bottle to her mouth.

I was alone and drunk and finally went up the hill for company. I vomited along the way, and felt marginally better. I pulled her to one side. I did not want to go to the other side, near the trees. That place gave me a bad feeling. I wished we had more champagne to distract me from that place. It seemed to call to me; then again, I was already drunk, and more alcohol might have made it worse. In fact, it got worse as we sobered up. Elisa sat with her head on my shoulder, singing "Purple Rain" off-key. "I'm bored," she said. "Come on, let's go for a walk."

"Let's go down," I suggested.

"Over there," she pointed at the very place I wanted to avoid. "There are stones. Do you see them? Big rocks!"

I saw them. Elisa squealed. I belched. I thought I might vomit again.

"No, please, stay here," I begged.

"Don't you feel well?"

"Horrible. Keep me company."

"You're not even the one bummed out over a break-up!" She stuck her tongue out at me. "Live a little."

"I have a bad feeling," I told her.

She looked at me like I was insane. I felt insane. On the other hand, part of me felt quite sane, absolutely certain that we would regret going near those stones.

"You're the rational one," she said, "I'm the superstitious one, remember?"

So it was. I had no strength to protest. She went. I went after her.

Elisa fell before she got there. She had stumbled and dropped the now near-empty bottle.

"Oops," she giggled. "Oh, well. Guess I'll just sit here, then. Look, Cat, isn't the light funny here?"

There was a glow around us. I looked down the hill. It was hazy. Quite a few houses were in sight. I pointed them out.

"There are more houses on this side," I said, "that's why it's lighter here."

I was feeling dizzy. I took a step closer to look at the houses below.

"Look at the stones, Cat. Do you think there was something here once?" Her voice was small and far away.

"Oh, no," I said, as pain seared my head. What was happening? I felt a strange tingling throughout my body. The two stones were on either side of me—I had been trying to get away from this spot all evening, but had somehow ended up here. I saw white, all around. I heard a deafening static. Elisa screamed.

I tried to move away, but my legs were held to the spot. I pulled, pushed, and suddenly, came to the ground with a thud, feet away from the stones, right next to Elisa.

She was ashen. She grabbed my arm. "Let's go."

We ran down the hill, she half-supporting me as I caught my breath, straight toward the beach behind our cottage. We fell into the sand, panting. We could hear my mother's laughter from here, which made me feel safe. Elisa must have felt the same—she didn't move, her hand was still grasping my arm. For a long time we didn't speak.

"I must have had some sort of attack, or something," I said after a while.

"Where were you?" Elisa asked. "I mean, where did you go?"

"What do you mean?"

"Cat, you disappeared. For a few seconds you just weren't ... there. At all."

"Don't be ridiculous, Elisa. I was dizzy, I fell. Everything went white. Oh, God, I hope I don't have a brain tumor!"

Elisa was staring at me, wide-eyed. She pulled away.

"No. You were *gone*. You disappeared."

"What are you—?" I couldn't finish my sentence. Not while she was staring at me like that. Like she was scared of me.

She whispered, "You knew it would happen, didn't you? In that spot."

I didn't answer her. I stared at the quiet sea, and let sand run through my fingers.

"I'm going to bed," I said.

We shared a double bed in the spare room. It was so late by the time we got to it that my mother and Roman were quiet, no doubt fast asleep. After I got into bed, the sheet pulled right up under my chin, I said to Elisa, not knowing if she was asleep or not, "I knew."

I also knew that I couldn't have said beforehand what it was I knew. I just knew ... something.

We talked about it, the next day, after we recovered from our hangovers. We decided we must have been totally wasted. I told her I was not fond of heights when I was that drunk. It was a version of history we agreed on, implicitly, and we did not speak any more about it. And where was the hill, the two stones? I looked for the spot, in the daylight, as we drove by it or walked near the hill below, but I never recognized it. Everything looks different in daylight. Or maybe I did not want to see it. Regardless, weird things happen when you're seventeen and have had too much champagne.

Somehow, after that summer, we drifted apart. Elisa started going out with Mark, and I finally started to sleep with someone, Olaf, the son of my mother's latest boyfriend. Then we went off to college and lost touch. It happens.

9

I tell Natasha, the next week, that I have heard from Elisa.

"Yes. Nice girl. You were such close friends. You two always reminded me of myself and Lilya. When will you meet with her?"

"I'm not sure I will," I tell her.

"Why not? Don't you want to call her, after all this time? Aren't you curious?"

"A little. But I'm not sure if there's a point."

"Ah, yes, I forgot. You fell out after that summer. I forget what happened. Did you quarrel?"

I am surprised she remembers the summer. "We didn't argue," I say. "It had nothing to do with that. We just lost touch."

"Oh, because I remember after that summer—didn't you go to the beach somewhere together? Oh, yes, that's right. Susan took you with her to Europe. Afterwards you weren't so close anymore."

She stands up and putters into the bathroom. When she comes back I am in the kitchen, making a sandwich.

"Don't cut yourself," she tells me. I am chopping the lettuce hard. I am irritated.

"Maybe I will call her," I say.

Natasha wanders into the other room. I bring out my sandwich and sit at the table to eat it. I got here late today. I lost track of myself and forgot about lunch. Now I'm ravenous. Natasha didn't even call to remind me to come. She said, when I arrived, that she figured I'd come when I came. She has already eaten, of course; it is almost dinnertime for her.

"I found a photograph of you recently." She bites her lower lip. "Now where is it?"

She rummages in the drawer of her cabinet, then goes into her bedroom, beckoning me to follow.

Natasha is wearing purple, bright purple. A cotton dress, ankle-length, with short sleeves and a scoop neck. She is radiant, almost cheerful. The evening light breaks and splays through the giant perfume bottles lining the chest of drawers, creating discordant splashes of color on the wall behind it. She is caught in its luminescence for a moment—she gives me a half-smile and I think, for a second, that there is something surreal about this scene, about my grandmother today.

Then she leads me to her bed and lifts up her mattress. Underneath is a photo album, which she opens to the first page. She takes out a picture of my grandfather and me. I was about six years old, and straddled his hip, my legs around his waist. I was laughing, my head thrown slightly back, and he looked content—not smiling, his lips just the slightest bit upturned. He was a strict man, a lawyer, living the American dream. I'm not sure he ever left the United States, and he was married to his Russian wife for forty years.

Natasha was like a small planet revolving around his sun, asking if he wanted this or that. She attended to him as if his life depended on it—motivated, my mother told me, by her appreciation for him, not any wifely sense of duty. She felt saved by him, according to my mother, though I don't believe her; I think it was the other way around. I saw how he watched her every move.

I never saw them argue. At a point of friction they would move their separate ways, my grandmother to a solitary pursuit like reading or doing her watercolors, my grandfather—if he could—to socialize. He would wander over to a neighbor's to chat about gardening or the weather, or he would have a drink with colleagues, or play tennis with friends. He was happiest in company. She was happiest alone.

Natasha turns over the photo, "It was ... let's see. Catherine, age six. It is true, what a picture says. I remember you so well when you were little. Your grandfather just adored you."

What is most clear in the picture is that I adored him, and I point this out to her.

She nods. "Well, I thought I would show you. I keep them here." She returns the photo to the album and slips it under the mattress. I return my attention to her. It has suddenly occurred to me what an odd place it is to keep a photo album.

"Why do you keep them there?"

"Oh!" She laughs. "I don't know." Her bottom lip pouts and she shrugs. "I suppose it is safe here. I feel it is safe. No one knows where it is, and it is always close by. I won't bore you now, but I have many pictures there, from long ago. You might like to see them. Another time." She jumps up. "Well!" She shuffles into the living room and sits down on the sofa.

"Natasha," I say, remembering Lilya, "do you think you'll ever go back? To Russia or Crimea?"

"I cannot go back, Catherine."

I rush to add, "I'm just curious. I've heard there are tours that go there now." I realize as I say it that she would never go on a tour—it would be too much like trips to Denny's. She'd rather ride a horse to Russia.

"I have nothing to do there, no one to see. I would like to go to China. I have read a National Geographic magazine about China. I think it would be very interesting. But, no I do not think I will go anywhere at my age. It is too late." She looks almost sad for a moment. She lifts both hands and brings them down, one on each knee.

"I wanted to tell you something Andrew said." She adds, "Your grandfather." Natasha moves to the kitchen now, fills up a glass with water from the faucet. "That is why I remembered the picture."

"I miss him," I say for some reason, but my intonation is all wrong, I sound like I am seeking her confirmation. I haven't thought about him in ages, but now that I've seen the photo, his face is clear in my mind. I wonder if Natasha still misses him, if she thinks about him a lot. Or about Refat. I see her in a different light, suddenly. She was once in love with someone else. I assume she was also in love with my grandfather.

She sighs, frowns, says, "Yes, I miss him, too." There is barely a pause: "He was of course very embarrassed when your mother became pregnant with you. He did not approve at all, but he was very excited about having a granddaughter." She continues, "Your grandfather said that a child must know even in the womb that he is wanted. I want you to know that you were wanted, very much wanted."

She pauses to check that I understand. I nod. I wonder why she is bringing this up. The thought has never really preoccupied me—after all, my grandfather had been loving and kind to me, so it had never occurred to me to wonder how he felt about my mother's pregnancy.

"It's nice of you to tell me that," I say.

Natasha remains at the sink and I move into the living room. I stand just behind the counter, at the opening above the sink between the kitchen and the living room. We stand on either side looking through at one another.

I ask, hinting at her motive, "And you? Did you approve?"

"No." She says it a little too quickly. "But I loved you the moment I knew you were there, inside my daughter. They are different things."

I sympathize with her as much I can. I never felt disapproved of or unloved, so I have no emotional need. I am not comfortable with her admission of disapproval, though. I wonder what she expects of me now. We have never done this sort of thing until recently, the admissions and confessions.

I say, "I suppose it is difficult when your daughter becomes accidentally pregnant, and she plans to raise her child on her own. It must be frightening."

I suspect Natasha is getting at something else, for she has not moved for several minutes, as if she is gathering her thoughts.

"Oh, yes. I warned her. It never would have happened when I was young, you see, but I knew I lived in another world with different rules. In this country the rules changed often. Susan, she did not have common sense with boys. Or men." She rolls her eyes. "The men she was involved with! I was not happy when she was pregnant, about who her boyfriend was. But then I knew, destiny brought you to me."

Is she alluding to my father? My mother claimed uncertainty about which boyfriend he was exactly, so Natasha couldn't possibly know.

"She had more than one boyfriend at the time, didn't she?" I ask. Natasha surely knew of her daughter's promiscuity—even I know how she was then, before me.

Natasha puts her empty glass on the counter and enters the living room. "Oh, yes, of course!" She waves her hand in the air. "Susan had someone new, all the time. I did not like *any* of them!"

There is a flurry of motion as she rushes to her watering can, fills it up in the kitchen sink, and begins watering her plants. I open the curtains on the sliding glass doors to the sun just beginning to set. The light is kind, warm. The air conditioner clicks on as I stand near the doors; it comes through a vent on the floor and blows my hair up, chilling me. Destiny brought you to me—the words repeated themselves in my mind.

"We are very alike in many, many ways." She laughs.

Now what was the point of all that?

Natasha is superstitious. She tells me that the Rooster likes to take center stage, is confident and assertive. That is how she is when she tells Lilya's story—she calls it that sometimes, "Lilya's story." I ask her not to omit her own, and she shushes me. "I'm getting to it now," she says.

Her words come to life. Her voice and manner obscure our surroundings. I enter another world via Natasha's memory. It is an alternate reality in its own right, and I am lost in it.

10

June 1937

Natasha had not forgotten some things from her first summers in Crimea when she was a young child, and she anticipated the joys of a Crimean summer with the passion of nostalgia: she would help pull down grapes and mash them to a sweet pulp for homemade wine; she would pick cherries, wild pears, and crab apples and eat them whenever her appetite demanded; she would drink wine at summer parties and eat the sweet pies and turnovers her mother could be persuaded to make. Near the house where she and her parents were staying grew great clumps of wild cherries, and no sooner had she settled in then she found a basket and a recipe for pie.

She and her parents were staying just up the mountain from Elmira Mamut's home, a ramshackle house with several side additions built to accommodate first a late child, then a newly married one. It was a very obviously lived-in home, very nearly buried in verdure; only at close range did it appear distinct from its environment. When Natasha had first arrived she thought this was to be their house. She had paused for a moment under the dark shadow of a large beech tree, wondering if she could bear to live in such darkness, when she noticed, just a hundred yards or so up the hill and behind a row of trees, another house, smaller and lighter. Elmira Mamut came out to greet them and show Natasha to her own room, which is when Natasha knew she had a home. Her own space, tucked away at the back of the house, had a view of the garden and was furnished with a bed and a desk. She spent many hours sitting on the bed reading; she sat there now, waiting for the Crimean Tatar girl Lilya to arrive.

Natasha's impatience to meet the visitor at last drew her out of her room into the living area. She sat near the window watching her father, who was sitting outside smoking in the shade while he read a newspaper. After a few moments Natasha heard a girl's voice call out in Russian, "Good day!" Natasha had such a burst of shyness then that she did not move from her position, instead peering through the window at the girl.

The Crimean Tatar girl, of average height with dark brown hair, stood just feet away. She had small features, and lacked expression. Natasha's father looked up from his paper and smiled broadly. His mustache twitched when he spoke. "Hello, Lilya, as you must be!" He nodded. "I am Aleksander Dmitrievich. You've come to meet my daughter on the orders of Elmira Mamut, no doubt."

"Yes. Natasha and I will be in school together," Lilya said, still without expression.

"So I've heard." He stood up and approached Lilya. He was tall and dark. "You are the daughter of Enver Bekirov are you not?"

"Yes, I am."

He nodded again, this time almost imperceptibly. "Perhaps I will call by, soon. I would like to meet your father."

"I am sure he would be pleased to meet you."

"Oh, good. I shall stop by quite soon."

Natasha waited for him to usher Lilya inside or call his family out, but Aleksander Dmitrievich just looked Lilya over and squinted. With an introduction like that, Lilya would surely not be exactly eager to meet the rest of the family. "Honestly!" Natasha thought in exasperation. Did her father have to introduce himself like that? No wonder the poor girl wasn't smiling—she had just met an army officer who had told her he was going to go talk to her father!

Finally he turned and called, "Natasha! Mira! Our guest has arrived!" He touched Lilya gently on the back of her arm to guide her inside.

Natasha moved into the center of the room near her mother. The living room was sparsely furnished, with a busy red-and-white wool rug hanging on the wall above a couch. The curtains were open, but at this time of the day very little light made its way inside, so the room was lit as if by twilight. At least it was cool there. So far it was always cool in that room, which was welcoming on a hot day like today.

Lilya came in with Aleksander Dmitrievich. "My wife Mira Vladimirovna," he said, introducing her to Natasha's mother.

Mira clasped her hands before her and said enthusiastically in Crimean Tatar, "Hello, hello!" Natasha remained somewhat in the shadows behind her mother, as if awaiting her cue.

"This is Natasha," said Mira, stepping aside as Natasha came forward, and then, in Russian, "Let's not stand near the door. Why don't we sit down and have a drink. Tea? I have some compote Elmira Mamut has made."

Lilya smiled tentatively and followed Mira and Natasha toward the couch. Within moments Mira had disappeared into the kitchen; then Aleksander nodded and said, "I will see you shortly," and went back outside. The girls were alone. Natasha guided Lilya to a chair; she took a seat on the couch so that they sat across from one another.

Natasha stared at Lilya and wondered what it was the Crimean Tatar girl saw when she looked at her. Natasha thought herself typically Russian-looking. She had the broad cheekbones of her mother, but was tall and slight like her father, with his dark hair and pale complexion. Striking, though not exactly pretty.

Natasha thought Lilya a true beauty (an opinion Lilya never shared): the Crimean Tatar girl was almost as tall as Natasha and just as slender, with long, chestnut hair and a near-olive complexion. With her small features, defined cheekbones, and dark eyes set under thick eyelashes, Lilya had allure, intensity.

Lilya stared at Natasha in silence, and nearly a minute passed this way until Natasha spoke up in Russian, "I do not speak Crimean Tatar very well. I have lived in Leningrad since I was just six years old. I did speak it better, when I was young and lived here before."

"I see," Lilya said.

"You see, we lived in a communal flat. All the neighbors were Russian."

"Your mother speaks Crimean Tatar?"

"No, a few words only. She speaks German and French—she studied them at university. My father is in the army; that's why he was stationed here once before, why my mother knows some Crimean Tatar."

Lilya stared at her companion, seemingly tongue-tied. She was, she would confess to Natasha later, impressed that Natasha's mother had gone to university, had been educated in a manner so worldly as to know foreign languages. She was also surprised by how forthcoming Natasha was. Lilya herself vacillated between shyness and bold curiosity, but rarely revealed much of herself. Curiosity won out for the moment, so she asked, "Leningrad—what is it like?"

"Oh, just beautiful! Though it is very cold and damp and my mother is ill, so it is not good for her health. She has a cough and the doctor says warm weather would do her good. But you do not want to know of that sort of thing, I suppose. You mean the theatres, the concerts and so on? The buildings are all yellow, a very majestic color really—it was Catherine the Great's influence, did you know that? And there are a great many shows one can see, and the museums—"

"Natashenka, will you come here?" her mother called out.

Natasha smiled apologetically. "Just a minute, please," she said to Lilya, and went into the kitchen.

Lilya was all alone. Aleksander had begun walking slowly back and forth outside as he smoked. When Natasha returned to the room, Lilya was sitting so still that Natasha nearly reached out to touch her cheek, to make sure she was breathing.

"Natasha says you speak Russian very well," said Mira as she came in with a teapot and a sugar bowl. Natasha set some cups down on the small table in front of the couch. Lilya looked down and denied she had any ability in Russian.

"Well, you must, and truly I am so glad, Lilya! Not just for Natasha's sake. I don't speak Crimean Tatar myself, and here we are," she coughed into her hands and brought a handkerchief from her pocket. "It is already better, my cough, and I've only been here for a few days!"

"It is so beautiful here," Natasha piped up. "The mountains just beckon to the sky, do they not?"

Lilya said nothing, but at last she smiled. Natasha felt a weight lift off her shoulders. She believed she had finally glimpsed the girl's character, her kindness. Lilya would tell Natasha later that she rarely liked girls, but that she began to like Natasha as soon as she had made that observation about the Crimean sky. She felt it to be true herself, though she had thought it took a lifetime of seeing it to realize its beauty.

When Mira stood and left the room Natasha leaned forward, whispering, "I have a secret to tell you."

It was 1937 and the height of Stalinist repression, even if a girl could be forgiven for not seeing things in exactly those terms at that time. In retrospect, there could be no doubt that the same Josef Stalin who was so publicly revered was—not so publicly—sending his henchmen to destroy every inkling of human freedom. Even in the midst of it all most people had a sense, as did Natasha—even if hers was half-formed and ill-informed—that a wrong opinion, a wrong step, and you could be fired, blacklisted from your profession, or disappear, or all of the above. It was a surreal time, a nightmare within an enigma that masked itself in paranoia and confusion. Since so little was known to the public, emotions reigned, a deep, abiding suspicion above all.

Natasha did not know the scale of Stalin's purges, but she knew that some of her father's colleagues had disappeared (because they did not serve faithfully, her father said, though not long beforehand her father had had nothing but good things to say about the very same people). She saw how he was almost always on edge these days, volatile in temper, prone to outbursts. She had overheard, late at night, her parents mentioning this or that prison camp on the fringes of the Eastern taiga. And her best friend from school in Leningrad had lost her brother, who was taken in the middle of the night and was now, it seems, in Siberia doing hard labor. The reason, her friend said, was no reason—his arrest followed his request that all workers comply with established safety procedures at his factory job. She did not say, as Natasha concluded much later in life, that her brother had done no more than voice his opinion above a whisper. He had merely revealed to his employers the Achilles' heel of his immortal soul, which sought the freedom to improve his human condition. Natasha's father, when asked by his daughter what it could mean, warned her that the laws were made to ensure safety, and should not be questioned; he asked her not to mention it again. She didn't, but she thought about it quite a bit, and came to the conclusion that bad things were happening for inexplicable reasons.

"Why Crimea?" she asked her father, when he announced, peering over the top of his newspaper, that they were going back.

"A job," he replied.

"We left there once already," she said.

"And now we're going back. It will be fun for you. Your mother's sickness ... she needs some warm air, and she can instruct the Tatars in Russian. They need to know it."

"What about you?" Natasha persisted. "What will you do? Are you being demoted?"

A man's pride, Natasha had worked out, was a sure route to truth, or at least a less-concealed version. Her father had a comfortable position in Leningrad, had been promoted, was always being invited to meetings. He seemed important; their city was important. Crimea was where you got sunburnt.

"There is important work to be done there!" her father growled.

"Like what?" Natasha scoffed. She could flirt with danger when her curiosity demanded. He might yell, deny her some privilege or indulgence, but he no longer smacked her as he had when she crossed the line as a little girl.

"Like making sure the minorities are not up to anything," he said.

"Oh, the Tatars," Natasha said, with a hint of sarcasm. "I suppose there are some dangerous ones, making mischief, who must be dealt with."

Her father glared at her, but nodded, barked out, "Satisfied? Don't forget the importance of discretion." He returned to his newspaper.

Natasha remained in the room, casually reading some book she'd plucked from the bookshelf. Gradually her father relaxed, and finally he said to her gently, "You want to know too much, darling. Sometimes it is better to know very little."

Never mind. She suspected that the Tatars in Crimea were in trouble. She did not have the words for it, but she understood implicitly that they were to be repressed, and that her father would be involved.

Natasha was too young and too preoccupied with youthful follies to be able to translate her suspicions into anything like empathy. She couldn't imagine any act that truly merited suffering in a labor camp. The inability to imagine how such suffering could be deserved meant she couldn't relate to it, either. Not unlike the bright young things her age in her country, Natasha's belief in the perfectibility of human nature existed undisturbed alongside her vicarious sense of political danger. But more than anything, Natasha didn't worry too much over the disappearances or the labor camps because she was a fifteen-year-old girl and loved what girls her age loved—to socialize, to gossip, to dream.

Moving to Crimea only amplified her girlish preoccupations. Natasha felt like she was on a different planet there, one without the dark cloud of politics looming overhead. She was inundated with smells and flavors, sunshine and sky—just as she had remembered, if vaguely, from years ago. Crimea was like a holiday land where nothing ever went wrong.

And so it was that when Natasha met Lilya, any sense of caution was lost beneath the desire to find a new best friend with whom she could enjoy her newfound Crimean world. Natasha liked Lilya immediately. What then could be more tempting than a secret to lure Lilya into friendship?

Natasha took Lilya outside, telling her mother she was showing Lilya their garden.

Nothing inhabited the garden yet except for overgrown grass, weeds, and the decaying remnants of a wooden fence, but the area to be cultivated was sizeable. Natasha told Lilya that her parents had big plans for their garden. They had never had a country house, and Natasha's mother especially longed to put her hands in the dirt and make things grow. Natasha took Lilya a good ways from the house, began to lower her voice with every sentence, and then she suddenly became nervous. What in the world could she say?

"So what is the secret?" asked Lilya.

There was only one thing Natasha could think of, and that fact—she felt it even as she decided to share it—she should not be sharing with a Crimean Tatar girl.

"My father is in the army," she began, and awaited a response so that she could have more time to formulate her next sentence.

"Yes, I know."

"Well ... I'm telling you this because it is only fair, and I believe in truth. Please do not say that you heard this from me."

"You have my word," Lilya said. She waited expectantly, but Natasha said no more for several long moments.

"No going back now," Natasha thought. She said the next words with a combination of nervousness and excitement (telling herself not to worry about the consequences): "The government has some plans to change things in Crimea, I hear ... I mean, things related to the Crimean Tatars."

Natasha thought that of course Lilya knew her father was in the military, and therefore would not be in the least bit surprised by her new friend's knowledge. Her words had clearly not had much impact, as Lilya said after a moment, "Oh. Is that it?"

"Well, I thought I ought to tell you just to warn you."

Natasha thought, "Well, what was the point of warning her? She already suspected as much. Only now, if she tells someone—I'm sure she will, too—it will easily be traced back to me." Would she get in trouble with her father, Natasha wondered, or would the Crimean Tatars begin to shun her? Or both? She already regretted what she had divulged in her impatience to befriend Lilya.

Lilya said, with barely a hint of smile, "I thought for a moment you had heard that Elmira Mamut was expecting yet another child."

"Oh, yes," Natasha giggled, "I hear she has many. No. But I have heard that the Crimean Tatar language will soon be phased out."

"Yes," Lilya replied.

Natasha could not tell from her tone of voice if she had known this or not.

"It's just, I was hoping to study your language," Natasha said.

Lilya brightened. "I can teach you."

"Oh, ah, thank you," Natasha stuttered, surprised.

"The truth is, I'm not so interested in politics," Lilya said. "Though of course I should be, since it is my people who suffer." Her eyes darted to Natasha and back.

How Natasha wished she had never broached the subject! She felt that Lilya was offering her a way out, and offered, gratefully, in return, "I'm not interested either."

"Do you believe in ghosts?" Lilya asked, apropos of nothing at all.

"Why? I might, I guess."

"These hills are haunted. Near your house a woman has been seen, an old woman who was Elmira Mamut's grandmother. She apparently died of a broken heart. I saw her here myself, once. Everyone knows about her. My thinking is that if a person can survive death, then life can't be all that important, and certainly not politics. After all, you're alive for a few decades, but you're dead for eternity. So how important can life be?"

In her excitement Natasha forgot all about the earlier discomfort of discussing politics. This was an interesting girl, all right. Natasha did not necessarily consider politics unimportant, but she would rather talk about ghosts. How many people did that? Certainly not her friends in Leningrad.

"I see what you mean. Life after death is certainly more interesting, isn't it? There are many ghosts in Leningrad. I think I might have seen one, one night when I was coming back from a concert, but I'm not sure."

Lilya took Natasha's hand and clasped it, excitedly. "There are ghosts of Greek soldiers here, too. I swear if you sit out in the moonlight on a full moon, you'll see them."

Natasha felt such a burst of joy at Lilya's impromptu gesture of friendship that she exclaimed, "Let's do it then!"

"Do you mean it? Would you dare?" Lilya asked.

"Yes. I think I would."

On the next full moon, only a week away, that's exactly what they did.

Natasha did not ever again mention politics with Lilya. Her suspicions, however, had been justified: the Crimean Tatar language was banned from schools, and several local men were arrested. One was a painter who worked as a clerk at the local government office with Lilya's father, another was a local representative, and she had heard rumors of a third and fourth, all of them sent away to prison somewhere, all of them uncovered as nationalists seeking to elevate their own ethnicity and undermine Soviet authority. On such topics her father was silent. Natasha guessed that he was involved. He had to be in one way or another (judging by their earlier conversation), but Natasha let her suspicion lie fallow. Her friendship with a Crimean Tatar girl cast politics in a very personal light.

She did not wish to contemplate what could become of Lilya's family. Lilya's father could find himself in trouble because he was a Crimean Tatar in local government, no matter how menial and unempowered his job, even if he was honest and patriotic. Nationalists came in all guises, using their positions to sway others to their points of view, or so warned the periodicals her father received from Leningrad. Natasha was unswayed, herself—what did it mean to be nationalist, anyway? It seemed to her that having pride in one's heritage was dramatically different from wanting one's people to take over the institutions of power. Different but the same. A label like nationalism might be no more than a means for their country's bureaucrats to make their lives simpler; still, it sent a tremor of insecurity through Natasha's life as she and Lilya grew closer. The insecurity grew despite the fact that both sets of parents treated the girls' friendship with kindness and inclusion—both girls were invited around to the other's house, each helped the other's family in whatever was needed at the time (Lilya's mother made Natasha's mother special soups for her recurrent colds, for example). Natasha wondered whether Lilya's parents were so welcoming for fear of the consequences of being otherwise; she also knew that no matter how kind her own parents were to Lilya, her father would remain complicit in the Crimean Tatars' repression.

Their first venture to see ghosts seemed to establish the common ground of their friendship. Of course, they did homework together (Natasha fine-tuned Lilya's Russian as the months went by), chased Tin-Tin around the house and garden, helped one another's families inside and out. Their passion, however, was to understand their souls. Perhaps it was just the need to develop a mutual interest—and why focus on the mundane when they could aim higher? Or maybe they were both independently fascinated by the supernatural. Whatever the case, somehow, over time, the big questions became the important ones, their daily lives plain drudgery in comparison.

In hindsight, Natasha believed that at the core of their friendship was a desire for freedom—from their lot in life, from the world they lived in. It seemed almost a kind of feminism before there could be feminism. Neither girl wanted to marry; they wanted to travel and adventure and live alone, in spinsterhood, free from chores and men. Only in their dreams could they entertain such a possibility, and only through sharing their dreams could the possibility of freedom solidify into something like an alternate reality. They were equal under God, whom they did not recognize as such—the concept was difficult to grasp in their atheistic culture—yet they searched to understand the unseen force they felt sure guided and protected them. The unseen force that, in fact, they hoped to glimpse.

They really tried to see ghosts. They hoped, prayed, and mostly just waited. They favored moonlight picnics where long silences predominated. And when they saw and heard nothing, and neither girl had thoughts to share aloud, they still looked and listened in solidarity.

Natasha would one day forget this quiet search for the Beyond. Lilya would one day disappear into it.

11

The doorbell rings for the second time in less than two weeks, but this time I will not open the door. Through the curtains in the living room I can see a young, nondescript white man in his twenties or thirties, I can't tell. I keep out of sight lest he notice me. He is clearly not a deliveryman, postal worker, or messenger in any other official capacity—he wears no uniform and carries no delivery. Probably a Jehovah's Witness, or a burglar checking the place out. I do not open my door to strangers. They make me nervous; you never know anyone's intentions these days, especially young, middle-class-looking white men, who fit the profile for serial killers. He rings the doorbell again. I watch him linger, then leave after a few minutes.

Today I am going out, and not to see Natasha. I am going to the state university about an hour away. Not Princeton—I avoid *that* university like the plague. I have decided to attend a lecture on sacred spaces given by an anthropologist/New Age researcher. Dr. Nelson Fitzwilliam has written quite a few articles on sacred buildings and their placement on sites of unusual electromagnetic activity. Normally I am quite disdainful of "granola" types whose theories are motivated in large part by their wacky spiritual ideas, but this man has done his research. My cautionary opinion of Fitzwilliam does take into account his impressive qualifications, of course, but not purely. His is well-documented, sophisticated research that nevertheless takes seriously the existence of electromagnetic fields and so-called supernatural occurrences—so-called because he seeks to understand them scientifically. I can even forgive Fitzwilliam his shared academic background with Edgar. Easy enough to do, I suppose; you can't dislike all anthropologists because of one bad egg.

I come here every few weeks to attend free public lectures and check out books on my indefinite inter-library loan rights, the happy legacy of my unexpired student card. Being in an academic environment again makes me claustrophobic and anxious—one of the apparent pitfalls of escaping an over-long institutional life, according to the astrologer at that dinner party. My predominant feeling is that somewhere, in these halls of higher education, looms a deadline with my name on it. Universities have, after all, always had expectations of me, even if since taking my leave of absence those expectations are confined to returning library books on time and not monopolizing the copier. Dr. Fitzwilliam's talk takes place, predictably, in a lecture hall which is just like every other lecture hall I've been to—I sit at the very back, low in my seat, hoping no one I know is there.

It's a far cry from the self-assured beginning of my academic career. Once this was the stuff of life for me, where I found satisfaction that bordered on ecstasy: listening to knowledge pour forth, echoing off the high ceilings and sloping seats in the lecture hall, myself at the center, in a spirit of perpetual delight. And of course, getting the highest grades, the private invitations to chat with professors. There was not a subject I did not excel in. Which, in hindsight, is to say that there was not a subject that touched me, at my core, above and beyond all others. I was the perfect dinner-party guest, the one who could contribute to any discussion. My motivation was to conquer the world of facts, which I did. I graduated in the top two percent of my undergraduate class, won awards, earned respect. For the likes of me, my professors said, there was no place else to go, so I stayed. A heady air of expectation surrounded me then.

Now I can see what the problem was. I built my life on facts without meaning, a beautiful ivory tower resting on sand—all around, a precarious business. Now I am not sure what I am—in fact, I am more or less lost, and not too pleased about it—but I am quite sure what I am not. I am not, and never was, a budding expert, an academic-in-waiting. Those types are focused on selective bodies of knowledge, obsessed with their passions, which makes grades and everything else secondary. They wake at night theorizing about the history of the Byzantine Empire, neglecting to do their biology homework. I neglected nothing. I fell into a postgraduate degree in history because I enjoyed it most of all, not because of any passion. My passion, which finally emerged from the one truly academic bone in my body, is so inappropriate to conservative academia that it has condemned me to isolation. Worse than an ivory tower built on sand, my passion is my sand castle. It has nowhere to go but down; it will collapse in on itself, eventually. How appropriate. I am alone. There is no one to suffocate but myself.

If I am stuck with myself, at least I can be honest with myself, which I wasn't really with my fellow doctoral students, and my advisor, to whom I cited maternal disease rather than my own inexplicable, unorthodox obsession as a rationale. I ran. I couldn't very well say that neglecting my thesis had nothing to do with my mother's illness. I couldn't very well say that, instead of writing another hundred pages of my thesis, I'd rather figure out what happened to the 21st Airborne—for no other reason than I had to know.

I have just faced this reality. This week, I withdrew from my PhD completely. Today is, in fact, the first time in almost a decade I have been not been listed, somewhere, as a student pursuing a higher degree.

Perhaps because of my recent emancipation, I begin to flush ever so slightly (but not too much) with the convivial fever of intellectual curiosity. The lecture is not part of a course and is open to the public. Most of those in attendance, like me, come obligation-free, purely out of a personal interest—few appear to be under thirty, and as is usual in such lectures, retirees make up a good portion of the audience. There is no pressure, no grade, no competition: complete anonymity. As I become more comfortable, as Dr. Fitzwilliam gets to the heart of his lecture, I relax enough to lose myself in thought.

I take notes in the way I always have—on pads of yellow lined paper, leaving room in the left-hand margin for subsequent comments or references. I am mostly concerned with the facts he gives, measurements of electromagnetic readings and precise locations, the majority of which display anomalies. He also reads historical and modern testimonies of visitors to the sites to illustrate how commonly lightheadedness, dizziness, visions of all types, and nausea are experienced in those locations. His argument is that people have always sensed differences in electromagnetic fields, and that the feeling of lightness or dizziness has been associated, unconsciously or not, with the Divine, which is why sacred sites have often been built in these spaces. I can find no reason to disagree, given that his facts support his argument. But he has said nothing new beyond what he has written, and his answer to the question what, exactly, is going on in those spots, does not satisfy me. He concludes speculatively—electromagnetic disturbances have the ability to induce altered states of awareness, such as occur during hypnotism and meditation. In such states, he further theorizes, we have access to our true spiritual nature, and are thus open to receiving insights.

I doubt that explanation. I'm not sure there is a higher consciousness, and even if there is, Fitzwilliam's reasoning cannot explain how in such spots people can, like the men of the 21st Airborne, simply disappear.

Something completely unexpected happens after Fitzwilliam's lecture ends and the audience has asked their questions (I realize then it is fortunate I did not pose mine).

There is Edgar, standing at the front of the lecture hall. He is shaking Fitzwilliam's hand and simultaneously patting him on the shoulder. Like old pals. I glance at the flyer for today's lecture, which I had put on top of my notebook so that I could find the room. Nelson Fitzwilliam's alma maters and former teaching posts are listed at the bottom, in a one-paragraph bio. My hunch is confirmed: Edgar attended the same undergraduate college where Fitzwilliam taught, and by the looks of things, Edgar was his student. What other reason could he have for being here today? I do not think Edgar is the type to have an academic mentor, much less one who is not mainstream. But there they are, acting like old chums, laughing and so on, and here I am, scrunching down in my seat to gather my bag and sneak out behind the old woman next to me.

A beautiful blond rises like Aphrodite from the sea of spectators and takes Edgar's arm. "Aha!" I think. I've caught him (I do not reflect that he is not mine to catch). The woman shakes Fitzwilliam's hand and nods, and the three of them chat for a few minutes. I watch, entranced, as Edgar turns to leave the room with this vision on his arm. People do not change all that much, I conclude. He must be here for her. She is probably a seeker of wisdom who practices yoga and goes to this kind of alternative talk regularly. I stand, move down the aisle feeling oddly assured that he will not notice me.

Edgar looks back over his shoulder in my direction—as if he can feel my eyes on his back. His gaze falls past me, but I get a good look at him. I have had no trouble forgetting him, Edgar the man, but his body, and what it could do, have been difficult to erase from my bored, lonely, after-hours mind. The jaw I found so kissable, the muscular arms, the small, dark crevice of his collarbone. He turns away but his image remains in my mind.

Then, a miracle, a revelation: I feel nothing, no fizz, no zing; my lust dissipates like a balloon letting out air. His physical presence evaporates from my erotic memory like a fog. And I had thought the day was wasted.

Thank you, Dr. Fitzwilliam, for tonight's lecture.

I am standing in the garden between the wisteria and the oak tree with Pinky, who has crossed the backyard in my arms under protest. She squirms so much I finally let her spring out of my arms onto the ground, but I do not leave the spot, though my instinct urges me away. Pinky, hiding under the bush next to the house, stares out at me expectantly. It takes a fair amount of willpower and patience to remain rooted to the spot. Within seconds I have goosebumps; moments later I see flashes of light—but I am not superstitious, there is something scientific happening here. I must wait and experience this, I decide; otherwise I'll have given in to weirdness.

I can see that the air around me is moving, despite all logical reasoning to the contrary. You can't see air move, I think to myself. And yet, as I watch, the air sparkles; now it is as if I am caught in a ray of light. I see something, a form in the distance. I see Victor—then I hear his voice—laughing.

I remember something Victor said to me once. I was sitting in the backyard in summer and the hydrangeas in my mother's garden were in full bloom. I sat next to them, on the grass, coloring in my coloring book. There were bees in the flowers; suddenly they were very close to me, flying across my vision and sometimes landing on my book. I was frightened. I decided to lie down and be still. I thought if I moved too much, especially if I stood up and walked away, they would be disturbed and sting me. Then Victor appeared from over the fence. He said, just like that, "The bees think you're just another flower. Blow away like a petal with the breeze." I think I got up slowly and crept off, which is what I thought he meant: to move gracefully, like a ballerina.

I think I hear Victor's voice (I tell myself that it's not really him, it can't be), and I see the bees in my mind's eye again, bees all around. I am back in that moment, lying on my back, unable to make out the sky. It seemed like there was a swarm of them. My heart pounded so hard I thought I would pass out. Then, Victor's head popped into the space above mine, peering over the hydrangeas, and I heard his words about being a petal. I heard him say something else too—how could I have forgotten it? "You've left part of yourself in another world, Catherine. One day you'll have to call it back." When had he said that? Now, as I remember it, his voice didn't seem to be above me; rather, it seemed to come from right beside my head, like he was a ventriloquist, speaking through the bees right into my ears. I shudder myself back to the present moment. I hear his laugh, him saying my name.

"Catherine."

I want to leave. I will myself away, then take a step backwards, and backwards again. I run to my house.

When I get home I see, among the bills and ads that have been pushed through the front door onto the floor, a letter for Victor Tehusa, another one addressed to my address. The letter now lies atop the pile of mail in the basket next to the front door. The next day, I place the morning newspaper on top of the pile, so that the letter is submerged beneath what has grown into a small, lopsided hill. I haven't read a newspaper in months, and don't intend to start now.

Natasha calls me in the morning. She says she cannot meet this Thursday, so I have a week of respite from Lilya, and nothing to do tomorrow but replay yesterday's events over and over in my mind.

12

I have run out of printing paper, so I go into what was Susan's study, an alcove in her bedroom enclosed by bay windows. She was not an office-type person, and refused to turn one of the guestrooms into a proper office; instead, she used the kitchen. The table was her desk, the fax machine was next to the toaster, an electric typewriter (which she only used while standing up) shared an outlet with the blender. The clutter gave me indigestion. Who wants to dine amidst paperwork? As a Mother's Day gift, when I had moved back in with her, I turned the alcove in her bedroom into a mini-study. I purchased a small used desk, and took an armchair from a guestroom and placed it nearby. I did not dare relocate her apparati, but did suggest that a small computer would fit perfectly on the desk, and a small filing cabinet next to it.

She was, she said, "delighted" by my gesture, which as it turns out accomplished very little. The alcove became a storage area for her office supplies, and the place where, after dinner, she would unwind with a glass of wine and a book. She organized the last two fundraisers of her life from the kitchen, and I bought myself a lap tray and ate in front of the television.

I am hoping that there is some extra paper in my mother's desk drawers now, since it is late and the stores aren't open. It is with surprising irritation that I remember, upon entering her bedroom, that Susan left very little in the way of "personal effects." Naturally, the drawers are empty.

Of course, there is ample proof that she lived here—her belongings are everywhere—but hardly any evidence of her day to day life. I encounter no piles of papers in the backs of drawers, no closets stuffed full of years' worth of clothes and shoes, no toiletries filling the bathroom cabinets.

Typical Susan: Before the last time she checked into the hospital, she embarked on a major clearout, without, of course, telling me what she was doing—and before, I might add, she knew she would have to be staying for long in the hospital. One day she called to me from around the corner somewhere, as if announcing that dinner was ready, "Catherine, come here!"

She told me to take some of her clothes, and explained, "I'm not going to live long and the ones you like shouldn't go to strangers."

Cheerful, as always. Of course she had something pithy and uplifting to say, something along the lines of, "Realism is not pessimism, darling, if the reality is not *bad*."

As weird as I thought her request, and as morbid, I did as she asked. (She had fine taste in clothing, after all). There were no other clues to her madness, though when she took two suitcases with her to the hospital I did think it was excessive. But who would argue with a sick person? I certainly did not want to acknowledge that she was going away for long enough to warrant so much luggage. My offer to bring her what she needed on a day-to-day basis went ignored.

Still, a woman needs fresh underpants (you can never have too many), so after she'd been in the hospital for a week or so, without consulting her, I ventured into her bedroom on a search for underclothes—only to find empty drawers, empty closets, empty cabinets. I panicked and began searching every storage space I could find. Even the front hall closet was cleared of her shoes and coats. Not even a speck of fluff on the floor. Nothing! When I confronted her, Susan admitted she had called the Salvation Army soon after having foisted her clothing on me, and given away everything she did not want to leave to me or my grandmother, then cleaned the house from top to bottom. She said, "My body can't take much more, Catherine. I'm not going to make it. I have to face up to it."

She had been preparing not just for her death, but for afterwards, for the business of death her family would have to confront.

Now, paperless, I stand in the alcove of her makeshift study and feel my irritation building to a rage. Just once I'd love to walk into her bathroom and find a half-used jar of face cream gone yellow and crusty around the lid, or an empty box of tampons, or an old pair of her shoes, in need of polish and with soles worn down unevenly, in the back of the hall closet, forgotten. I'd like to go into her bedroom and find she'd forgotten to clean up some spilled wine on the carpet, or had not vacuumed beneath the bed. I'd like to find something of hers that isn't perfect and wasn't perfectly planned!

I am so angry with her right now I wish she were alive just so I could throttle her.

"How am I supposed to mourn you?" I ask. I give a little shriek, not too loud, just loud enough to let off steam. "You haven't even left me a measly scrap of paper to clean up!"

I storm out. I turn on the television and pour myself a glass of wine.

Two weeks since I've seen Natasha feels like a long time. As I am driving to meet her I begin to remember where she left off with her tale, and suddenly I find myself eager to hear more about Lilya and herself, to learn about this Refat character. By the time I make it to her door I am so impatient that I skip over the niceties of greeting and practically pounce on her, announcing, "I'm so excited to hear what happened next, after you and Lilya met!"

In a second I am in the kitchen to see if the tea is made or I can make it, if lunch is ready or we can talk first. Natasha guides me back to the dining table.

"You have hungry eyes. Shall we eat first?"

This is not a suggestion; she is in charge here. I am a bit embarrassed by my unbridled enthusiasm, and say (attempting to mask my deflation, as if lunch had simply not occurred to me), "Oh, sure."

Neither Natasha nor I have much to say over lunch. She asks me how I've been, and I say fine, without giving any details. She seems to accept this, and gives me a similar reply when I ask about how she's been.

So, we are left to eat. It must seem to her that I haven't eaten since the last lunch she fed me, that I am ravenous. Truly, I have rarely inhaled one of her roast beef sandwiches so quickly. Natasha takes her time, as usual, probably because of her age. She's utterly slow; I'm too fast. She tells me as much after I finish my sandwich, and chastises my speed in all things ("For example," she says, "I could hear you sprinting down the hall.")

On the contrary, I tell her, my life is slow, too slow. I say that today I feel impatient with the slowness, and am operating in fast-forward for a change.

Natasha doesn't fall for it; she does not resume her story straightaway. She can't help but notice, of course, that my life holds very little right now, though as of yet she has not asked me what I am doing. Thank God. Whenever someone does ask me what I do, meaning for a living, I become tongue-tied. Where words fail me, my imagination steps in: I see a vast emptiness, and my insignificance in it. I imagine that my life is a big, empty bowl and I'm a marble, rolling around and around the sloping insides, never reaching the center, with nowhere to go but with nothing to stop me. Finally, when my interrogator looks sufficiently confused by my silence, I give some garbled explanation about my course of study, trying my best to put myself across as an eccentric academic type who is doing something so esoteric, so complex, so important ... Half the time people look suitably impressed and say I must be so smart, so driven. Or else they appear to be trying not to roll their eyes, which they no doubt do as soon as I turn away.

My grandmother tells me that life should be slow, and then makes a point by starting a conversation about family, indicating that today, at least, could be very slow indeed.

"Did your mother ever talk to you about your grandfather, after he died?" She asks.

I have noticed that Natasha does not do anything to keep her hands busy when she is not smoking. In fact, she has an uncanny ability to sit perfectly still, her hands motionless, fully concentrated on her listener. Her perfect stillness has—at times—a trance-inducing tendency.

"Hmm?" she prompts.

"She enjoyed speaking of him," I reply, and think a moment. I would rather not have to talk about my mother today, but I see I have no choice. "Susan seemed proud of him."

"Oh? Well ..." she says and frowns. "Your mother and he had a very close relationship. Probably to compensate for her poor relationship with me. She was a daddy's girl."

"It seemed that way," I agree.

It is now, for the first time in my life, that I realize my grandmother and I share some mannerisms (or lack thereof)—for I cannot think what to do with my hands or feet as I sit there bored and restless, wishing I had the outspokenness to change the subject. I wish I were a fidgeter, because this is a perfect time to find a bit of lint on the couch, or a piece of paper on the table, and work it with my fingers.

"He told her things he never told me. I always wondered if, somehow, he turned her against me. Did it seem this way to you?"

My grandmother wants me to comment on her relationship with my mother? This is new. From where she is sitting across from me the sun is in her face and she is squinting, which she normally does only when she removes her glasses. Her slanted eyes give the impression of mild aggression. She awaits my response and seems to grow impatient by the second, staring at me hard.

"If so, I never noticed," I say.

How had my grandfather been against my grandmother, I wonder? I can remember how my mother was with my grandfather, but my memories blur around the edges. Susan's relationship with Natasha is clearer in my mind, but then somehow it had always seemed pre-defined, wrapped in its own bubble, and in a kind of stasis as long as I could remember. My grandfather's role in it all seemed peripheral. His orbit made a wide loop around his family.

"Humph," my grandmother grunts. Apparently, we are both at a loss for words.

I grow uncomfortable. I want to distance myself from wherever it is Natasha is taking me with her questions, but I feel the need to reassure her.

"She did love you."

"That is *not* what I am saying!" she says rather more fiercely than I expect. "I often wonder, what did Andrew say to her, near the end of his life? Why was she so bitter toward me? What had I done to her?"

"Why would grandpa turn her against you?"

I worry I am overstepping my boundaries here, but she opened this topic of conversation, and anyway, I don't want to talk about my mother.

It's begun to rain. Just a moment ago the sun was out, and now, suddenly, the sky is dark. Fall is coming, I can tell just from the way the rain smells. Natasha can't squint at me now; there is no sun to avoid, no masking her emotion with a hard glare.

Natasha remains quiet. The rain begins to come down harder outside and fills the silence. "Oh dear!" she suddenly gasps. "I think I watered my plants yesterday. They will have too much water."

"They're not happy out there, anyway," I tell her.

She is flustered and rushes outside as if it's some kind of emergency, and I follow her the few steps to the balcony. I can't understand why she is acting so bewildered, so helpless. We bring in the plants. We place them on the floor in front of the closed sliding glass doors.

"I think I would like a cookie and some coffee. Would you like some?" she asks, equanimity restored.

"Yes, that sounds good."

"I did not mean to interrupt you." She fills the kettle with water and puts it on the stove.

I don't know what to say. I hesitate to remind her of what I asked. I feel like it would be prying to ask if she and my grandfather had problems, so much so that I almost don't want to know, but now that we both have broached the subject, it's awkward to turn back. To make matters worse, she is clearly not going to just respond. In fact, she appears to be waiting for me to prod her, so I do.

"You said you were worried grandpa turned Susan against you, and I just wondered why he might do that."

She opens the freezer and takes out a glass container filled with fresh ground coffee. She pours it into a coffee plunger. My grandmother has never owned a real coffee maker. They do nothing for the taste of coffee, she says. She used to have some funny Turkish-looking contraption that sat on the stovetop, in which she brought her coffee to the boil three times before pouring it out. Now she is lazier, and uses a plunger, a "cafetière."

"Well, he might have had reasons."

"Oh, God!" I think. "It's about him, the Crimean Tatar boy she loved. She must have told my grandfather."

"Because of Refat?" I ask quietly.

"Your grandfather never knew his name."

The cuckoo clock against the wall chirps the hour. I have always hated that clock. It seemed so loud and offensive, although somehow it is less painful here than it was at my grandparents' house years ago. I don't know why. Maybe the acoustics are kinder here—the harrowing cry might not reverberate as much with wall-to-wall carpet and low ceilings. My grandmother once confessed to me that she never liked it, but that she kept it for my grandfather's sake. He had, she said, shopped far and wide for the perfect clock. He had a love for them generally: the tall grandfather clocks that cooed, banged, sang, and beeped out the time; the ones that stood upwards of six feet high and had more than one face, a little one near a big one, and lots of dials and hands and decorative adornments. The bigger and busier, the better—fortunately he did not collect them, as they were very expensive, but he had at last found one he adored. The cuckoo clock was his favorite possession. He even provided for its future, apparently. (Meaning it will be mine one day.)

I guess I should not be surprised that Natasha has kept it. They were married for thirty-odd years, of course they had a deep connection, right? They must have been in love at some stage, surely. She would want something of his that he loved, a testimony to her love for him.

I've tried not to imagine it, but just this moment I can't help thinking of Refat and Natasha. It is odd to think of my grandmother being young and in love. I wonder if she felt the same way about my grandfather as she did about Refat? Or was it convenience?

Natasha's mouth quivers; I cannot tell if she will smile or frown.

"Catherine?" she asks, to draw my attention back.

"Yes?"

"I told your grandfather that I had been in love before, long before I met him. I don't know why I did. It was one of those conversations that at the time seems so innocent, and afterwards you realize it was only innocent for one of you. I told him that I had been in love as a young girl, and that it hadn't worked out, and he asked me a few questions, and I answered truthfully. Andrew was never in love with anyone but me. He told me so, right then, after I'd told him of my past. He said there was never anyone else on the planet he could love like he'd loved me, and he could not believe that it was not the same for me. I didn't realize how much I had hurt him with the truth, but around that time he began to spend more time with Susan, and around that time Susan began to change, to be difficult with me. We'd never had an easy relationship, mind you, but something had changed. I always suspected it was because of what I told Andrew. I don't know. I never asked. Until now."

I can feel how hurt she is. I hate moments like this, when you want to say something reassuring, but can't think of what, or how. I feel so awkward, just standing there with a sympathetic look on my face. I am simultaneously curious to know more about Refat and pissed off at my mother. Susan the serial faller-in-love—she would have had no right to get upset about my grandmother's love life. Why is it, I wonder, that people consistently fail to apply the same standards to themselves that they apply to others?

Natasha goes to the large cabinet next to the dining-room table and opens it. On top of her good china is a carton of cigarettes. She takes out a pack and opens it. "Let us open a window. I will put a towel beneath the door."

I open the sliding glass doors in the living room. The rain has stopped for the time being, and the air is heavy and wet. The thermometer on the balcony reads nearly eighty degrees, almost cool enough to turn off the air conditioner. Natasha comes out of the bathroom with a towel and goes to the front door. She gets on her knees and pushes the towel into the crack, patting it firmly. I go to help her up. "The alarm!" she exclaims, and brings a chair from the table, shifting it a few feet backwards, and while I support her, climbs onto it. She fiddles with the smoke alarm on the ceiling and then I help her back down. The kettle on the stove emits a whistle which rises to deafening in a few seconds. I rush to take it off the stove, and fill the coffee plunger.

"Here we are," she says from the dining area.

I bring the plunger into the living room and place it on the coffee table. Natasha brings in a pack of chocolate chip cookies and two mugs. We both take our coffee black.

I sit across from her in the armchair. She lights a cigarette.

"I don't know why my mother would have been mad with you about … *that*," I say, not quite comfortable enough to actually say, "about you having been in love." "Are you sure grandpa was upset enough to tell her? It doesn't sound like him." (He was quite softly spoken, and as far as I remember, avoided all confrontation).

"It is funny," she begins, then eats a cookie. Again, I wonder if I am meant to encourage her, or if she will continue on her own. It begins to drizzle. With the door open the sound is loud enough to notice. Soon it seems to surround us, the gentle pitter-patter, steady and calming. I have the sense of being closed away in a safe place, only it's a slightly foreign place and I'm unsure of the language.

"What's funny?" I ask.

"Life, you know. Maybe it's all in my head. Andrew seemed to get over it. He was distant for a little while, and then no more. And Susan, well, she was going through some tough times. You were small, and she was a single mother. I think when you become a mother it's natural to think differently about your own mother, and she probably started to think about all the things I'd done wrong that she didn't want to do with you."

She shrugs, up-down, in one jerky motion. She plunges the coffee and pours me a cup.

I say dryly, "I can't imagine what conclusions she came to."

"What are you referring to?" she asks. She is smirking.

"Oh, I don't know," I sigh. "Never mind. It's not worth talking about."

"Your mother was a very different kind of mother than I was, and look, it had the exact same effect on the mother-daughter relationship. It just amazes me. Does nothing work?"

"She did the best she could," I say, unconvinced.

"She loved you terribly, you know. She was so proud of you."

"Yes, she said so. I loved her, too. How can I complain? She was fabulous in so many ways."

I should tread carefully, I suddenly think. This ground is unstable; I could be leading myself in an uncertain direction.

"No one is perfect, of course," Natasha says. "God knows I wasn't with her. I was too short with her, too critical. I had certain expectations without realizing I had them, and she rebelled. But, you know, she turned out very well. A warm, generous person, if eccentric."

I nod. I have decided not to venture further. I feel guilty that I am on the verge of speaking ill of Susan (not because she is dead, but because I didn't say anything to her face when she was alive, so it seems unfair to say it now).

"Hmm," Natasha says. She is biting her lower lip and looking at me askance, like she's sizing me up.

I want to ask, "What, already?" I can tell her thoughts are brewing something, some observation about me and my mother, and I don't like it.

"Nice coffee," I say.

"You're angry with her about your father."

As if that's the only thing I could be angry about. Plenty of kids grow up without knowing who their fathers are. No big deal.

Natasha takes a deep breath and seems to hold it on its way out.

"No," I say at last, "I'd like to know who he is, but I'm not angry about it."

There: end of conversation. I hope.

I used to imagine that my father was some scoundrel who had left my mother pregnant and alone. I concocted fantasies of him now married to a bimbo half his age, a cruel misogynist prone to physically abusing children, especially his own—for which reason I was better off without him. From about age five on (when it dawned on me that other kids had fathers, or at least an explanation for not having one), I began nagging my mother to tell me who he was. She gave me nothing, as if she didn't realize that it was more than mere curiosity. "Oh, darling, don't worry about him. I love you so much!" she would say and then kiss me on the forehead as an abrupt full stop to the conversation.

When I was sixteen my mother finally caved in, and told me that it didn't really matter who my father was. She said that, it being the 70's when I was conceived, she had been having an affair with three or four men, and sometimes went to parties where she ended up in bed with God knows which of them, and they were all dark-haired or dark-complexioned anyway (the type she preferred). I asked her straight out if she were implying that she did not know who he was, and she said she knew he was a good-looking man, and that's all that mattered—so I assumed she didn't know. She said I should consider not knowing his identity liberating, or a mystery if that made me feel more special. I suspected that, secretly, she wanted me to appreciate how hip she was, how modern and liberated. Besides, I reasoned, she did not care so much who fathered me because *she* was my family. Love is what makes a child, not genes, she said. It was not a time in her life she regretted (I don't think she regretted anything, ever), and she saw no need to apologize for not having provided me with a father. Anyway, as she was fond of saying, life was so generous as to have given me to her, and didn't we have a most wonderful time together? Wasn't she a good mother and didn't we have an extraordinary relationship? Moreover, she added, my grandfather was around for a good part of my childhood, most importantly the early, most influential years of my development.

It's true. I can't complain that I lacked a fatherly influence. Maybe it was because she tried so hard to convince me that I had everything I needed and wanted that I saw all the more clearly the empty spaces that needed filling. Maybe if she hadn't tried so hard, I wouldn't have seen the spaces so well.

"Isn't his name on your birth certificate?" my grandmother asks me. "I thought your mother had put it there, just as a matter of fact."

My heart seems to stop. Would Susan really have put a name on my birth certificate? Could she have been lying to me all those years about not remembering who he was? "You, who think of everything," I harangue myself silently. "Shouldn't you have thought of that sooner?"

Natasha seems to be waiting for an answer.

"I've never actually seen my birth certificate. I guess I haven't exactly gone looking to find out who he was."

"Well, your mother had it somewhere. I remember her needing it to get you your first passport. Maybe it's around the house, or you could just request it from the hospital where you were born."

I am so small, so silenced, so dumbfounded by the sheer simplicity of the thought, that I have at last forgotten why I was so excited to see Natasha today.

Until she says, "Let me tell you about meeting Refat."

13

April 1938

Hitler annexed Austria in March 1938. Of these goings on Lilya and Natasha knew very little—even as Europe slid toward war, nothing of importance seemed to happen in the now-entwined lives of Natasha and Lilya for almost a year after their meeting.

Among their activities: Lilya helped Natasha learn some Crimean Tatar and, in turn, Lilya read all of the Matveev family's periodicals from Leningrad and most of the books they'd brought with them. The girls made a trip to the sea together in August (with Natasha's parents), stopping along the way to picnic in sight of the Dzhur-Dzhur Waterfall. Together they rode homemade sleds down the hills after the first winter snow—and together they were sick with influenza for two weeks afterwards.

Yet, however much they were oblivious to world events, they could not avoid hearing of news closer to home. They learned that Crimean Tatars were being arrested on various accusations, and news filtered into their hamlet of prison camps and further crackdowns on ethnic minorities in Crimea and elsewhere. Lilya and Natasha did not dwell on such news. It was upsetting. Moreover, it was difficult to make sense of. Mundane village gossip and spooky stuff were far more deserving of their attention. They explored local caves at dusk and swore to the presence of powerful nature spirits. One night in early spring, after many attempts, they finally spotted the ghost of Elmira Mamut's grandmother behind the Mamut's garden shed. She was as fat as her granddaughter and hovered, a cloudy form that cast no shadow in the moonlight, her stricken face turned toward the girls. The girls screamed; the ghost vanished.

One might assume two teenage girls would be social, or at least have the desire to socialize—not Lilya and Natasha. They hardly ever spoke to anyone else outside of their families, though they were not conscious of being so socially exclusive. When Natasha recalled, in adulthood, her first meeting with Refat Chobanov, she could find no explanation for why they had taken so long to meet (she had been in Crimea a year and a half by then; it was a very small village and she thought she had met everyone within the first few months). Her memory of the day gave no clue as to how, finally, the particular occasion for their meeting came about. It was as if she and Refat had both fallen from the sky and landed on the bench outside their school together, when out flew a scrap of paper from a book ...

"I'll get it," Natasha said.

"No!" the young man cried, but in vain. Natasha had picked it up and read it. A poem, about Crimea.

"Hmm," she said. "Here you go. I rather like it."

He murmured something under his breath.

"You're Refat," she said, "I can see your name written on your book."

"I know who you are, too," he said, eyes averted. Then he snapped, "It's just a poem, not a very good one. I was trying to describe something about the land, so don't read too much into it."

"What are you saying?" Natasha asked. "I just told you I liked it. What's your problem?"

"No problem at all," he said. "It's no secret that your father is an officer and I just wanted ..."

"Yes?"

"I'm not frightened. Just the opposite. I'm telling you that this poem means nothing, in case you had any ideas now that you've read it."

"Shut up," responded Natasha, sulking, "Who do you think you are? You really don't know what you're talking about, and I don't see the point anyway. What has it got to do with your poem?"

"Poets have been arrested on less evidence," he grumbled, "accused of being Crimean Tatar nationalists."

"You're poem is beautiful, Refat. My father is not going to arrest you. I'm not his informant."

"I see."

"Do you? You are noticing things that aren't there. Either in me or your stupid poem. Are you that worried you'll be branded a nationalist or something? Is that it?"

"No." He grew hot. "I shouldn't even be talking to you like this. We should pretend this never happened, for your own good."

"What do you know about my own good, Refat?"

Refat was silent at that and in his turn began to sulk. Natasha hoped he had noticed that she was not the typical gracious female; that she was someone who, in the company of men, would not retreat to the kitchen, but would hover, interject, object.

"You are just being sensitive," Natasha rolled her eyes now. "As all poets are. Your poem, it seems to me, is about love, about this village," she made circles with her arms and pointed up, "about this mountain. It is innocent. It is beauty, if you can understand such a thing, and we will discuss it no further."

Despite her irritation, Natasha did not want this conversation to end. She hoped to think of something especially galling to say to him, but her mind went blank. She tried working herself into a huff, hoping an idea would come. He sat there, so smug, so.... stubborn.

Refat exhaled deeply.

"Aren't you going home now?" he asked her.

"Yes."

"Well then, let's go. I bet you've never gone this way before, up that side," he added, pointing at the path away from the school.

"Okay. Let's go," she said. "But I'm not the type to forget an argument. I'm not done with you."

Natasha thought she saw him smile, but probably he was sneering.

What Natasha learned from Refat later was that, of course, he had noticed her when she began school, he had heard all about her and her father, and he had seen how she had become fast friends with Lilya Bekirova. But Natasha had only just caught his special attention recently. She could not imagine then, or ever, how he could have been attracted to her. She was not, in her own eyes, very pretty. And she was a typical know-it-all; the teachers favored her, not because she was Russian, but because she always had the right answer. Refat apparently did not view her classroom behavior as irksome, instead finding it alluring.

He admitted to her later that when they climbed the hill together the day they met, he knew he had a crush; when her hand brushed against his and a lump formed in his throat he realized it was too late to protest it. Natasha in turn told him that she—who had never noticed him before in her life—felt by the end of their first meeting as if she had always known him. She felt they had an intimacy at the soul level that committed her to him instantly.

In the few days after Natasha and Refat first met, Natasha was ever on the lookout for another chance encounter (Lilya had been at her side after school every day since the meeting, and Natasha did not want to speak to Refat with her friend in tow; nor did he, apparently, for he ignored her altogether). They both knew instinctively to keep even their innocent acquaintance a secret.

As it turned out, Natasha only had to wait until the weekend after they met to speak to him again. At the occasion of Lilya's cousin's wedding celebration,

Natasha, who was one of many guests, spied Refat at the end of a long table. Then, after the feast, she saw him dancing with one of Lilya's aunts. She felt like an intruder, and wondered if their meeting were just a fluke. Refat would always have been there that day after school, or tonight at the wedding, no matter if she existed or not. The day was scripted, a matter of inevitability. She was the unscripted onlooker, the character who wasn't supposed to be, and unable, she thought, to change the plot.

Everyone danced. Lilya danced and her cousin the bride danced, uncles and aunts, grandparents, strangers, all got up and moved, hands in the air, swaying, clapping, laughing, twirling. Through all this human commotion Natasha and Refat were pushed by the mass movement toward one another until, in a corner, they stood face to face. Natasha glanced around with apprehension. Her feelings were written all over her face, she thought; she didn't want anyone to see her this way.

"It's you," Refat said.

"Yes," she said, with a wide grin. Here they were, once again. "So," she thought, "I have made it into the plot!"

"You dance like a Tatar," he observed.

"Is that a compliment?" she teased him. "Anyway, Lilya taught me."

"Lilya Bekirova?"

"Yes, my friend."

His dark eyes swept up her body from toes to head.

"Lilya invited you?" he asked.

"Do you think I don't belong?" she asked, not at all seriously.

"No, of course you do." He became flustered.

Natasha edged away from the party-goers.

"I can hardly hear you," she said. There were some guitarists, and some old women singing, and everyone clapped.

Refat followed Natasha as she moved away from the noise.

There were at least fifty guests dancing, more people eating, in all far too many people to take notice of Natasha and Refat speaking to each other with the kind of bodily electrification you'd expect in young lovers. Lilya was far away, out of sight. Natasha and Refat stood as if invisible. Their momentary silence was awkward.

"How is your poetry?" she asked him.

"Fine."

He sounded so serious that Natasha had to smile. "It's not an interrogation."

He blushed. "I haven't written anything in the past week," he said.

"I'd like to read more."

There was an uproarious clamor of voices cheering a couple who whirled around one another. A crowd had gathered, clapping and hooting, flowing through and around Refat and Natasha like water, separating them. Lilya appeared and bumped against Natasha in an effort to see the pulsating center, but she did not even see her friend.

Natasha and Refat could no longer hear one another over the voices, and they came into and out of view of each other as people came between them, pushing them further apart. Natasha thought she should go before Lilya noticed her speaking with Refat. Refat was in no apparent hurry though, and for a moment they both simply stared at one another, helpless in the ocean of people. Natasha raised a hand, meaning to say goodbye before she was swept away. All that emerged above the crowd were white fingers, delicate and unreachable.

Despite the brevity of their two chance encounters, Natasha and Refat were already united in their commitment to see one another regularly, so long as they could manage to escape anyone's notice. Their association would be sure to provoke disapproval, as Crimean Tatar boys were expected to court only Crimean Tatar girls. Their dates came primarily in the form of walking home together after school, usually with others in a mass exodus which camouflaged their mutual longing. If they were lucky, when no one was around to notice them dash off ahead, and when Lilya had errands to run or relatives to visit, they walked alone. Natasha and Refat got to know one another discreetly, which is how, at age seventeen, they fell in love.

Their romance was not hindered by the fact that their interests did not coincide: Refat loved Crimean Tatar history and engineering—he could take apart a radio and put it back together in five minutes; Natasha loved reading novels and fairy tales and being with Lilya (she did not tell him about her forays into spiritualism). Nor did politics or culture affect their courting. Natasha tended to avoid all mention of her father. As for Refat, although he was uneasy lest his parents discover their romance—since they were planning to find him a suitable fiancée before his eighteenth birthday—his family's expectations did nothing to prevent what was happening with his Russian girlfriend.

They had nothing in common save intelligence, wit, and curiosity about the world. Refat was attracted by Natasha's mind, and vice versa. Natasha made Refat think about things even if he disagreed with her opinion. For her part, Natasha loved how he considered everything she said—although to her mind he took the most banal statements far too seriously. Even if they had ten minutes together they often quarreled lightheartedly, leaving them both breathless.

Moreover, Refat was obviously befuddled by Natasha's mere proximity. To Natasha, though her attraction to him was great and she enjoyed looking at him—he had dark hair and olive skin, brown eyes, was taller than she and of slim build—such details were insignificant in light of their soul-deep connection.

Moments alone together were as rare as they were fraught: in the woods before a schoolmate caught up with them; a weekend meeting in some secluded spot. Natasha used every wile she had to keep Refat near her longer, and he also found compelling reasons to prolong their walks, by wandering away from town, their school and their homes, dragging her along and pretending not to notice how far they had gone.

Natasha tried not to allow her thoughts of the future to mar their romantic encounters. She wanted to ask when, where, how—can we be together?—even though she knew there was no way. She would have preferred to pretend that a life with Refat was not just an idle dream, but she knew better than to do so. By the time they had been meeting for six heady months Refat had spoken of their future only once, when he said, "I hope you will write me one day, to tell me how your life turns out."

Natasha replied, "I would rather not." For to her, nothing could be worse than admitting they wouldn't be together, other than having to actually write her beloved when it was so.

Their love was like a terrible secret that you wished you didn't know and had to guard with your life. It *was* a terrible secret, since it could come to nothing. Refat would one day have to marry a Crimean Tatar girl, Natasha a Russian man.

14

My mind is a jumble of images and there is a weird tingly sensation somewhere in my chest; I am jittery, and a little bit queasy. Maybe it was the five cookies I had in the lead-up to Natasha speaking about Refat. I don't know, and the worst thing is that I don't know what I actually do know. I'm not even sure where I'm driving as I drive home, and I make a wrong turn past the street I've lived on for most of my life. I feel like I'm in one of those snowglobes you see around Christmastime, with the tiny scene inside, tiny people and tiny reindeer, a tiny Santa and tiny houses, with snow on the ground everywhere. I feel like someone has shaken it upside down and everything is falling, not just the snow but the Santa and the houses, and the people—and me, and I still haven't come back to earth.

Maybe it is Lilya and Refat and Natasha. Natasha's story of her past is so immediate and vivid; it draws me in until I am so immersed that for a moment, or two, or three, I am there. When my imagination lures me inside Natasha's past life, it is so real to me that the smallest details are perfectly accessible, like they are my own bits of memory, preserved like exhibits locked behind airtight museum glass.

And there is something disquieting about this, too, something I try hard to rationalize, and can only accept at face value: Ever since she told me about the day Lilya found out she would meet Natasha—that day of Yusuf's birthday party, her visit to the market stalls, Tin-Tin—ever since, whenever Natasha recounts her story, I find myself imagining that I am Lilya.

Perhaps I am confused, and this confusion is part of my grief, and it is relieved by imagining life from another person's perspective—and not someone who is related and also grieving. But maybe not, because memory is playing other tricks on me. The past is all coming up now, bubbling and churning and spilling over from one era to the next. I am beginning to wonder what the past really is, anyway.

If the past has fully concluded, why is its presence so palpable, as if there are no boundaries between my current awareness and my memory? Why does the recollection of the past (mine, Natasha's) impose itself so fully in the present such that the slightest smell, the slightest taste, the slightest stray imagining, and I only have to close my eyes and I am there, in that past moment? Natasha's past speaks through her with such immediacy that I feel its breath on my face; the elderly woman I know recedes and it is someone else looking out through her eyes. Then we are both in her past, and I feel as if I am being thrust into a play and acting out my role. Moreover, it is as if the process of remembering dissolves all boundaries and all conscious control. Often, just as I slip back into my role as Catherine, I find myself in my own past. Today, for example, the fading of Natasha's voice lulled me almost back to the present, until my consciousness slipped on the silence and I found myself in a child's body, my own young body, my mother standing over me as she told me that I would be in big trouble if I removed anything from the box because she was looking for something very important. We were in the attic, engaged in something akin to spring cleaning, and I was close to twelve years old.

I had not noticed the box. I was looking for my old Holly Hobbie Easy-Bake Oven. I thought I had spotted it in the corner, and though I was too old for it (I was already helping my mother cook on the real stove), I got excited just remembering the little cookies and pies I used to make.

"What box?" I asked her, my eyes accustoming themselves to the dim, dusty light, straining to see the pink of Holly Hobbie's oven box.

My mother did not hear me. I noticed she was shaking in that not quite inconspicuous way she did when she was angry (as if, on the rare occasion she felt this emotion, her body rebelled against it). She withdrew a small dust-covered object from the box marked "Daddy's Things" and blew on it. Dust exploded in a small puff and the object revealed itself to be a deep, majestic purple bottle. It had a light sparkle which lured me to my mother's side. She stood staring at it. I asked, with incredulity, "Are those grandpa's things?" The purple sparkly glass was so pretty that I couldn't really believe it had belonged to a man.

"It belonged to his mother, and he gave it to me."

"Doesn't Natasha want it?" I asked.

My mother gave me a withering look and said, "He wanted me to have it."

I could not fathom why she had looked at me like that; not unreasonably, I assumed grandpa would want his wife to have his mother's pretty bottle. If I were married, I would expect my husband to give me his dead mother's things.

I slid back into the present without warning, like in a lucid dream when you realize you are dreaming, that you are the narrator rather than the figure in the dream, which realization then wakes you up. I found myself, at that moment, reflecting: was this scene related to what Natasha said about my grandfather turning my mother against her? There is no other proof in my memory.

This was one of the many moments over the past few days when the past has intruded on the present. It might happen when I am sitting with Natasha after she finishes speaking, or later, at home, when I am thinking about her, Lilya, and Refat. I don't know what the trigger was today—maybe the look of Natasha's eyes, so like that of my mother's that for a moment I actually thought of her as "my grandmother." Reliving the moment in the attic passed quickly, but even now I can smell the dust in the open box, and I can see clearly the old button-up shirts and moth-eaten wool sweaters that spilled out after my mother took the purple bottle.

Natasha watched me for some time after she finished speaking, and I could think of nothing to say, and dared not flinch, dared not give the slightest hint that my mind had wandered for just an instant. She took a breath—and for another second she looked just like my mother did; the resemblance was never strong between them, but at that moment it was uncanny. She *was* my mother—and the sadness in her eyes took me back, again, to Susan in the attic.

My mother was tall, just like Natasha. Not statuesque, though she gave the appearance of it when she wore high heels. Her height that day was in the way. She had to bend down to keep her head from hitting the attic ceiling and one hand was permanently braced against the small of her back, as if it hurt to be standing that way.

She wore khaki shorts and a red button-up cotton shirt, the top buttons undone to reveal her cleavage, as usual. On anyone else it would have looked preppy, usual, casual, but on her it looked typically glamorous. I never figured out how she did it, because not a single one of her features was particularly stunning or even extremely pretty: mousy brown hair, brown eyes, a medium size nose that looked large if you glanced at it from a particular angle, a too-small head and slightly pointed ears. Yet the individual imperfections seemed to disappear when you took in the whole package—together, every little bit of her worked with every other little bit so well that somehow, she was movie-star stunning without any special effort. In the attic that day her allure was never more effortless. She was not wearing a speck of make up. Her long dark hair was pulled back into a messy ponytail at the nape of her neck; long strands repeatedly fell across her left eye; there was a smudge of dirt or dust on her cheek and beads of perspiration on her forehead.

Natasha must have been caught in a similar loop: she drew me back from mine with the words, "I was sitting here watching you and thinking how much you remind me of your mother. Remember the city council party you went to with Susan, when you wore very similar red dresses? You told me that you were offended that everyone told you you looked so alike."

She was amused by the memory—she was over that evening for one reason or another, and saw us out. Even Natasha had said we looked alike, like sisters. I was no more amused at the time than I was when Natasha reminded me of it today.

I was polite but said little; it was time for me to go, anyway. All the way home I tried not to think about that night. But now I'm home, and there is no one to be polite with, nowhere I have to be, nothing I have to do, and even with the television on I feel myself slipping, sliding into a cocktail-party daze, and there is nothing I can do to stop the remembering. Nor, anymore, is there any inclination to; I have been beaten, and I accept defeat gracefully.

I was fifteen and it was the height of summer when I went to a formal cocktail party hosted by the city council at the Mayor's house. It was a social gathering of city council officials, community leaders, politicians-in-the-making—anyone who was or wanted to be in local politics, including philanthropists. My mother chaired the arts committee, and she also organized the annual Spring Music Festival (jazz in the park, salsa on the square, et cetera)—and schmoozing big spenders was part of her job description, so of course she had to go. She dragged me along, despite my objection that it would be full of old, boring people with whom I'd be forced to make polite, if not intelligent, conversation. She told me she wanted me to get out of the house for a change. I didn't put up much of a fight. I think at that age I said "Whatever" and shrugged a lot when the stakes weren't high enough to object.

It was, of course, her idea to put me in a red dress that was similar to hers, to which I responded, "Whatever." Actually, it was a gorgeous dress, tight-fitting, cleavage-hoisting, and I secretly hoped to look devastating in it. I looked pretty good—it was at the beginning of my pretty phase. The dress wasn't as overtly sexy as my mother's, which had slits mid-thigh on both legs, but managed to convey as much with an age-appropriate cut and shape.

Still, I was not thrilled to have to attend. As soon as I walked in I knew it would be as boring as I had predicted. Davis Culpepper and his band were playing low-key jazz music. Davis was a former beau of my mother's from about four or five years earlier. He was good at playing jazz for old, immovable types, as it was a repertoire he had refined, my mother had told me in their days together, over years of working on cruise ships.

"I thought Davis had a reputation, now," I whispered to my mother as we came in. I had heard he had a new album out, that post-Susan he had begun playing some New York clubs.

"Background music is good bread-and-butter work," she whispered, with a mock slap on the wrist.

Everyone was standing around in small clusters, speaking quietly, sipping their drinks, nibbling their dainty bits of pâté on crackers. My mother went off to make her rounds, leaving me at the long hors d'oeuvre table with Ada, her secretary.

"You and your mother look like twins, tonight, Catherine! You both look so beautiful!"

"Thanks," I murmured. ("Whatever," I said under my breath).

Ada stood around for a while, then went off to get a drink and never came back. Not that I blamed her. I wasn't the most interesting company.

I was standing alone trying not to look too awkward and fuming at my mother for abandoning me when I noticed that to my right stood Joe Clarkson, the director of the local Catholic church's community service programs. He saw me and did a double-take, then came around to face me, exclaiming how much I'd grown up, asking how I was, if he could get me a drink. Joe loomed over me; he was an oversized teddy bear—hairy and thick with curly black hair that would have put him in the hip crowd in the 70's. I was uneasy. I was beginning to realize just how much I disliked large social gatherings. I think this one proved responsible for keeping me from them in college.

After we had a brief, requisite exchange of pleasantries, I gave him a terse smile and allowed my gaze to wander, rather obviously. I wanted to escape him altogether and tried to position myself for a subtle exit. As I turned away he leant toward me confidentially. "Hey, listen, Catherine," he said. I felt a hand on my back, and smelled his sweat. "Yuck!" I thought. He was about to say something when my mother arrived and took my arm,

"Sorry, Joe, I just wanted to introduce Catherine to the Petties." And we were off. Susan whispered in my ear, "A leech, a pervert."

"He is?" I asked. I'd known him for as long as I could remember and I didn't know that about him.

"Now that you're womanly, darling, absolutely."

The thought of Joe being a pervert kind of grossed me out, and then: "My mother thinks I'm womanly?"

Before I could process my mother's comment (was she just observing that I now had breasts, or that I was attractive in a sexual way, or that she thought I was a woman?), she was introducing me to Mr. and Mrs. Pettie, who, she told me later, were wealthy and wanted to help fund local arts. Susan said, a little too loudly, and in the direction (I thought, if I wasn't imagining it), of Joe Clarkson, beached at the hors d'oeuvre table,

"Believe it or not, she is only fifteen, I have her birth certificate to prove it." She directed a pointed glance to Joe, "It's packed away with other unbelievable documents, such as those which prove *my* age, for example!"

Mr. Etzel, some secretarial-accountant type who came to anything hosted by my mother and just drooled all over her, approached and ogled me this time, his wife in hot pursuit. I found his attention creepy. After a moment his wife took him by the arm and steered him away. I edged away from my mother and her embarrassing chitchat. Susan was lost in the moment and laughed uproariously at something Mr. Pettie had said. Joe was walking my way, when my mother grabbed me, said, "Excuse me," to the Petties, and dragged me onto the balcony.

"Sorry, I didn't expect him to be this persistent. That's okay. You and I will have a nice chat outside."

"Don't you have people to schmooze?" I asked.

"Don't worry about it. It can wait."

We stood in the darkness, the light from the living room falling past us. It was sweltering outside, and the air buzzed with insects, but I didn't mind. It felt like a relief to be away from the chatter and music and light.

All of a sudden my mother said, "Catherine, sometimes I don't feel like I know you at all."

"Well, maybe you don't," I replied.

"What I mean is that I'd like to know you better."

"You didn't say that very well, then."

"No, I didn't, did I?"

She put her champagne glass on the balcony railing.

"Sometimes I think you disapprove of me," she said.

I tried not to blink, not to give anything away. "That's not true," I said, stalling for time, to think up a better response. "I'm not making a judgment, Susan."

"I've never really liked you calling me by my name, you know."

"Sorry. Mom. It became a habit, and then … I guess I never really thought of you as the maternal type."

"Ouch. Fair enough. So you're not judging me, aside from the not-maternal part."

"I don't disapprove of you. I just can't relate, that's all. Other moms are at home baking, or working in some traditional job, they're mom-like. I don't know. They're not glamorous and they don't have boyfriends."

"You think I'm glamorous?"

"Yeah." I couldn't help smiling. I don't know why, maybe because she seemed so pleased.

"Well, what can I say to that, Catherine? I am not like other moms, I guess that's true. Just tell me this. Do you plan on becoming like them, just to spite me?"

She was on the verge of giggling, I could tell. Give Susan a couple of glasses of champagne and she would laugh at anything. In the end, her mirth was infectious, even from the other room, even if I was in a foul mood. In a crowd of people her Tinkerbell giggle carried from one end of the room to the other, uninhibited, ending in a single loud "Oh, my!"—as if she couldn't believe the hilarity herself.

"No, I'm *not* going to be like them," I insisted, and stopped her cold—her smile vanished.

"Yes, you're too ambitious, my little Capricorn. You'll be making a name for yourself formulating some theory of something, probably taking some unexplained mystery and turning it into science."

"I thought you said you didn't know me well. And I'm going to ignore your tone of exasperation."

"Well, maybe I do know you well. Just lately, we haven't been connecting."

I took her champagne glass and said, "Can I finish it?"

"Go ahead. Shall I get you some more?"

"See, not mom-like. Not at all."

"You have a sense of humor, darling, I've always appreciated that."

It made me distinctly uncomfortable talking to her about personal things. She did try, occasionally, to get personal with me. I wanted to open up, but somehow was never really able to.

"Maybe I will have more champagne, since clearly we're going to continue this heart to heart."

"Well, given that you're so perceptive, I'm just going to ask you something. Catherine, this is going to sound … well, I don't know how it's going to sound so I'm just going to say it. I've been wondering, that is, lately I've been doing a lot of thinking, and it occurred to me that you might be angry with me. About your father."

"What father?"

"Precisely."

"I'm not angry."

"Well, if you are, I'm sorry. I had always hoped to give you positive male role models. There just didn't seem to be a lot around."

"I'm not angry."

"If you are, it's okay. It's normal."

"I'm going to get myself some more champagne."

I hoped that when I returned, my mother would have left, and I could be alone. On my way back I drank half the glass and it went straight to my head. Which was a good thing. She was waiting for me.

"Where's mine?" she asked.

"I didn't know you wanted any," I said.

She actually looked sad, which surprised me. Susan rarely looked pensive, much less sad.

"I can go get you some now if you want."

"No, that's okay."

We stood for a long while without speaking, and I thought, expected, that any minute she would wander off, or that someone would find us in our dark spot, or find Susan, and drag her back into her more familiar limelight. No such luck.

She said, "Have I told you that I've been meditating lately? I've been reading about Buddhism and detachment. Really interesting stuff."

"Oh. Religion."

"I know, Miss Scientific Rationalism. Not your thing. I like that you're such an independent thinker. I've always told you the most important thing in life is to be your own person, to make your own decisions."

"Thanks, I guess."

Susan just sighed. I always knew how to bring our conversations to a full stop.

I was a teenager, and independence should have had unreserved allure to me, but I didn't want to be independent, not then. Maybe to spite her, who was so independent herself, and imagined everyone wanted the freedom she thought she had. Maybe because I'd never had a chance to be very dependent, seeing as my mother always appreciated "my independence" so much, gave me such free reign, more than other kids had, not to mention how she was always telling me to travel and see the world when I finished school, to get away from her and "spread my wings."

Susan gave me a big kiss and told me to stay far from Joe, then wafted away into the crowd, circulating like air while I half-watched, half-hid in the dark corner until I needed more food. I thought I had it all figured out: When Susan said I was womanly that night she was chalking up another point for my independence, which meant she didn't know me at all, even if I couldn't say how, being that I hardly knew myself either. I only knew that the problem with being one's own person, with being self-initiating and self-sustaining, is that there is no one and nothing to give you structure, to tell you what to do. There is too much freedom, and too much freedom is chaos.

Really, I don't know how much longer this can go on, this inertia that might be gradually transforming itself into dementia. What is this la-la land I'm inhabiting lately? I am not exactly worried, more wearied, like I'm resigned to a life lived in a daze and already tired of it.

I have eaten dinner, watched television, re-lived a party when I was fifteen, and now I am too exhausted to work, so I suppose I will go to bed—but what have I accomplished? Lately all my days and nights are like this, an endless series of meaningless events, and at the end of the day I go to sleep hoping that it will again be Thursday and I can go to Natasha's and escape into her past for the afternoon.

So I wash my dishes, take a shower, and crawl into bed (tonight: the guestroom). And I lie there, considering my pointlessness.

Then I remember what Natasha said about my birth certificate.

My birth certificate!

I leap out of bed and stand in the center of my room, arms out, biting my lip, thinking, looking around the room as if the document were about to jump out of a shadow and get me, realizing that I have absolutely no idea where to begin, all the while still reeling from the shock of my stupidity. Have I been sabotaging my subconscious into never, even for a moment, thinking, "Hey, maybe my father's name is on my birth certificate?"

I'll just start looking, I decide. I go to my mother's bedroom, intending to tear through her chest of drawers, her desk, her closets—until I remember that everything is empty. Empty, empty! Here I haven't even begun and already I've run out of places to look. My breath comes fast and I can hear the pumping of my heart as if it were being transmitted via earphones. Damn it! Where could it be? Why have I not bothered to look for it earlier?

I go inside her closet and start to pat the walls, absurdly. I slap my hands hard against the white plaster, half-expecting to find a secret compartment, as if I'm in some spy film.

I place my hand to my forehead, pressing hard, and concentrate. I try to recall exactly what my mother had ever said about it. Suddenly the bedroom door slams shut with a gust of wind through my mother's open window—have I left it open? I don't remember—and the cocktail party blows into the room with its jazz and tingling champagne glasses and Susan's voice: "It's packed away with other unbelievable documents, such as those which prove *my* age, for example!" I almost jump out of my skin. Now I am as creeped out as I am frantic.

Would she really have been truthful with perfect strangers, or was she just making a joke? And why had she never shown it to me? She had gotten my passport by using it, of course; it was strange that I had never seen it.

I was the person she confided in, at least during my teenage years, the person who sat with her at the kitchen table at three AM hearing out her sobs and rants on another boyfriend who had proved a big disappointment. I listened as she voiced her dismay that she had not learned to be closer to her own mother—she always said it in the context of how lucky she was to have me. So why would she have hidden my own father from me?

"Forget all that," I tell myself. "Go to the attic." I know that despite her tornado-like sense of organization, she was meticulous about her files. And I know that, despite Susan's pre-death purge of all her belongings, for our sake (and for that of the lawyers and insurers), she kept all of her files in tidy boxes lined up in the attic. I can only assume she was referring to her own birth certificate at the party, and that she was not making a joke.

There are boxes, stacked against a wall. They all have labels ("Arts Festival 1983," "Music Festival 1985," "Tax Return 1989"). I start to move them around, to take the ones off the top and get to the ones on the bottom, whose labels are not facing me. Fifteen minutes later I am covered in sweat and dust, but a calm has overtaken me. I feel certain I am on the right track. At last, a box I'd moved earlier but had overlooked now draws my attention. Its label says, simply, "Et Cetera." Leave it to Susan to be creatively imprecise.

Inside I find all matter of random documents: her birth certificate, old driver's licenses, university transcripts, Eurorail passes, a dried flower, friends' wedding invitations and baby announcements, a certificate of achievement for fundraising, an invitation to the Met for a party in 1979, bits of paper I can't bother reading closely, and then, among it all, in no particular folder, is my birth certificate. On it is my father's name:

Kenneth Alfonso Metcalf.

The phone is ringing. I stuff the paper back in the box and go as fast as I can down the stepladder.

"What a ridiculous name," I think. "What kind of heritage did he have, exactly?"

"Hello?" I say.

"Sorry it's so late, Cat. I hope I didn't wake you," a woman says.

"What time is it?" I ask, and see it is past ten.

Silence. I am breathing too fast. Kenneth Alfonso Metcalf? Was that a stage name? And why did she put it on my birth certificate, anyway? (Could she do it without his permission?) Was she assuming that he would be involved in my life? Or did he insist his name be there, and if so, why did he disappear afterwards? Knowing my mother, she probably would have preferred he leave it off, to take all the responsibility herself, in writing and in deed. Then again, maybe she would have put his name down just to piss him off, to have on paper that he had sired an illegitimate daughter.

"Cat, it's me. Elisa," she says in a small voice. My mind comes rushing back to earth.

"Elisa!" I say. "Sorry, I was in a daze. How are you?"

"Good," she says, her voice still hesitant. "Did you get the message I left you earlier?"

"Oh, yeah, sorry I didn't call. I've been meaning too."

"That's okay. It's just that I'm in town a lot lately, and I wondered if you'd like to have coffee, or lunch or something. I don't know what your schedule's like."

"Yeah," I hear myself saying. "That would be nice."

"How have you been, Cat? I mean, since Susan ... you know."

"Oh, fine." I don't feel like I can be bothered to come up with a more appropriate answer. "Hey, you remember how I never knew who my father was?"

"Yeah?" I can hear her perk up. I feel like we're teenagers again. I put the receiver close to my mouth, afraid I won't be able to say the words out loud.

"Well, I just found out his name. Kenneth Alfonso Metcalf."

She laughs from the other end of the line, and I laugh with her. I haven't laughed this way in a while. I feel like a snake shedding its skin, like something old and used up is peeling off of me for good.

15

I am taking Natasha out for her birthday today—my idea. We have never been people who eat out much, probably as my mother loved to cook and Natasha, who also enjoys cooking, believes eating out is frivolous. I do not know if her opinion reflects her age or cultural origins, or even her personality, but in any case when I was growing up, all important events were celebrated at home over food that had been prepared and presented with loving attention—even if it was not especially gourmet. We only ever ate out as a special, impromptu treat; eating out was an event in and of itself.

I have not, as far as I'm concerned, inherited either my mother's or Natasha's culinary inclinations, nor their energy for celebrating, so for Natasha's birthday I break with tradition and suggest a new French restaurant. She is turning eventy-one.

Natasha arrives before me. I can see her as I walk toward the door, her profile turned to the road. She doesn't see me coming; in fact, at first I do not recognize her at all. Out of the context of her home, in a place where senility is not a given, age is not present in the same way, or perhaps its social relevance is merely absent—initially I notice an older woman who is extremely well-dressed and I think nothing of her, until I realize I am looking at Natasha. This realization leads me to another: I have been seeing her as old, as if her age were somehow crucial to her character or to our relationship. Now I cannot help but see the lovesick schoolgirl in her. For the first time, I recognize Natasha as a woman whose life was fully lived before the thought of me ever existed.

Our eyes meet as I approach our table. She is wearing a long, slender turquoise dress and a colorful orange scarf. She wears pearl earrings and smells of some kind of Estée Lauder perfume—I know it's her favorite, but I've forgotten the exact name. Today she is almost sophisticated. Susan would be proud.

Only when I sit down do I notice the book on the table. *Angels*, it is called.

"A good novel?" I ask her.

"Not a novel, dear. True stories."

It takes a moment for what she is saying to register in my literal brain, and when it does I am shocked.

"You don't believe in angels, do you?" I ask.

"Why does it surprise you that I might believe in such a thing?" she asks me. "I am an old woman; my death is not that far off."

I give her a pitying smile, and say to my near instant embarrassment, "That's not why you're interested, though, is it?" Oh, how condescending I sound! As if it isn't perfectly normal to have spiritual musings after the death of a loved one. I immediately apologize. Naturally, I assume her interest in angels relates to Susan.

"No need to say you're sorry, Catherine, though I am puzzled that you cannot imagine me being interested in supernatural things. I take it you are not?"

"Not what? Interested in the supernatural?"

"Yes."

"Well, not exactly … not."

I should be ashamed of myself, really. Firstly, she has told me how she and Lilya were interested in such things, so I should know better than to question Natasha's present interests. Secondly, here I am, questioning the disappearance of some planes and a bunch of men. I mean, not that I am convinced it was a supernatural event, but the disappearance is hardly natural either.

"I'm open-minded," I say. "Anyway, I'm apologizing for projecting my own neurosis. I just don't want to think about Susan … I mean, you know …" I falter, "if angels exist, then Susan might be …"

"She might be okay?"

"She might be around. Like, around me."

"Isn't that a nice thought?" Natasha asks. Two menus have been handed to us—neither of us have even glanced at them. A waiter stops by and I raise my hand and mouth to him, "Just a moment."

"In short, no," I say.

"I see. Is that because you cannot bear any sort of ambiguity?"

"Well, yes, and don't smirk like that."

I can see Natasha is amused by my reply. She raises her eyebrows, and I feel compelled to continue.

"If she's not entirely gone, then I have to communicate with her, don't I? I mean, I *should*, right? And then what do I say? What does she think? It's too complicated. If she's just gone, I don't have to worry about all that. Now," I lean forward toward her, "it's your birthday, Natasha, so let's move on to more cheerful things."

Natasha smiles at me. Two glasses of champagne arrive and she makes a toast to life and its mysteries. Then, just as I am settling in for more mundane conversation, reading the menu and trying to remember what "haricots verts" are, she says, "Anyway, I am reading this book really because I have been thinking about

Lilya. I have been feeling like Lilya is around me. Not Susan. Does that shock you?"

It does, actually, but I have had a big gulp of champagne and now that I've got the glass in front of me, our conversation is a bit less daunting.

"You think she's around, and not your own daughter?"

"Yes. I don't know what Susan is doing. Maybe she is gone. Or maybe she does not feel any need to communicate with me, or I with her. Lilya, on the other hand ... I swear sometimes I can see her, but then maybe it is just that Refat has brought it all back to me. I do not know. So, I am reading this." She lifts the book so I can see the cover, a diaphanous white form against a blue background. Very cliché. "It is interesting. Some people feel that after we die, we hang around to help others. To guide them."

"Guide them to do what?"

"You are so literal, dear. I mean, to guide them toward a more spiritual understanding of life."

"I see."

"You may not, but never mind. Let's order some food."

I fear my relief is transparent. I don't want to come across as some naïve materialist who has never thought of my immortal soul, especially when Natasha has clearly given hers some thought and we both have a loved one who is either *only* a soul or nothing at all. However, I prefer to focus on some tasty French delicacy and the deserts I see being taken to nearby tables.

Still, if only a little bit, if only to reach that part of Natasha, and understand Lilya, I wish I could talk about souls, angels, whatever.

We order, then I make a toast. "Happy birthday!" I offer cheerfully. "May this year be full of mysteries resolved, fun had, and health and happiness."

We eat crusty rolls and have another glass of champagne and attempt small talk. We shouldn't bother. Neither of us is good at banter and I find myself wanting to ask her about Lilya and Refat. I can't; I know I can't. Not here, in a restaurant, and especially on her birthday, when any and all recollections should be solely of merriment.

In the middle of our idle chatter Natasha asks me how I am really doing, as if our conversation so far hasn't covered that point. I avoid answering her, since I can't really say how I am without launching into a half-coherent self-analysis with no conclusion. Fortunately, my recent exploration in the attic comes to mind. I am relieved I have something to say. I put down my champagne glass to say it and steady myself for her reaction.

"Well, guess what? My father's name was Kenneth Alfonso Metcalf. It was on my birth certificate. Which I found in the attic."

I wasn't going to tell her, I really wasn't ever going to mention it again, but now it's done.

"You were right," I add.

"That it was on your birth certificate?" she clarifies.

"About other things, too, I'm sure," I laugh. "But yes, I meant you were right that it was on my birth certificate."

"I remember Kenneth." She says.

I can feel myself suppress all enthusiasm. Then, "To what end?" I think, amused at my ridiculous self-awareness. Why should I edit my curiosity? Anyway, Natasha's expression is of someone trudging through memory to locate facts—it is apparent that she could care less whether or not I want to hear them.

"He was Spanish-looking. I think they were together for a while. They must have been, since I actually remember him. He was doing some sort of study ... let's see ..."

"He wasn't a musician?" I ask.

"No, Susan wasn't exclusively involved with musicians at that time. In fact ..." she looks close to a revelation.

"Yes?" I prod. I have given up all attempts to stifle my excitement.

"That's right. He was studying business. Something to do with computers. In those days no one knew much about computers, as far as I know. He did play the guitar, in clubs, on the weekends. I seem to recall he was very logical. Susan never told me who your father was, of course. She was seeing other people at the time," Natasha laughs. "But I guess she was sure he was the one. Come to think of it, I can imagine he was!"

"You're laughing because my father was a computer geek," I say, "and it doesn't surprise you."

She is scanning her memory again. "I can see him now. Long dark hair, leather jacket, but very polite. Very goal-oriented. Actually, I didn't really like him all that much, but he was better than the others. You know," she leans across the table and pats my hand, "if you wanted to, you could look him up!"

"No thank you," I say. "I've had enough family revelations for now."

"You surprise me, Catherine. All my life I thought of you as this serious little girl with her head in a book, and when you grew up and stayed at the university for so long, well, I thought you wouldn't change much. I have to admit to you that I feared you were reading too much about life and not living it. Now I see your seriousness was a defense against Susan's frivolity. You've changed since she died. I can't say how you've changed yet, but you have. It's still happening," she wags her finger at me. "You will surprise me some more, I think. When one long phase of life ends and another begins, you change. It's like when I left Russia to live in Crimea, and then Crimea to go to Germany, and then to the United States. You change on the inside. I have to say, in your case I think it is good."

I know I am blushing.

"In your case it wasn't good?" I ask, to shift her attention away from my imperfections.

"It became good."

The waiter returns. Natasha says, "We must order." She quizzes the young man on the menu choices, and, while I attempt to think up a neutral question about how she changed on the inside while her life was transformed on the outside, the moment is lost. We are in a deep discussion about steak tartare and then champignons, which becomes a conversation about where in France the *garçon* is from, then where Natasha is from, only I think of it as "conversation lite." My grandmother's past is reduced to geography and delicacies, my present to the unfortunate absence of cultural references and proper French pronunciation.

Thanks to Susan, I am at least well traveled, but that hardly touches the core of my identity. I am two generations removed from my Russian ancestry; I am a hopeless monoglot and fully American.

I am the daughter of computer geek Kenneth A. Metcalf.

16

December 1938

Lilya might have been in the dark longer about her friend's romance if not for the day when Natasha's father asked his daughter to stay home from school. Aleksander Dmitrievich had to leave for Simferopol on Friday morning and wouldn't be home until Saturday evening. He left Natasha in charge of the house and of her mother, as Mira had come down with another of her rattling coughs and fever. There was no way Natasha could let Refat know she wouldn't be on the path to and from school that day, but she assured herself that one missed meeting would not matter.

It did, she realized by lunchtime—she missed him too much—but she did not know what to do about it. There was no justifiable excuse for leaving. Still, Natasha was not one to suffer silently, and imagined all manner of excuses which might allow her to escape the house. Snow lay many inches thick on the ground; the blinds were kept shut to block drafts, blankets shoved under doors to keep the heat in the main living spaces. Natasha's mother was covered up in bed to her neck and claimed she was amply comfortable, but the warmth would not last long inside without Natasha's vigilance to the fire. She drank another cup of tea and chopped potatoes for the soup.

Natasha stepped outside to breathe the frigid air, to clear her head, and when she did she glimpsed a figure in the trees down the path. Her heart leapt—she nearly called out to Refat before catching herself—for she realized not a second too soon that it was Elmira Mamut collecting firewood. A moment later she saw that her neighbor had seen her too. Natasha braced herself for the inevitable deluge of greeting, inquiry, and so forth, but Elmira did not approach her, and did not call out.

Natasha swallowed the hard knot in her throat. She knew perfectly well why the busiest busybody around had no time for her. Try as she might to avoid thinking on it, to pretend otherwise, there was no other conclusion she could draw. She was being shunned. She felt the blood rush to her head. Everyone she had met in Crimea had initially been civil, even welcoming—despite what they must have suspected about her father's presence among them. But lately, things had changed. Kindness had turned to avoidance: the averted eyes of schoolmates, the silence of neighbors, even Lilya, whose behavior was so pointedly normal—pretending not to feel the obvious chill that descended whenever she and Natasha encountered other villagers—that it was abnormal. "Of course they don't trust us," Natasha thought. Lately, mistrust felt like something closer to fear.

And why should she be so taken aback? Four local Crimean Tatars had been arrested in the past month—not by her father, but he had been there when the officers came in from Simferopol to take the men away—nationalists all, two of them writers. Naturally her father was somehow involved, enough to give any reasonable person cause to be nervous around him and his family. Her preoccupation with Refat, she realized, had insulated her, by and large, from the surrounding fear, allowing her to act as if nothing were profoundly amiss. Now, however, as she stood alone, within shouting distance of her neighbor, suddenly the atmosphere of terror flooded into her awareness. "Oh my goodness," she thought, as the enormity of what was happening seemed to hit her all at once. "What is going on here?" If she stood alone at her back door long enough, the tide of arrests could very well sweep her village of Tatars. She knew it made no difference what "nationalist" meant, nor if a person was or wasn't one. Labels were the authorities' excuses to conceal plans.

She went back inside to check the soup. She did not like being mistrusted; she did not like what was happening around her, and felt a great sympathy for the Crimean Tatars' plight. She did not understand if her father was actively supportive of the government's agenda, or was merely doing his job. In any case, she disapproved of his involvement. She was not his ally, much less his informant, yet impotence and indifference were uneasily married in Natasha's world. She could hardly explain her feelings to anyone. What else could she do but carry on with her life?

Her mother fell fast asleep after lunch and Natasha decided she could not stand her confinement for another minute, even at the risk of discovery. She stoked the fire and added a blanket to her mother's bed, then ran out the door and down the hill toward the school—after twenty minutes, if Refat were not there, she would return home. The fire would last at least until then, if not longer.

On her way she passed Elvedin, Menube, and Mehmet, all of whom kindly called out a greeting but hurried by her all the same. She stopped. Snow flurried down and for a moment Natasha was alone, almost poised to turn and go back when she heard a bird and listened instead, eyes closed. When she opened her eyes Refat was there, smiling, and it was just the two of them in the quiet snow surrounded by birdsong, like in a fairy tale.

"Did you think I wouldn't come?" Natasha asked.

"Things come up," he shrugged.

"My mother is sick and my father is away until tomorrow. I'll have to go back now."

"Come here," he invited her, and took her hand. "Let's walk back together."

They had to stay on the path where it was worn by footprints, as all around them the woods and the path merged into snow banks, pristine but treacherous. Refat held Natasha's hand firmly, and several times she leaned against him to stop slipping. He was trying to slow her down, she knew, and she allowed him that. She was not far from home, and, she hoped, her mother would still be fast asleep.

"Where has your father gone?" he asked her.

"To Simferopol. Business."

"I see," he said. She tried to scrutinize his face, to judge the meaning of his tone (flat, impersonal), but she had to look ahead to concentrate on walking.

Natasha felt distress well up inside her. Could it be that Refat shared the sentiments of Elmira Mamut and her schoolmates? The sun slanted through the trees and reflected off the white ground; the glare gave her a headache and she could not think. With a whoosh and a scream a little girl came sliding down the path on a sled, an older boy behind her, both of them nearly straight into Refat and Natasha. For a half-second Natasha locked eyes with the little girl as she sped past; then the girl came to a slow stop into a pile of snow. Natasha's heart thudded, though not from fright. The girl was okay. It was what Natasha saw in her face that was so affecting: a daughter she might never have, a Crimean Tatar girl like one Refat might someday parent, but never with Natasha.

Her mood shifted to gloom.

Natasha pulled away from Refat and stopped. She faced him.

"You do not resent me, because I'm the daughter of an officer?" she asked.

Refat smiled, "No more so than you resent me, a nationalist."

"But you're not a nationalist."

"I am a Crimean Tatar, aren't I?" he asked.

"Don't be sarcastic," she said.

"I'm not."

"I'm afraid for you," Natasha admitted, breathless.

"Don't be. I'm not."

Natasha shuddered and leaned her head against Refat's shoulder; he opened his coat and stretched it around her shoulders.

"My father is a farmer," he said. "We're not nationalists, just simple folk."

It didn't matter what he said, not to Natasha, not to the Fates, who had a plan for them both regardless. Natasha and Refat forgot the world they lived in for a moment as together they grew warmer, as the snow fell harder, and then—they kissed. When footsteps brought them apart it was too late. Enver Bekirov, Lilya's father, had just passed. He had seen them, no doubt, but he trudged away as if he had not, only grunting under the weight of a big sack thrown over his shoulders.

"Don't worry about that," Refat whispered, but Natasha worried.

"I should be getting back," she said, "before my mother needs me."

He was motionless as Natasha broke away, up the hill, without a wave goodbye. She never turned to see how long he stood there. She began to run home, but decided to risk another half hour or so away from her mother, and headed toward Lilya's house.

It was perhaps amazing that a secret such as the relationship between Natasha and Refat could be concealed between best friends, that the unknowing friend could not see the secret plainly written on her besotted friend's face, yet such was the case. Natasha hid her feelings so well because she knew her secret was scandalous; she feared Lilya would not approve, or even worse, that she would not understand. Lilya truly had not a clue. Her attention was focused elsewhere—if not on her friendship with Natasha, then on daydreaming of supernatural curiosities.

Natasha felt that, now that Lilya's father had seen her and Refat together, she was obligated to tell Lilya. It was unfathomable that Lilya learn the news from her father, who might—it alarmed Natasha to realize—cause a scandal. Natasha could not bear to consider the consequences now, which was beside the point anyway. The point was, if anyone were to find out the truth, it should first be Lilya, her dearest friend.

Natasha ran down the path and off to the left, where Lilya's house was. Enver, still ahead of her, was headed around the back.

There was Lilya outside, greeting her father and following him around back. Natasha stopped at the side of the house; Lilya saw her and smiled, walked over. Enver turned; he looked right at Natasha and waved hello, and Natasha felt reassured. Perhaps he would keep her secret for her, she thought.

"I have to talk to you, quickly, my mother is ill and I must go home," Natasha gasped, taking her friend's arm and guiding her around to the front of the house.

"What is it? Are you all right? You look rather pale," Lilya commented. "Come inside, we'll be alone. Have a cup of tea to warm up."

Natasha would have refused had she not suddenly felt her fingers and toes going numb.

"Just for a minute," she agreed.

"You're in a funny mood," Lilya observed, leaving Natasha to wait for her in the living room. Natasha didn't even bother to take off her coat or hat. She could hardly sit still in that room, alone. She prepared the words in her mind and rehearsed them.

"Lilya, I have a secret to tell you, a real secret," Natasha told Lilya when she came in with the teapot and cups. Lilya poured Natasha tea and handed her a plate of biscuits. They never met like this anymore, so formally, even when it was as cold as it was. They sat in the kitchen or went for walks, arm in arm. Now here they were, sitting as they had been in Natasha's house on the day they met, when Natasha first confessed she had a secret to tell.

"Yes?" Lilya said. She thought of who Natasha's father was, and the recent arrests—instinctively she shrank back from her friend.

"I'm just going to say it," Natasha began. "I'm in love with Refat Chobanov, and he's in love with me, too."

Lilya blushed. She giggled. Then she sighed with relief.

"You have my blessing," she said, then begged her friend to stay for just a few more minutes. She had to tell Natasha what had happened to her two nights earlier.

Lilya could not sleep. There was no particular reason, save, perhaps, for a late dinner. She could see a cloudless sky through the curtains as she lay in bed, so she did something she never would have done before meeting Natasha: she snuck outside to see the stars. She'd never watched the stars at night until she and Natasha had met. She wished her friend was with her now. Still, even alone, she might as well enjoy the night so long as she couldn't shut it out through sleep, she thought.

Dressed in her warmest clothes, scarf wrapped twice around her neck and face so that only her eyes and nose were free, Lilya trudged through the snow around her house to sit out back where the woods began. It was not all that late, only nine o'clock, but late enough for the rest of the family to be asleep, or so she thought. She didn't expect another living soul to be up at this hour in this cold, and nearly fell over when she heard the voices.

Men, approaching, talking, her father among them.

Lilya jumped up and went to hide behind a bush. It was covered in snow, so, luckily, she could not be seen. It was a silly thing to do in retrospect—what if someone saw her footprints and found her? The voices stopped nearby. The men were sitting out behind her house. She peeked around the bush and saw them. They were smoking. Brooding. Complaining about things, again.

Lilya tuned the voices out. She wondered when she could go back inside without attracting notice, for surely she would get in trouble for being up and out of bed at this hour. She sat down in the snow. It wasn't so bad; she was warm with all her layers, the air was too cold to melt the snow so she stayed perfectly dry, and most importantly, she could still see the sky, immense and bright with stars. The smell of tobacco wafted her way and she enjoyed it.

At some point Lilya's attention drifted back to the men. They mentioned something about agriculture, then impending war, Germany had forcibly taken over the Sudetenland in Czechoslovakia in September, and later that month Western Europeans agreed to appease Germany by signing the Munich Agreement, offering to Hitler all the German regions he wanted. At some point the discussion shifted to nationalism. Lilya could not help but follow their discussion now, once she'd begun to pay attention. In the towns of Yalta and Alushta there were reports of Crimean Tatar teachers being accused of nationalism, taken out into the woods and shot. One of the men said his cousin, a simple farmer, was sent to a prison camp in Siberia because he had written a poem, published in a local magazine, describing the beauty of the countryside. Lilya's father and his friends named local political figures they knew, or writers, or artists, all accused of nationalism, who had disappeared in the middle of the night, or been taken away at gunpoint from their homes or offices, or had left for work and never come home. As the names went on, the lament grew quieter, first tense, then fearful. One man said he had lost hope for his people, that their cultural figures were taking Crimean Tatar history to their grave. He said the daily fear of arrest and persecution, so groundless and random, made life an almost unbearable struggle. Enver Bekirov said a life lived in such fear was a kind of death.

Lilya did not wish to hear anymore, and had begun to block it out when she heard her father say, "We must carry on with life. I will have my daughter engaged if not married by the end of the year, before all the men leave for war."

That was it. Lilya had had enough of dire news. If that was to be her life, it would have to await her arrival. Now she would journey elsewhere, away from plans and tragedy, into the woods and the night. She would have some fun, even if the end of her freedom was inevitable. So she waited until the men laughed uproariously, ten painful minutes of fuming in her hiding place, then leapt up and ran. They would think she was Tin-Tin, or a wild animal, and she gave up worrying about being caught. There were worse things in life than being caught outside eavesdropping late at night.

Like marriage.

She stopped up the hill a ways, out of sight of her home, not yet to the Mamuts'. She decided to just sit and look at the stars. Gazing upwards, not knowing what patterns existed, she invented her own: a man and a troika, a cross, a house with a funny long flagpole. She was by now freezing cold but determined to enjoy herself. If only Natasha were with her, they would know precisely what to do now—there was some kind of alchemical reaction when the two girls were together that always gave them a purpose. When Lilya could no longer discern patterns in the sky and was just trying to imagine what next to do, an awful howling began. Someone's dog, no doubt; it wasn't her Tin-Tin, that was for certain. The cry might have given someone else a fright, but not Lilya. She sat resolutely, shivering with cold but not fear—for if there was one thing she could face up to, it was darkness and the unseen. She had screamed alongside Natasha when the ghost appeared to them, but only in camaraderie. Her instinct had been to watch it carefully, to approach it, but it had disappeared too soon.

The howling ceased; she thought of the ghost now. She hoped that if she thought of the ghost hard enough she'd see it again.

She didn't.

A little while later she noticed someone else who didn't look like a ghost at all, a man with long black hair, wearing a strange outfit like a Gypsy or an Indian—what looked like a blanket wrapped around his chest and shoulders, with long, dangly bits hanging off it. He had been watching her, it seemed, from behind a tree. Lilya was not startled, or upset. They stared at one another as he came out from the tree, soundlessly stepping through the snow toward her. He was not wearing enough clothes to keep warm, she thought. His forearms were bare. She saw he wore an amulet. She could not take her eyes from the symbol:

Then it seemed as if it were the symbol coming toward her and not the man.

"Lilya!" a voice called out in the dark. It was her father's voice; she turned toward it and looked back to say something to the strange man—but the man was gone.

Lilya did not get in trouble, she told Natasha. Her father brought her home and told her she was silly for running off. He told her she was nearly a woman and could go outside at night if she wanted, but not to wander too far because it was dark and she could get lost.

"Though politics is not for the likes of you, and I would prefer it if you left us alone when we are discussing it, next time," he said, "as you did tonight."

"I heard your plans for me," she told him.

Enver's face softened, and he stroked her cheek. "I will make sure you are well taken care of, don't you worry," he said. "That's not why you ran off, is it?"

"No. I had been meaning to go, but I was waiting for you all to make some noise so that you wouldn't hear me."

He laughed and kissed her forehead.

"Next time wear even more clothes," he said. "You looked nearly frozen when I got to you. You could have become confused."

Lilya hadn't thought of that possibility, and she told Natasha that perhaps the cold had made her delusional.

Because she was convinced that the man was too alive to have been a ghost. He seemed to have come from another world.

17

Natasha says, "Those were different times, weren't they?"

I am numb; I only gradually feel my senses rushing me back to the present. Natasha has not noticed. She is half here with me, and half there, in her past.

"What do you mean?" I ask. I have actually forgotten her question, and my own is a cover-up.

"Everyone was so worried about getting married then."

"Oh, yeah," I say absently. I am still gazing in wonderment at the man Lilya saw in the woods, his amulet cold and glowing against his collarbone. I can see his every feature and let my mind go over and over all the details, hoping some pearl of meaning will be revealed to me.

"Well, I should make dinner now for me. Did you want to stay?"

I hear her speak, but cannot make sense of her meaning. I notice now that the sun is low in the sky and realize that we must have been sitting here in her living room for hours. I think I should be going, but do not move, and I can tell that Natasha has no apparent inclination to get up either. I wonder if she is exhausted, like me, from the details. So many details, so well excavated. I wonder if her mind also goes numb from the effort, if she finds that bringing up the past saps her energy for the present.

"Catherine, I asked what will you do for dinner. Are you okay?"

"Sorry. Yes, I'm fine. I need to go home."

"Fine," she says, with an air of expectation. She still does not move.

"It's just," I say, "I can't get that amulet out of my mind. I wonder what it means? Did Lilya ever work out what it was?"

Natasha's head juts forward, as if she's leaning over me to hear me better. She looks confused.

"What amulet?" she asks.

"You know, that the man wore in the woods."

She squints at me, quizzically. "The man Lilya saw in the woods? The ghost?"

"He wasn't a ghost," I say. "He was real."

Now she looks taken aback as well as confused.

"I never said he wore an amulet. Lilya never mentioned an amulet. You must be embellishing."

She closes her eyes for a moment, as if overtaken by fatigue or just tired of our conversation, at last.

A weird warm glow spreads over me. I can see the amulet even better in my mind now, the triangle, the infinity sign inside it, and I can feel the man's eyes on me. They are familiar, somehow, but then Lilya's story feels strangely familiar.

Lilya's story.

Natasha opens her eyes and we look at each other. For a moment, just a second that passes as quickly as it arrives, I think she can read my mind. That she knows I really did see the amulet.

But she can't, can she? Nobody can read minds. "Except me," comes the thought before I can stop it. "I can read Lilya's."

I want to think that it isn't possible, that I am delusional, "embellishing" as Natasha puts it, but the reality of it is too tangible.

Something else nearly escapes my notice, an elusive feeling or hunch. For a moment I cannot figure out what it is; then, as I look at my grandmother, she is transformed before me from the older woman I know to a teenager. The young Natasha, the girl in love. I see her like this as clearly as if we have both been whisked back in time, and I realize what it is that almost escaped me a moment earlier: I see her from the perspective of Lilya Bekirova. For a moment, I feel that I *am* Lilya, fully and completely.

Then as quickly as the feeling came in, it rushes out.

Now I am a bit worried—is this what it feels like to go mad? But, no, I must admit to myself that I feel perfectly sane, absolutely lucid. In fact, so lucid that my rational self struggles to integrate the experience and, naturally, falls back upon logic. First I must understand if I do, in fact, have some sort of insight into Lilya's mind. I attempt to recall what I know of Lilya Bekirova, what I know of her life—the bare facts that Natasha did not tell me. Immediately I hit upon names. Natasha often struggles to pronounce Crimean Tatar names correctly, and she sometimes leaves them out of the story completely unless I nag her.

Before she has a chance to change the course of our conversation I ask, "Do you remember Lilya's brothers?" Because I do. Gentle Yusuf, wise Ayder, baby Fevzi, and the many images and impressions surrounding them.

"She had three. I remember a few things. Why?"

"In case I'm embellishing," I state matter-of-factly. "Do you remember their names?"

"I'm afraid I don't," she says. "What are you getting at?"

"Do you remember anything about them at all? Because I could have sworn you mentioned their names, their ages, something."

"I met them, of course. But it was so long ago, I remember very little of them. I don't know what they were called. Lilya never spoke of them, as far as I recall."

"I really am imagining things," I say. My spine tingles, I have goosebumps. Could I have imagined Crimean Tatar names? Could I have fabricated this deep feeling of familiarity?

Natasha is watching me, perplexed.

"Are you all right, dear?"

"Sure," I say, in a falsely cheerful voice. "I guess you describe everything in such detail that it's easy to fill in the gaps. Anyway, I've got to go. I've got a lot of work to do."

"Oh," she frowns. She gets up, with obvious stiffness, and comes to embrace me.

"You are a funny girl, sometimes," she says. "Maybe you read about an amulet, and it's just on your mind."

"Maybe."

"Well, sometimes my mind plays tricks on me, too. Usually when I'm hungry. You don't eat enough. Make sure you get enough to eat tonight."

I am out the door before she can ask me any more questions, before I am forced to explain myself.

I go straight to my favorite bookstore, speeding to get there before it closes. There is a book I saw last week in passing, on a special display between Science and Health, a row away from the New Age section where I have never gone. The book's title had something to do with past lives and hypnotherapy. On any other day I would say I didn't believe in reincarnation, but right now I am desperate for answers.

I find the book right away and turn to the back cover. There are rave reviews by other authors of New Age books, two of whom apparently have PhDs. The book is about a psychologist's work regressing patients into their past lives in order to heal present trauma. My skepticism stands no chance against my need—qualifications and methodology mean nothing when I see the words of one reviewer: "Explains how memories can have a past life origin." I'm sold.

I am so impatient that I stand in front of the display and begin to read the introduction: the author's background, why she began to use hypnotic regression, how she stumbled upon a patient's past life while trying to go farther and farther back in time in search of the cause of the patient's claustrophobia. How her patient was cured of her phobia after describing in incredible detail, fraught with emotion, being left locked up in a cupboard to die of starvation in sixteenth-century England. And then: how years later the psychologist confirmed the historical detail, detail which the uneducated patient would not possibly have been able to uncover on her own.

Of course my mind throws up doubt. Perhaps the woman had watched an historically accurate period drama or read some historical romance novel, or had overheard some conversation between historians on a bus. Something. I am heartened—if surprised—to find that the psychologist shared my doubt (I assume anyone who writes books in this category is utterly lacking a skeptical faculty).

I read about how initially she scoured historical records for evidence of her patient's past life, and found record of a Mary McKnight (which her patient claimed was her past-life name) who died in what the patient claimed was her past-life hometown, in Kent, 1542. The psychologist could find no more information, and labeled the case "unconfirmed." A few years later, she was at a conference in England near where Mary had presumably lived and died. She searched the local archives to find the cause of Mary's death, where she came upon records confirming that Mary had been found post-mortem, locked in a cupboard. It was enough to send the psychologist down a whole new career path, resulting in the book I am now holding in my hands.

Already, I am feeling a peculiar sensation—what I can only call confidence—that I have stumbled upon something true. Not the kind of truth I normally encounter, hard-bound, cross-referenced, lauded and accepted—but the kind of truth that is instinctive and right. Like manners, or style, or like when you know you've done the right thing. Like locating my newly-purchased ficus next to the office window, or like agreeing to meet Elisa for lunch.

I am tucking the book under my arm to take it to the check-out when I notice an older man staring at me from the corner under the Military section. I can't seem to budge as I take him in, wondering who he is and if I know him. I feel like I ought to know him, that there should be something familiar about him, but I can't work out what it is. The man wears glasses that keep sliding down his nose as his gaze goes from the book he's gripping to me and back. He has big bushy eyebrows that look as if they should get in the way of his vision—even from where I'm standing I can see hairs overhanging his glasses. He must be in his seventies, though he has a fit look about him. Short and slim, wearing a tweed jacket that looks like it's come from another era; he looks not dissimilar to any old physics or mathematics professor at the university, although there is an air about him that is alien to the typical collegiate scene. For one thing, he is not giving off the cocky self-assurance that professors here bear like a birthright. For another, he is fumbling around with a book and staring at me wide-eyed like someone who is not comfortable in his environment—like someone not from around here.

He continues to peer at me from behind the book which he is holding at chin-height. I can feel his eyes boring into me when I am not looking at him. It is not the gaze of a dirty old man. He is staring at me as if he knows me, with unguarded curiosity, even fascination. Does he think that I won't notice, and doesn't he see that I see him, too?

If I were feeling more self-confident I would approach him, but I am uncomfortable saying anything to this man. It's as if he knows something I do not. So I sneak away to the check-out to pay for my book while his nose is stuck in his, and slip out of the bookstore before he catches sight of me again.

When I get home, as I'm washing my hands before making myself dinner, I take a good look at myself in the mirror, wondering what it was the man at the bookstore had seen, if anything, that had had him staring at me with such intensity.

I am cooking a spaghetti bolognese tonight, with a side salad and bread rolls. I never have salad or bread with dinner when I'm eating on my own. What's the point of making more work? Yet tonight, for some reason (and not because I am taking to heart my grandmother's injunction to eat a lot), I fancy a feast. At the last minute I take a frozen roll of cookie dough from the freezer, slice it, and put it in the oven. It's like I'm cooking for company.

As I come into the living room from the kitchen I see a man going down the front steps. I sidle up to the window and peer outside. I think that he looks like the same young man who knocked on my door two weeks ago, though it's difficult to say at night, seeing only the back of his head. I did not hear the doorbell, or a knock, though he must have tried both. I close the curtains. I wonder what the man could want, then forget about him as soon as I turn on the radio in the kitchen and pour myself a glass of Chardonnay.

Later that night, relaxing with a plate of cookies and a cup of coffee in front of the television, I notice a bit of paper below the front door. I go to pick it up and read it:

I guess I've missed you again.
I have come. I recognize your house from my dreams.
My name is Sam Hunter.

I go tingly all along the back of my neck and shudder. I check the locks on my doors and windows. Initially I am so shaky that my mind goes blank and I cannot imagine what the note means. When I have calmed down I presume it must be the man I saw earlier, the one who came by two weeks ago. "Holy shit," I think, "am I being stalked?" I resolve to notify the police, then I go to bed.

I don't know why I don't call the police right away. I just have a feeling that it can wait, which is totally illogical, and contrary to my temperament. I wonder if this is the kind of self-delusion I've observed in horror movies, when the victims decide they must venture into the dark corridor in the haunted house in order to investigate the scary noises, as if they are immune to danger.

It is the next Thursday and Natasha is looking through her mail as she answers the door, squinting through her reading glasses.

"Hmm," she says, pausing at one. "From New York. Is there more?"

I see a subtle upturning of her lips as she painstakingly opens the letter. I am still standing in the doorway. She pulls out a single piece of paper and begins to read.

I go sit on the couch while she reads the letter. She remains where she stood when I entered; the door is still open. After a few moments she takes off her glasses and puts the letter back in its envelope. I think she might be tearing up.

"Well!" she sighs. She sniffs and wipes her nose. She goes into the kitchen and I stand up and follow her, watching as she opens the dishwasher to grab cups and plates and begins to put them away, her fistful of mail still in hand, shoving the cutlery and the letters all into the same drawer. I wonder if I should offer to help, if I should say anything, or if she will eventually notice me.

After a minute or two of silence she suddenly begins to talk. She begins chopping a cucumber as she says, "I used to read all the time. Now it's too tiring to read!"

I take this as my cue, and begin to help her with lunch.

"You don't read much anymore?" I ask.

"I watch *Days of Our Lives*," she says.

"That's only an hour a day, though," I point out. "What about the rest of the day?"

"There are others," she says. She hands me a tomato to slice, then begins to detail her favorite soap operas, recounting the characters and their antics. I want to ask her about the letter but do not. I'll ask later. Anyway, in her stream of one-sided conversation she gives me no entry-point. She can hardly believe that she is watching it herself, she confesses. But she finds the predictability soothing, how the characters react to the most ordinary and tragic of occurrences with an equal degree of overreaction. She shakes her head. "What garbage!" she says, and laughs at her own enjoyment of it.

Then, for the first time ever during one of my visits, she turns on the television. We eat while watching some typical daytime drama (I only know it is not *Days of Our Lives*, which—she explained earlier—she tapes so that she can enjoy it at night, on her own, with cup of hot chocolate). After the program is over, my grandmother surfs through the channels and I gaze out of the window down at the pool. It has recently closed for the winter season.

After a half an hour of channel surfing and no conversation I become anxious. I realize that I am worried Natasha will not continue her tale. It has never occurred to me before that she won't, but what if she did suddenly stop? What if she just said, "That's it. I can't bear to talk about what happened next"—then what would I do?

This should just be a random thought, an insignificant and irrational worry, the kind that pops in and out of my mind all day—but it doesn't leave me. It pesters me and gradually metamorphoses into something big and needy. "Oh, dear," I think, noticing my hands have gone cold and clammy. "It cannot possibly matter that much, can it?"

Natasha has zoned out. She is absentmindedly using her forefinger to wipe every last crumb from her plate into her mouth. I want to intervene. I need to intervene. I must know what happens next in the lives of Lilya, Refat and young Natasha, because I am incomplete without the ending.

Even as I ask myself, "Do you really mean 'incomplete?'" I realize, with a small shudder, that I do. As if my life is half-lived by me, only completed by Lilya's. And then another thought hits me: How can I have some of Lilya's memories and not know what else happened to her? My facility for logical consistency does not fail me, even in my state of agitation. It is illogical that I can recall what I believe only Lilya knew, and not be able to know any further events in her life until Natasha recounts them.

I must get a grip.

"Should we have some tea, or coffee?" I ask. We are usually at the tea or coffee stage when she begins to talk. My suggestion works.

She turns off the television and gets up, wordlessly.

"No, you stay there," I tell her. "I'll make it."

She looks relieved. Natasha hardly looks at the coffee when I bring it out, but sniffs into the air approvingly.

"I've been thinking so much about your life before you came to America," I tell her. "You're story is so intriguing. You know, I can hardly wait to visit you. I love hearing about your past. It kind of makes me feel connected to my past. You know, to our family's past."

I'm not just saying it. Now that I think about it, I have never thought of myself having a family history, as being a branch of a family tree. I've always felt more like an island, alone and unconnected.

My grandmother smiles at me. She has to turn her head to do so. She is in her armchair, on the same side of the room as me. Normally she sits on the couch facing me to talk.

She turns away and says, "You know, Lilya was nothing like you, and yet, you remind me of her sometimes."

I get chills all up and down my arms.

"Really? How?"

I hold my breath.

"Well, I'm not sure. I was thinking about it this morning. Maybe it's your will. Lilya had a strong will."

I can think of nothing to say, but I murmur something monosyllabic, something that doesn't give away in language or tone my impatience to know all about Lilya. We are silent for some time, and I wonder if she will tell me more today, if I can ask her what she is thinking when she has that look on her face she has now—distracted, dreamy, just that tiny bit anxious.

"You know, my life in Leningrad seems so far from me now, like it was just a dream, whereas my life in Crimea seems real. I have recollections of life in the city, but they seem all the same. Big buildings, walking to school, our small apartment. The long winters. But when I think about Crimea I remember all the details."

I decide to encourage her.

"So what happened with you and Refat next?" I ask. "Didn't the war happen soon?"

Victory! Natasha takes the bait. She comes to sit across from me, moving wearily, sitting slowly, coffee in hand. She crosses and uncrosses her legs, licks her lips.

"Yes, the war was coming, not that it was on my mind."

She begins to tell me about the war; she begins to tell me about herself and Refat. But it is Lilya I see and feel and hear with all my senses, and only half in my mind. My body stirs with the cold air of autumnal Crimea, the shadows in this apartment go long and draw close, and in the darkness I think I can see, from the corners of my eyes, the figure of Lilya Bekirova standing just over my shoulder.

I can feel her presence. I can feel her in me, waiting for Natasha's words to draw her out.

18

October 1939

In 1939, the madness taking hold of Europe had not yet reached the Crimea, although German forces now occupied Czechoslovakia, ever closer to Soviet borders month by month. To avert his country's involvement in war, Stalin sealed a deal with the Nazis promising mutual non-aggression, or rather, non-interference in parallel aggression: the Germans would not interfere with Soviet designs in Finland and the Baltics, while the Soviets would not thwart the Germans in Poland. Stalin, history tells us, aimed to widen the USSR's sphere of influence under the threat of Hitler's territorial ambitions. After the non-aggression pact was signed, Hitler invaded Poland and Stalin launched the "Winter War" in Finland.

That was how war reached Natasha's family, long before it reached Crimea and Lilya or Refat, before it even reached Russia. In October 1939 the Matveev patriarch was called back to Leningrad, then sent to Finland to participate in the Soviet invasion. Natasha and Mira did not know until after the fighting had begun that Aleksander Dmitrievich was in the midst of it; even had they known they would not have worried excessively. The outcome was certain to be successful. The pomp and circumstance, the every communication from above (the authorities, the trusted leaders) reiterated a simple message that gave the Matveevs and countless others hope: the Fatherland's power was historically just and, accordingly, invincible.

It was a month and a half since her father's departure when Natasha left home around eight AM. She walked ten minutes down the hill, diverging left and away from the Bekirovs before going down into a dip behind another hill, where she saw Refat waiting. Winter was well on its way, a change evident especially in the mornings when frost became a thin veneer of ice causing Natasha to slip as she crossed the grass. Her frozen fingers fumbled to pull her hat down over her eyes as the wind cut through it and stung her face.

Natasha and Refat had been a couple for a year and a half now, but only several months ago had they devised a method of meeting when they were not at school. Each morning on weekends, and every day during school holidays,

Natasha would go to a particular spot after breakfast and await Refat. Their rendezvous point was much closer to Natasha's house than to his, so she never missed a meeting, whereas Refat came only when he was able to spare the time away from farm duties, given the twenty-five minute journey it took him each way. In any case, Natasha never had more than ten minutes to spare in the mornings; it was all around a hurried affair. Yet she and Refat were grateful for even those few minutes alone together.

On this day Refat did not kiss her hello; instead his first gesture was to place a hand roughly on her arm, then ask when they could meet there later, for longer.

"You're in a fine mood today," Natasha observed. She pulled back her arm.

Refat gave Natasha what seemed to her to be an indulgent smile. He said, "I apologize, it's just that I cannot talk right now."

He took her hand in his, and kissed her fingers.

"You should wear gloves this time of day," he said. "You're freezing."

Natasha let her hand relax in his. He took her other hand and blew hot breath on her fingers. She was embarrassed that she had reacted with such irritation.

Refat explained that right now he was supposed to be tending to a sick cow, one of their milking cows, desperately needed this time of year. He knew without doubt that his hour-long absence would earn him a rebuke. He could not afford to stay a moment longer, but needed to speak with her soon.

Natasha could see that Refat was bothered by something. He had never before exhibited such urgency in his need to arrange their next meeting. She went cold inside.

"I can come this evening," she said. "I'll say I'm seeing Lilya."

No sooner had they agreed on the time than Refat ran off, and she turned away, refusing to watch him go, refusing to entertain any speculation as to why he had to speak with her later.

Natasha came early for their meeting. She had come with her paper and pencil so she could sit high on the hill and sketch the mountain Ai-Petri in the distance.

Drawing was a very recent hobby—she had tried it before every once in a while, but never with any passion, nor determination to improve her skill. Her interest crystallized after her father was posted to Finland. The connection between his departure and her artwork was not, at the time, evident. Later, in a foreign country, when her painting went through its first big transformation, she suddenly realized that the absence of her father had been the catalyst for exploring her creative urges. Despite the passion of young love, which should be an artist's first muse, her father's quiet judgment had stifled her. "What is the point of those clouds, and that tree? Do they communicate something of importance, or are they distractions?" he would say, or something similar, on the few occasions Natasha showed him one of her drawings. To be fair, his remarks weren't comments on her talent so much as a convenient entrée to one of his favorite lectures. To him, art for art's sake was just another form of bourgeois loafing. Art needed to be socially useful, to inform and celebrate through its depiction of peasants in landscapes, suffering at the hands of Kulaks, the beauty of a factory, and so on.

Then, within days of his departure, after years of pretending away her interest, she was overcome with a compulsion to draw everything. Especially distractions.

She drew from memory. First, of people she saw. A young Tatar at the market. Her mother Mira. A child. Four weeks into her new hobby, as the leaves changed color and dropped, she began to draw what she saw around their house. She and Lilya had a picnic, and Natasha brought her pencil and paper and drew the trees and rocks. She drew for herself, for the elation she felt when lines became an image. She drew to distract her mother from loneliness. Since Aleksander Dmitrievich's departure, Mira Vladimirovna either babbled or said nothing, but she no longer conversed—except when she saw her daughter's drawings. Natasha drew for Refat. He acted very pleased with her pictures, which sent Natasha over the moon. She dreamt of owning oils one day, and painting things exactly as she saw them. For now her pictures were in shades of gray and black; only in her imagination were they full of color.

Today would be the first time Natasha drew Ai-Petri. Every beautiful place seemed to tell her a story, and for her this mountain told of its age and wisdom. Its trails of snow dipped down irregularly from the top like a beard, and around it were smaller hills, as mild and flat on top as Ai-Petri. Ai-Petri looked to Natasha like an old man surrounded by the small tables where his grandchildren sat, meek and awed by their grandfather's presence. She was a realist, though; she drew it true to life. She had come here before to be inspired by it, but had never quite felt the confidence she needed to put pencil to paper. Today she had no doubt she could sketch it. Even without color Natasha felt she could finally capture it—the angles and the perspective, and the dramatic contrast of where the dark mountain met the brilliant, bright sky.

Natasha saw Refat walking toward her when he was just a dot on the horizon. Even then she could sense something was wrong; as he came closer she saw that he was slouched, and when he came closer still, that he was looking at the ground and did not notice her. She did not call out to him and kept drawing.

Refat did not wave when he saw Natasha, nor did he smile. He climbed to where she sat and sat next to her. Neither spoke. Natasha could feel a weight of expectation and fear pressing down on her, and she dropped her pencil.

Refat took her hand, but looked out at Ai-Petri, as did Natasha.

"See what I've sketched?" she handed him her work-in-progress.

"You have true talent," he complimented her, but his voice was empty and dull.

Natasha's hand went limp in his. She wanted, but did not have the courage, to take it away.

"You are talented at a lot of things," he went on. "You are a very special person."

Refat cleared his throat. His hand twitched in Natasha's.

"So what do you want to say?" she asked him, dreading the answer. She did not look at him, could not do so, though she looked toward him. "I can't bear for you to just sit there."

"I wanted to tell you in my own way," he said. "I wanted to tell you how much you mean to me, and not just say it."

He was bumbling, but Natasha knew he was not as good at expressing his feelings out loud as he was writing them into his poetry. She could see he was uneasy.

He said, "Certain things have to be in my life, and then there are the unexpected blessings. Like you."

It was the most beautiful thing anyone had ever said to Natasha, and she never forgot those words; even then, sitting by him, trying not to cry in expectation of the words "It's over between us," with her attention overwrought and waning under the crush of an awful foreboding, just then his words repeated themselves over and over in her mind for several long seconds. The words were themselves blessings—"unexpected blessings, like you"—until Refat said,

"I am leaving in a fortnight to join the Red Army. There is war."

Natasha did not cry. Maybe he thought she was being stoic, her typical stubborn self, because after a minute he asked her what she was thinking.

"So that's it?" she asked him. "You're leaving? What about us?"

It was the only time she asked him outright about their future. He never could, of course, make any assurances, not before, not now. And his heart had already spoken, it seemed. He groped for words, started numerous sentences without finishing before the explanations came pouring out, in and among them declarations she would go over again and again in her memory. Ones like, "I cannot forget you," and "You have changed me," and "I wish we could marry."

His country needed him, he told her.

"But this is your homeland," she said to him.

"Still, my country needs me," he said.

Many of the young Crimean Tatar men he knew had also enlisted, he told her.

"Then," she could hardly whisper. "You must go."

She refused to wish him farewell. They had two weeks left together. Two weeks that would be for Natasha the ultimate lie, or from another perspective, the final realization of truth: she and Refat were not really a couple in love as they had as much as broken up for eternity, yet they were in love and it was their destiny to be forever apart.

On her way home, once Natasha became aware of her vice-like grip on her drawing pad, she ripped out her sketch of Ai-Petri and crushed it into a ball. She threw it hard onto the ground. Smudges of clouds and mountains darkened one side. The ball of paper got caught in the grass, then rolled away with the wind. She could see the light and dark places and was glad there was no color. She did not ever want to use colors to draw this landscape even if she had all the money in the world to buy oil paints. There was no color here worth painting. There was no color left in her. The mountain was a silly old man, not to be counted on at all, and one day it would decay and crumble and amount to nothing, just like everything else in this place.

One week later Lilya arrived at Natasha's house in the late afternoon. She came unannounced—which was not in itself out of character. On that day, though, she brought a cherry pie made from one of her family's last jars of preserves. It was a rare treat, an unusual gesture that went unexplained. Lilya had baked the pie herself, she said. She was flushed despite the cold and could not—did not—look her friend in the eye. Lilya insisted on helping prepare tea, as Natasha's mother was not feeling well and was in bed at the time. Lilya said very little in the kitchen, still less when they sat with their tea. Natasha waited for some sort of explanation as Lilya sliced the pie and offered her friend a plate.

Natasha felt no impatience or apprehension. They were always comfortable together, used to both chatter and silence. Natasha did not ask her friend any questions, perhaps because she had not yet told Lilya about Refat and the news weighed on her. To know he was leaving was one thing; to voice it made it real, imminent, and infinitely worse. For the time being, with her dear friend sitting across from her over tea and pie, life was not so bad. It was almost as it had been, with her beloved nearby, where she could touch him and see him and pretend it would always be this way.

She knew she had to tell Lilya sooner or later, and since they had finished their first slice of pie and Lilya had said nothing at all, Natasha decided she might as well gather her courage. She managed to look her friend in the face and say, evenly,

"Refat is leaving for the war."

"I know," Lilya said.

"Oh," Natasha replied with some relief—she would not have to speak about Refat any more that day. She assumed that since so many young men were enlisting, news traveled fast.

"I know because his father met with my father last night," Lilya said, staring hard at the crumbs on her plate.

"Oh," Natasha said again. She thought, "Well, men meet at night. In a small village people know one another, and they meet."

Lilya stared at her friend. She leant over and took her hand. Lilya's hand was cold and Natasha shuddered when she felt it. She was not paying a lot of attention to Lilya other than to feel her hand, not really. She was trying to clear her head of fear and loneliness in order to find hope. That Refat would not have to fight, and he would come home, and somehow they could be together.

Lilya stroked Natasha's hand, and said firmly, "Natashenka, you know I must marry. My parents have been looking for a fiancé for me. Refat's father came, and … need I say more? Please don't make me say it."

"Say what?" Natasha thought. Then: "Lilya and Refat?"

It couldn't be.

One look at Lilya told her it could. It was.

Natasha gasped. She did not take her hand back, she felt too weak; her hand was lifeless. Lilya stroked her friend's hand again but Natasha had lost all sensation. Then she felt herself fall inside, as if off a high, high cliff. She felt a plummeting sensation she had only ever felt before in dreams. "Perhaps this is what dying feels like," she thought, and then became aware that she had stopped breathing. The room dimmed, then brightened, and her free hand instinctively went to her eyes.

Lilya came around the table and knelt beside her.

"Oh, dear, please breathe, dear Natashenka," Lilya was pleading. She cried, softly. "Please don't think I want this."

Natasha fell off of her chair. She would never have thought such a thing was possible, that a woman could faint and need smelling salts, but here she was, not unconscious exactly, but immobile. She could not sit up and the room spun and spun. Lilya helped her to stand, half-lifted and half-dragged her back onto the couch.

They sat for some time, Lilya and Natasha, arms around one another, rocking back and forth, as the news sank in.

"Before you say anything," Lilya said, "I must speak—"

"—I cannot speak," Natasha whispered.

"I agreed against my will, at first," Lilya continued. "As you know, at some point it was inevitable that I agree to marry, and Refat's father and mine were very firm about their decision. I considered my options, then it occurred to me that this was the best possible option. Refat loves you, not me, and he can never love me, nor I him. So he is safe with me. And Natashenka, I managed to delay the wedding until Refat returns from war. Anything can happen—"

"Don't say that," Natasha whimpered. Lilya had handed her a handkerchief and Natasha dabbed at the tears falling onto her cheeks.

"Not *that*, my goodness, not at all! I mean, in time, maybe we can work something out! Maybe it can work between you two. By the time he returns, things could have changed, and because of our engagement, I am holding him for you, you know what I mean? It could be worse, my dear, he could be promised to someone who insisted on marrying right away, and then what? But that is not the case."

"This is all possible only if he comes back from war."

"And he will, my darling."

"So," Natasha said, balling up the handkerchief in her fist, eyes red, "you are engaged."

"Yes."

"That makes things easier for you, doesn't it?"

Lilya said gently, "By doing my duty I have pleased my parents, so they will not be so worried anymore. It is easier in some sense, yes."

"No one knows, still, about me and Refat. Except you." Unless, Natasha thought, Lilya's father had told others. Somehow she did not think he had.

"Perhaps it is better that way," Lilya said.

Natasha thought, "It is final, my fate. Refat will either die in battle, or survive to marry Lilya." Her best friend was to marry her beloved! She wished she could embellish this ridiculous, twisted story with anything to give her hope, anything to make her smile, but it was not possible.

From that moment Natasha sank into depression. The days passed, undifferentiated. Lilya did not come to call, Mira tiptoed around her, and it seemed to Natasha that not only had she forgotten how to live in the world, but the world had forgotten her. She stayed in bed for days.

Then, on her fourth bedridden day, Natasha awoke to her mother's call.

"You have a visitor," she said. "But if you are still feeling bad I will tell him to come back."

"Him? Who?" Natasha asked.

"A schoolmate of yours, Refat."

"I will be out in a minute," Natasha said.

She fumbled in her drawers for a brush and couldn't find one, then used her fingers to comb her hair into place. She pinched her cheeks and wished she could sneak into her parents' room for her mother's perfume and rouge. "Silly girl," she told herself, "that you should care at a time like this; this could be last time you see one another." Then she froze, unable to face the thought. Every moment with Refat was a gift, she realized, so she vowed to look for the eternal in the temporal. Natasha told herself such lofty thoughts as she entered her living room and saw Refat standing, hat in hand, coat on but shoes off.

"I cannot stay," he said. "Your mother is insisting."

Mira Matveeva hovered, teapot in hand. She was clearly bewildered by whatever it was she was seeing, and looked searchingly at her daughter. She looked again at the young Tatar man before her.

"Mother," Natasha said, "I will be right back—" and without explanation she threw on her coat and shoved her feet into shoes, leading the way outside.

Mira stood in the doorway as the kettle whistled, as Refat put his shoes back on and her daughter drifted off in the snow with the young Tatar shuffling behind her.

"I won't do it!" Natasha said, her voice still and calm, yet emphatic. She was still gliding off ahead of Refat, still bent on being philosophical, even as reason crumbled in her brain and she began to pant anxiously. Before she knew it the words came tumbling out, "What have you come for? I know about your engagement. I should congratulate you. I guess you've come to tell me, and then—"

"Slow down, Natashenka," Refat said.

"I will stop," she said and faced him. "I will enjoy this moment," she said and gazed at him, his every feature. She breathed slowly. They said nothing.

"I cannot come back again. You see, the train is leaving early and we, the other guys who have enlisted, we must all go together."

"So you're leaving early," Natasha said.

"Yes."

"It shouldn't affect you," she thought to herself. "What's a few days, anyway?" She drank in the sight of him, imagining that time had stopped.

But it could not last, she realized, and if she could not be that way for a few short seconds, how could she last for an eternity without him? A lump rose in her throat and she coughed.

"You're flushed," he observed. "Are you going to cry?"

"Does it matter?" she asked.

"I've never seen you cry. It bothers me."

"Well then, you can go." Natasha gave a little shrug.

"Are you angry?"

"No."

But Natasha's lips began to tremble and she feared the tears would come. She sniffed and rubbed her eyes with her bare hand.

"This is not how we should part," he said.

"Then let's not. Let's say it's otherwise," she began, and took a deep breath. "Say you're going for a short while, and we'll see one another again soon. We don't know, it might be true ..."

"Yes, that is true," Refat smiled. He took her bare hands in his gloved hands and covered them.

"Because we have a lot to discuss, you and I," Natasha said loudly, as if announcing this news to whomever was around to hear it. She lowered her voice, "I mean, lots. You know, about our future, and yours, and mine, and Lilya's. I mean, we are rational adults now, aren't we? We can discuss things and work them out. It will all work out. We just need a plan."

Refat might have set her straight had it been any other day. Indeed, he began to correct her, saying, "But you must understand my darling ..." he said, then his words fizzled to a stop. He searched Natasha's face, then lowered his eyes. Something must have clicked in his mind.

"A lot to discuss," he said, almost whispering. "Yes we do, don't we?"

"So," Natasha said. "You be sure to come back as soon as you can, to discuss these issues."

"Yes, I will," he said.

He kissed her hand. They kissed each other three times on the cheek as people did in greeting, in parting.

"We will see each other soon," he said.

"And have so much to talk about," she said.

Refat took a step backwards, then another step, then he waved, and Natasha waved back.

And he was gone.

Natasha had relied on Refat to take away some of the awful burden of their love's ultimate hopelessness—as he had, with a kiss, his hand in her hand, or some pointless conversation. Now in his absence the load she carried grew heavier and she began to sink. She was alone, even with Lilya, who tried to no avail to talk her friend out of her misery. Natasha seemed not to hear properly, as if they were both under water, Natasha sinking to the bottom while Lilya spoke through the depths to try to save her. Natasha could not be saved.

Then word came in April of the next year that Natasha's father had been killed, a month earlier, along with other Red Army soldiers in Finland. She cried, but beneath her tears was a fear that, deep in her soul, she did not, could not, feel any loss. There was nothing left inside herself to lose.

Decades later, Natasha learned that the Winter War cost the lives of two hundred thousand Soviet soldiers. It was a bloody affair that only slightly expanded the USSR's northern border and did not, in the end, quash Finland's independence. Stalin's regional brutality did not end in Finland. Thereafter he threatened the Baltic states with invasion if they did not voluntarily become Soviet republics and cede control of their governments. He sent in the secret police, the NKVD, to arrest or kill leading economic, political and cultural figures; many more ordinary people were sent to the Gulag on various other spurious charges. At the time, though, in the midst of her own private war, Natasha knew nothing of the world outside beyond the fact that it had claimed, in different ways, both her father and her lover.

19

Natasha ends her account so abruptly and with such a pained look that I find myself lost for words and, after a few seconds of silence, I give her a hug and leave.

Yes, I can feel her loss. Her grieving is so acute—has it never abated, or has retelling it brought it up again? I cannot imagine. Yet, as soon as I shut her door behind me Natasha's despair glides off of me like dry sand. Against the background twinge of my sympathy, Lilya preoccupies me. I feel like a traitor to Natasha that my instincts are shifting my attention from her to her best friend, and I want to run back inside and hug her again, tell her how sorry I am, that I love her, that I am there for her—even as my mind speeds toward Lilya.

There is something going on with Lilya, I know, some worry or problem that only hints at itself in my mind. I will have to wait until our next meeting to find out. Meanwhile, Lilya haunts my imagination, hovers in my dreams.

Since my visit to the bookstore to get the book on past lives, my research into the disappearance of the 21st Airborne has taken a sudden turn to the absurd.

The reincarnation book introduced me to the New Age section, and, having hit a brick wall in my research, I decided, why not see what the kooks have to say about unexplained disappearances?

By today, after my last visit to the bookstore I have already gone through all its New Age books—everything from fairies, angels and aliens to energetic healing, meditation and yoga. Some things I read are pure crap, the ramblings of doddering fools with no credentials and overdeveloped fantasy lives. Other books are surprisingly believable, well-written and well documented, many of them authored by educated sorts (no doubt exiled from the academic establishment).

Some theories presented in these books can be neither proven nor disproved by our science for the simple fact that they cannot be measured or tested or categorized according to the methodology of science as we know it. So much is experiential; how can one establish control conditions for a person's encounters with ghosts, ghouls or fairies, or alternate realities? The only part of New Age thought that has any validity to the scientific mind is reincarnation, as documented by hypnosis. Again and again I come across books claiming that hypnotized subjects exhibit abilities or a knowledge of facts that they could not have acquired from their present life experience. For instance, hypnotic subjects have been documented as flawlessly speaking languages unknown to them when not under hypnosis.

All this is not to say that anyone understands what reincarnation is. The soul traveling through time, coming back again and again? Genetic memory of one's ancestors? A kind of morphic resonance shared by the human species—are we all connected psychically through space and time, and in certain states of consciousness we attract to us memories of lives and eras which mirror and/or make sense of what is happening to us in the present?

Truthfully, I have been reading mostly about reincarnation. I have no other convincing explanation for what seems to be my experience of being Lilya—or at least having her memories. I have also perused psychology books, but I can't believe I have some kind of psychosis, and I don't believe my imagination is sufficiently well-developed so as to create a believable fantasy all in the name of wishful thinking. On the other hand, reincarnation has evoked in me as much confusion as clarity, and I am hesitant to make too much of it.

For one thing—setting aside for a moment the fundamental question of what reincarnation, if it exists, actually is—what is the point of it?

That's the problem with all this New Age stuff. It purports to give people answers about the mysteries of life without addressing the point of life in the first place.

Take my experience of Lilya's memory. It is so uncannily real, so much my own, that of course I cannot help but accept that at some level Lilya and I share consciousness (a concept which is problematic in and of itself). That perhaps, for want of a better explanation, I am the reincarnation of Lilya Bekirova. It certainly explains my memory. It does not, however, explain why I have been reincarnated as Catherine. Most contemporary spiritual writers, following the Hindu and Buddhist beliefs, assume that the human soul improves itself life after life until it is so pure and good that it can return to God.

I'm not at all sure I'm an improvement on Lilya. I'm not so sure I'm improving on anything. Then, of course, there is the perennial question: if God indeed exists, and is as perfect and good as religions contend, why would he curse his creations with the need for improvement?

So as not to be seen in the New Age section, I gather my books and read at the in-store café, drinking coffees and eating whatever is for sale (mostly cakes and cookies). I must have an air of desperation about me, with my books piled up on the table, empty plates, notebook paper crumpled on my lap, as one day a middle-aged woman sitting next to me in the café catches my eye and says, "Looking for answers?"

She is wearing a large crystal necklace and I am pretty sure that means she thinks she knows the answers. I nearly snarl at her. Inexplicably, I have become enraged.

I pretend that I haven't heard her and squint more intently into the book I'm holding, imagining all kinds of caustic, brilliant retorts to put the woman in her place.

Perhaps I really am wasting my time with reincarnation.

In any case, today I have put all reincarnation books to one side and am limiting myself to books in which strange phenomena are linked to specific locations—disappearing people, UFOs, crop circles, altered states of consciousness. Immediately I am drawn to a book about "ley lines" (a term I have so far avoided because of its New Age connotations). Ley lines, as I already know, supposedly run through many of those places where scientists have reported electromagnetic anomalies.

The concept of ley lines originated in 1921, when a British amateur archeologist and photographer named Alfred Watkins, noticed that some ancient sites were in alignment. He thought these lines, which he dubbed "leys" (an old Anglo-Saxon word for meadows or cleared land), marked old traders' routes. Good science fell prey to counterculture when ley lines became synonymous with streams of energy crisscrossing the globe, intense sources of mystical power which cause as well as attract supernatural occurrences.

Since then, the term has expanded to mean, in addition to the invisible lines connecting ancient monuments, invisible lines linking stones, the lines drawn in earth carvings (such as the Nazca lines in Peru), and lines known by local inhabitants as marking paths of spiritual significance (such as the fairy paths in Ireland, or, according to many indigenous peoples, the paths souls take upon physical death). Science has not proven the existence of ley lines as such; that is to say, there is no proof that there are linear, energetic features anywhere on the Earth's surface. But scientific research has found that specific locations said to be on a ley line, such as at sacred sites, exhibit high background radiation and other kinds of electromagnetic anomalies.

In the book I'm reading now, ley lines are linked to shamanism—a generic term used to describe certain features of spiritual practice found in different cultures, and also often used to describe the religious practices of the world's first peoples. Shamanism was, and in some places still is, a way of life that recognizes the interdependence of the natural and supernatural worlds. The men and women who preside over shamanic rituals are high priests, political figures, and "witch doctors," and are often called shamans. In their cultures they are the ultimate interpreters and predictors of reality, the ones who, it is said, can walk between worlds. Shamans travel between dimensions in order to seek counsel with spirit beings in human or animal form, to discover the future, to heal the living and help the dead. The worlds, I have learned, share common descriptors across the board, the accounts only varying slightly according to the people in question—be they Native Americans or pre-Hindu hunter gatherers. There is a lower world, the world of elemental spirits and animal totems; the middle world, where we humans reside; and the upper world, the domain of wise spiritual teachers.

This is where my interest peaks: some New Agers claim ley lines mark the paths shamans take to travel between worlds. Apparently, ley lines occur at sites of rock carvings where it is known that shamans practiced their craft; moreover, students of shamanism using narcotics to reach higher states of consciousness have reported seeing straight lines which, they claim, led them out of their bodies.

I have to concede that my research has uncovered examples of places with anomalous energy, and I have documented strange occurrences at those sites, but until today nothing I've read has even hinted at a hypothesis for what could be happening. The connection between ley lines and shamanism offers an interesting avenue of inquiry concerning the disappearance of the 21st Airborne.

Okay, so the theory is bizarre, unprovable, and perhaps insane, not to mention partial. I have yet to find an explanation for how shamans travel between worlds, if only they can do it or if—at these high energy places—anyone can just disappear. The descriptions of those worlds in books on shamanism do not satisfy me, no doubt because I am too literal. I am impatient with sentimental depictions of wafting spirits and predictable landscapes (pristine, Technicolor, hyperbolic). Yet, I cannot deny it: the ley-line/shaman hypothesis is the closest I've gotten to conceptualizing the 21st's unexplained disappearance.

There must be other worlds. The men of the 21st Airborne must have disappeared into one of them.

When I accept this hypothetical conclusion today I shake with laughter and nearly choke with the effort of keeping my mouth—full of berry friand—closed. There is no hippie woman to ask me if I've had a spiritual epiphany, only geeky types with accounting and computer books looking down their noses at my hysteria. They can see the books on my table and probably think I'm a fruit cake.

I am high on caffeine and sugar and, I decide, I have finally lost it. The real world of serious theses and political theories has no hold on me anymore. It was never helpful in explaining reality, anyway. Without it I can believe what I like. I speed home through pouring rain, skidding as I turn the corner onto my street, imagining for a moment what it would be like if I sped right through a portal and into another world.

I remember, suddenly, how I stood on the hill in Croatia and disappeared from time and space, and I grow cold.

How could I have forgotten?

Now, for the first time, like a person awaking from a coma, I am aware that it is no accident that I of all people have to know where the men of the 21st Airborne disappeared that day. It is partly an epiphany, partly an admission to myself: there is no complexity driving my intellectual pursuits. Human motivation is, I decide, ridiculously, embarrassingly simple. Not knowing what happened to me in Croatia has driven me all these years.

Several hours later I am dozing on the couch when a knock at the door brings me back to consciousness. It is already dark, and cold. I turn on the lights outside and look through the peephole. A young man is hugging himself and shivering. He is completely soaked. Without thinking, I open the door.

I realize, with a shock, that he is the man I saw walk down the front steps the week before, the same man whose knocking I didn't respond to before that—the man who probably left the creepy note! I don't even have a chance to slam the door back shut when he says,

"I'm sorry to disturb you. I was looking for Victor Tehusa. I was sure this is the right house but no one's ever home and no one's responded to the note I left him, and you're obviously not him, so maybe I'm lost or … maybe you can help me?"

"Victor's dead."

I think first, "Oh, the note wasn't for you—way to overreact." Then, "Oh shit!" I can't believe how unceremoniously I gave this young man the news. "So tactful, Cat!"

"I'm sorry," I say, "Please come in and dry off."

My response is unwitting, instinctual, and surprises me. The young man's Southern accent has disarmed me at once, I reason, or maybe it's his face (kind), or his manner (sweet, harmless). Normally I will not even open the door when I am home alone, not to mention stand there talking to the stranger who knocked on it.

I hope he wasn't close to Victor. He doesn't look in the least bit shocked or upset, fortunately.

"What are you doing, letting in this perfect stranger?" I think, yet the words that come out of my mouth sound instead like, "Please let me get you some dry clothes. I'll throw your clothes in the dryer."

I am still trying to compensate for my insensitivity concerning Victor's demise so I hardly look at him as I insist, pay no more attention to his appearance than I already have, and do not question his motives, either aloud or in my head. I am unrelenting as I interrupt his polite protests with instructions to wait just a minute, as I hand him a towel, as I put the kettle on, as I leave him alone downstairs so I can find clothes for him upstairs. I come back with the biggest t-shirt I own, and some roomy sweatpants with an elastic waistband, and direct him to the bathroom.

"Thank you, really, you don't have to …" he says, for the third or fourth time.

I shush him, and when he emerges from the bathroom (the t-shirt fits, the sweatpants look a bit short, but otherwise fine.) I ask, "Tea or coffee? Please wait out the storm, have a hot drink, while I dry your clothes and think of how best to take my foot out of my mouth."

I finally look him in the eyes, "I'm really sorry about Victor. I hope it doesn't come as too much of a shock."

"Not at all. He was a friend of an acquaintance. Coffee sounds like a gift from God."

I freeze, as my brain dings, "Kind of an odd comment!" and I wonder again what in the world I'm doing.

Only when he sits down at the kitchen table, dry but for his hair, does it strike me—I must know this young man already, that's why I am comfortable with him, that's why when I read the note he left I didn't call the police in a panic. I can't explain it, but now that I've had this thought I realize my familiarity with him was there as soon as I saw him through the front door. I fill the coffee plunger with fresh grounds and try to smile—convincingly, I hope—and say, "By the way, I'm Catherine."

"Sam."

"Nice to meet you. Sugar? Milk?" He takes both. "Victor was our neighbor for as long as I can remember. He died about five years ago."

"I don't know you, do I?" Sam asks. "No, I know I don't. It's just...."

"Yes," I say. "I was just thinking the same thing."

Sam folds his hands in his lap and, I notice, does not look closely at me or the house at all, as if he's seen me or it before, or at least like someone with benign intentions, not like a stalker or killer or thief.

Or maybe he's just shy. He stares at the table, until I engage him directly again.

"So, you don't think we've met before?" I ask.

"I don't see how. I've never been to this state before."

I don't bother pointing out all the ways it's possible we've met. It's not as though I've never left the state, but for the moment, I ignore it.

"Well, maybe we'll figure it out," I say, and ask, "So why were you looking for Victor?"

He clears his throat. I pour hot water into the plunger just as the kettle begins to whistle. I dislike the sound, as shrill as a fire alarm. The kettle was my mother's, of course; she said she loved it because she could hear it from the other side of the house even when she was on the phone.

The rain slows to a slow drizzle and the aroma of strong coffee fills the kitchen. It feels warm and cozy here, and I feel very much at home, suddenly—it's not often that I feel this way in my mother's house. "Even though there's a stranger here?" I ask myself. I remember Sam's wet clothes, and before he has a chance to answer my question about Victor I ask him where they are. He brings them to me from the bathroom and I put them in the dryer.

I say, feeling that I've slighted poor Victor's memory again, "You were saying?"

He says, "Victor was supposed to help me out some."

My back is to Sam. I am pouring milk in his coffee. I practically keep on pouring when he says next, "Hey, maybe I was meant to find you instead."

Normally—not that this is the least bit normal—but in any other circumstance I would have grabbed a knife and chased him out. It should have felt creepy, the idea that he feels he might have been meant to find me. It *was*, intellectually—just like the note he left for Victor. I feel just fine, though. I only pause for a half-second in surprise at my reaction. I give him his coffee.

Sam says, "Oh, I must sound nuts. I apologize. I'm not crazy, I swear. Well, I was looking for Victor because he's a Native American medicine man, so if that's crazy to you, then I empathize, but that's my life. I never set out to find Victor any more than I meant to drag myself dripping wet through your house to drink your coffee, but I reckon when you're as apparently aimless as I am, seeking all manner of things on nothing but a whim or on unexplained advice, well, all that unpredictability seems to mean something after a while. Since I feel like I sort of know you, I'm just hazarding a guess that it's no accident I'm here."

I've had to sit down to concentrate on his stream-of-consciousness speech. It seems a lot for him to say. There is a natural quietness about him that, until a moment ago, I would have assumed implied reserve in all things. Still, in spite of his loquacity, he speaks so softly and evenly that it is less like talking than conveying.

"So you're deterministic? You believe in fate?" I probe, trying to understand just what he meant.

"Not as such."

I almost don't know what to say next—our conversation is not following the typical getting-to-know-you banter I am used to. I want to ask him about what he said, about Victor being a medicine man, seeking things, but I don't recall well the words that came spilling out of him and I don't know how to phrase my questions. Despite my bookstore rampage, I don't feel I yet have the right vocabulary for supernatural talk.

Sam is drinking his coffee and looking blank-faced. He sees me watching him and smiles.

"I knew Victor my whole life," I say. "I didn't know he was Native American. I mean, he looked like your average middle-aged white male to me. I believe he died from a heart attack. It was sudden. We didn't know for a few weeks, and then his nephew turned up in the back garden, trimming the hedge. I asked about Victor and he told me. My mother and I were very sad. I didn't know him well, but he'd always been there. I used to chat with him now and again, especially when I was little."

"So I found the right place, at least."

"I guess you did."

I glance out the window over the sink. Through the fogged-up glass the drizzling rain looks like a solid wall of mist.

Sam looks up at me now and again as he sips his coffee. Somehow I find it uncomfortable to look at him directly. I have the sense he sees too much, that he will see all my insecurities.

He runs his fingers through his wet hair. He is handsome. Slim, average height, brown hair that was probably once blond. His fingers are long. Aristocratic. Fingers that could play instruments. Susan taught me to notice a man's fingers straight away. She said you could tell what kind and quality of musician he was, and how good he was in bed.

I can't decide if I find Sam attractive or not. There is an aura about him—the only way I can describe it is to say that he doesn't seem fully embodied. That is, he doesn't seem to be in the here and now, as if his mind and spirit are far away. Somehow that makes him unreal, and a person can't be attracted to someone unreal, right?

"So … why did you want to see Victor?" I ask for a second time. I don't mean to be nosy, though I'm curious, and truly, I haven't really processed what he said earlier.

He waves a hand dismissively. "That requires a story," he drawls. He smiles again. He seems to be weighing the pros and cons of telling me. I bring the coffee over to offer him some more; he raises his cup in response.

"I don't want to bore a stranger with my life, though, so I'll just give you a shortened version, one that will about last through this second cup of coffee, and that way I won't expend your hospitality." He takes a big sip. "I was at an Indian reservation in Oklahoma, and I hadn't been there long when I had a dream—it was what the Native Americans call a Big Dream—you know the kind that can wake you up and you lie in bed, feeling as if you've been there, the place in your dream, all the emotions alive in you and so on. I had to get up and walk around, just to ground myself before dreaming further.

"My dream told me to find the Butterfly Man. I mean, that's what it sounded like. You can imagine I had a good laugh. I thought I might be going for a trip to the circus or to a Vegas show or something."

He stops then, asks me, "Are you okay.? You look pale."

"I'm fine."

Victor had told me he was the caller of butterflies, so why should it surprise me so much that other people call him the butterfly man? But it does. Hang on—not somebody, somebody in a dream. Now *that* worries me. Isn't it a bit strange that I've let a stranger into my house, a stranger who tells me something he could not possibly know from a dream? I am beginning to feel like I'm getting into something too deep here. I recall Victor's description of himself, the butterflies all around him as they were sometimes, in the spring, when he seemed to call them like it was a party trick. It never meant much to me then, but now Victor's words feel loaded with all kinds of mysteries that are beyond my understanding.

Sam is watching me attentively.

"You were saying?" I ask. "You had a big dream … it sent you to Victor. It was that specific? You got an address?"

I am being tongue in cheek, but Sam takes me seriously.

"No. Unfortunately it's never that clear. I've been having these dreams for some time now, and I've sort of worked out a symbolic dictionary of the language of my dreaming. Victor's reputation, his energy if you will, his appearance, and his surroundings were clear, but it wasn't enough to find him. It took some time asking around other elders who might have known him. But I tracked him down."

"So they didn't know he had died."

"Maybe they did," Sam replies. "But they knew he'd called me here anyway."

After several seconds I say dumbly, "Oh."

I remember I have a box of unopened cookies and jump up to get them from the cupboard. The dryer whirrs softly in the background. I set it to one hour. I wonder when it will go off. It seems like we've been talking for ages. The familiarity underlying our new acquaintance tugs at the edges of my mind. Then again, I am a nice person, after all, my mother's daughter. Perhaps her spirit has finally claimed me, has switched on the genetic coding for hospitality and warmth. Susan would invite a stranger into our home, not me. Maybe I am, finally, becoming my mother (not too much, I hope).

Apparently I find myself compelled to feed him, too. I take the cookies to the table but stand there with them in my hand.

"Dead Victor called Sam. Dead Victor called Sam." I can't stop the silly little mantra from repeating itself over and over in my head.

"So what do you do?" I ask, meaning for a living, meaning with his life. I feel we've risen above what's real and familiar into some ambiguous la-la land, and the language of careers and professions seems like the quickest route back to reality. I need a context for understanding this man, since I invited him into my house and we are alone.

"I do odd jobs," Sam says. "I guess you could say I have a calling, not a career, and the jobs I do just support that. Listen, Catherine," he says. He pushes his empty mug away from him slightly. "I should go. I mean, I will go. Here I've told you I was meant to meet you instead of Victor Tehusa, and I've said these things about my dreams—it must sound crazy. I usually get a good sense of whether I can speak my mind or not, but maybe I've got it wrong here. I don't want you to be uncomfortable. You've been so hospitable and I'm really grateful."

I can't believe it, but I'm speechless. Because the fact is I really don't want him to go. I can only smile to excuse the silence.

"Anyway," Sam says, and scoots back in his chair. "My clothes are probably almost dry."

"No way, they'll be wet," I blurt out, then, "Sam what, by the way?"

"Huh?"

"Your name."

"Oh. Sam Hunter."

"Of course. I should have remembered it from the note you left at my door. I'm Catherine Moore." And then, in an effort to entice him to stay, I say, (failing to display any wit or intelligence whatsoever), "Um …"

He is waiting for me to finish my thought, so I try really hard to articulate what it is I mean, even if I ramble a bit. "I never let people in. Strangers, I mean. Strangers don't normally knock on my door. But I let you in, without thinking. I am a rational being. Analytical to a fault, at least I like to think of myself that way. You could be crazy, even dangerous, but I don't think so."

I take a breath, and he laughs at me. I guess he thinks it's funny, anyone thinking he could be in the least bit dangerous. "Not with fingers like those, anyway," I think, noticing them again, delicate and harmless.

"Anyway, do you really expect me to send you away now? I mean, now that you've said what you've said I'm curious. I hadn't thought of Victor in ages, and then when you were sitting there talking about your dream I remembered something he said to me one day in the garden, something that didn't make sense at the time. And you—all this *meant* to do this, being *led* here ... If it's one thing I need it's direction in my life. You seem to have something of the kind, maybe that's why ... Look."

I stop there. I sound like a bumbling idiot. What do I want from him? I take a deep breath and focus.

"If you don't have plans, Sam, let me make you dinner. I'm holding these cookies, but really I was going to make dinner before you came. Just spaghetti, nothing special. Join me?"

"Are you sure?"

"Do you have anywhere to go?"

"No."

"Well, then."

Sam rises from his chair and brings his mug to the sink.

"I'm not much of a cook, but I take directions just fine."

I joke (in a last bid attempt to lighten the tone), "I promise my directions will be a bit clearer then the ones that got you here."

I wonder if he knew he'd be spending time with me all along, then dismiss the thought. I don't believe in fate. Sometimes people just get along.

We do manage to engage in mundane chit chat, which is a relief at first, but soon becomes maddening. Minute by minute I grow increasingly desperate to tell this almost-stranger about Lilya, because—let's face it—he is the only person I know who probably wouldn't laugh at my experiences. I restrain my impulses, however, because first I want to understand this young man better. After all, I don't know him, and (I tell myself at ever less frequent intervals), we are alone in my house. I want to feel absolutely safe and comfortable before I tell him too much.

"Sam," I say, as I take out the spaghetti and the jar of pasta sauce from the cupboard, "I'm trying to understand what it is you're doing, if you don't mind explaining again?"

"Not at all. I'm making garlic bread I take it?"

I have, without thinking, placed a baguette, a cutting board, knife, and a several pieces of garlic in front of him.

"Yes, oh, and here's the butter." I take it from the fridge and hand it to him. "If I put you right to work then I can reason with myself that I let you stay because I need the help. I know I've said it before, but this *is* unlike me. It sounds like you're always meeting people and finding yourself in strange situations, though?"

"Yes, that's true."

Sam begins to chop the garlic. He is quiet and seems comfortable being that way, whereas I feel I must busy myself by taking out pans, searching for the right wooden spoon, finding the placemats—to fill any awkward silences, and because I don't want to just blurt out everything on my mind.

When I've found everything I need to cook, and since Sam has not answered my question yet, I ask, "So … you travel around looking for teachers, wise people, who tell you … What do they tell you?"

Sam says as if he's said it many times before, "They tell me what they know, and what they see in me."

"I don't really get it."

"You see, the people I visit have usually spent a lifetime in spiritual practice, so they have a bit of wisdom. I go to them and ask to be their student or follower or whatever. And situations come up, conversations happen, and they help me, give me insight."

"It's kind of like never-ending therapy then," I deadpan.

Say replies earnestly, "Yes. Though I have to say that my dreams guide me more than people in the world do."

So far we're not facing one another, though after he says that he turns his head toward me and half-smiles. I avoid looking at him. I still don't know what to make of what he is saying.

I have put water in a pot and am fishing around for a bottle of wine. Red, preferably. I have a few bottles stashed away, leftover from Susan's collection—meaning it's decent wine. I find a nice cabernet and open it.

"Wine?" I offer Sam.

"I don't drink," he says.

"Well I do," I say, and pour myself a glass. "You're not a monk, right? I'm starting to look bad here."

"I'm not a monk," he says, "don't worry, I just don't like what alcohol does to me. There's enough in my life to keep my head swimming."

I laugh. So far I find him relaxed and genial. Just now I notice that he's also, evidently, not the best chopper (which is a surprise given the look of his fingers), organized though he may be. He has a little pile of chopped garlic on one side of the cutting board, and a pile of unpeeled garlic on the other, with not a speck in between.

"For the record," he says, "I don't follow a particular religion or philosophy. I think wisdom is wisdom, that there is one truth out there."

"So did you just wake up one day and realize this was your path in life?"

Now I'm standing next to him, facing him as I lean against the counter drinking my wine (probably too fast, I'm a bit nervous—partly it's Sam and the topic, partly it's how I always am when entertaining—wanting to make the guest feel welcome and feeling somehow I've failed, not like Susan with her gift for hospitality).

"I was called to it. I had an initiation. Many people on a spiritual path have one. In my case, I called myself. I mean, an aspect of my consciousness appeared to me and told me to follow this path in life. The part of me that transcends time and this body I'm in."

I think I am warming up to the topic, at least intellectually. "I'm not sure that makes sense to me, but that's okay. You're saying that you, Sam, are just one manifestation of your consciousness. By consciousness do you mean soul?"

"Sort of. Different traditions use different language, but the concept is basically the same. You could say that the person I am is just a dream the real Sam is having, but dreams can disturb the dreamer and affect their experience. It was desirable for me to follow this particular path in life in order to be aligned with the real Sam. Does that make any sense?"

He lays down his knife and seems to be searching my face for a flicker of understanding.

"The metaphor makes sense."

"But you don't buy it?" he asks. He uses the knife to push all the chopped garlic bits into his neat little pile. I think he is smirking, good-naturedly, as if he's smug about what he knows, though so far he strikes me as being too humble for smugness. Maybe he's just amused.

"I didn't say I didn't buy it. I'm not sure I understand, that's all."

"I know how it might sound. It's a bit far-fetched."

I move to the table and sit. Then I get up and bring the bottle of wine over.

"I might be needing this," I say.

I've forgotten all about the water on the stove, which is coming to a boil. Sam asks if I need to put the pasta in and heat up the sauce. I find it amusing that he is so concerned about doing the right thing at the right time. I tell him to leave it for a minute, and to sit with me and have a drink. He sits but again declines the drink.

"I don't have any doubt about your experience," I say, "or your conceptual understanding of consciousness. But let me ask you this: what does it all mean for you?"

"What do you mean?"

"Let me put it another way, and please don't mistake my tone for doubt, or rudeness. I'm just being very particular here. This is your life, right? Moving around, meeting wise people, seeking answers. I mean, you have no career, or professional aspirations—I'm not being critical, believe me, because my life has none of those things either. What I mean is that you don't sit around thinking about retirement or supporting a family—I assume you don't have a family? I'm sorry, I shouldn't assume."

"I don't."

"Could you have a relationship in these circumstances, though?"

"I could. I haven't."

The way he says it, I'm not sure he wants to, or that he's ever tried. His life certainly seems monastic.

"You're right, of course," Sam says. "It's not a real life. Is that what you're getting at?"

"Almost." I struggle to find a combination of clarity and politeness, and as I rehearse in my head the balance of the two dangerously resembles nonsense. I take a slow sip of wine and drum my nails on the table. Sam sits back in his chair. I don't look like I've put him off just yet, which brings me some relief.

I try aloud, "You are a perpetual student of wisdom. Would you say that's accurate?"

"Yes."

He is sitting there watching me, so patiently and without the least sign of discomfort. His face is the sort that might be an open book, although now it is blank.

"If you don't mind my asking, what is your ultimate goal? Is it enlightenment?"

Sam's gaze drifts elsewhere; he remains without expression and hardly moves. At last he says, elongating his vowels in that lovely Southern way he has, "We-ell, yes." He looks thoughtful and adds, "I've never put it in those terms."

"I see."

"I guess I trust the journey."

"Okay."

"The more I learn, the more I realize I don't know."

He appears deflated at the thought of his unknowing.

"I can imagine," I say.

"There's no other life for me but spiritual searching, and one day guiding others."

"Mm-hm."

Sam squirms a bit in his chair.

"That's extraordinary," I tell him, "to spend your life on that kind of quest. It makes my life look comparatively frivolous."

"Why?" Sam asks. He brightens a bit. "What do you do?"

"Well, nothing, really. I was doing a PhD, then I quit."

"Do you mind if I ask why?"

"Seeing as I've asked you all those questions? Hardly. Because I found a conundrum that no one would take seriously, and I decided to find out about it myself."

"You're doing research, then?"

"Yes. Of a sort. And I'm visiting my grandmother in her retirement home once a week. My mother died not long ago, and there's no one else alive in our family."

I'm not sure why I've told him that. His face changes. He looks very sympathetic and says, "I'm sorry to hear that."

"That's why I can afford to be frivolous," I tell him. "This is her house. I've inherited enough to support myself for a while."

I've no idea why I've told him that either. "Wow," I think, "Big step, finally admitting to someone that you're living off your mother's legacy."

"At least you've got that," Sam says. I nod my agreement. Telling someone how I'm supporting myself makes me see my circumstances in a new light, and I wonder, have I been ungrateful or am I just ambivalent?

"What is your research?" he asks.

"Oh, my research. I don't usually go into the details, but I guess I might as well tell you. You might not think it's so strange. I'm trying to figure out what happened to a group of soldiers in the Second World War. They and their planes disappeared one day in the Pacific and no one ever found any trace of them. It's not the kind of research that has any promise in terms of career."

Sam says, "I'm not someone who's going to tell you that has any importance. So do you think they disappeared into another world?"

I feel myself go pale at the casualness of his suggestion. To that he adds, "By the way, can I put the pasta in?"

Is it possible for a stranger to have this kind of effect on someone? Sam may seem reserved, but evidently he is forthright when he feels comfortable enough. His frankness is the bait I need to open up; with this lure Sam Hunter reels me in from the open seas. It's like I've been floating on a vast expanse of solitude for so long I have forgotten what it is to have a long, rambling conversation, like I have stored up impressions and opinions but am so out of practice that thoughts come out incoherently, are overlong and have to be sorted out by the listener. Even though Sam's life has a direction and purpose, in its own way it is at least as unconventional as mine, which feels like common ground. And his garlic bread is pretty tasty in the end. We eat pasta and toast the unexplained, my wineglass clinking against his glass of water. I should eat more, but I've had so much wine by the time the food is ready that I'm almost full, and anyway I'm too excited. Sam doesn't tell me much more about his metaphysical search, but by the time we have finished our meal I have told him all about the Crimean Tatars, Nastasha, and my strange affinity with Lilya.

I learn a little more about him, too: he has no permanent home; for several years he lived on Native American reservations and has rented apartments for short periods of time as well. He has traveled to South America to meet shamans and has studied with several spiritual teachers in this country, including a visiting monk from Tibet and a former Catholic priest who writes books about his visionary experiences.

The odd jobs he does to support himself include handyman work, house painting, gardening, and occasionally tutoring children in high school subjects (he did this a lot on the reservations, he tells me). When he travels he stays with friends of friends, if there are any, or he camps at parks when the weather is warm, and when it's not, he stays at budget motels when he can afford it, or else at homeless shelters. Tonight he's going to a motel; then he's finding an acquaintance of an acquaintance in the city and staying there for a while—until, he tells me, he figures out what to do about Victor—specifically, about there not being a Victor.

So, within the space of an evening, the ex-stranger Sam Hunter knows more about my life than anyone else at the moment, and the level of intensity generated by our mutual divulgences has more or less disrupted the delicately balanced routine of my aloneness. I forgo television and we talk until midnight. Then, in a complete reversal of my every cautious instinct, I insist he stay overnight. Since, I remind him, he has been living off the kindness of others for some time, who am I to break the habit? He hardly protests—it is so late, and still raining. I put him in my mother's room, warning him of her presence, not in spirit, but in the substance of things.

"The flowers," I tell him, "are hers," referring to the silk lilies in a vase on the bureau, the silk roses on the bedside stand, and the rose pattern on her sheets. It is all so girly, so secretly Susan (as opposed to her fashionable extrovert side). I've not had company in this house since Edgar and I split up, and I feel awkward about putting a man in such a flowery setting. I throw a wool blanket over the bed, bring him some extra toothpaste, some soap and a towel.

"I usually have a new toothbrush lying around, but I'm out," I tell him.

He thinks that's funny, that I keep extra supplies around as if I'm expecting a shortage. He thanks me a few times as I spread the blanket over the bedspread.

"So this is where it all happens," I say. "Your dreams."

He tells me that they can happen at any time, that a true dream is less a vision than a journey. He says that they sometimes happen when he is awake, and it is as if he slips into another world, fully aware he is doing it.

As I lay tossing and turning in bed that night I think about dreams and other worlds and slipping from one to the other. I decide that this Sam Hunter is a lost soul, but I can't help thinking that he is also a shaman without a tribe.

20

When I wake up I lie in bed a good five minutes gathering my senses. The clock says ten A.M., which is a record as far as I can remember. I get out of bed, yawn, and stumble on the perfectly smooth floor. I grab my bathrobe and am halfway to the bathroom when I remember Sam, and the phone rings.

"I'm calling to say that I'm running late."
Then I am running down the hall to see if Sam is still in bed. He's not. The bed is made.
"Catherine?"
"I'm here," I say, registering that it is Elisa on the phone.
"Oh, shit," I remember, "you have to meet Elisa for lunch."
"Is everything okay?" she asks.
"Yeah, I'm fine. I just overslept."
Sam is not downstairs either. My t-shirt and sweatpants are folded on the sofa. There is no sign of him in the kitchen.
"Oh, I woke you up. It's unlike you to sleep late, isn't it? Did you have too much fun last night?"
"Um," I grope for words. I look out the front window for any sign of Sam, peek into the bathroom and the office. No Sam. "I couldn't sleep," I say.
"Oh." (She sounds disappointed).
"It's just insomnia."
"I guess it happens, given the circumstances. Do sleeping pills help?"
(By circumstances she means my mother dying. Anyway, I just say no, because I'm too distracted to discuss it. I don't use sleeping pills. I tried them once and felt like a wreck the next morning—still tired, and hungover, too).
"Look," she says, "I won't make it until noon. Is that all right?"
"Sure," I say, just as I find a note from Sam on the kitchen counter next to the kettle. I start to unfold the paper. It's from my desk; he must have gone looking for something to write on and seen my office, and I wonder if he noticed the books I have out, the ones I've just bought from the bookstore on ley lines, shamanism, and reincarnation. When I hear Elisa's voice speak again into my ear, I'm surprised. I have forgotten I've been holding the phone.

"So I'll ... see you soon."

"Oh ... yes," I mumble—the phone in my ear goes dead but I'm too busy to put it down—and open the note:

> It was nice meeting you, Catherine, and thank you for your hospitality. I can't leave you my number as I don't have one and I don't know the number of the people I'm staying with, and yours is not on your telephone so I can't call you. Unfortunately, I have to go and don't want to get you up, so the compromise is that I'll drop by soon.
>
> So, we'll meet when we meet.
> Take care,
> Sam

It has been nearly a decade since Elisa and I last saw one another. We meet at the local diner-style café, where they do breakfast all day and specialize in pancakes and waffles. It's not that crowded—we've missed the rush hour—so I know I won't miss her. At least, there will be none of that awkward, unsure guessing, when someone looks familiar but it's been so long you don't want to risk making a rash assumption. I doubt anyone could miss Elisa, of course, and I don't. She's unmistakable, looking sophisticated in her brown pantsuit, still gazelle-like, only a little fleshier than she was in school—slender and curvy at the same time.

When she sees me she grins and runs toward me. We hug and exclaim over how we've changed (we can't believe how much older we look; I tell her she's gorgeous as ever; she tells me I'm the one who's thin now, that I look great, but I think she is being polite—she asks me in the next breath if I'm taking good enough care of myself since Susan died—suggesting I'm too thin?).

I have already claimed a corner table—I like having walls on two sides of me and sitting away from the door. Elisa sits across from me and we smile at each other like we're on a date.

It's slightly awkward trying to think just what to say. I've hardly even spoken to her since we left for college, and we've changed so much. I can't imagine how to fill in the years, where to start or even if its worth trying.

"Are you working today?" I ask her.

"Yes, I did. I mean, I went in early. I've taken tomorrow off. Trev and I are going to the Adirondacks for a long weekend."

"Trev?"

"Oh, sorry. Trevor. My boyfriend. He's a lecturer here, at the university. That's why I'm home so much. I work in the city."

"Oh."

"I'm a junior editor at a magazine."

I can't believe I haven't asked her what she does, in this world where profession is identity. I rally my enthusiasm and exclaim, "Great! What kind of magazine?"

A health and beauty magazine, of course. Elisa tells me about it. She writes all the pieces on women's' health. It suits her. Elisa has a bachelor's in some kind of science, I remember that. And she's always been a magazine junkie. I can see that she's happy. I can see that she and Trevor are happy. She asks me if I'm happy, adding, "Given the circumstances."

"You mean since my mother died?"

"Oh, gosh, I didn't say it right!" she looks alarmed.

"No, no," I reassure her. "You said it fine. It's a logical question to ask." After all, we used to tell each other everything.

"I'm fine," I tell her. "I mean, I'm getting on with life. I'm visiting Natasha weekly. She's been living in a home, you know."

"What do you do, Catherine? I mean, have you finished your PhD?"

We're to that so quickly? I feel mildly annoyed. I wonder if she expected great things of me, the straight-A student and Ivy Leaguer. Probably everyone else she knows our age has a career already, pays a mortgage, plans for children. "She should meet Sam," I think. "That would blow her mind."

"No, I haven't finished it." I shrug. "I've decided I don't want one."

I can see she's waiting for me to tell her more—what else I'm doing with myself, if I'm working or not. The waitress comes just in time and we order. When she goes I tell Elisa, sounding confident, I hope, "I'm taking some time off life now."

She says, "I think that's a good idea."

I'm glad I've dealt with that. Now we can talk about other things. I'm not ready to tell her much else. Actually, I'm still reeling inside from my evening with Sam, from having divulged everything to a stranger. I have no energy left to say much more about myself today.

Fortunately, Elisa has a lot going on. Career, boyfriend, a social life, and over omelets and salads and a few cups of coffee, we cover a lot without mentioning my life anymore.

"There is another reason I wanted to meet with you after all this time," she says. Her comment is an abrupt full stop to a discussion of how she loves and hates New York City. I put down my coffee. Now what will she say? We haven't run out of conversation, and the way she says it, I feel like an interrogation is coming.

"I just," she says, running her long, polished nails along her napkin, and tearing a bit of paper off at the end. "I've always felt bad about losing touch with you, and lately I've been thinking about you a lot."

"Don't worry about it," I reassure her. "I mean, of course at the time I wished we hadn't lost touch, but it happens. I haven't lost sleep over it."

Elisa frowns. "I have. Lost sleep over it."

I say nothing.

"I mean, you know, that summer in Yugoslavia. In Croatia, when we were drunk and went up that hill ..."

I begin to get goose bumps.

"It kind of freaked me out. I couldn't understand what had happened."

I feel the blood drain from my face. I wish we'd ended on New York. Hugged, said goodbye. But here we are. No choice but to participate.

I say, "You mean what happened on the hill, where I was standing." I'm sure I could say, "where I disappeared," but just now I have an urgent need for her to clarify my memory. To validate it.

"Yes." Elisa looks right at me. "Where you disappeared."

We let the words hang in the air.

Finally I say, "Yes, I did, didn't I?" as if I am confirming it myself.

"It really scared me, you know? I had no explanation for it. After that, I just wanted to forget about it. I guess since you never talked about it, I started to think I was the one who was crazy."

"You weren't crazy. I didn't know what happened either."

"Well, that's the thing. I went back."

My heart starts to thud. "You did *what?*"

"Trev and I. Well, he's a political scientist and had some research to do there. I went with him a few months ago. We weren't that far away from where you and I had been, at least I didn't think we were, and I wanted to visit the place we'd been to, so Trev and I hunted it down. I remembered the village, and the hills, and I found it. The hill."

"You mean the one where ..." Now I can't bear to hear the words again.

"Yes. Where there were two big rocks. Do you remember the rocks? Like there used to be a stone something there, a monument or something."

"Of course. I stood between them."

"They were huge, weren't they?"

"Yeah."

"Well, when I went back, they weren't there anymore."

I don't think this means anything much and stare at her blank-faced. She is waiting for me to respond, and I can't. I shrug.

"They were huge, Cat! How could anyone have moved them?"

She's right, of course.

"You must not have been at the right place," I tell her.

"I was. I walked up every stupid hill there. I dragged Trevor with me all day long, climbing hills, asking locals about stones, all to find a similar hill, and guess what? No stones like that anywhere. I found the right hill, and there was nothing. And do you know what else?"

She is scaring me, I can't explain how or why. She has started to gesticulate a little too close for comfort—her fervor intimidates me. I want to cower in my corner. I don't remember her ever being this intense.

I say in a meek voice, "What?"

"The locals say they never go up there, because weird things happen. A little boy disappeared once with his dog, and other people have seen strange lights, and fairies, and other weird stuff."

Elisa's eyes go wide and it's as if she isn't blinking, like she's going to suck me in with her eyes, and I don't know if she's gone mad or if I'm the one who's mad, but I feel a sudden release of tension and I relax. I must be going slightly crazy, which certainly explains a lot, and excuses just as much. Only yesterday I had thought about when I stood on the hill in Croatia and disappeared, after reading about shamans traveling to other worlds, before a shaman appeared on my doorstep. Of course today I am meeting the only other person on planet Earth who saw what happened to me on the hill, and of course she is confirming what happened! There is a neat synchronicity to it, and I feel an overwhelming urge to surrender—as if my life is a movie and I'm stuck here watching it, the plotted action, the foregone conclusion.

"Actually," I say, "I don't remember what happened. I seemed to be somewhere else for a moment." And as I say this to Elisa the sensation of being there comes over me; the light goes fuzzy and the café hushes around me—then everything is normal again, back in this movie theater of my life.

"I know," she nods, "I know, that's the thing. I didn't know then, I didn't have any context for understanding something so ... weird. But I know now that it was real, whatever it was that happened there, and I don't know what did happen, but it was real. I'm sorry for acting so weird about it. I feel like it affected our friendship. I was there this summer, and since then, I haven't been able to stop thinking about you. Then I heard about Susan ..."

"You don't need to explain," I reassure her. "I know it really happened. It's okay. I'm figuring it out."

"You are?"

She's obviously still trying to figure it out herself. I try to look reassuring, and tell her I've had some insights lately, that I'm doing some research. She looks doubtful, then talks about how she's been reading about Judaism, her family's religion, to make sense of "spiritual things." It may be inconsistent of me given my current interests, but I can't help feeling indifferent to her searching. Spirituality is a concept that, frankly, I have never known how to relate to. Don't you need to know what a soul is in order to experience its relationship to God? Not to mention needing to have a concept of God in the first place. This isn't a discussion I can contribute to, so I change the subject. It's not easy to move on to mundane things, but I manage, somehow.

By the time we leave the café, promising we'll meet again soon, Elisa is pensive and looks tired. I feel like I've stolen her fire.

I don't have a word for what I'm experiencing, but something in my life is falling into place, and I feel like it should, and it will, and who cares if I *am* a bit insane?

That afternoon I notice that somehow, autumn has replaced summer without warning. The leaves are falling off of the trees so quickly now that great heaps are building up behind our back gate where the hill slopes down on the other side of the oak tree, and the neighbor children are coming over to jump in the piles.

It's funny—watching the children jump in the leaves makes me realize that all this time at my mother's house I've been feeling homesick for the home this used to be. I make myself a pot of coffee for the smell alone (I can only manage half a cup after brunch with Elisa). I want to bake cookies, like Susan sometimes did when the cold came for the first time in the fall, sugar cookies with chocolate chip smiles or oatmeal raisin cookies. I am sitting, now, alone at the kitchen table with my cup of coffee, listening to the children laugh outside, and I can hear the wind and smell the change of season: the newly crisp air, cookies, and something else. I think it is the smell of cinnamon and freshly toasted bread.

Maybe it's not the smell of autumn at all but my mother's memory wafting through the house.

I can feel a warmth in the air around me and I feel my homesickness dissolving inside of me, like I've arrived home after a long trip.

There is no denying it: the permanence I have so far managed to avoid has been coming all this time. I can't explain why, but I know it has to do with Lilya.

With each word of my grandmother's story I feel more rooted in this house and, for the first time in ages, in my life as well.

"First I should tell you what became of me," Natasha says the next morning. "Then I'll tell you what I know of what happened to Lilya. After today, though, her story is all speculation."

She looks up from where her eyes had been glued to the floor. Her words come in a steady stream; I am lulled and slip into my other awareness. Today, for the first time, when Natasha begins to tell her story, I am no longer conscious of when I leave the present and find myself in the past.

21

May 1940

Natasha and her mother Mira moved to Simferopol and there they waited, life on hold. They planned to go back to Leningrad but were awaiting the proper documentation and some money from the government to help widows of officers. Meanwhile, through her contacts Mira found work teaching a few classes in an elementary school and Natasha began to study at the university. Their activity was of necessity and they derived from it neither enjoyment nor the feeling that it was settling them in a new life. Indeed, they both felt trapped in a no-man's-land that contained neither their past nor their future. For Mira, Crimea had always been a colorful postcard with no substance, unlike the sophisticated city of her roots; for Natasha, without Lilya and Refat even Crimea's charms—previously such a source of joy—held no allure. They both longed for the wet autumn and bitter winter of their northern city, where, in the midst of its buildings and urban throngs the warm, white cliffs and rolling hills of Crimea would recede into fairy tale—along with the memories they contained.

Natasha's mother did not cry at all for her husband, though she sat, morning and evening, knitting a blanket that would have reached from one side of the house to the other had she had the material for it. Natasha also counted her losses in secret. She studied half-heartedly and made no friends. She sat alone in the evenings and drew pictures of Leningrad, as she remembered it.

She told her mother nothing about Refat, but her behavior must have given her away finally, as Mira could no longer wait for a voluntary confession and asked her daughter if the loss of her father was the source of her obvious pain. Natasha said she was not only mourning that loss, then told in as few words as possible about her meeting and falling in love with Refat, their long courtship, and its ending.

"The young Tatar … who came to see you that day," Mira stated, as if she struggled to recall any clues there might have been of Natasha's lovesickness, and had found only one. Natasha merely nodded.

She thought that might be the end of it, that she and her mother would not discuss love again. Mira began to ask questions though, little ones in the middle of conversations about other things, probing gently into the nature of her daughter's affair. Mira managed to discover, over the next few months, what exactly Natasha had felt for Refat, what they had said to one another, what future her daughter had hoped for. In such a way Natasha and Refat's love gave its final gift, for in return for her daughter's willingness to share her story, Mira told Natasha about her own experience with love.

Before the Revolution she had always dreamt of moving to France or Germany—she had a cousin who had left to marry a Frenchman when Mira was fifteen and she had always meant to visit her. When the Revolution came she couldn't leave, and as her adulthood wore on she became cynical and frustrated, until she sought relief in lust and then marriage. She married Aleksander Matveev as if in his arms she could escape life, but the years wore on, bringing the responsibility of a child, the military career that took her husband from her long before he died, and the arguments. Mira said that Natasha and Refat had had the perfect love: it demanded nothing and existed on its own terms. It would never know compromise or decay, for it had died in its youth. Mira warned Natasha that love was not everything in the world. She said, mincing no words, that everything her daughter had felt would begin to fade one day, that it would have faded even if she had married her beloved, because that's what love did.

Mira Matveeva began to speak more of her first youthful fantasy soon after their earnest conversation on love. She began to speculate about what life was like in Europe, and for distraction her daughter joined her mother in fantasizing. Together they began to imagine a future that could never proceed from their past. They imagined it with such conviction that its alternate reality took hold of them; they began to believe in its existence somewhere, sometime, just ahead of the dreary present. As a consequence of their imaginative yearnings, it came to be that Natasha decided to live for life's possibilities, specifically for her own mysterious future and the joy it might hold. And, then miraculously, a mysterious future of a sort came to life, bringing with it if not joy, then at least the enhanced possibility of future happiness.

Nearly two years after they arrived in Simferopol, in the first half of 1942, the Germans took Crimea. A few months after that, Mira Matveeva met a German officer and fell recklessly in love. Their love was so infectious, so inspiring, that Natasha, in the spirit of hope for her own capacity to feel love again, with composure and the desire to mend at last her broken heart—wrote what was to be her very last letter to her friend Lilya:

Dear Lilya,

I have released Refat from any obligation he has to my soul, to my heart. I think you should marry him, my dear friend. You are as much a soul mate to me as he was, and in this horrible bloody world we must all stick together. The most precious people should abide in the most special company as a bulwark against all evil and despair.

I have heard no word of his whereabouts or well being, have you? I pray for him every day. I pray for him to come home to you, and that you will keep each other safe for me.

Please write me about your life, and think of me when you see the stars over Ai-Petri.

Yours,
Natasha

For Natasha, the release she felt was a long time in coming. However, it was a mystery to Lilya how it had come about. During the two years since Natasha's move to Simferopol, Lilya had received scores of letters from Natasha in which she rarely mentioned Refat and gave no hint of her emotional state. This was despite the fact that Lilya had sent as many letters in which she pledged again and again to keep her word and delay her marriage to Refat. Lilya had assumed that her friend's silence on the matter meant Natasha had not even faced the thought of Refat's marriage to Lilya—and Lilya could not imagine how she and her friend had grown so far apart that Natasha had not even mentioned this great shift in her emotions.

Lilya and Natasha were only two hours apart by car, yet neither had the means to visit the other. It had felt to both, at first, as if a continent lay between them, save for their shared expectation that one day the short distance between them would cease to be a barrier—when they had money, or a car, or a relative who would take them. Their expectation of meeting again melted away the miles and each imagined that one day, suddenly, the other would simply appear and it would be as it had been before they parted.

Months passed and then more months, until their separation began to be measured in years. And to both girls it felt as if the distance was growing larger, and then all notion of distance lost its relevance when the European war—once imagined to be far—was all around them. The girls wrote each other less frequently, but did not fret so much over their waning contact. Natasha's loneliness was steadily being healed by her mother's company and their fantasy life. She did not feel in danger in the midst of invasion; the invaders behaved themselves well in Simferopol, she thought, given the situation. And then her mother was involved with a German man. It was at this point that ethnicity began to divide the friends, before distance and political borders took them farther from one another.

Lilya's creeping loneliness, not assuaged by her own fantasies, was replaced by dread in December 1943. So much of Europe had already fallen to the Germans—Holland, Belgium, Denmark, Norway, France. Her own country had entered the Great Fatherland War in June 1941, after the Wehrmacht crossed the river Bug into the Soviet Union and launched Operation Barbarossa. War was undeniably closer to Crimea from that point on, but its presence in Lilya's village remained unfathomable to her even as Nazis laid siege to Kiev, Vyazma, and Leningrad. Only when the Germans took Crimea in the first half of 1942 did the inconceivable become an everyday reality. Now, nearly two years later, on the day Lilya was to receive her friend's final letter, she sat by the window and watched smoke rise in the distance. It was so far that it was like watching the smoke of a bonfire on the hill behind their house, which meant that it was quite a way away indeed, and that it was many times over the size of a bonfire. War had not seemed real before, but the burning of Crimean Tatar villages one by one was all too real.

As Lilya watched the smoke for the third day in a row she had an urge to make a notch somewhere, on the wooden floor or perhaps even on the inside arm of the chair. She wanted to draw three small straight lines, three for the number of times she had seen smoke in the distance rising above the hills and the tree line. She expected there to be more, which is why she thought she should begin the count now, before there were too many to remember.

She expected, also, that tomorrow someone would come knocking on their door to tell them that another village had been burnt to the ground by the Nazis, the inhabitants shot or left to fend for themselves. And she half-expected that her village would be next.

But just then she did not let her thoughts run too far ahead, and she made no notches, for despite the sense of doom that loomed over their household, her mother still became most upset about disorderliness. And there was something mesmerizing about watching the smoke rise, so Lilya sat quietly and just watched. It had been a wide column just two hours ago, the size of her thumb when she held it up to the window. Now it was a dark, thin line drawn against the deepening colors of the evening sky.

She felt her mother's presence somewhere behind her but did not turn her head. Ayshe hovered nervously in the shadows nearby. Lilya listened as she moved first to one side of the room, then out and into the kitchen, then back and to the bookshelf, where she could hear a book being pulled out, and then the footsteps were louder and closer. Her mother held a book out to Lilya and said, "Here." Lilya took it without turning around. She pried her eyes with difficulty from the sight outside.

"You should not preoccupy yourself with doom," Ayshe said with a half-laugh. She stood uncertainly behind her daughter and then put her hand out to stroke her hair. Lilya sat still for a moment, ignoring her. She suddenly reached up and took her mother's hand, calming it.

"I wanted to show you something," said Ayshe finally. She leaned over and ran her hand along the smooth, burgundy front cover of the book. She opened it to the first page. It was the family photo album, and Lilya said at once, and rather impatiently, "I've seen them all before, Mother."

"You have not seen all of them, because I found some more in your father's things, in his books. I put them in yesterday."

Her soft, gentle voice contrasted with the brusqueness of her daughter's. Even if Ayshe had wished to soften her daughter's mood then, there was little she could have done to take the fear from Lilya, or from herself, or from her other children for that matter. Lilya sensed that her mother's inability to serve as a source of protection for her children weighed upon her heavily, and she wished, for her mother's sake, that she could bring herself to be more cheerful.

"There now," Ayshe turned several pages, past familiar photos of Lilya as an infant, with her parents and aunts and uncles picnicking when the first brother was a few years old. She shut her eyes to the photographs for a moment and tried to remember those first years of young motherhood.

Lilya had turned back to the window and now said quietly, as if to herself, "Another will burn tomorrow, I feel certain." She looked to her mother to judge her reaction. "Will she admit it?" she wondered. But her mother ignored her, and instead pointed to the picture she had sought.

"Here is your Uncle Mahmedi. Do you remember him?"

"Yes, a bit." She looked at the photograph intently, calling to mind the man who had held her so often as a baby, whose beard was an endless source of fascination, so long and coarse. She could recall its wood-ember scent, its speckled reddish-brown color.

"He came to live with us not long after you were born. He was already in his twenties, but he had a young spirit. Silly as a child, he was."

Lilya peered up at her mother. Her face was drawn.

She felt guilty for having mentioned the fires and said, for her mother's sake, "I remember how he used to throw me up into the air, even when I was so big I did not go up very far."

Ayshe laughed, "Yes, that was him. He helped me a great deal when you were young. You were a handful, and I had so difficult a time ... I didn't know what to do! I was only nineteen, and suddenly a mother. It came easily to others, but to me ..."

Lilya traced the image with her right index finger and recalled being about five years old when her mother reprimanded her for knocking over a jar in the kitchen, spilling the contents in a slow stream from the table to the floor. Ayshe's manner was usually steady, calm, though she was often stern when her children created messes. She had wagged her finger threateningly that day, her voice gone high-pitched, and then slapped Lilya, eliciting a red-faced wail. Uncle Mahmedi had come running into the kitchen and scooped Lilya up. The adults exchanged looks, then suddenly Ayshe began laughing, hysterically, great whooping laughter, impromptu and infectious. Uncle Mahmedi, Ayshe and then Lilya, laughing, laughing.

Her mother had lost control that day, and Lilya tried to remember if it had ever happened since. Lilya knew why her mother was bringing this up now. At twenty-two years of age Lilya should by rights be a mother herself. She could imagine how demanding a small child would be. She searched her mother's face, thinking what she was trying to say by bringing out these pictures. Ayshe flipped the page in the album and said, "There is your father and Uncle Mahmedi together."

They stood side by side for the camera in a stiff, formal pose, arms straight at their side. Ai-Petri was behind them; they were squinting into the sun. Uncle Mahmedi was somewhat shorter than her father. They looked nearly identical but for the height difference and Mahmedi's beard. But it was Mahmedi's eyes turned slightly toward his older brother that betrayed the nature of their relationship. Uncle Mahmedi looked up to his sibling, it was plain.

"Well!" Ayshe exhaled deeply. "That is all. I wish we had more pictures. They tell so much." She closed the photo album and withdrew it from her daughter's hands, then held it to her chest. Lilya returned her gaze to the window. She could no longer see any smoke. She wanted to comment on it, but thought she should give her mother a rest. She had, two evenings prior, insisted to her parents that they should leave, somehow, take the children, sneak out at night, something! They knew what was happening; how could they wait and watch?

"Do not watch, then!" replied her father. Her mother, face awash in tears, said, "They will kill us if we are caught!" It seemed the whole countryside was teeming with German soldiers, waiting for such an excuse.

"We will do nothing, then?" Lilya had asked, slamming her open hand onto the table, bringing herself only stinging pain and no relief from anger.

"No!" Her father caught her by her shoulders, breathed cigarette breath into her face. "We will survive. We will keep our eyes open." But his resolve seemed so ineffectual, and a part of Lilya closed up into a tight fist. Her father released her and went outside. Her mother gave her such a mournful look. "We must not speak of it, we must not …" she moaned, and then tears. Lilya could not, would not, cry. Nor did she mention their situation again. In the end, who was the more honest of them? Truly, they could do nothing. So Lilya took on the role of patiently waiting. An air of expectation, sometimes fearful, sometimes resigned, hung about them all.

Ayshe still stood behind her daughter with the album in hand. Lilya could imagine her face: defeated, tired, downcast. Lilya wished she had it in her to put her arms around her mother and tell her it would be all right.

"The young men will return soon enough and you will marry," said Ayshe to her daughter. "You will marry and I will become a grandmother."

And if the men died, if she and her family all died? Lilya foresaw impending loss, and wondered what part of her own life she could possibly lose. She had no carefree youth, nor the freedom of a bachelor's life.

It was a short while later that evening when her mother came to her with the letter from Natasha. Ayshe had forgotten to bring it to her daughter earlier, and it had lain on the bookshelf all day long. Lilya's memories of nights beneath the stars, spirit-hunting and fairy-spotting, all came flooding back. For a moment she forgot the rising smoke and experienced for a moment the magic of her time with Natasha. She composed what was to be the last letter her dear friend would ever receive from her:

Dear Natasha,

I, too, have heard nothing from or even about Refat. You dear, silly, girl. I do not love him, and I have no wish to marry. I will try my utmost to avoid that path, or at least to put it off eternally. I am quite happy with my father and brothers and have no further need of men. I will write you if this changes, and wouldn't you be in for a shock?

I wish we could visit one another; you are not at all far. But as you know, that is impossible. I will write you more news when I can, but remember this single fact: we have seen ghosts together! Life remains a mystery, dear friend. Let's remember that, okay? Come what may …

I embrace and kiss you,

Yours,
Lilya

22

Natasha falls silent, and her silence sends me plummeting back to the present.

She pushes her coffee cup away from her, to the far side of the coffee table, and runs her hand across the table, as if clearing away the crumbs. She moves the *TV Guide* from the table to the couch. What is she making space for?

I have said nothing. I breathe slowly and look out the window. I will rouse myself soon, I think, I just need time to assimilate what she has said.

I am thinking about how it is possible for two friends to lose touch, for a friendship that has defined one's day-to-day life to suddenly fall away, to become part of memory. Elisa crosses my mind, but all thought of her vanishes as I catch a glimpse of Natasha. She looks so remote, her eyes so cloudy, her face so still.

Natasha gropes for a book beneath the coffee table. I cannot see what it is—a reference book of some sort, an atlas or encyclopedia. She opens it and pulls out an envelope, and from inside it she withdraws a letter. She places it reverently on the coffee table.

The handwriting looks familiar, then I look closely. It is in Russian. I do not know the language, nor the Cyrillic alphabet, but I know the name at the bottom of the paper. Lilya.

"Here is the letter she wrote me," Natasha sighs. "I received it on the day she was deported."

23

May 1944

By May 18, 1944, after more than one hundred Crimean Tatar villages had been burnt to the ground, when Crimean Tatars thought there wasn't much left to destroy, and as Lilya and her family held their breath, too afraid to be grateful that their village had been left standing, the worst happened.

In the middle of the night, Lilya awoke at the first knock and went to her parents' room to rouse her father. He lay still in his bed, eyes wide open, his expression rigid. An air of expectation, and his immobility, lent an obstinate look to him. It was this obstinacy which made the biggest impression on Lilya as she stood over him.

He stared straight ahead and made no move to get up.

"Stay here." he said at last, "Do not go." He rose slowly as the second series of knocks fell upon the door, which shook in its frame with every bang. A deep, rough voice rang out in Russian, "Open your door at once!"

In total there were only a few minutes between Lilya rising from her bed and her father reaching the door, but the actual event unfolded as if in slow motion. Her father purposefully lingered in the far corner of the main room for what seemed like minutes that ticked on painfully as the door and then the walls surrounding it shook and the chair next to the door trembled and appeared to slide forward slightly, and to Lilya it seemed she and her family would soon be tossing about like they were aboard a small ship on an angry sea. She feared for her life.

Her father stared at a photo of Stalin on the cover of an old newspaper. She wanted to usher him to the door, to take him by the shoulders and shake him and tell him not to give up so soon, it could not merit such defeat as was so plain in his demeanor, where was his obstinacy of only a few moments before?

But she did as she was told and stood back. No one had turned on a light. It was pitch dark.

Implicit in her father's icy glare when he finally went to the door was a sense of betrayal that had, really, never been a stranger to him, not after those nights in the garden with his comrades, not after what Lilya had heard him them all say, not after the burning of villages. Lilya knew that once her father opened the door he would relinquish his power to history, his power and hers, all of theirs. Together they would be swept up by the tide along with the rest of the Crimean Tatars who had suffered before them.

He opened the door to the sounds of Elmira Mamut, who was walking down the hill with her husband and children, now just within sight behind the soldier who led them. Lilya heard the older woman whimper. Elmira carried a huge bundle inside a sheet that was knotted at the top to hold it closed. Her hair was a gray mop hanging disheveled about her face, she who normally took great care to pull and pin it back. She held her bathrobe tightly around her, and she walked as if resigned to whatever fate awaited her. In a few more minutes Lilya and her family would follow her down onto the main road into the unwelcoming night. It would have been difficult for Lilya to imagine now the slow, lonely death that would greet Elmira twelve days later in the hot, overcrowded railway cattle-wagons where many much younger people and even small children would also die.

It was a Soviet soldier who stood at their door shouting instructions as Lilya huddled in the dark, her three siblings surrounding her with wide-eyed stares. Fevzi, the youngest at not quite eight, grasped Lilya's hand and whispered, "Where are we going? Can't the children stay here?" Lilya squeezed his small hand and whispered "Shhh" in as calming a manner as possible. Her mother remained silent, yet lying in bed.

"You have fifteen minutes!" the soldier shouted, and just then her father reached out and turned on a light.

How does one collect a lifetime of memories in fifteen minutes? How do you choose between those things that you hold dearest in your heart and those things that might sustain you physically? How can you banish the fear and sleep that weigh you down, so that you might have the clarity of mind to gather yourself together?

Of course, there were those among the villagers who did not believe they would be gone permanently. They left after attempting, in those hurried fifteen minutes, to make their beds even as they went empty-handed. There were those who went taking what they thought necessary for a short journey, neglecting their dearest possessions as they grabbed whatever useful items they could carry. Some left, taking what in that rushed moment they thought meant the most, if not defiantly leaving that very object so as not to admit the possibility of no return. Most left knowing deep down that they would never be back, and these took only their memories, their traditions, their history. Those most treasured things, at least, would not be left lurking in empty houses—in homes that were to reverberate with silence and the intermittent wail of pets who, hungry and abandoned, shared in the suffering of their former caretakers and companions.

The deportation was an experience that is still etched in the minds of the survivors, but is for the most part overlooked by the outside world. Those who are old enough to remember their own experience relive it, if not by speaking of it, then as it plays itself out in their everyday lives: a sudden hot flash of fear brought on by a heavy knock at the front door, or the need to take obsessive care of any surviving family heirloom. Indeed, after the deportation Lilya would have recurring dreams of having to pack everything she owned into only a few bags as she escaped some imminent peril. Sometimes she would watch as a tornado approached. She would feel the wind of the giant swirling mass beat against her skin while she frantically packed her bags as more and more objects appeared out of nowhere to be packed. Sometimes fire pursued her, rolling balls of red flames, hissing and spitting. She never awoke from these dreams having successfully packed full her bags—and when she was back in the land of the living she repressed all memory of the dream ordeals.

On that spring day shortly after midnight, Lilya's father had little uncertainty about what to bring. In contrast to the many people who had heard stories of Nazi concentration camps and therefore left only with the clothes on their back—or those whose bags contained various hastily thrown together combinations of food, clothing, and memorabilia that would be taken from them by the soldiers anyway—Lilya's father was admirably practical in the chaos of the moment. He permitted only Fevzi anything personal, and that only because this youngest child did not go anywhere without the small toy soldier, a near identical representation, ironically, of the Soviet soldier who at that very moment stood with his regiment on the hillside path directing people toward an open field. The Bekirov family's one modest bag was filled with all of the food the house contained, including onions, beets, cabbage, potatoes, and tins containing various meats and vegetables, a jar of compote, nearly stale bread, a bag of apples and a small pocket knife. Lilya's mother grabbed the family photo album when her husband was not looking. She hid it in the folds of her nightgown, bunched up around the waist and held to with the cardigan she put on and tied about her tightly. It was the one thing of sentimental value that was to survive their long journey across the green mountain passes, lowland fields, and the never-ending desert steppes of Central Asia.

That and their memories, of course, and their traditions, and their pride. They and their fellow Crimean Tatars were infused with a strong sense of justice which would outlive Lilya's generation and pass on to the next, and the deportation only strengthened their convictions.

But the soldier who barged into their home knew no such thing. He was doing his job, and he noticed their bulging pockets and demanded to see what they had. No one moved, and Lilya's father said, "We have only food." Lilya's mother was still frantically eyeing the rooms, wandering around and touching things. Her hands had taken on a life of their own, petting and squeezing as if the memories conjured up in the feel of objects would lead her to safety. She could not decide what else to take. But the soldier did—he grunted and took the small bag of apples which Lilya's father had been clutching tightly and yelled, "Well, you have too much food! Do you think you're going on a holiday?" and he muttered under his breath, "Traitors!" Then louder, "There is a limit per family!" His comrade stuck his head in the door and gave the room a once-over. He smiled. He had two gold teeth in front and the light reflected off of them. It was a grin that reeked of greed. "Get them out and down the hillside to the field!" he shouted, then more quietly, but intended for everyone to hear, "We'll come back here later," he added to his comrade. The two of them chuckled and ordered the family to leave.

"But it's only been ten minutes, we have five more yet to get ready!" cried Ayshe. She stood in front of the bookshelf and was pressing a book to her chest as if it would protect her. "Shut up and go! NOW!" came the response, and then a hand grabbed her arm so hard that the book fell to the floor and she gasped. The children were still wide-eyed in fear and groggy from sleep, and although none of them made the slightest noise nor movement, tears were streaming down Fevzi's face. The two soldiers pushed the whole family outside and left the door open behind them. The light was left on. The soldiers marched behind them and yelled at the children to keep up.

Along with Lilya's family there was Diana Seitosmanova, a part-time schoolteacher, with her five-year-old son. And Necip Kubedinov, the oldest local collective farm chairman their village had seen yet at sixty years of age, the only candidate for the job since all the young men had left to fight. Also Reshat Sevdiar, a shepherd, and his wife Adshigulsim (Lilya knew their son was fighting for the Soviets in Leningrad). In the back of the crowd was Luda Asanova, her sick husband Server Asanov, and their three children. Also Numan Abduhamitov, Mustafa Kerimal, and Mahmedi Ablaev, colleagues of Lilya's father she had seen several times, as well as neighbors who lived farther up the mountain whose names she did not know. Menube Dzemileva and Ayshe Seyhislamova, already widowed by the war, were quiet and resigned; other women Lilya saw were silenced by fear, as they had already pleaded—"Our husbands are fighting for you!"—only to be hit by rifles. Lilya saw Refat's parents arriving, and many others she did not know and had seen only a few times in her life.

It was a sea of people lined up in their nightclothes. The Bekirovs learned that they had been lucky to make it there unharmed and with the few provisions they had taken. Others were not so lucky. Soldiers had forced their way in not with knocks but with automatic weapons; they prodded the sleeping inhabitants to wakefulness, jabbing at ribs and doing worse.

Lilya carried Fevzi into their train car, his head against her shoulder. She held her mother's hand and helped her up. In the bustle of leaving, in the weakness of sleep, Fevzi's hand lost its grip on his little toy soldier. It fell to the damp green earth, small and forgotten. A soldier walked the length of the cattle car ensuring that no one could jump off. He paced back and forth and in an instant that went almost unnoticed, inadvertently tread upon Fevzi's little soldier, crushing it with his heavy military boots. Only Lilya, her eyes and mouth glued to the slats in the car, gasping for a breath of fresh air as the bodies crowded in around her, saw the two broken pieces and the smaller bits that would most likely remain there forever, sinking into the soil and oblivion.

Later, death and despair broke out around them: there was no food or water, no toilet, and hardly any space for breathing. They traveled like this day after day, with no explanation other than the vague statement that they were being relocated east. When people began to die from starvation the soldiers merely threw the bodies onto the side of the tracks whenever, for no known reason, they stopped every few days.

In such a time, when focus on survival eclipses all else, when nothing grander than obtaining a breadcrumb or a drop of water could gain entry into one's consciousness, Lilya saw something in her littlest brother Fevzi she had never seen before.

His seven year old body was painfully thin after five days of traveling; she could hear his stomach rumbling louder than hers, and yet he insisted that every scrap of food go to his mother Ayshe, who died unaware that these surreptitious gifts were his. This youngest child watched his own mother slip away, his eyes trained on hers, too dehydrated for tears. Lilya could not think for her grief and hunger, yet she could not take her eyes away from Fevzi, and would not release his arm for the comfort it brought her.

He had serenity. Where did he find the spirit for it? At his age?

Lilya had not spoken to him about important things before. He was her baby brother, who gave what you would expect a baby to have to give: a cuddle, a giggle, several minutes here and there of playing.

"Why are you so strong and brave?" Lilya asked Fevzi when he lay beside her, as there was room to lie down once so many had died. Fevzi was too weak to stand. Lilya feared he would not survive.

Fevzi shrugged. "I'm just small. What is life to me? Don't you remember where we were before? Don't be scared. Whatever happens, we will be all right."

"What do you mean, before, Fevzi?"

Fevzi toyed with the frayed blanket someone had given him. Lilya feared for a moment that he would not respond—it was as if he were in a state of trance, connected to some greater power that kept itself hidden from her, from all adults, and if she probed it would pull itself back, withdraw into the shell of her small brother like a crab.

"With Allah," he said, and he added, his eyebrows raised, "of course. I only came here for a short while. I only came to tell you about your strength."

"My strength?" she asked him. "I have none left."

She felt his arm slacken, and shook it gently, to rouse his circulation and keep him awake.

"Life here is so small, Lilya," he said quietly, "don't you remember? Where we were before?"

Then, just as Lilya had feared, Fevzi drifted on his own small ocean of sleep, as the car traveled across the land, rocking him just the slightest bit. His eyes fluttered, then lay closed.

24

This time the present comes down crashing with a loud, urgent ringing and I feel like I've fallen and just landed on the sofa. Here I am flat on my back, rigid and conscious. My head aches.

For a while Natasha and I say nothing; I rub my temples. I can't shake the image of Fevzi and his toy soldier, the memory of grief.

"Fevzi died," I say, to confirm it.

"Who?" Natasha asks.

"Lilya's youngest brother, Fevzi."

"Did I say that was his name? I can't remember his name. I'm not sure which brother died. I know one did. And her mother, too."

"I know," I think matter-of-factly, "I was there." I dare not say it aloud.

"What happened to you, then?" I ask. "How did you end up in the States?"

"My mother remarried during the German occupation of Crimea," Natasha replies. "A German soldier. His name was Karl. When the German army retreated in 1944 we went with him to Heidelberg, which ended up being in West Germany. He died of a heart attack when I was twenty-six and we moved to France, then to the United States where his family had relatives. My life was unremarkable after that. After Crimea, really. Marriage, children. Well, one child anyway."

"Your poor mother."

"Why? She had a good life. She escaped the Soviet Union and grew old and fat in New York."

"Still, to lose two husbands."

"There are worse things," Natasha says. She sounds tired, and I think I should be going, only I haven't regained the strength to stand up.

"That is the end of my part in the story. Now it's about what happened to Lilya, that's what has been bothering me. Do you remember the day you, your mother, and I went to Central Park together?" she asks. "Just a couple of years ago."

The question is incongruous, and my mind fogs over. I try to recall that day, then I smile as the memory floods back.

"Yes, I remember. I was wearing a turquoise dress."

It was cotton, sleeveless. The only dress I owned; it was long and loose, like wearing a soft sheet. I remember my mother telling me, with disapproval, that it completely hid my figure, but I loved it for just that reason.

"God, I loved that dress! After that afternoon I could never find it again."

Natasha looks almost smug, almost pitying, and it occurs to me that after all that, the tale of deportation, deprivation, escaping war—it might seem unimaginable, if not inappropriate, remembering a day because of an article of clothing. Then again, this is my eccentric grandmother with her bright, gaudy get-ups. I can't imagine how she might react to my comment, and especially now that I've learnt of this past I didn't know she had—I ask myself, "Do you know Natasha at all, even now, after all she's told you?"

I think I might have destroyed the moment. She frowns slightly, then turns to the window. She reaches distractedly for a cigarette, and for the first time I notice how her hands shake slightly. I am reminded again how quickly she has grown old, but also how much I overlook her ageing—and how I am surprised by it.

"That was such a lovely autumn day, wasn't it?" she asks. "I haven't seen such a nice one since." She pauses thoughtfully and then picks up the TV guide.

Is this my cue to leave, I wonder?

"On that day I first received a letter from Refat."

I feel a surge of excitement, as if it is *my* past reappearing in my life, and exclaim, "After all those years!" (Of course, she'd mentioned before that he'd written her; now, however, it has real meaning for me).

"Yes, and after my marriage, my whole life. I was, I mean, I am a different woman now. You can imagine my shock to receive a letter from him. It brought up all kinds of memories."

I can see the thought of it is making her uncomfortable.

"I began receiving them periodically after that," she takes a deep breath.

"When Lilya disappeared, Refat wrote me to tell me what had happened. It was the first I had heard from him since we'd separated, and the last I ever heard from him until that day we went to Central Park. He had tracked me down through a Russian woman I used to know in New York who was involved in charity work. She went to Simferopol to investigate the possibilities of giving aid to Crimean Tatars. She mentioned my name, as her "dear Russian friend who had lived in harmony with the Crimean Tatars before deportation"—and Refat was one of the people listening to her. It was pure chance. He told her right then and there that he used to know me, and she gave him my address. She never told me, though, can you imagine? There I was with this letter out of the blue!

"He wrote me about where his life had taken him, how he'd married a Crimean Tatar girl, had four children of whom he was immensely proud, of how he had made a career for himself as an electrical engineer. His first letter was very polite and very informative. He had taken part in the Crimean Tatar National Movement by petitioning the Soviet government for the right to return to Crimea, and he was one of the first to return in 1989 when the Soviet Union fell apart. He became very active in the national movement and has been working with a charity raising money to give to families who lost everything with the economic collapse.

"I wrote him back to tell him about my life, and I thought that was the end of it. But he kept writing! Not right away. I received his second letter a year or so later, several months after I had finally sent him mine. He told me all about how he had returned from the front to Crimea, about how he had walked through the forests and hills he so loved only to find his village empty—and be met by militia who deported him to Uzbekistan. He told me about how when he arrived in Uzbekistan he was put to work, about finding Lilya, about how she didn't want to marry right away and he did, because their people had lost so many and he felt obligated to have children. I knew something of what must have happened to Lilya in deportation and exile from research I had done years earlier, and Refat filled in the gaps with more personal detail. My goodness, what long letters! And I always wondered, why? He never said why he wrote, but three letters after his first one, he just stopped."

Natasha pauses, opens her mouth to speak, then closes it again.

"Did you write him again, too?" I ask.

"Only once more. I thanked him for telling me what had happened, and told him I was sorry for all he had suffered, and wished him well. I assumed that was it. Then your mother died and I started thinking about Lilya, and dreaming about Lilya. I began to think about you, and the fact that Susan never knew about her. I began to think that *you* should know about me and my past. Because if there's one thing I learned, it is that time ..."

She is starting to choke up. I look around for tissues, but she calms herself.

"Anyway, then Refat wrote me again, just recently. He said he'd been thinking about Lilya, too, and had gone back to Uzbekistan to make inquiries about what happened to her. He said he has some information for me about her, and will visit me soon. I don't know when, since he doesn't know when his work will bring him to New York. Certainly in the next few months, though."

"He's coming to see you? Here?"

I vaguely recall her telling me this before; still, it meant nothing then, and comes as a shock now.

"Yes." She shrugs. As if there is nothing she can do about it. "Actually, in my last letter I was living with you and Susan, so that is the last address he has. He doesn't know my mail is being forwarded. I imagine he'd go to your place."

"Won't he call?"

"I never gave him a number."

"Directory assistance!" I practically shout. "You need some kind of warning!"

"If he can work that out, I guess. He might just show up one day."

"Well ..." my head swims, I'm sure my mouth is gaping, "how do you feel about it?"

She looks around the room and settles her gaze on her lined and spotted hands. She turns her wedding ring around and around her finger.

"Well, I've been wondering that myself. I don't know if I have the words," she says. "What I almost said earlier is that time changes everything, and nothing. It is somehow important that I tell you that, that you know that."

Natasha looks pained. She stands and begins clearing away the coffee cups, the plates with crumbs (we had cake today). I stand up too late to help her, but follow her to the kitchen anyway. My arms are folded at my chest. I am cold, and self-protective, like I'm the one giving away too much of myself. I wish that I could wrap my arms around Natasha, but I have never been like that, nor has she.

"I should have told Susan about Refat when I told your grandfather, when she was running around having love affairs. I always thought she saw me and your grandfather and—though we loved each other very much—I always thought she detected something in me she thought was dissatisfaction. She was very perceptive. She would not have understood that what she saw had nothing to do with the happy marriage I had with Andrew. I'm sure she thought I had settled because she didn't see the passion. She pretty much told me that once, not in so many words. She was only a teenager herself then and I didn't have the courage to tell her the truth. I think she decided she would never settle. She would never end up in a marriage merely satisfied. It wasn't like that with Andrew, though. I have had two loves, very different from one another, and I would never have given up the love I had with your grandfather for Refat, or vice versa.

"I think Susan of all people would have understood if I'd given her the chance, if I'd explained properly. She was good at understanding. Doesn't that sound funny?" she chuckles. "She didn't understand everything. I never thought she understood me, for example. Then again, maybe it was because I didn't let her.

She was good at imagining what it was like to be someone else. She had empathy. She was kind, and warm. I never told her I thought so. I should have told her."

Natasha's eyes well up with tears, which catches me off-guard. This time I manage to I bring her the tissues. I think the emotion of the day has worn us both out. I try to say something supportive, but I can find no words; I'm in a daze and inured to tears—she can't take me with her, even if I wish I could cry just for some kind of release. I hand her more tissues. I hand her the entire box. Then, because there is nothing I can do about her crying, and she is doing nothing else, I do nothing at all.

One by one, lone, disjointed memories come floating into my mind: Susan baking cookies and letting me lick the bowl; a picnic at the park with Julio, one of her boyfriends, whose grandmother had made me my favorite Mexican dishes to take along that day; the song my mother made up to sing me to sleep at night as long as I can remember, until I was a teenager and told her I didn't want to hear the song anymore: *Sleep, my precious baby, sleep* ... I remember how she put Barbie Doll Band-Aids on my scrapes even when I was sixteen. I remember how once I thought bliss was lying in bed next to her in the middle of the night, when she was so fast asleep she didn't notice, and I could snuggle up against her and let her warmth envelop me. I remember how she always told me I could do anything I wanted with my life, as long as I was true to myself, and how I never really understood—but she expressed such confidence in me that I assumed she was right, that I *could* do anything.

Except be depressed. Because she was always telling me to cheer up and giving me too many suggestions for how. She was so busy with her gorgeous, perfect, sophisticated self that even when she looked right at me she sometimes saw through me to her next conquest, her next event, the next ball or dinner or whatever. She never saw that hole in me that she created when she wrote my father out of my life.

"Oh my God! Is that it? Is that the source of your resentment of your mother?" I feel like yelling at myself. It annoys me that it is so clichéd—the absent father—so Freudian!

Meanwhile, Natasha is still crying.

I am angry. That she assumed because she could raise me on her own without a man, that I didn't need a father. That she was so good at being happy and enlightened that she assumed it would be just as easy for me. That every single tear, every single hurt, every single disappointment was an occasion for her to go into Buddha mode and inspire me to rise above suffering. Even her own death!

How can I mourn? How can I deal with my own suffering when my mother didn't believe it existed, when she was the one who was supposed to teach me how to live?

Of course! Why has it never occurred to me that Natasha is the same as me? She has suffered—so she must never have understood her own daughter's denial of suffering. And here she tells me her story has ended, as if nothing of interest ever happened after she moved to Germany, as if the only story she can relive is one of heartache—the unspoken sadness in her life, the part of herself she could never really have shared with Susan, the part that needed validation. I suspect I will never know the rest of her life, the years between Germany and meeting my grandfather. I fear her story will forever be incomplete, lost, subsumed into Lilya's drama—but what can I do? I am left to wonder who Natasha became after Crimea, and who she has become since.

Natasha takes my hand.

"Here, you need one, too."

She hands me a tissue. Here we both are, crying. What a ridiculous, maudlin sight. It's enough to make me laugh. Susan would like that. Laughing at tears. She was never good with tears.

Susan let me do anything. She never told me I wasn't good at anything, and she took my every whim seriously, my every goal, ambition, preference. If I had said I wanted to be an astronaut, she would have found me a space suit. When I was four and developed a fascination with firefighting (my preoccupation with avoiding emergencies surfaced at a young age), she introduced me to the only firewoman at the fire department, who took me on a tour of the station. She was that kind of person. She believed in potential.

Natasha says, "Enough of that."

We recover and I take my coat and kiss her goodbye. I don't think we will mention my mother again any time soon, and I don't think Natasha will speak much more about herself, either.

When we meet a week later Natasha says she will tell me what she learned from Refat's letters: first, of his homecoming to Crimea, then about his and Lilya's life in exile in Uzbekistan.

25

August 1944

Refat had the good fortune of surviving the war, though for a month he lay in a field hospital with a wound to the head. It was summer when he was finally discharged and sent home. Only five days earlier he had taken off the bandage covering his left eye, and it was still swollen half-shut. His head ached with every effort to see clearly into the distance, but that did not deter him from walking the long route home from the train station—so that he might savor his reacquaintance with his land. Refat made his way up and down the shallow mountain passes and deeper into the thickening vegetation until he knew he was at the center of things and soon would sense the familiarity that comes with being home.

Refat went from clearings to woods where trees were clumped and twisted together as if coupling. He realized that he'd been gone so long that he had forgotten the smell of these mountains and he breathed the sweet air in deeply. It had been years, of course, but he didn't want to think about that. It had been as many weeks as the number of German soldiers he'd seen killed, at his best estimate. But he did not want to ponder that either.

It had been longer since he'd seen Natasha than the whole time they had been together.

When he came out of the woods and was on the road to his village he met some uniformed men from the local security forces.

Like the rest of the Crimean Tatar soldiers in the Red Army who survived the war to return to Crimea, Refat made it home only to be forced into exile. He did not get to his house, or even to his village. On a lonely country road less than two miles from where security forces had woken his parents in the middle of the night to send them away, the local militia summarily arrested Refat and deported him to Uzbekistan. Like his compatriots before him, he was charged with treason.

Several weeks before Refat's arrest, and after more than three weeks crammed into wagons on the train traversing two thousand miles of soulless terrain, after tens of thousands of dead had been tossed out onto the side of railroad tracks like so much rubbish, when near-starvation and disease threatened the survivors of this cruel journey, Lilya's train arrived at its destination.

Roughly one thousand Crimean Tatars were deposited on the outskirts of the Samarkand district of Uzbekistan—in the provinces where there were factories and fields, and a settlement which the Crimean Tatars were told was now their home. It was a penal colony that had not been prepared for its first residents; it was without visible boundaries, living arrangements or food. Lilya, her father and brothers and several other families were escorted to a barn where they would share their quarters with horses until barracks could be built. The other exiles occupied two existing barracks originally built for factory workers and meant for a few people at a time. The deportees slept seventy to eighty people in a room, crowded together on the floor, which was not the worst arrangement. Still others slept in the open air. A camp commandant was assigned to the exiled Crimeans, to ensure compliance with their new regime. They were not allowed to go more than three miles from the settlement on pain of a twenty-five year sentence to hard labor, and they had to check in with their commandant once per week to confirm their whereabouts. There was nowhere to escape to in this place, anyway, in a foreign land and foreign climate, not while their homeland was kept from them at gunpoint a world away, and the rest of the world waged war.

They did not know then that they were in for twelve years of the harshest kind of internal exile—before the regime ended and there was freedom of movement (only locally; it would be fifty years before they could return to their homeland). Their destination was a dusty, dirty, lonely stretch of nowhere in the southeastern part of Uzbekistan. There was no gentle sea nearby, and the fertile cotton-growing valleys were beyond view, as were the rivers that cut through them. It was a desert place with views of the stark, brown ranges of the Tien-Shan and Alai mountains, flat near the settlement, hilly just beyond, and everywhere brown and lifeless. The region's ancient minarets and madrassas did little to prettify this alien land for its newest inhabitants. To the Crimean Tatars it was a place that by rights should have itself been exiled from the earth, so bereft was it of sympathy for its inhabitants.

They were told right away that they had been "resettled," that this was their home, and that likewise they would have a life here and therefore would be given work—but it soon became clear, homeless as many were, that the Crimean exiles were the very last priority in the midst of a world war.

One old Tatar woman (ancient at fifty-two, who had survived despite all the odds) said over and over again, "The road in at least leads back out." She slept beside Lilya at night and talked in her sleep to her three daughters, only one of whom had survived the journey. That daughter spent the first week in their new settlement on the brink of death, rocked with a fever that clung stubbornly to her malnourished body. Lilya slept poorly, ever on the ready for the next emergency, and could not help but notice the daughter making her mother comfortable in her sleep as the old woman mumbled instructions about baking and cleaning, and awoke, every day, in tears to the nightmare that had stolen two of her children. Her daughter did not succumb to fever, and the old woman praised Allah, and said once more that the road in led back home.

"What could our home do for the dead?" Lilya despaired to herself. She was surrounded by the bodies of the dead, piled up, left in ditches, because there were no proper burial places and camp commandants refused to help. Hunger and disease claimed about twenty of the surviving Crimean Tatars before Lilya stopped counting. And she was surrounded also by the bodies of the living, sick with disease and despair. It was hard to find any good in life, so distracting was their struggle for physical survival. The sun was at first one of the most relentless sources of discomfort. But as the temperatures soared into the low hundreds, it soon joined other sources in a masterly conglomerate of displeasures that stemmed no less from the daily trials of finding nourishment or the impossibility of fulfilling the ordinary human desire to clean oneself, than from the sheer psychological horror of realizing their inability to leave the prisoner's life.

There would be physical labor, camp commandants promised, something to distract them and maybe provide an income to improve their conditions, but there was no work immediately. In this desiccated reality survival was the only responsibility; it structured the days and nights and dictated every last minute. As the weeks went by and the survivors gained back their strength, people passed time in whatever ways they could—with a deck of cards here, a bit of talk there. More often than not, it was spent in warding off further ill-fortune. That is to say, keeping a vigilant watch on others, especially children, for signs of illness, making sure that you had what was needed (doctorless though they were) and if not, trying your best to procure it—everything from food and water to cigarettes to medicine. For those sleeping out in the open, it was fashioning some sort of shelter. Soon the landscape was littered with makeshift houses—earthen huts, wooden lean-tos, tents—and their human inhabitants. Then, finally, local authorities began to build barracks.

The attitude of the local population did not facilitate the Crimean Tatars' transition to a new life. Uzbek residents were not shy in voicing their assessments of the newest settlers: they were traitors. Locals had been prepared for the

Crimean Tatars' arrival with propaganda, had been told the exiles had collaborated with the German invaders against the Soviet Army.

"My son died fighting the Fascists!" one Uzbek woman screamed with a frightful passion as Lilya walked back from the well to their barn. The woman's age was indeterminate as she sagged, face and torso alike, her body and spirit weighed down by gravity and grief. She stood in the distance with a shopping bag, staring at Lilya as if she had herself killed the woman's son. Lilya felt the woman's venom and thought bitterly how lucky it must be to have someone to blame. Lilya's grief had no such clear target; she might have blamed Stalin, or the army, or history—but she did not have the strength, and the anger she initially felt was hard to maintain in the face of all the physical challenges and discomforts of exile. Her new life—if you could call it a life—was so awful and so unfathomable that sometimes she felt there had to have been an error, and wished she could stop believing in it. Perhaps that is the answer, she thought. This is not real because it *cannot* be real.

"A traitor doesn't seem like the very worst thing to be," said Yusuf to Lilya. She stroked his head. His eyes were hollow. "It is worse to be dead, surely."

They did not speak of Fevzi, ever, nor did they speak of their mother. Yusuf looked at his sister in a searching way, though, and she wondered if he were asking about those they'd lost.

Lilya had no proof of eternal life, but she felt the truth of it in her soul. She kissed her brother's forehead and gave him this thought: "Death is peaceful, Yusuf. It is like spending an afternoon at the seashore with plenty of food and perfect weather."

Her description gave them both something pleasant to contemplate for many minutes after.

Two hundred and thirty-eight thousand Crimean Tatars were deported. By the end of the first year of resettlement, one hundred and twenty-eight thousand of them had died.

Some weeks after their arrival, the Crimean Tatar deportees were informed of their participation in building the economy of the future, of contributing to Soviet greatness: the local cotton fields needed sowing and picking, and the nearby textile factory made fabric. All able-bodied adults were to work at either one or the other. From then on Crimean Tatars were woken before dawn for twelve-hour workdays.

It was punitive labor, the kind that killed workers by the thousands at prison camps (though Lilya and most of her compatriots knew little of Stalin's camps yet). But it came with a salary. The local market was a sad affair with few stalls, but a salary would give them access to produce and meat and other needed things, and hungry people dream of naught but food. Once work began, a feverish frenzy descended on some, those who, like Lilya, spent nights dreaming of the tiniest sprouts of cabbage emerging from the desert, of bucketloads of potatoes, tomatoes, of clean, fresh green leaves forming dense carpets of growth over the bleak brown landscape that surrounded them.

Lilya went to work at the textile mill, monitoring fabric as machines fed it from one mechanism to another, learning to clean the machinery as the men operated it. She spent much of her work time remembering her mother's many recipes, imagining what she could prepare had she the proper vegetables, and whom she would feed. She worked twelve-hour days and still in the evenings prepared food for her brothers and father, with the help of the old woman and her daughter, both of whom worked all day too. As the meager wages began to be distributed, the families who shared the barn pooled what money they had and bought whatever their rubles could buy. Evening fare was paltry (potatoes, an onion, one small piece of meat divided among many, cooked out in the open over a pit). On weekends Lilya's sole task was food—imagining, choosing, chopping, cooking. The work became easier many months later when more barracks were built. Each family was allotted a single, bare room without toilets and a kitchen shared with ten or so other families—but it was somewhere to cook. Lilya and the other women prepared as much food as they could for as many people as they could, desperate to put meat on their bones and bring the ruddiness back to their cheeks. Still she battled pessimism. What good could food do if they were stuck here? When would the children be sent to school? What future did they have in Uzbekistan, and what future did she have?

Marriage and children. That was the great hope of many, who had lost so much, but not Lilya. She gave little thought to it still, and her father only advised, "Wait. Refat may yet return from war." There had been no word of his death.

Lilya waited, and tried not to think about him, or Natasha.

Crimean Tatar soldiers routed into exile arrived in an unsteady stream, seeking their loved ones in a foreign republic. Many arrived with bandages testifying to their sacrifices for their Soviet homeland; there were more than a few amputees. It was an especially painful irony that many of the Crimean Tatar men branded traitors to their country and sent into exile returned to their families wearing Soviet medals for valor. As they arrived along with Central Asians, local Uzbeks began to understand that these poor, bedraggled exiles were not traitors at all, and friendships between peoples were tentatively formed. They had common ground; they were Muslim, their languages both Turkic. Already so many Crimean Tatar men had died on the front, or in transit to exile, that Crimean Tatar women, widowed or yet unmarried, had begun to go out with Uzbek men.

And so husbands returned to wives; fathers to sons and daughters; the living to the dead; but in and among the happy returns, to the living came news of death. For Lilya, first came word of cousins dying en route to exile, an uncle's death in hard labor, and then news of those who had died in war. It was not unexpected. Still, it was enough to sap the will to carry on. And, of course, Lilya had her own troubles to confront. She had heard from a cousin who survived that Refat had survived, too, wounded but well. He would soon come for her.

She did not want to see him; she wished that he could see Natasha and not her, could leave her free of men and family—she had her brothers to care for, she didn't want more responsibility. She wanted more freedom.

Now that she had a routine (watching machines digest fabric, shopping and cooking), her mind started to wander and her hunger for autonomy grew. Though she was often tired and short of time, whenever she could she walked through the markets and toward the hills beyond, down and back around buildings and into quiet groves where trees and grass grew (despite the aridity) among the few ugly, tall apartment buildings that passed as homes. And because in her heart she could not confront the reality of her people's suffering, she began to daydream of something more permanent than life. Afterlife. She thought often of the man who had appeared in the woods that night in Crimea as if from another world. In her memory it seemed as though he had actually said something straight into her thoughts, a few words she had missed in the stirring of the bare branches or the crunch of the snow underfoot. As the weeks went by and she grew more bored by the daily routine of work, she became more and more convinced the man in the woods had spoken to her. The words which she could not remember gained form over the months until they existed just on the tip of her tongue, until one day her mind spoke them as clearly as if the man were repeating them in her ear: "Come with me."

She laughed when she heard them, and doubted the soundness of her mind straightaway. How silly and pointless the man's words were, if in fact he had even said them! Where would she have gone? If only he had said something wise that she could have puzzled over in her desert exile.

Lilya wished for a revelation that could give some kind of meaning to or understanding of her life. She knew what she wanted, she knew it in her heart, and Natasha would have understood, as she was the only other person who knew

Lilya well. Once they had hoped for a revelation together. As her exile wore on and Refat came closer, Lilya reminded herself that her and Natasha's adolescent search for mystery had not just been folly, despite their youth and inexperience. They had watched the moon and talked of ghosts because they hoped for a modest blessing. Life had to have more purpose than what their small lives contained.

Lilya wanted to disbelieve the world she saw around her with a passion that increased day by day—she had seen enough unfathomable misery since she left Crimea and could bear no more of this so-called reality. Finally, at some level in her being, she rejected it.

Refat returned. Lilya told him on their reunion that she was not prepared to marry yet. She needed time to know him better, she said in confidence, and asked that he be patient with her. He was not in a hurry himself, and visited her several times a week just to talk, always, as the custom went, in the presence of her father. To anyone who asked Refat deflected the details of his and Lilya's engagement, claiming that he wanted to earn the money for a proper wedding first.

He found work in the factory and there he lost himself in labor, believing, as he learned to operate the machinery and was made to sweat from morning until night, that this work freed his mind from his body's captivity.

Many of Refat's compatriots (the ones from their homeland, for there were exiled minorities from other Soviet regions working alongside them) told stories at night, five or six men over a single bottle of beer and three cigarettes, sharing remembrances of their peninsula. How very different was the air in Crimea, the sky, not to mention the verdure, and Refat began to write poetry about his homeland in the hope of capturing something of what had been lost. In their desert exile the men did not yet speak much of their families. Those with wives and children who had been placed in different settlements quietly tried to locate their loved ones. Every once in while news filtered through—of death, of birth, of life lived in exile not that far away, but with their prison-like regime, in places that were as unreachable as the moon.

Refat's losses were comparably few: his mother had survived; his father, too, though he had almost died from disease upon arrival, and was feeble and stayed at home with the old women. Refat had no siblings. Once a family curse, it was now a blessing, for his parents had not lost a child.

There were very few older men like Refat's father who had survived deportation, but there was another old man Refat worked with at the factory who gave Refat some direction he had lost in the course of war and exile. Mustafa was in his mid-forties but was as old as some men are at seventy, and it was not just the look of him or how he shuffled and no longer stood straight. In the past week Mustafa had heard word that his wife, to whom he been married for more than twenty years, had died upon reaching a settlement in another part of Uzbekistan; his youngest two children, both girls, had died en route. His son had survived; he was fourteen and now lived with Mustafa's sister, a hearty, middle-aged woman who had recovered from pneumonia just a year before deportation.

"So it goes," Mustafa told Refat, after learning of his losses.

On this day during lunch, Mustafa was whittling, making yet another of his small wooden figures of maudlin women in scarves and men with hard expressions. He was an artist, really, though he didn't see himself as one. He had made wine before and had an appreciation of grapes, their pulp, their sticky sweetness, a talent for bottling and fermentation, and he could recall every tactile experience from planting to harvest, from gathering and crushing to the first taste of his latest vintage. His hands had been doing rough work for two decades and now were comparatively idle. Empty hands grasp at fullness, he told Refat, and Mustafa found fullness in the wood.

"This one is you," Mustafa said, carving the small figure's hair with his pocket knife. It was not at all the likeness of Refat, so thought Refat. The wooden man had cavernous eyes all out of proportion to his other features.

"I'm sorry about your family. Allah willing your son will have many children," Refat offered.

"Yes, that is my hope. I had expected this news. I have no tears left."

Mustafa proffered Refat the small wooden figure. Refat fondled its head. It was so smooth. A soft wood of some sort, porous; Mustafa had warned him not to allow the figures to get wet.

Somewhere nearby someone had begun to sing, some simple melody. Unfamiliar to Refat, it could have been a traditional song, or perhaps it was the singer's invention. Someone called out to get back to work. Refat slid the figure into his pocket.

"Have many children," Mustafa told him. "So many that your children's children will overrun this place, and when we return to Crimea ... there will be so many."

Refat's thoughts turned to Natasha. He did not speak of her at all but hadn't succeeded in banishing her from his thoughts. He told himself that one day he and Lilya would wed and have children and life would carry on. Love had brought him nothing but heartache; it had given him nothing tangible, certainly nothing that could redeem his present difficulties. Lilya, on the other hand, could redeem him. Through her his people would continue, and that, better than just survival, was what life was about now. Survival and fertility, to sow, from a plundered land, a population to reclaim it.

Refat suddenly saw his future through Mustafa's eyes, as if it were as tangible as one of the older man's wooden figurines.

Refat heard humming. Whoever had been singing had continued on with the melody and nobody had stopped him. There was banging in the background, and it gradually grew louder. Still the humming continued.

Refat began to imagine Lilya and his life with her. He began to imagine life.

That evening Refat went to see Lilya, and asked her father if he and his fiancée could have a word alone.

He told her they had a duty to their people, that theirs was a fate greater than that of just any couple. He explained that he had no money to provide for her just yet, just the promise that he would be a kind and loyal husband who would always respect her and care for her well.

Lilya did not seem surprised, or upset, Refat thought. In fact, she hardly reacted. She took his hand, and said, "Of course. Let's share the news." Then she smiled.

It was a such great relief, Refat thought, and so very easy in the end, to succumb to fate.

26

Someone bangs at the door and our hush is interrupted by a raspy, old woman's voice calling out for Natasha.

It is timely, at least. Natasha says, back over her shoulder as she opens the door, "Of course, that is Refat's version. I never heard from Lilya after the deportation."

She excuses herself and I get ready to go. Natasha, it seems—against all my wildest expectations—has joined the home's bridge club, and is being summoned to her game.

Nothing can interrupt my mounting anxiousness, not even the otherwise happy thought that my antisocial grandmother is at last developing a social life.

She might not have heard from Lilya again, but what about me? Will I? I descend into a state of suspense, racked with nerves.

I'm just waiting for something to happen. I know it is coming. I hear whispering in the rustling leaves that settle outside of my office window and I imagine the sound is meant to reassure me, to hush me like my mother's voice used to do when I was little and she lulled me into sleep with our bedtime song. I can't think for the sound and I can't think for the anticipation. I am so tightly drawn into myself and so finely balanced on this precipice of moment-by-moment waiting that the merest indication that something is imminent—what will it be?—would send me toppling into life, because I am half-alive in this waiting for someone, or some event to breathe life into me. I hear the leaves and the wind whoosh through them, and the whispering rises to a murmur. "Shhh," I try to calm myself. "Shhh." I cannot bear to hear it anymore. I leave the office and turn on the television. I must tune out from reality. I must have patience that whatever it is that is so unsettling me will rise to my awareness in its own time.

Before her neighbor knocked on her door, Natasha wondered aloud what could have happened to Lilya that would make her decide to marry Refat after all. I told her it must have been the shock of deportation and the need to carry on with life as usual, but I suspect I'm not the only one of us who doesn't buy that explanation.

I have never been in a trance, nor meditated, nor undergone hypnotherapy, but the state that comes over me while watching television later that night is what I imagine an altered state of consciousness must be: physical immobility, light-headedness, calm, and an uncontrollable parade of images and feelings that leads to a focus within and a gradual forgetting of the world around me.

I suspect at first that I am dozing, until I have a moment of clarity: I see Lilya in my mind's eye, then I am her, then there is nothing incoherent about the images appearing before me as I find myself inside her life. I am there.

27

February 1945

Lilya was stalling for time with Refat not only for the reasons she had given him (which were valid), but also because she sensed a shift in herself and had a feeling that something was about to happen that might change things. That change was just out of sight, awaiting her discovery.

She told no one of her thoughts, but her younger brother Ayder, the oldest sibling after her, knew her well enough to suspect she was keeping something from him.

"You do not seem excited to marry," he observed. "I wonder what you are thinking about so seriously lately."

"I'm thinking of other possibilities."

"There are not many for us, Lilya."

"Well, I don't know. You never know what could happen. For example, I could go to university."

Ayder asked with all sincerity, "Is that what you would do instead of marriage, if you had the choice?"

"I don't know. But I do know that life can change in an instant. One minute you think you are going in one direction, then something happens and suddenly you're going in another direction entirely. Isn't that what happened to us, to get us here?"

"You're dreaming," he laughed, not unkindly.

"Yes, I know."

"It could be disappointing, just waiting for life to change dramatically."

"It could be disappointing expecting it not to."

Lilya could not possibly convey the strength of her convictions to her brother, who was himself consumed by thoughts of marriage (he was already in high demand, being one of the few Crimean Tatar men of marriageable age around). She didn't mind so much waiting for the unknowable or intangible to happen. She did not fear disappointment, because she could not fathom any more tragedy.

To quell her restless sense of anticipation, she walked, no matter how tired she was, no matter the weather (unless there were dust storms). Lilya walked three miles outside the perimeter of the special settlement like a prisoner in the jailyard—it was as far from the settlement as the Crimean Tatars were allowed to go. From the barracks to the market, she counted the buildings (ten barracks and three apartment buildings), the bus stops (two), the benches oddly placed in front of buildings and ditches (she rarely stopped and never sat on the benches—they seemed to be continuously occupied by old, immovable Uzbek men and women). The siren song of the hills beyond the invisible borders of the settlement tempted her to escape. She ignored their summons, though she dreamt of responding despite the burning, sinking feeling that held her back—not just because she would be caught outside the settlement, but also because outside there was no life for her, and no way back to the life she knew. There was nowhere to go. Naught but a desert mirage. Confronting this reality was certain to cause misery. Better to expect miracles in captivity, so she did.

As day followed day, Lilya came to take her expectations for granted, and it was in this state of mind that she met Sumai. She had noticed Sumai's companion first: her attention was drawn to an old Uzbek with dark skin and slanted eyes wearing a cloth sack around her neck. The woman frequented a particular stall at the market. Lilya could not tell what was sold there and she did not approach to find out. There were many people in the market, so many Lilya was surprised she had noticed one in particular, yet the woman's dark gaze often met hers, as if it were no accident that they should single each other out.

Then, when Lilya was in the neighboring stall, the old woman's eyes boring into her, Sumai appeared next to Lilya quite abruptly. Lilya recognized her straightaway as the old woman's companion.

"I need your help," she said.

Lilya eyed her stony-faced. She was also an Uzbek, and, given the delicate relations that yet existed between the Crimean Tatar settlers and the local Uzbeks, Lilya expected rudeness, or at the very least a perfunctory demand.

"Please come with me," she said. "I need help carrying some things to my home."

"Why are you asking me?" Lilya asked, taken aback.

"You are going that way anyway. I have seen you walking before."

"What do you want?"

"Just your help."

"There are plenty of men to help you."

"I am not comfortable in the company of strange men, and no one here is familiar. You are strong enough to carry my load."

Lilya did not want to be rude, and so she followed this woman to the stall where the older Uzbek woman stood. The woman who'd dragged Lilya there disappeared behind some boxes and the older woman with the sack on her neck smiled at Lilya, and said:

"If you're looking for something, I can help you. Go with Sumai and talk to her. We will meet again."

Sumai appeared then, her arms nearly collapsing under the weight of small boxes piled one atop the other, some filled with potatoes and carrots, others with bottles, yet others with contents not visible. Lilya looked around to see if she knew anyone. Not a soul. No one was even looking at her. There was an urgency in the moment she could not have explained to anyone, much less herself, but also, strangely, an innocence. It was as if some part of her thought no more of what she was about to do than a small child would think before running off with a stranger promising sweets. Lilya took a few boxes out of Sumai's arms, and followed her. She saw, as she left, the old Uzbek woman finger the sack on her neck and smile.

Lilya and Sumai trudged through the market briskly, despite the weight of their loads, in the direction Lilya normally took—just as Sumai had said. They passed three identical apartment buildings and went behind the third one, then up a slope to another identical building that Lilya had not seen earlier. There Sumai put the boxes on the ground to open the door for Lilya. They climbed the stairs together until Sumai said, "Stop."

"Just help me inside," she added.

Her apartment was just like any other apartment of the time: small, ugly, dark. There was nothing hanging on the walls, which were all bare cement except for one wall which had on it what looked like recently applied wallpaper. Lilya had not seen a Soviet apartment building before. She saw how small it was, and saw her future.

"I should not be here," she said, not meaning to speak aloud.

"You're living in the barracks, aren't you?"

"Yes."

"Unmarried."

"Not for long."

"They will build more buildings and then you will live in an apartment like this one, too."

"I have a house, in the mountains. It has many rooms, a big living room, a garden ..." Lilya did not know why she was sharing this with a perfect stranger. Sumai nodded, her back to her as she stacked the boxes.

"It seems to matter a lot to you, where you are from, who you are?" Sumai asked.

"Shouldn't it?" Lilya realized she had not moved two feet from the front door, and stood defensively, arms wrapped around herself.

"Well, that is what we all want to know, isn't it?"

"Doesn't it matter to you?" Lilya asked.

"Yes, and no." Sumai faced her. "You'll have tea, and then go," she announced. It was a statement of fact rather than an invitation. Lilya did not reply, but moved toward the kitchen, just a few feet off to her left.

Sumai went past her.

"If I told you that your life is insignificant, what would you think?"

Lilya found herself staring at a bare wooden table. She said, "Ha! It *is* insignificant. That is a joke, isn't it? I mean, what significance could it have? I've not done much with my life so far, and look at where I am now."

"Yes, indeed. You're not far wrong."

Now Sumai grinned at Lilya, revealing a row of gold teeth. Somehow Lilya was reassured by that smile. What was she, a deportee, doing in the home of an Uzbek woman, someone she ran into at a market stall? Lilya dismissed the question out of hand. "Eh, why not," she thought.

"Did you need any more help?" Lilya asked Sumai, for truly in that moment she felt that there had to be a reason for their company.

"Oh, my. Don't we all!" Sumai said.

"I see," Lilya replied. "Perhaps she is mad," she thought.

"Did you know that the people who are indigenous to this region practice shamanism?"

"Shamanism?" Lilya gasped. "Oh! Do you know anything about it?"

"Yes, it is my people who practice it." She turned to Lilya, peering at her as she placed a teapot on the table. "Would you like to know more?"

Lilya nearly blurted out "Yes, yes, yes." She bit her tongue, held her breath to calm herself. Was she just ecstatic or insane? Her mind reeled with supposition, fantasy, excitement; if only Natasha were here, too. Shamanism was not supposed to exist anymore in the Soviet Union. It was illegal, like other expressions of faith, and her involvement in it would put her at risk, especially as she was a Crimean Tatar, a special settler under the constant eye of the law.

But it actually existed! People who knew the ways of communing with spirits and other worlds, who knew about herbal remedies and magic to heal the ill, or manifest a wish. She had only read stories about it, and had imagined if it were true she would like to find out more …

"But I'm getting married!" Lilya exclaimed. Her heart fell.

"And? Your husband will not own your soul." Sumai placed a teacup at the edge of the table.

Lilya approached and sat. She held the empty cup and traced its edge with her thumb. So many unexpected things happened in life, so few of them joyful, or even interesting. Yet now, here was something that was truly intriguing. And how else, for her, could there ever be joy apart from intrigue? She who was destined to marry, to follow a well-traveled path, she could not pass by unexpected sidetracks. Was this the change she had been expecting? Yet, she had hoped the change—the miracle—would replace the destiny of married life, not exist alongside it.

"Eat," Sumai said. "I made some meat pies."

Sumai brought out the pies and placed them in front of her guest. Lilya realized she was starving and ate, without shyness. Sumai watched her eat two pies and insisted she have more. Lilya could not believe there could exist this kind of delicacy in such a time.

"I'll send some home with you," Sumai said.

There was a softness to the Uzbek woman that Lilya was just beginning to see. Lilya wiped her mouth and thanked her for her hospitality. She was eager to hear more about this woman's people, their spiritual practice. She could not disguise her excitement, no matter how much she tried.

"Will you tell me about shamanism?" Lilya asked, her voice meek with desire.

"No. That is a job for Tilgar. She is our shamaness."

Lilya wondered if she were referring to the old Uzbek woman from the market. The one who had spoken to her earlier.

"She is the one who found you," Sumai said. "She will help you, if you want, to understand what is hidden in your soul."

"I see," Lilya whispered. She had been found. What did that mean? Had she been stalked? Was this a trick to lure her outside the boundaries of the settlement? She detected no trickery. It was if she had agreed to meeting the shamaness beforehand ("Before what?" she wondered). She realized she was beginning to panic, for what would it all mean? She drank her tea in two gulps and stood.

"I have to go," she announced. "Thank you for your hospitality. I think I am frightened now, so I should leave."

"Don't be scared." Sumai stood, too. She had a warm smile, at least just then, a mothering smile. "Tilgar has helped me, too," she said.

"Well, I'm going," Lilya opened the front door, then asked without turning back around. "How will I meet her?"

"At the entrance to this building, tomorrow, an hour before sunset. You will walk together."

The strangest thing happened next.

When Lilya reached the bottom step, as her hand reached out to the entrance door, the world fell away and she stood on a hill looking out over a huge expanse of green, a meadow with flowers here and there, and the old woman standing beside her. She saw nothing familiar. The ground upon which she stood was solid, the air smelled of grass. She opened her mouth to ask the old woman what was happening.

"Would you know true freedom if you experienced it?" Tilgar asked.

Suddenly the earth seemed to go soft and Lilya lost her bearing. Her foot slid. She began to respond, but her tongue was tied. Then, as quickly as the scene she was in appeared, it was gone. She was standing in the stairwell. She opened the door to the courtyard.

Same dusty day. Same bright sun.

Only it wasn't quite the same. Lilya wasn't quite the same either, despite having taken the same route home, appearing as usual in time to help prepare dinner over the same hot stove, for the same godforsaken people.

After dinner she went outside behind the barracks where she could be alone. This spot was her *terra sancta*. She needed natural light and fresh air as a panacea for a strange sense of inner movement which unnerved her—how else could she describe the flutter in her chest, or the indigestion, or the dizziness?

She loosened her belt and inhaled deeply. She imagined oxygen infusing every cell, sanitizing her like antiseptic, and she thought, "Something bad has simply, quite unexpectedly, gone. Poof!" She opened her eyes half-anticipating a disintegrating cloud of dust. What was happening? Then a sudden wind came from both her right and her left, blowing so fiercely that it blew her back against the wall and she squinted as sand flew up into the air and all around. People went running inside for shelter and her brother Ayder came out to see if she was all right, but she refused his suggestion to follow him back in.

The dust storm didn't bother her. She felt that she was part of it, that she was inseparable from the natural world. She shielded her eyes and dared the sand to attack her vision. Then she closed her eyes to the force of the wind and sand and lost herself to the sensation. She imagined the wind as a giant creature sweeping her into its arms and swallowing her whole. It washed her with currents like small prickly tongues, and spat her out like rotting meat. Then, a kinder current came, warm and soft, and Lilya felt herself rise like smoke over the camp. She returned, smoldering like embers, glowing hot-bright.

Freedom seemed to have come to her with the speed of the wind.

Compared to what she felt now, it was as if all this time, for as long as she could remember, she had been bound by her belief that marriage was a restriction, a hindrance to true life. It was as if she had been wearing clothes that were too small, but was so numb she didn't notice it and therefore could not change it. Her freed self, however, could not ignore the frays, the unraveling thread, the seams that angrily withstood an expanding inner force. So Lilya could not remain clothed in her old beliefs, confined within a worn-out self. When, after the dust storm, Lilya's senses returned, she gathered around herself a larger belief, she stretched and settled into the expanded space, she saw a different world than the one she had seen before, and she believed in its possibilities.

That evening Refat arrived at Lilya's barrack as he often did, and asked her father if he and his fiancée could have a word alone.

She was welcoming, as usual, but not prepared for what he was about to say and how he said it. He spoke as if defending himself before a judge.

Refat told her that they—he and Lilya, just like every other Crimean Tatar couple—had a duty to their people, a duty that went beyond the simple act of marriage. They had to ensure the survival of their people by having many children, by teaching the next generation about what they had lost, and what they would one day find again in their homeland. Refat wanted Lilya to marry him right away, to put aside her hesitation and honor her parents and her grandparents by continuing the generations. He explained that he had no money to provide for her yet, but he promised her that he would be a kind and loyal husband who would always respect her, and care for her well.

For an instant Lilya considered his words. She realized she had effectively made the decision to accept his proposal after her visit with Sumai, when she stood behind the barracks as the sand flew around her. She had never meant to make him wait forever; she had been stalling for a revelation and today she had had one. And she could hardly ask for more in a husband given that she did not want a husband to begin with.

Lilya now understood that her search for meaning would not suffer in the cocoon of marriage. Instead, her marriage would be the perfect building to house her mystic searching. She would hide herself in it so that no one would suspect her true passion. The mysteries she was intending to explore were all inside her head, anyway, where she had always been free.

Lilya took Refat's hand, and said, "Of course. Let's share the news."

Oh, how it lightened her spirit, she thought, to just surrender. She composed her last letter to her best friend.

Dear Natasha,

I don't know if my letter will ever reach you. I have not heard from you in so long I begin to doubt your existence and pray you are well, and happy, and that life is bringing you some joy wherever you are.

I am writing to tell you that I will marry Refat in one month's time. My decision may seem strange to you, but please know that it is my choice. Something happened to me the other day when I was standing outside. The earth seemed to disappear from beneath me and I seemed to float up into the sky. I was not drinking, I promise you! Natashenka, now my life does not seem so difficult. I do not know if I will ever see you again, but I am certain that time does not stand in my way, nor loss. I feel a strange certainty that things will work themselves out, and it is fine that I spend my life being a good wife to Refat. He is a kind and honorable man. Do not worry about me.

The tulips are in bloom. Everywhere you see them, red ones and white ones. It is otherwise so brown and dull here. Whenever I see the flowers out of the corner of my eyes I think they are little fairies dancing on the dusty brown hills. Do you remember the crocuses in Crimea? Have you seen any fairies yet?

Please write to me.

Yours,
Lilya

28

My vision of or, better still, my excursion into Lilya's life—I don't know exactly what to call it—was not dissimilar to when I felt myself slip back to my mother's city council cocktail party. I was sitting on this same couch, in front of this same mumbling television, and there was the same loss of control, and the same willingness to lose it. Only this time I slipped back much further and I returned as if from a long sojourn abroad: fatigued, ungrounded, the very air of my familiar home unfamiliar and unlived in.

This time I became Lilya, and I have come back as not quite the same Catherine who left.

I turn off the television. Sit stunned for a while. And then it really hits me. I leap off the couch and pace frantically.

Did that really just happen? Did I just become Lilya in the past?

I do not feel any doubt. It was all too fantastically real.

What else happened with Tilgar? My memory ends with Lilya's decision to marry; I can go no further. Why can I not remember? I know Lilya disappeared, but I cannot fathom how.

Natasha is the one who allows me to know. When she speaks of the past she opens up something inside me, connecting me to Lilya through her words. I need her to tell me what happens next, so that I can remember it.

My conclusion sends me into a frenzy. I can't bear to wait another week to see Natasha and find out what happened. How could I possibly wait in this state of agitation? I *have* to know. Nothing else matters. If Lilya's story is incomplete, then so am I. It is an irrational thought, but I cannot rationalize it.

I call Natasha. I never call her. She is surprised to hear from me. I ask her if I can come by the next day, in the morning. She doesn't ask me why and I don't tell her. She probably hears the impatience in my voice, probably thinks I have some important news to tell her.

29

I tell her right away that I hope I am not disturbing her, that I just had to speak with her.

"Not at all, darling. I love to see you," she says. "Let's make some coffee. I haven't had any yet. I was waiting for you."

Immediately I am guilty. I can barely contain myself and here she just wants company.

I wish I could still my unquiet mind, but I learned long ago that my mind cannot be stilled by wishing alone, especially not when it comes to unsolved mysteries.

I wait for the coffee. I try to make pleasant chit-chat; it has never come naturally to me, and certainly doesn't today. We discuss her bridge game the previous evening; she tells me some of the residents here aren't so bad, after all. They are "tolerable." She asks me if I've had breakfast and I lie and say I have. She makes herself some toast. She's eaten, but is still hungry.

"I still don't like bread in this country," she says. "It took me years to accept it, that a person could consider this breakfast."

She has thrown me off my track, and I ask, "But ... aren't there good bakers in the city? I mean, couldn't you find some decent European breads?"

"Oh, yes. But then I met your grandfather."

This does not seem to follow. I have nothing to say, and cannot help imagining what he was like. I have utterly lost sight of why I came.

"When did you meet him? How? Had you been here long?"

Natasha finishes her toast and wipes her mouth. She is casual, almost too casual, close to indifferent.

"Oh, about five years. I had already studied English, and done some university studies, so I just enrolled at the city college and kept studying English, and that's where I met him. I had no friends, and still had a big accent, and there was Andrew, a fellow student. He liked my accent. I liked him. He was easy to be with."

Natasha shrugs.

"And?" I prod. "And? You haven't told me any of this. I can't imagine you with a big accent."

Her accent was almost absent, but for certain vowels. She sounded like a native speaker most of the time. Only the occasional oddly constructed sentence or unusal word choice gave her away.

"What's there to tell? We moved to the suburbs where all they had was sliced white bread! It's not interesting, dear. At that point my life became pretty much the same as any other American woman of the time. We got married and had a child. My husband worked all week and played golf on weekends. I raised our daughter and learned to cook hamburgers."

"But, I remember your friends—you used to go out a lot. You even took dance lessons, didn't you? Ballroom dancing? I thought you were adventurous!"

"Hardly, Catherine. I was just doing whatever we did then. Someone had an idea to do ballroom dancing so we did it. Really my life has been predictable in this country. I am not complaining. Being married to Andrew was like ..." Natasha falls silent. Her face wears a blank look of concentration, devoid of emotion.

"It was comfortable like putting on a warm coat after hours of feeling chilly. Comfort is not exciting, though, is it? You don't go around desperately searching for the perfect warm coat—you just need one, don't you? And once you've got it, you take it for granted. You don't realize it was the perfect one."

Natasha frowns.

I feel like I've intruded on an intimate moment. That's ridiculous. She is freely offering me her thoughts. I stroke her arm.

"You fell in love with Andrew, didn't you? I've never thought about it before, really. You had an entire life with him."

"Yes, we did have an entire life. Sometimes I cry. Of course, I laugh too."

I can't help but laugh at that. "What do you mean?"

"Look at me! How can a person go from Leningrad to Crimea to the life of an American housewife, to this? This apartment? This home, alone? It's not one lifetime, it's many!"

Natasha's words have reminded me why I'm here. She is smiling now, so I have to ask while we're on a good note. "Natasha, I need to know what happened next. After Lilya decided to marry Refat. I'm so sorry, Natasha. I love to see you, but I couldn't wait!"

"Oh, dear, I knew it had to be something urgent for you to be back so soon. Don't you worry about it. For goodness sakes, you could have told me over the phone and saved yourself the trip."

"But I enjoy your company!" I protest, now even more guilty. The truth is, of course, there is alchemy in her presence; hearing her voice through a little plastic hand piece couldn't possibly achieve the same effect!

"That's nice, darling. I enjoy your company, too. I do hope you'll keep coming to visit me from now on, though."

"What do you mean?"

"Now that the story is over."

I can see her holding her breath for my response. I just don't get it.

"In Refat's first letter to me he wrote that not long before they were due to marry, Lilya went to the market one day and just never came home. No one saw her there, and no one ever saw her again. So that, my dear, is the end of my story."

This is where it ends? I cannot comprehend how that can be. I ask Natasha, again, what happened next. She says she really doesn't know, though she might know something else soon if Refat learned more during his recent trip to Uzbekistan.

I am the one who should know—I am the one who has relived Lilya's life so far. I am angry that my mind draws a blank. Without Natasha's voice carrying me away, without this room, this coffee, her little cakes and cookies and secret cigarettes, how will I ever go further? Natasha says it's over for now, that we know all we can know. She reminds me that Refat will be in town soon, tantalizes me with what he may have discovered. Anyway, she says, meanwhile life carries us on even when we fight it.

"What do you mean? Who is fighting?" I ask her.

"You. Get back to your life, my dear. Enough tales of troubles that should have been laid to rest long ago." She mutters under her breath, so that I can barely hear it (but as if I am meant to), "Refat should take that advice, too."

Natasha rises from her chair. She opens the sliding glass door. I pull my sweater up around my neck. She smiles, breathes deeply.

"There now," she says. She glides over to the table, moves the flowers to the bookshelf in one swift motion. What is this lightness in her? Where did it come from? I get up and close the door. She opens the cabinet and brings out a pad, some colored pencils.

"What is going on?" I ask her. "You are so happy, suddenly. Not that there's anything wrong with that ..."

"Oh, Catherine. I am relieved. I've carried it around inside me for so long. When Susan died, it seemed the cruelest twist of fate, another loss before I had properly dealt with this one. Now that I've told you about Refat and Lilya, suddenly the pressure is gone! It is a surprise to me as well. I'm sorry that I've given it to you, this sad story, darling, but I had to give it to someone."

I am uncomprehending, shell-shocked, and there she is, drawing something. Her eyes are so clear.

"Go on, now. I'll see you next week. You know, you are my hope, Catherine. I think you'll have a long life, that you will be with a man you adore. I am not certain of most things, but I have a good feeling about this. I think that it has taken three generations to heal. To have one love, and no regrets."

She says nothing else and it takes me awhile to grasp what she's said. Then I get it. It is so simple.

Her losses began with Refat, then Lilya, then my grandfather, then my mother, and they end with me. Because I'm the one who lives.

Alive and unresolved. More than that, I am a total basket-case. Catherine, two generations removed from Natasha Matveeva, may have a long, love-filled life ahead of her, but right now the shit is hitting the fan.

I drive home in a cold sweat, and collapse on my bed when I get there.

There is no stopping the images that come, that hurl me into a cinema of short takes, visions and vignettes one after the other. White limestone cliffs that plunge into azure. A long table. Pastures. Voices laughing, shouting—a table laden with food, relatives of all sizes, their gaiety echoing through a low-ceilinged room, out windows. A white bulb drooping heavily from a tree, pregnant with life and destined to die. Trains racing through the desert. The smell of death. Loss. Sleeping on the cold earth and walking to market in the blazing heat. Wanting to escape. Wanting to live. Tilgar.

My memory is dense with ghosts that I cannot escape. I hear them, voices of Fevzi, Ayshe, voices I know and some I don't. They are drawing my attention across the globe to the deserts of Central Asia, to a small, empty place in Uzbekistan. They call me back to Lilya, and into the depths of myself. Then I realize I don't need Natasha to get me there after all, and I never did. I am being drawn by something else, some force beyond my comprehension.

I can see the gauze separating my reality from Lilya's; it stretches across my vision, thin and cottony. I close my eyes to the sight. Part of me is there with her already, the other part demands answers. Who am *I* in this drama?

On one side of the veil is Catherine, an American woman of unremarkable parentage. Nondescript. Hair limp and mousy brown. She once was all I could remember, but that woman is not who I am, not in my entirety. On the other side of the veil, in another dimension of space and time that is somehow unified with my own via the murky depths of consciousness, is Lilya. I lie on my bed and sail into and out of my memories and wonder. If the memory of Lilya is my memory, and I am a future dream of hers, then who is the person who can remember both lives at once? I must be that third person, not Lilya, not Catherine, but someone who at once contains and transcends them.

I fly through the veil and into Lilya, and see that I am proven correct. It is not Catherine who moves toward Lilya's life; Catherine is still there, lying on her bed in the future, succumbing to a supernatural episode. For just a moment, a tiny, easily missed segment of time flying from one mind to the next, I enter an in-between place and am neither Catherine, nor Lilya. I am the third person who contains them both.

30

February 1945

The first time Lilya met the old Uzbek woman Tilgar, she did so as a woman betrothed and a woman free. Her freedom did not mitigate the hardship of life; how could it, with the death and poverty and exhaustion that lay all around her? Lilya's Crimean Tatar brethren still lived in barracks like farm animals; children were still dying from malnutrition and accompanying diseases; the adults endured twelve-hour workdays in factories and fields; camp commandants checked up on their whereabouts and the compliance with the regime. There was no word of ever going home.

But in this soul-destroying environment, Lilya's imagination took her elsewhere: to Crimea, to the mountains she could see from this godforsaken town, to an adventurous future of out-of-body travels and the gaining of wisdom. During her small breaks at the factory (for a weak cup of tea at lunch, to pee in a hole in the ground), time seemed to stop and each moment marked an infinity. The weekend held a world of drudgery, yet she went for a walk before arriving at the market, walked slowly as she went, and took the long way home unless her load was too much to bear. And today, of course, Tilgar. Skipping her evening chores, she went into town on the pretext of finding more potatoes (which in any case were always needed, and ever scarce).

Lilya had only once before met a spiritually wise person, a highly placed Muslim cleric in Crimea when she was young. He was a guest at a family gathering and engaged Lilya in conversation. She did not recall what he had said to her, though she wished she did. She remembered vividly his air of wisdom and peace, a kind of self-satisfaction that she assumed came from having direct access to Allah. She assumed a person highly regarded in any faith would have as much wisdom. So on this day Lilya had a few assumptions and expectations—among them that the shamaness would have answers to many of life's questions, that she would share some with Lilya.

Then, when she saw the old woman standing near the entrance to Sumai's apartment building as promised, Lilya lost her courage. "She is just a crinkly-wrinkly old granny who probably engages in dubious animist rites which are highly illegal—what are you doing here anyway?" she berated herself. The old woman had none of the quiet, godly aura she had seen in the cleric, nothing of the sort.

Tilgar nodded when she saw Lilya approach, then wandered off. Lilya followed and caught up with her.

"Did you not see me?" Lilya asked awkwardly, even though she had seen the old woman nod at her.

"We have a destination," the older woman said.

"Isn't it dangerous, to be seen in public?"

Tilgar did not look at Lilya directly, but stared straight ahead as she walked.

"Those who have eyes for their world only see very little, indeed."

They would surely attract attention, Lilya thought, a young woman and an old Uzbek.

But as they walked past the buildings and further away from the town, the few people on the street seemed not to notice them, as if they were looking right past them, or through them.

Lilya looked at the old woman again and saw some of the fierce self-confidence and intensity she had witnessed at the stalls the day before. She felt a bit easier in her company and tried to formulate the many questions she had, then felt a bizarre compulsion to justify her participation in this risky endeavor.

"I'm not sure if I am mad, or if you have a strange influence on me, or if this is all some foolish mistake. But you should know that I am sensible above all else, and any interest I have in spiritualism is purely one of intellectual curiosity—"

"Is that so?" Tilgar interrupted.

"Why yes, of course. What else could it be?"

The old woman slowed her step just slightly and asked, her voice sweet and melodious, as if she were asking a favor of a small child, "But did you not stand with me upon the hill as I dared you to seek freedom from your illusions?"

"Oh!" Lilya exclaimed, recalling that strange moment at the bottom of the stairs after she had met Sumai the evening before. "The vision."

"Call it what you like."

"It was real," Lilya stated, confirming the reality of it to herself.

"Listen," Tilgar said quietly, and her words seemed to take on the tone and rhythm of a mantra or prayer, her voice rising and falling ever so slightly as she spoke, with a pause for breath at the end of each sentence,

"I have read your books and heard your radio and I know your world. But I do not live in your prison so I can see outside of it. I understand what has happened to mankind in the past centuries, and I see what is coming. Before the first World

War came I knew of the second, and now I can see the third. Before it is over the hope of my people will be lost if we do not leave this world altogether. It is only getting worse. You will never go home. Your people will return to Crimea in another fifty years, but it will not be the place you left behind. Your world holds little joy, my dear. Only those like you who seek true peace will find it."

By now Lilya was fully entranced; she felt as if she were swaying as she walked, but it was just her head that bobbed as she tried to lean closer to the old woman, who was much shorter than she and had never raised her voice loud enough to be heard even a foot away.

"My people have a prophecy. Long ago we stumbled upon a hole between worlds and left our world for this one. According to our wisdom it was an accident, if not a sin, for we left behind our one true home in the mistaken belief that we could easily return. Ever since we have suffered, knowing not how to get home. But the day will come when a shaman of our people will locate that same hole between worlds and return us to our true home. If we do not, we shall die before the third world war marks this planet for its destruction."

Lilya could not imagine how to reply, so strange was Tilgar's revelation. After a few moments she managed, "That sounds fanciful ... and intriguing." And she wondered, "Could it be true?"

There was no emotion in Tilgar's voice when she responded, "I'm not asking for your acceptance; that will come on its own. I'm telling you so that you may understand better that what you see is not all that exists in this universe."

The old woman picked up her pace, and Lilya stole a glance or two at her ancient features. She thought she detected the shamaness' sadness, but did not see how that could be. It was out of keeping with a spiritual teacher—isn't that what she was? Someone who had answers? Having the answers to life's questions surely made one joyful, Lilya thought. She dismissed the idea and waited for further instruction, until she could not help but ask, "How did you find me?"

Sumai had said that Tilgar had found her—hadn't she?

"You do not know?" Tilgar asked.

The town had given way to desert. The hills were upon them and Lilya was outside the boundaries of her settlement, in breach of regulations, flirting with a twenty-five year sentence. Yet she had no fear. Indeed, it seemed as if they were invisible, a law unto themselves.

"Why would I know?" Lilya asked.

Tilgar walked straight on and Lilya hurried to stay at her side. For an old woman she was fast. The air was hot and breezeless.

"The Guide brought you to me. Did he not tell you to come with him? And did you not follow him to me, in the market, that day?"

"Guide? What guide? I met Sumai ..." then Lilya stopped talking to think, and climbed the first hill after the old woman. The man in the woods on that winter night. With the amulet. She only later remembered he had said something to her: "Come with me." Did Tilgar mean to imply that this man was a guide, that he had meant for Lilya to come to Uzbekistan and find her? Was that possible?

"But I had no choice to come here!" Lilya exclaimed. "I was forced against my will! It was a travesty! A crime!"

"Shhhh," Tilgar said, leading her down the hill now, toward a tree. "Of course, of course. Destiny leads us too, you know. Even if against our will. Even if unfairly. Sit under this tree, sit in the shade. I will sing for you."

Lilya did as she was told and Tilgar began to sing.

It was not a language Lilya knew; it was not Uzbek, nothing at all Turkic. The words were not beautiful, they clicked and bumped, but the melody was nice and Lilya was suddenly tired. They had not in all probability come that far today after all, but it felt as if they had been walking for hours. Lilya sat and watched the sky, the uninterrupted blue, as Tilgar stood nearby swaying and singing her strange song. "The man with the amulet," Lilya thought, "maybe he was a ghost after all, and, invisible, he brought me to the shamaness." The melody of Tilgar's song wound its way around her like a heavy net, and Lilya felt her eyes drifting shut, then she felt the old woman's hand on her arm, her neck, her forehead, and she experienced surrender. She was unconscious, yet aware. Perfectly comfortable. Lulled by the song, Lilya slept and knew she slept, the shamaness beside her, now whispering her magical song into her ear.

"Open your eyes now," she commanded.

Lilya opened them.

The scene before her was breathtaking. Below her were hills so green and lush she instantly wanted to roll down them as she had done in Crimea as a child; in the center was a lake of dazzling blue water and as she peered, attentively, she could see fish, and plants, and the shimmering white of pebbles. All around the lake were fir trees, and orange and lemon and apricot trees drooping with fruit, and a large outcropping of rock on one side perfect for sitting on or diving off of.

"Is it Crimea?" Lilya asked. Though she'd never seen this place before, she could not imagine such beauty could exist elsewhere. She noticed that the shamaness was not with her, that she was standing, alone, at the bottom of a hill just yards from the water. "Why can I not see you here?" Lilya asked.

"It is your home," Tilgar said, "existing inside you, for you to visit when you need to rest."

"Is it real?"

"It is the best representation of reality your mind can remember at this time," she said.

"Why are you showing me this?" Lilya asked.

"It is your birthright to know. I am only helping one who asked for help."

It seemed to Lilya that she spent ages at the lake, alone, washing her feet in the water, watching the sky and the trees, drinking in the scene like oxygen. Yet at some point she felt a tug and turned her back on the lake, and darkness enveloped her and she spun, fell, and slowly woke up to her other reality—where it was still evening. Not much time could have passed at all.

For several seconds Lilya sat under the tree, adjusting her eyes to the light, to the sight of Tilgar, to this reality. She did not know if it was awe or fear that moved her. She said, "I should go now," but she wanted at the same time to beg for another visit to that place.

Tilgar sat next to her, staring placidly into the distance.

"You go. No one will see you, I promise."

"Is that your magic?" she meant their apparent invisibility.

"It is my will."

"Will we meet again?"

"Oh, yes."

Lilya tried to gauge Tilgar's expression. One would never think, to see her, that she had such abilities. She looked liked any other world-weary old woman marooned on a park bench waiting for life to run out.

"Do you have any questions?" Tilgar asked Lilya.

Lilya said, "Just—one thing. Why did the Guide bring me to you? Why me?"

Tilgar shrugged. "You were seeking wisdom. He knew where you could find it."

"But what am I to do for you in return?"

When the shamaness smiled, as she did now, her smile erased her age, her wrinkles became laugh-lines.

"In every student lives a teacher. Who knows what I might learn from you!"

Before Tilgar could transform back into a crone she began to shoo Lilya away. "Go, go! Meet me in a week's time in the same place. We will walk."

Lilya took with her doubt, awe, a tinge of fear (though diminishing), and joy. She savored the memory of the lake and the green rolling hills. She no longer could say for sure which world was more real, or even what it meant that she was here one minute and there the next. The only constant was her, she realized, and she began to question who, or what on earth, she was.

31

There is a message from Elisa on my answering machine. Actually, I am home when she calls, and listen as she speaks. She says that her boyfriend has accepted a post in the city, so he will be moving in with her. That is to say, she won't be around here much anymore, except periodically to visit her parents. She leaves me her number in the city again (she says I should have it, and I probably do, stuffed away somewhere), and tells me to call her sometime when I'm there.

It is not particularly newsworthy to me that her man is leaving town. It is as if she is using his job change as an excuse for telling me that we needn't see one another anymore. As if either of us needed an excuse.

I don't really understand how people change so much that they lose one another. I sometimes wonder if I will ever find that kind of friendship again, or if it only ever happens in school when we're unformed and fragile, before we put up walls. With this thought fresh in my mind, as if enough weird things haven't already happened in my life, through the window I see Sam Hunter walking down my quiet, suburban, tree-lined street as if he were any other yuppie going for a walk on a weekend. I go outside to await his arrival.

"I assume you're heading this way?" I ask him as he turns into my driveway.

"Catherine!" his face lights up, "I've come by a few times and you haven't been home."

"Why didn't you leave a note?"

"I have too much to say," he says.

We're already walking inside, he's right on my heels. We're like Lilya and Natasha would have been, like Elisa and I were when we were kids after two weeks apart when one or the other was at summer camp. "So charming and affecting," I think. How is it that this man has gotten through my emotional barricades? It is a mystery to me, but I recognize that whatever it is I've found is as special as what I've lost, and I am grateful for Sam's friendship. Sam is hardly through the front door and he's pacing to and fro like he's lost and needs someone to sit him down.

"You can sit," I laugh at his agitation.

"I can't, I'm too ... I'm just too full of nerves."

"I have something to tell you, too," I say. I can hardly wait to tell him about my visions—he, of all people, is sure to have some insight.

"I don't want to be rude," he says, "but I think I have to say something first."

His combination of Southern drawl and unnecessary politeness makes me want to giggle. Sam does not wait for me to turn on the lights, or get us a drink, or even sit down. He begins to speak, glancing at me first for approval, which I silently give him—I bite my tongue and try to serve as an example, by sitting down at the kitchen table. He is still pacing in the living room.

"You really opened up a can of worms!" he exclaims.

"Oh I did, did I?" I ask.

"It's infected my dreams," he says. "I don't have any direction! I've never thought about before, until I met you. I think Fred was hinting at it, but I was just too dense to get it—"

He is so agitated he bumps into the side table, knocking it against the couch. He rights it and continues to pace.

"Fred?" I ask.

"The ex-Catholic priest. He went on and on about the mundane world, about how a spiritual person tries to extend himself beyond it, but must be in it, and I didn't get it. I didn't get it at all, but then you started saying all that stuff about what was I doing with my life and what was my goal, enlightenment or what. It made me think. That is always the goal, in any life, but that doesn't mean there isn't anything else. My dreams have been telling me, all this time."

"Dare I ask what exactly enlightenment is?" I interrupt him.

"Catherine, that's a big subject, I don't want to lose my train of thought. Look," he gives me a guilty look, "to summarize, not that something like that can be summarized, but it's basically the realization that we are one with God, the universe, whatever."

"Whatever," I say. I can see my sarcasm has been noted. "I didn't mean to interrupt."

"The thing is, I'm not sure I can get to enlightenment without working out some things first. Like why I'm here, in this body, in this life."

"It's not to be enlightened?"

"Yes, but how? Everyone is different, right? With different life circumstances, different choices to make. We all take different paths, don't we? I'm not a carpenter or a stockbroker, am I? I'm out there seeking wise people, travelling, studying, practicing devotion. My path is particular. I think it's starting to make sense. Of course there has to be more to my life than just this. I think everything I've learned so far has brought me to this point!"

Sam stops. He comes to join me at the table, sits quietly for a moment. He appears ecstatic, on the verge of revelation. I lean forward. I wait. He says nothing and his expression shifts.

"What do you mean?" I ask. "Are you okay?"

"When I first started out, it was just a leap of faith. When I decided to explore my own spirituality, to pay attention to my dreams and follow them, I had been living a fairly normal life. Not that strange things had never happened to me. But I was from a small town in the South, and there was nothing special about my background. Well, my grandmother was psychic and I'd had some strange experiences—"

"That's a pretty big caveat to this supposed normalcy of yours," I say.

"Okay, yes, there were some unusual things that happened to me. I had a recurring dream that turned out to be precognitive, for example. But what I mean is that my family was not religious. I never went to church and spirituality was just not something we talked about much—I was not prepared for the life I was to lead."

Sam says after a moment, "I went to college. It was just a small community college, but I did really well. The professors thought I should carry on, get a graduate degree at a state school, but I didn't want to study anymore. I wanted to live in the world. The problem was, there was nothing in the world that interested me, as a career I mean. Anyway, so I chose this path. The first person I met was Robert Sherman. I had a dream to go to this huge reservation, in the desert, and so I followed it. It took me a few months. I had dreamt of this old man with long white hair, and I had to ask around a while. It was really weird at first, you know? Telling people I was looking for an old white-haired Indian who lived in the desert and had a fox. But, synchronicity happens in this kind of life, and almost as soon as I found the Navajo Nation I met a man who said there was a mystic in this one settlement who had a fox as his totem and matched my descriptions. I had no idea what a totem was. The language was all new to me, and the concepts. I didn't know what I was doing, I just followed my instincts.

"So I found Bob Sherman. He was a Navajo. It wasn't like I thought. It's a beautiful country, but you can just see how people really struggle with poverty and alcoholism. The federal government set up legalized gambling there to improve things, but according to Bob things have only gotten worse with unemployment and so on. I didn't expect the place to be so big with so many people, either. There are twenty-five thousand square miles in the Navajo Nation, a reservation with portions in three states. There are like almost three hundred thousand Navajos—which is all to say that it was more than just a fluke that I found Bob.

"He lived in a trailer at the edge, and pretty much kept to himself, except for the women who came to him for love potions."

Sam rolls his eyes. "When I got there and asked where to find him, most people told me he was crazy, and if I hadn't dreamt about him I would have thought so too. When I found him he was smoking pot. He only had on shorts and he had a beer belly like this," Sam laughs, gesturing to imitate Bob's girth. "What a sight. Anyway, I told him who I was, and that I had dreamt of him with a fox. He got a devilish look in his eyes and said, 'So it's you. I've been expecting you. Now, take off your clothes and put them here.'"

"He said *what*?" I say.

"Take off your clothes. I said that wasn't what I thought I'd be doing, and he asks me, 'So what did you think you'd be doing?' I said I didn't know, and he said, 'Well, then, take off your clothes. If it makes you feel better, I'll take off mine too.' And he did. Just like that.

"It was a hundred degrees outside, so I wasn't worried about being cold, only sunburned. I stood around for a while thinking about it, and finally it dawned on me that I wasn't in control here. I mean, he'd come to me in a dream, right? And I fully expected him to know better—in my dream he was clearly a wise man, even if here he looked like a doped up eccentric. What the hell else was I going to do after spending months searching for him? So I took off my clothes."

"Wow. Some initiation."

"It gets better. We didn't do much the first day. We cooked dinner. To say I was self-conscious is the understatement of the century. All I could think about was my penis, his penis, was he looking at mine, and how could I not look at his? It was just terrible."

I start to giggle. Soon I'm laughing so hard I have tears coming out of my eyes, and Sam's no better. It takes a few minutes to calm down, before Sam continues, a cheeky grin stuck to his face.

"Fortunately, Bob lived at the edge of his little town like I said. There was no one else around. I slept in a sleeping bag outside his trailer. The next day we just hung out, literally."

We both giggle.

"I asked could I put my clothes back on and he said no. He didn't either. We didn't do much. He asked me about myself, I helped him cook. We stayed in the shade all day long. I smoked pot for the first time in my life. Didn't much like it. After a day I was used to being naked. Not comfortable, mind you, but accustomed to it. Then on my second naked day he asked me to go into the settlement to get some things from the shop. I asked him where my clothes were. He shrugged. There was no way I was going to go anywhere else naked, and I said so. So he said he'd come with me."

"This is unbelievable," I say.

"You're telling me. I was not the most popular guy in school. I was used to not being noticed. I was good at not being noticed. It was something else to have everyone, I mean *everyone*, staring at me. I thought we'd be arrested. But no, people looked, then looked away. A few people called out to Bob. I guessed it wasn't the first time he'd been naked. I wanted to just hide I was so embarrassed. I told myself that I'd give it a few more days, and if by the end of it the only wisdom I'd learned is that I could hang out with an eccentric old Indian in my birthday suit and feel comfortable, I'd move on.

"The next day was the same. Into town for the shopping. Hanging out. I was determined to give it another day and then go. The only problem was, I hadn't dreamt at all since I'd been there, so I didn't know where to go next. I started to get depressed—here I'd decided to learn about my spirituality and follow my dreams, had had a really specific one about a wise old man, had spent considerable time and effort finding him, and at the end of the day I was naked and not the least bit wiser."

I can't stop myself from laughing again. I decide it's time for coffee, so I tell Sam to continue while I make a pot. I rummage around in the cabinets and come up with crackers, and bring cheese from the fridge. He keeps talking, in between mouthfuls of cheese and crackers—he eats like he's starving, like he's forgotten to eat all day.

"I guess about the fourth day of being naked I stopped caring about anything except getting away. I decided I'd leave the next morning. Bob was a nice enough guy. He had interesting tales to tell of riding around the country on a motorcycle, of once when the local police came and searched him for drugs. He was colorful, but not the wise man I'd expected.

"So night came around and I declined his offer to have some beers, and I went to sleep. In the middle of the night he woke me up and told me to come quick and follow him. I was so sleepy I just went. He handed me a blanket to wrap around myself since it was the desert and it was cool outside. We were both barefoot. We started walking. We were walking away from the reservation into the desert. The moon was full enough to see somewhat. It looked like we were heading toward canyons through nothing but scrub. My feet were starting to ache and get all scratched up, and I was getting grumpy. The weird thing was, I didn't once ask him where we were going, or why. I just followed him like a sheep. I don't even know how long we walked. Hours, though it was still dark when we got to where we were going—which was a cave in a canyon.

"He led me inside and there were others all around, all naked, men and women, wearing masks. There was a fire in the middle. We went to sit in a circle, and no one talked, and nothing happened for a while. I was beginning to wonder what was going on when a woman got up and started dancing. She wore the mask of a wolf, and her hair was all matted and thick and wild, and she was dancing and howling. I didn't know what was happening, and the energy there was weird, you know, very intense and I was getting nervous. At least it was more like what I'd imagined, right? Yet I had no idea what was going on and Bob said nothing, and it wasn't exactly the right time to ask.

"The wolf-woman kept dancing, then everyone started to sing. I was tired by then, and confused, and I couldn't take my eyes off the fire. At some point I became mesmerized by the fire, and the woman dancing, and the singing, and I seemed to go into some strange state of consciousness. It's weird, I can't even describe it, it was like a trance. Before I knew it Bob had pushed me forward into the circle, and he yanked the blanket right off me. I looked around to see where he'd gone and he wasn't there. Right where he had been sitting was a fox! It should have clicked. I should have thought it was his spirit animal. You may know that Native Americans have animal spirits that guide them? Supposedly we all resonate with a particular animal and its energy can be supportive if we're open to it."

I have heard something about it, and nod him on.

"Anyway, at the time my thoughts were all muddy, and I was feeling higher than a kite, and there was this fox staring at me and naked people dancing and then whoosh! In flew a hawk that landed right at my feet. It looked me right in the eye and I felt this strange kinship with it. Then it stepped closer and closer and I swear to God it had walked right into my body. I could feel it going in beak first through my abdomen, and it hurt like hell! Bob's voice spoke right into my ear then, and he told me, 'The true shaman is unadorned, Sammy. His body is merely the clothes his spirit wears to look human. Now your spirit animal is with you.' I thought he was gone and that I was losing consciousness, when he whispered, 'I certainly hope that you now expect the unexpected.'"

Sam goes quiet. The crackers and cheese are gone, and the coffee is still percolating. All I can say is "Wow," and respect the solemnity that seems suddenly to have come over him.

"After that I can't say what happened. I either passed out or fell asleep. When I woke up it was light and I was alone just inside this cave. Wearing nothing, I might add, but a blanket. And there was a hawk sitting not five feet from me. It flew off, and I followed it." Sam shrugs. "It sounds crazy, but that's what happened. It took me across the desert for a day until I came upon another settlement, and then I met someone else. Though I got to wear clothes after that."

"I won't even ask what kind of reception you got, showing up naked and barefoot."

"And painfully sunburned, I might add. I spent the rest of the summer in the shade. That was my first experience with shamanism. What I learned was that I had to have no expectations, to give myself up to the experience. What happened with Bob didn't make a lot of sense until later, and even then, I was still learning. From that moment on I made a decision that I would just trust the journey. I never really thought about a destination, I just followed my dreams and intuition."

I think it doesn't make sense at all. I would have stopped then, before it got even more weird and nonsensical. Clearly it was a pivotal experience in Sam's life, though, and who am I to judge? I fill two mugs with coffee and bring them to the table, along with milk and sugar for Sam. I'm settling in for another long afternoon and evening with him. I'm even wondering what we can have for dinner, then decide we'll order in.

"Are you warm enough?" I ask him. "I'll turn the heat up."

"They call me the Dreamer, Catherine. That's what they all call me."

His words stop me in my tracks. They ring a bell, but I can't be sure.

"Who call you that?"

"The teachers I've met since Bob. Victor called me that, too, in a dream."

I rush to adjust the thermostat and am back in my chair before he's said another word. He is evidently preoccupied, but has lost the nervous energy he arrived with. My excitement seems to be rising on the other hand; I can't wait to tell him about Lilya and my visions. But I savor the wait. I enjoy his company, even in silence, watching Sam bite his lower lip and pour milk into his coffee. When he speaks again he's looking distractedly beyond me into mid-air.

"Shamans believe that every soul has two tasks in any physical life: to construct the physical reality that surrounds us, and to develop the inner self that must live in the outer world. If you concentrate on the outer life to the exclusion of the inner life, you are like the proverbial rich man who is surrounded by wealth and privilege but is miserable. If you concentrate on the inner life you are like Siddhartha before he became Buddha. At the beginning of his journey he believed that he had to deny his body sustenance in order to overcome the physical body and experience pure spirit. He did not eat or drink until he was so weak he couldn't think straight. Finally he realized that deprivation was not the way to reach enlightenment, that without a strong physical body the mind lacks the clarity needed to experience spiritual insights."

Sam takes a breath, and asks for a glass of water.

I get up to get us both water, and ask him, "So, are you saying you think you've focused too much on your inner journey? That you've been neglecting yourself in some way?"

"Maybe I'm not finding the balance," he says. He looks dispirited. "I thought I was close to understanding, but maybe I'm not. Do you know what the truth is? It's that I don't know if I am looking for enlightenment. I could tell you all about it, we could talk for ages about what people have experienced, what the Buddhists think, and the Christians, and the Native Americans, but I'm not sure it can even be described. I don't know that I'll know what it is until I experience it, so how can I say what exactly I'm aiming for? Remember the initiation I told you about?"

"The naked one? Or when you told yourself to go on this path—I mean, a part of your consciousness appeared to you?"

"The second one."

"Right. I'm still not sure I understand that part."

"It's not so much conceptual as experiential, Catherine."

If his tone of voice weren't so kind I might think he was being impatient or patronizing. Maybe it's his Southern accent again. I have the feeling he's figured me out, somehow. That he knows I need a challenge.

"Okay, I think I get it. You mean the experience of encountering someone you recognized as being somehow part of yourself is what matters."

Sam smiles, almost indulgently, but not unkindly.

"Yes. His message is why it mattered. Of course, I believe it actually happened literally. By the way, if you're looking for proof of my sanity—"

"I'm not, Sam," I reassure him.

"Good, because there is no proof," he laughs. "But don't tie your mind in knots over literal interpretations. The main thing is, my experiences are leading me to some kind of better self-understanding. Anyway, I was told—by this aspect of myself—that I had to follow my dreams wherever they took me, but the advice was more specific than that. I was told that I'd meet someone who would guide me to the next step in my journey. I have. I've met lots of people who've guided me. And there's no doubt it's been a journey. But the journey has become the end, so to speak. I've just assumed that my journey was about the unfolding of wisdom, and my role was just to seek it. There's just one thing I guess I had forgotten about, until now. Actually, until I met you."

I sit up straight in my chair, and raise an eyebrow.

"I have a weird question for you," Sam says then.

I laugh, despite myself.

"You're hilarious, Sam. You have a weird question, do you? *That* would be new. Just one?"

"All right, I know it's all a bit strange. But this one's actually not as weird as it is random."

"Well, I don't remember ever being abducted by aliens if that's what you want to know."

"Me either, yet." Sam takes a sip of water, and becomes solemn. "Catherine, is there—I don't know how to say this right—um …" he takes another sip of water. "Is there any symbol that has meaning for you?"

"What? Like one I like in particular?"

"It could be."

"Not that I can think of. I'm sure when I was a teenager I wore ankhs and peace signs and stuff, but so did every other teenage girl I knew."

"There's nothing else you can think of, I mean, some symbol you've seen or had around the house?"

"No. Sorry. Why? What does it mean?"

"It's just, in my vision I was told that someone in particular would guide me, and that I would know the person by a particular symbol."

I shrug. "So maybe you're looking for the Artist Formerly Known as Prince?"

"Huh?" He looks dumbfounded.

"Oh, Sam. See? Too much inner work. You're obviously neglecting pop culture. No wonder you feel you're out of balance."

"Never mind," he sighs. "Maybe I'm grasping at straws. It's just that it really seems that something is going on here. I always assumed my life was about the journey, but now I feel that maybe I have some specific task to carry out too. Like I'm supposed to be here, and having this conversation, and that I'm supposed to be doing something next, with your help. Victor's not here, but you are. And I turned up here, this was the house I saw in my dreams, not his. Do you have a piece of paper and a pencil?"

"Sure." I go to the telephone on the kitchen counter and take the pad and pencil back to Sam.

"Might as well," he mumbles. "Here," he draws something and slides it across the table to me. "That's the symbol I've dreamt about. Have you ever seen it before?"

"Hmm," I say, taking a sip of coffee. "It does look familiar."

And then I gag, nearly spitting out my coffee. I stare and stare at it, mesmerized: the necklace the man in the woods wore in Crimea, the necklace Lilya saw. The symbol I remembered, that my grandmother knew nothing of.

Sam's eyes go big and round. A grin spreads across his face.

"You know it, don't you!" he exclaims.

"And it gets even weirder," I say.

After a pot of coffee, Chinese takeout, and some hours, I've told him all about Lilya. I tell him that I've researched the possibilities, that my memory of Lilya is so uncanny that it can only be explained by shared consciousness.

I tell Sam that I think I might be the reincarnation of Lilya Bekirova.

The words don't sound as silly as I've feared, and he receives them with a chuckle.

"Isn't it your feeling that matters most?" he asks. "If you don't doubt your experience, I would say that's exactly what has happened. The vast majority of the world's population believes in reincarnation. There's even some proof Jesus taught it, that Christians believed in it until the Church destroyed some early texts that made reference to it."

"So, in your experience, it is possible?" I ask.

"It's likely."

I stare at the symbol Sam drew.

"You know, when my mother got sick and we knew she wasn't going to make it, it was like, everything I thought I was sure about suddenly I wasn't sure about at all. Life didn't seem to be a sure thing anymore. I'm not saying it very well."

"You're saying it fine," Sam encourages me.

"Reality started to go fuzzy." I look at Sam full on. "Now reality is taking a different shape altogether. Past life memories, shamanic initiations. At least it's solid! Life feels nothing if not real."

"Do you ever dream of your mother?" Sam asks.

"No."

"I'm sure she's around, Catherine. Looking out for you. Souls often stay behind to help the living."

"What if she has something better to do?" I ask, half-joking. "But maybe you're right."

Sam reaches out and takes my hand. I appreciate his effort to comfort me, but physical contact makes me squirm. I smile wanly and take my hand away to push my hair back behind my ears.

"We had a complicated relationship," I say, "my mother and I. I hope she does know, somehow, about all this stuff that's happening to me. She would be excited. She was into this sort of thing. Well, at least she had some sort of metaphysical belief system to make sense of it."

Sam is listening so patiently that it's like he's egging me on with his quiet stare. I wish he would say something to change the subject, since now I feel almost compelled to keep talking.

"The day my mother died, I saw Victor Tehusa in the garden. Life has just been getting more and more interesting ever since."

Sam chuckles. "I'm sure you did see him. Victor's not the kind of soul who just passes over."

I don't say it, but I think it loud and clear: "What if Susan is that kind of soul?"

"Do you believe in Heaven?" I ask Sam.

"Yes, I just don't think you go there on a one-way ticket."

"I see. So you think souls are free to come and go."

"Of course."

"Do you really think Victor sent you to meet me?"

"I'm sure of it. I dreamt of *this* house."

"It's weird, you know, because he's had a couple of pieces of mail sent to him at this address. He's been dead for more than five years and I've never gotten mail for him. I don't actually know what to do with it. As far as I know his relatives still own the house and they used to stay there every once in a while and do some gardening. But I can't remember the last time I saw them. I don't have any way to reach them, either."

I suddenly have the compulsion to go fetch Victor's mail from the basket in the front hall.

I've never even looked at them closely. One is a package, the other a letter. I look at the package first, and see something I never expected under the name Victor Tehusa:

"[re: the Dreamer]"

I pull out the letter and see that it says the same thing.

"Look," I say, handing them to Sam.

He mumbles, "Oh, my ..."

"It's you, isn't it?" I ask.

"Well, I don't know what to make of it."

"Take them," I say. "Since you're the Dreamer, and Victor called you that in a dream. It's probably not entirely ethical, but he's dead, and I don't know what else to do with his mail. Just take them."

Sam stares at the package and the letter. He folds his hands across them.

"So what happens next?" I say.

He shrugs.

"I don't know how to invoke the visions, or whatever they are. I don't know how Lilya disappeared. I need to know."

I don't expect a reply and I don't get one. I am alone in this.

Sam goes, with Victor's mail under his arm, promising we'll meet again very soon. As usual we make no firm plans in that regard, but it doesn't matter. I know we'll just find each other again like we have so far.

32

Natasha calls me the next morning. I'm groggy and not expecting the phone to ring at 8 AM. I haven't even gotten out of bed, much less had any coffee. I don't recognize her voice.

"Who is it?" I groan.

"It's me, dear. Your grandmother. Good morning."

I ask her what day it is—am I due at her place this afternoon? She reminds me that it is Monday, then asks, "Please come with me to a talk tonight. It's lecture series night, and tonight it's on near-death experiences."

"On *what*?" I ask. I sit up and pull the covers around me. I am far from clear-headed, but unwilling to leave the warm bed.

"Near-death experiences."

"Lecture series?" I mumble, more to myself than to Natasha. I seem to remember her going to a bridge club. What is going on with her social life?

"Yes. I am not a hermit, Catherine. I thought you might like to go with me."

But she always has been a hermit, or so I thought. I *like* her hermit ways, and I think I need it today. My mind is a blur of otherworldly remembrances and metaphysical discussions and I feel sorely in need of predictable company, friendly companionship. Since she has no more to say on her past, we can settle into the present, eat sandwiches and chat, or even say nothing, just enjoy each other's company. I switch on the bedside lamp and try to remember what I have planned today. Nothing. The fog of sleep lifts. What am I thinking? She just said she is going to a talk on near-death experiences, as if I need more of this kind of thing! I cannot even breathe my reluctance before Natasha has agreed to the time of our meeting, and hangs up abruptly.

She meets me at her front door and promptly shuts it behind her.

"I didn't even know you had a lecture series," I say.

"Once a month. They are sometimes interesting."

"You go to them?" I ask. I do not bother to conceal my shock.

"A few lately. On different topics. Let's see … there was one a few weeks ago on feminist literature."

"Are the residents interested in that?"

"Why not? Not that they know what feminism is, but they'll go to anything around here."

We have made it to the end of the hall and Natasha is breathless. She is walking quickly and looking at her watch.

"Did you ... enjoy the lecture?" I cannot bring myself to ask what is to me the obvious question—what does Natasha know about feminism? As stereotypical as it might be, my impression is that women of her generation had for so long been kept out of the public arena that they not only did not know what the feminist revolution was, but did not particularly care.

"I did enjoy it. Though I don't like Jane Austen."

"Natasha!"

"Yes?"

I don't know why I've exclaimed like that, and fall dumbly silent.

"Were there any feminists among you?" I joke.

"Just me, I'm afraid."

I am astonished.

"You're a *what*? I don't even call myself that!"

"Why not? An intelligent, educated woman of your time should be proud to call herself a feminist."

Now we are downstairs, walking toward the main entrance. Off to one side is a conference room where the lecture will be held.

"Well, it's not that I'm not a feminist," I say defensively, "I just don't see myself as an activist."

Natasha sighs. "It's not about activism, though, is it darling. Anyway, here we are," she says as we arrive in the conference room. The oddity of Natasha-the-feminist falls away. The room is filled to capacity with old people. For a moment I feel out of place, and I am, but then, I realize, so is she.

She whispers, "Just look at them all!" as if she is not one of her contemporaries. One could be forgiven for thinking that she is not.

Dressed in black, with a bright red scarf, she looks formal and sophisticated, if overly serious. Natasha rarely wears black, and I have to wonder if she is mocking her peers and the topic of the seminar. Probably so. I'm not sure if it is the loud earrings (busy gold baubles), or her expression—a combination of self-satisfaction and bemusement. She stumbles a bit on the carpet, at which point I notice her high heels. I had no idea she still wore them, and more surprising, that even at her age they look good with her slim ankles and slender, long legs.

A middle-aged woman stands at the front of the room and tells us she is about to begin. She is, she introduces herself, the author of a book on near-death experiences, and has had a few herself. I am, admittedly, more curious about Natasha's interest than in the actual topic at hand. I remember only too well from earlier that she has an interest in death, or at least angels. Still, I am surprised by her insistence that I attend with her today. So far I have not had a chance to ask why we are here.

The audience is eager—years of experience ensure I know the signs immediately—quiet murmuring, fidgeting, and, when the speaker says "Hello," rapt silence.

"My name is Joan," the speaker begins, "and five years ago I was in a car accident. The paramedics pronounced me dead as I floated above their heads. That's when I finally realized that my body is just a vehicle."

We are all hypnotized before she even mentions the white light, angels, spirits of dead relatives, and the hundreds of people she's interviewed since her accident. Natasha and I sit through an hour or more of Joan's talk before question time begins—by which time I have forgotten all about why I am there. It is fascinating, I must admit, never mind what brain chemistry might be producing these near-death experiences, or if they may be, in fact, real. My mind drifts to Lilya, and I have to catch myself from tumbling into that memory—of Uzbekistan and Tilgar. I refocus on something in the room—Joan's earring, just barely visible from our third row seat. I think I have had enough of weird states of consciousness. The synchronicity of my attending this talk does not fail to impress me, even if I don't know what to make of it.

Once glance at the other faces in the room clues me in on the desperation motivating their attendance. The faces of my grandmother's co-residents are filled with longing mixed with excitement. So many of them have, no doubt, lost loved ones, so many will soon take their own journey out of life. I don't have a firm opinion on these things yet. I have hardly had a chance to assimilate Lilya's experience with Tilgar and yet there has been a definite shift in me: I don't doubt any experience any longer, my own or others. My head swims. What is the difference between Tilgar's world, my remembrance of Lilya's life, and the near-death experiences Joan describes? I feel as if the entire world is tilting into another dimension where all familiar things lose their reliability, taking every one of us along with it.

One look tells me Natasha believes it all. She turns toward me as others raise their hands, and I think she might be about to cry.

"Catherine, dear, what do you think?" she asks me softly.

"About what?" I ask.

"Do loved ones wait for us, on the other side?"

I am totally at a loss. Sam says they are there but here, in their world but still visiting us. I can't agree or disagree, and anyway, doesn't Natasha have her own sense of these things? Why ask me? It was she, after all, who stalked ghosts in her youth, who read the book about angels. She must have an opinion. People her age are supposed to have opinions about matters of death and the beyond by the time they all start to die. We're talking about a generation of church-goers, my grandmother included. I don't know what to make of her asking me, her agnostic, rational granddaughter—as if I can bring some insight to this topic—after all, she can't possibly have any idea about my recent experiences.

I ask her, "Don't they say they wait for us? I mean, that's what they say at church, right?"

Natasha went for years. She stopped going because it became inconvenient for her to get there.

"Sure. But they just say it. That doesn't make it true."

Others have begun asking questions. Some have had their own experiences. I want to get out of there fast—I don't know why, because Natasha expects some kind of something from me, because I've had enough of this business.

"Anyway, I only went because of your grandfather. It's what people did." She pats my knee.

All those years at church, and she was just acting out of marital obligation?

"I've always thought that part was true, though, about the people waiting for you."

She speaks so casually. Obviously she didn't find it all true. I wonder why this surprises me.

Then I smile. It makes sense. Of course Natasha questions everything. I feel a sense of kinship with her, even if I can't pinpoint how, exactly, we are alike in our metaphysical questioning.

Joan asks if anyone has any questions, or would like to share an experience. A woman raises her hand eagerly. She introduces herself as Margaret Wilkins, and tells how she and her husband were in a car accident which took his life, but spared hers. We gasp collectively at the tragedy. Then Margaret shares with us how she did not have a near-death experience at the time, but how at the hospital, as she later recovered, her husband appeared at her side. He told her all manner of things, she recounts, including about life with the angels.

"He told me they don't wear just white," she says with a note of disappointment.

There are titters. Joan pauses thoughtfully and the room falls silent. Someone else raises a hand and volunteers a classic near-death experience, replete with the tunnel of light, angels, and an old friend holding a deceased dog.

My attention wavers. Natasha whispers that she has some port upstairs we should drink before I go home. I wait for the right moment to stand, hoping that the talk is over soon and I can give my mind a rest from metaphysical things.

Margaret Wilkins raises her hand again.

"Walter told me to buy shares in Microsoft," she says.

Natasha grabs me by the knee so roughly I nearly melt onto the floor. When the pain stops blurring my vision I see that Natasha is trying hard to stifle a giggle. Joan makes a comment about guidance coming from deceased loved ones, and asks if anyone has any particular questions—and Margaret Wilkins speaks out, "Walter told me to stop feeding the cat meat, too, and he was right, her indigestion is gone now."

Natasha cannot contain her giggle, and I just manage to stifle mine, and then I take my grandmother by the hand and tug at her arm as I ease out of my chair, crouching, trying to sneak us both out of the room without attracting too much attention. A lost cause when there are only thirty people in the room, all of whom make a sport out of spotting fodder for gossip.

We get to the elevator before we laugh out loud—thankfully, so that Mrs. Wilkins does not think we are mocking her, the batty old soul.

Natasha's laughter changes her entire demeanor, and I feel myself relax. We are schoolgirls. I can see right through Natasha's wrinkles into her unlined smile. I can feel Lilya laughing in me, I can feel our friendship come alive, hers and Natasha's, mine and my grandmother's, and it is the strangest feeling. I can't remember this woman from my childhood—here is a woman who was intimately involved in my toilet-training, but surely she is another person altogether now? Surely we both are? I feel a miraculous absence of age, of time or relationship. We are two women. We are girlfriends giggling in the elevator.

My eye catches a glimpse of her hand, the wrinkled, loose skin, and it means merely that she has had more life than me, just enough to put my life in perspective.

Mine is not a bad life, actually. In some ways I feel like I'm just beginning to live.

33

It is like Sam just knew it would happen again—my visions, slipping into Lilya's life—that his knowing accounted for his silence on the matter. I am beginning to wonder if at some level he is tutoring me in his weird world, if he is leading me, by what he says and by what he doesn't say, to my own revelations. Or is he merely a convenient decoy, and I am the one guiding myself?

In any case, it doesn't take long. That same night it happens again, this time by my will alone. Or call it silent pleading—a feeble attempt at meditation that ends in a desperate prayer for guidance. I wouldn't say I have it all under my control, as I have almost given up by the time it happens, and only fall into my past over the precipice of sleep.

34

February 1945

The week after her initial encounter with Sumai, Lilya twice stopped by the Uzbek woman's apartment in the evening after work, her justification being that it was on her way home. The first time she arrived on a whim, curious about this woman who was a friend of the shamaness and had so oddly brought them together. On that occasion Sumai behaved as if she might have been expecting Lilya. Without hesitation, though equally without warmth, she set the table. The two women had tea and cookies and chatted about nothing in particular. It came as a surprise to Lilya that there was no trace of the secrecy and intrigue that had marked their first conversation, and it gave her the confidence to tell Sumai, openly, that she had been meeting with Tilgar. Sumai asked how her apprenticeship (as she called it) was progressing and then promptly begged for no more details, insisting that it was not her business to know—that Lilya should not mention it henceforth. Merely having a secret without a best friend to confide in was a burden, so Lilya was greatly relieved that Sumai at the very least knew about her shamanistic encounters. By the time she and Refat had set their wedding date, Lilya was visiting Tilgar several times a week. Whenever she wasn't, she often found herself drawn to Sumai's apartment instead.

Refat insisted on meeting the Uzbek woman who sent treats home with his bride (Sumai was always giving Lilya cookies, or pieces of fried bread with meat inside, or pastries). His insistence was justifiable; it was his right as her husband-to-be to know who her friends were. Lilya put off telling him her address for a few days. She was nervous about sharing Sumai—on principal, and for fear Refat would somehow discover that she met with Tilgar.

When Lilya voiced her fears to Sumai, the Uzbek woman asked her, "What difference does it make? I promise you he will be none the wiser. He will see that I am a married woman, that I am just a housewife like you will be, and nothing will come of it."

"You have a husband?" Lilya asked.

"He is not here. He's in the camps. His name is Nikolai."

Lilya could not overcome her shock. "In the camps ... you mean ..."

"Yes, prison camp. He was arrested. He was taken to Siberia, several years ago now."

Lilya went quiet; she did not ask Sumai on what charges Nikolai was taken.

"So you see, Refat might have more in common with me than you ever suspected."

"And your husband, does he ... know about ... you know?" Lilya abided very strictly to Sumai's once-spoken request not to discuss her activities with Tilgar.

"You mean about Tilgar? No, of course not. Now do you see now how much you and I have in common, too?"

Lilya recalled then her revelation about marriage and freedom, and resolved to have the same confidence in the matter as Sumai seemed to have. That night Lilya gave Refat Sumai's address. He thanked her, with a blush, and asked,

"Do you think it is intrusive, that I care to know who your friends are?"

She replied, "I assume it is because you wish to know me. I suppose that is nice."

He fingered the bit of paper with Sumai's address for a moment, then spoke again. "I knew Natasha, so I do have faith that you have friends of a good character. I suppose I am curious. Maybe just forget about it. I do not have to go."

"If it puts your mind at ease, then go. Go soon," Lilya said. "She is expecting you."

Lilya had not seen Sumai for several days when, while sitting with Refat in the evening sharing a cup of coffee (a happy luxury), he announced, "Nikolai Aleksandrovich, Sumai's husband, was arrested for possessing leaflets of a subversive nature." Refat glanced askance at Lilya, squinting, "of a religious nature."

"I did not know that," she said.

He finished his half of the coffee.

"I'm not saying Sumai is someone I would choose as your friend. But I am glad you have a friend," he told Lilya, and they never spoke of Sumai again.

The preparations for Lilya's and Refat's wedding, few in this time of need and urgency, were almost completed two weeks after their engagement. Their extended families and friends helped to find the proper authority to legalize their union, to organize the guests, to find a location for the ceremony, and to request that those who were able bring a sweet or two for the bride and groom and their families, perhaps something for the guests as well. Lilya and Refat participated as little as possible in the preparations other than to build upon their acquaintance, a slow-going process, but one holding some promise. It always felt to Lilya as if Natasha were the invisible third party sitting between them, yet rather than making their meetings feel awkward, somehow Natasha's presence legitimized their union. Whenever they mentioned her name out loud (infrequently though it was), the warm feelings her memory invoked made Lilya feel closer to Refat. She could only sense, judging by Refat's reaction to the mention of Natasha, that his response was the same. Very soon after their engagement Lilya no longer minded Refat's company at all, and it seemed that he grew fonder of her every day.

In all of this courtship Lilya participated somewhat unbelievingly, for her reality, the real, true life she perceived herself as leading, did not really involve a wedding, marriage, the continuation of a dreary factory job, the promise of children, and so forth. Those inevitable life passages were like smoke, a fleeting consequence of being alive; Lilya was the fire, the true center, and what fanned her flames were her thrice-weekly evening strolls with Tilgar, no matter how short and fleeting. Though it felt like hours to her, she was never gone more than thirty minutes, which she assumed was the special magic of the shamaness.

It was all happening perfectly: student and teacher, side by side, walking outside the boundaries of Lilya's prison in body and spirit. They were like escapees who returned to their cell, knowing their place of imprisonment by a less pessimistic name—not home, or anything like it, but a familiar way station. Someplace that Lilya, for her part, was accepting as being as insignificant and as temporary as life itself.

She went to that other place often, with the lake and the hills, where she walked deeper and deeper into the water until she worked up her courage to swim. The water was warm and she could see the bottom. Tilgar was always there but not there, somewhere invisible in the background.

Bit by bit Tilgar began to tell Lilya things, about the reality of the lake and the reality of her life in Uzbekistan—to teach her the difference. How to meditate, to see things properly. Lilya never felt she had stumbled into esotericism, for there was no obscurity. Mystery, perhaps, surprising revelations, all of which were—once the veil was pulled back to see things as they were—beautiful in their clarity and simplicity.

Tilgar never made promises; Lilya never asked what her path would be or when her apprenticeship to Tilgar would end. She had to put aside the past and future and focus on now, that's what Tilgar said. Lilya was lost to time anyway. As she meditated in her bed at night, she blocked the past and had no thoughts of the future. Instead, she went over and over her journeys with Tilgar into the strange beyond.

On one Thursday, Lilya and Tilgar walked in twilight from the market beyond the town into the hills as usual. Tilgar took Lilya by the wrist and pulled her brusquely this way and that, so that they wove up and down, right and left in a strange zigzag dance to an unknown destination.

"I will tell you about time," Tilgar said. "Yours, and others, and how once it did not exist, and where still it doesn't."

"We've never gone this way before, have we?" Lilya asked. She only ever knew where the sun was in relation to them, and she did not recall it ever being straight ahead of them as it was now.

"I want to show you a special place, one I have not been to in a long time."

Tilgar let go of Lilya's hand and marched off ahead. They did not walk for long and when they stopped the sun was still directly ahead of them.

"Do you see that rock?" Tilgar asked.

Lilya looked ahead, squinting right into the setting sun. She wondered how in the world the old woman could see clearly without holding a hand to her eyes.

"Yes, I see it."

"Do you really see it?" Tilgar asked.

Lilya looked again. She was not sure. The glare was so bright she only saw light falling, the little white dots of her vision fogging and clearing as she squinted—somewhere in her line of sight she could make out the rock, just as before. She stared at it. It moved toward her.

"It's moving!" Lilya cried out.

"No. You are moving."

Lilya had to close her eyes for a moment and think—was this true? She wasn't moving, she was standing still, wasn't she? And then she felt herself sway forward, and take a step.

"I wasn't moving before …" she stuttered.

"Ah, time. It has no relevance here," Tilgar said.

"What do you mean?" Lilya asked. "Oh," she gasped. "Do you mean I saw the rock in the *future* at the moment when I stumbled forward?"

"Yes. You saw the rock from your own future perspective."

"So …" Lilya lurched forward. "Can we, I mean, can I….?" She stepped closer and closer, until the sun was not in her eyes. Tilgar reached out and grabbed her from behind.

"You must hold on," she said, taking Lilya's hand in hers.

"Is it only a little bit in the future? The time between my seeing the rock appear to move and my moving was just seconds."

"It is linked to your consciousness, my dear, and therefore as inconstant as the wind. But that is time."

Lilya knelt before the rock and ran her hand across the surface. Tilgar still held her other hand. Lilya looked up at the older woman, quizzical, as if unbelieving. She turned back to the rock.

"What is my consciousness?" she asked. "What do such words mean? I don't understand."

Then, involuntarily, drawn by a sudden dizziness, she fell forward onto the rock. When she looked up she appeared to be in a different place altogether: there were flames all around her, near-darkness and the glow of recently scorched earth. The sound of explosions and a monotone, background whine that began—second by second—to sound like the screams of people.

"Take me back!" she shouted, and felt herself tugged and then, eyes shut, the whining disappeared and there was a hand on her shoulder.

"It was awful," Lilya said. "Why, why did it take me there? What was happening? The end of the world? Where was I in the future? Oh, Tilgar, it was terrible, just too terrible ..."

"What?" Tilgar asked, trying to help Lilya upright, but Lilya preferred to stay on the ground and resisted the old woman's aid.

"What does that have to do with my consciousness? What does it mean? Is that my future?"

"Calm down, child. What did you see?"

"Destruction. I don't know ... the earth was burnt, there was screaming." Lilya was too distraught to continue and squatted, face in hands, breath shallow.

"You saw the war, the final war. Let's go then," Tilgar said. She helped Lilya to her feet. They began to walk away.

"I don't know what that means," Tilgar said. "I am the only other person who has been shown that. Don't fret. It will happen many lives from now, far into the future, not in yours or my lifetime."

She sounded like she was trying to convince herself more than Lilya.

"Look at me, my dear." Tilgar stopped and faced Lilya. They stared at one another for a few moments. Lilya felt calm come out of the old woman's eyes and move into hers, and she melted into stillness.

Tilgar whispered, "You and I, it seems, might have a shared destiny."

Lilya looked into Tilgar's eyes. The old woman slowly turned, and took a step away. Lilya followed.

Lilya gave only a brief moment's thought to what Tilgar meant by 'many lives from now.' They had not ever discussed the concept of souls being reborn life after life. Lilya was not in the mood now. She became sad, pensive. If her future held such horrors as she'd seen, what was the point of living? Wasn't there some kind of evolution through gaining wisdom? Some improvement in one's life once certain mysteries were understood? Or was that a stupid assumption?

It was darker. Maybe a half hour had passed. "Time to get home," Lilya thought gratefully, and picked up her pace. They had not travelled more than a few yards when Lilya stopped. She turned around and took a few paces back the other way.

"I saw something flash back there; did you?" she asked.

Tilgar said nothing and stared in the direction Lilya faced.

"It was a strange light. I saw it, out of the corner of my eye," Lilya said.

Lilya began to walk back the other way. She had seen something that beckoned her directly. Somehow, she was sure it was meant for her. She would claim it. It was her discovery. All of a sudden she felt utterly certain that there was more to her future—in this or any other life—than doom. She would find proof of it now—she didn't know why she felt that way just because she'd seen a strange light. But she had no doubt.

This time it was Tilgar who followed.

Lilya stopped, and looked down. They stood at the top of a steep slope, rocky and sandy. Tilgar came to stand beside her.

"It was there," Lilya said, pointing down."You see the light? See? It's strange here. Just there," she pointed again, "like a glow that seems to emanate from a spot, down there."

Without thinking, Lilya took a step down, stumbling. She fell to her knees, scraping them badly. Tilgar stepped down after her.

"You mustn't rush into anything!" she said, "Wait!"

"I just want to see," Lilya said, scrambling down the hill. Tilgar came after her, sliding on her feet and then as she fell, on the palms of her hands.

"The light!" Lilya exclaimed. Its radiance grew as she approached; even Tilgar was blinded by it. The old woman caught her breath.

"You've found it," she said softly.

"Tilgar, what is it? Some kind of nature spirit? Or ...?"

"No, no. Stop, Lilya. Stand back, you mustn't stand in the light."

"I just want to see," she said, as the ground levelled out. Before them was a column of light in plain view. The sun was an orange glow on the horizon and this beacon, this radiance, lit up a circumference of several feet and cast no shadows.

"You have found the portal, my dear." Tilgar's voice was weak with incredulity. "I don't understand, that is *my* future—we must have a shared destiny—it's the only explanation. I can't believe it. Wait! We must talk!"

Lilya advanced. "It's beautiful," she said. "Not at all like your rock. There's something special to be found here."

Tilgar called to her, "It wasn't supposed to happen like this." Then, as if gathering her senses, she said loudly and firmly, "We must go immediately!"

"I want to feel it." Lilya took a step closer, then closer still. Tilgar dashed forward and tried to push her aside, but Lilya was too fast and she stepped right into it. Then Tilgar stumbled on top of her.

For Lilya, the world began to spin as she fell into the light. Her thoughts blew away like mist and her body disappeared into weightlessness and she knew nothing but falling, falling.

35

And what am I to do with this revelation? Where did Lilya end up? Or did she fall off a cliff and die?

I don't even have the strength to imagine it. My mind is numb. I need a break. I fall back asleep and wake up in denial. Acceptance can come later, after a strong coffee.

I have abandoned altogether my research into the disappearance of the 21st Airborne. Now I spend my days reading about things like shamanism, reincarnation, ley lines—at home. I have ordered books from bookstores and borrowed from several libraries. No longer is it my aim, however, to find explanations or uncover new facts. I no longer wish to clarify or analyze anything at all. I'm seeking validation. My reading is part of an ongoing inner dialogue that seeks to make sense of my life. Lives. And all the unexplained events therein.

I am bursting with information, firsthand accounts, facts and figures. My mind is inundated with stories of the supernatural, both banal and sublime, transformational and forgettable. Only now, after my latest Lilya revelation, I realize just how muddled I am; how my head is buzzing. I am dizzy, and very, very tired.

Today, very uncharacteristically, I put all the books away and I sit. Staring into space, unwilling to do anything but let my mind go blank. Hoping for clarity, resolve, something to do now that I don't know what to do. An idea. Motivation.

I can't call Sam because he doesn't have a number.

I turn on the television. It is on all day.

For dessert I bake cookies and for dinner I prepare a lasagna. As I mix and chop and layer I look through the kitchen window over the sink. Evening comes early now; the backyard is shadowy and cold, the trees almost bare. It is windy. I close the curtains, which I never do, and turn on the radio. Stupid pop music is better than the dull roar of my thoughts.

The phone rings.

"I'm sorry if I've interrupted your dinner," Natasha says.

I tell her I haven't even begun yet, the lasagna is cooling. I haven't chosen a wine.

"Well, what do you know," she says. I detect nervousness. She breathes the words out too fast, "Refat will be here tomorrow. I just got a letter from him today."

"What—so soon?" My appetite disappears and I reach for the first bottle of red wine I see in the cupboard. There are three.

"It's not much notice, I know. The letter came from Ukraine, then the post office obviously forwarded it from your house."

"Oh, right. He still has my address from when you lived here."

"Yes. That's why he'll be arriving at your house, actually."

"What? He's—" The cabernet nearly slips from my grasp. I can't be sweating, can I?

"He's coming here *tomorrow*?"

"Yes, Catherine."

I tell her to hang on a minute. I put the receiver down and then the wine bottle, and I wipe my hands on a dish towel. Then I take a few deep breaths and pick the phone up again.

"What do you want me to do?" I say. "Shall I drive him to you, or—"

"I'll come in the morning," she says.

"What time is he arriving?"

"I've no idea. Probably the afternoon. He's in New York. He'll have to find his way here, which will take a little while I imagine."

"Didn't he give you a number to reach him, something? Can't he call first?"

"I think that's just how things are, dear." Natasha's voice is fading perceptibly. "Please stay with me, if you don't mind," she asks.

Oh, Natasha. It is a plea. I can almost see her trembling, and I'm no better.

"Of course," I tell her.

36

The smell of cookies has, somehow, overpowered that of lasagna. When Natasha arrives the next morning she says, "It smells like Susan has been baking."

"I bake too," I say. I sound tetchy and defensive, which isn't how I'm feeling and not how I want to come across.

Natasha has not noticed. She is too nervous. Her eyes are roving around the room even as she holds her hands in a tight ball at her chest, clutching her purse. She is dressed relatively conservatively. Black pants, a brown top. Hair tidy. Just one adornment, a hair comb with sparkly bits tucked neatly above her left ear. She is wearing a bit of makeup, and red nail polish. I think she looks beautiful and I tell her so.

"You haven't changed a thing," she says, meaning the house. "But it feels completely different in here."

This is the extent of what we say to one another. We turn on the television at nine-thirty in the morning, and at noon we turn it off when a taxi pulls up to the driveway. My grandmother disappears into the bathroom without a word.

The door is open and Refat simply walks in.

My heart is in my throat, which is my excuse for saying nothing. I stare and stare. I seek Lilya in him. I know I seek Lilya as soon as he enters the room and hesitates at the door. He hangs his coat on the coat rack, wordlessly, and nods to me in greeting. His eyes have almost passed over me as they search for my grandmother. He looks as if he is shaking. As if in sympathy a shiver crawls up the back of my neck and through my scalp.

It is all over in a moment—the anticipation. I have no chance to say, "She's coming," or, "Please sit." A smile transforms him, and me. He beams so brightly that I feel like I am caught in a searchlight, that I have been discovered—not I, Catherine, but Lilya! I see Lilya reflected in Refat's lit-up eyes, in the gleam of his yellowed, crooked teeth. I know on the other side of time Lilya has been caught in his light. I feel her glowing presence swell within me so that it is as if I am reflecting the brilliance back to Refat and he is lit up too—and, for the briefest second, Lilya's image gazes back at me from Refat's eyes, and for the briefest second I see in Refat the fiancé Lilya knew.

Then Refat's smile finds my grandmother as she appears in the room and I am lost to the shadows.

"Natasha," Refat says.

"Refat."

My grandmother pronounces "Re-fat," as if she hasn't been saying the name to me over and over again for months, as if the foreignness of his name surprises her. Tongue on tip of palate, stuck for a second or two or three, until she draws breath to say it again, this time easily.

It slowly dawns on me that this is the man I saw at the bookstore. The same man I saw at my mother's funeral!

"I have seen you," I say with hesitation, my voice croaky.

Refat turns to me, "You recognize me? So sorry if I scared you. I wanted to visit earlier, but I was afraid." His accent is cumbersome and unfamiliar. "You look just like her—as she was."

"Like who?" my grandmother asks, with surprising courage.

"Like you, of course. You were never around when I came by your house, so once I followed your granddaughter."

He followed me?

"You've been in town?" Natasha asks. Her face goes paler—if that is possible—her eyes widen.

"Once or twice, after your daughter's funeral."

"You were at Susan's funeral?" my grandmother gasps.

"I did not know it was a funeral until I got there that day. I followed you there. I am sorry, Natasha. I was afraid if you knew I was here you would refuse to see me."

"I would never—" she says, and loses her breath.

I don't for a moment comprehend—has he been following us, me—does it matter?

Refat says something to Natasha in Russian.

A smile sweeps across her face, and she replies, a long, Slavic sentence rolling off her tongue. The words seem to come easily to her, as if she has never stopped speaking her native language.

I have never heard my grandmother speak Russian. For some reason, it brings tears to my eyes.

The room is so charged that I can hardly stand it; my curiosity is slowly overwhelmed by it, and I realize I should go. Natasha says to me, "Don't forget your coat,"—she means it is okay that I leave. I almost wish I could be a fly on the wall—I cannot imagine what they will say to one another, yet I am so relieved I don't have to participate.

I tell Refat it was nice to meet him, take my coat from the closet and go.

37

According to Ben Jamison, there are physical locations on Earth which are distinguished by the recurrence of particular kinds of events. For example, the same clearing in the woods may have been used to skin and cook animals over centuries; the same hill for ritual sacrifice; the same mountainside for religious pilgrimage. Dr. Jamison has some important questions to ask about this phenomenon—so explains the blurb on the flyer Sam left me under my door this morning. Sneaky Sam. I was home, of course, waiting for Natasha and Refat—he should have knocked. Instead he scrawled on the flyer, "Please meet me there tonight." He knows me well enough by now to know I'll not have other plans.

I have never heard of Jamison and am sufficiently disengaged from my own quasi-academic pursuits that I don't feel terribly curious to find out. I take the photocopies handed out at the door to the auditorium and only glimpse at the bottom of the covering handout: Jamison's credentials. He is an archeologist. He must have an excellent reputation in his field, as the auditorium is packed with sweaty student types, academics, and visitors alike.

Sam and Dr. Jamison enter the auditorium together. I have the feeling I'm witnessing a scene of reunion. There is an intensity and magnetism between them. When they part they shake hands and Jamison pats Sam on the shoulder like men do when they want to hug. Sam arrives at the seat I saved for him looking dazed.

I ask him what his connection to the lecturer is. He says that Dr. Jamison did his doctoral work in Sam's hometown. His meeting with him before the lecture today was their first since that time. Sam says he will elaborate later, if there is time—"Since when do we not have time?" I wonder? Clearly, Sam has something planned for after the lecture.

I look down to the bottom of the handout again and note the dates Jamison obtained his various degrees.

"You must have been in school when Ben was doing his research." I say.

He is fidgety and brushes off my question.

"It was a small town. Not hard to meet strangers. I was curious about his work and we got to know each other."

"Then I can see why you wanted to come," I tell him. "Why me though?"

"Isn't this the kind of thing you're interested in? With the disappearance of those planes over that spot in the Pacific?"

I tell Sam that I'm here because he asked me to meet him, and not because, as he suggests, the lecture is germane to my research. I tell him that I don't go to university lectures anymore. That, in fact, I've abandoned my research—but Sam will have none of it.

"It's not just about your research, or because I wanted to see Ben again," he says. "I want to talk to you about what he has to say. I've read his latest articles and I think you'll find it interesting."

"Well, possibly," I think with some doubt. At least it's a break from my life. I'm comfortable in the familiar auditorium. I'm happy to see Sam again.

The auditorium goes quiet as Dr. Jamison turns on his microphone. He introduces his lecture as a series of questions and conjectures which, he hopes, will eventually metamorphose into a book.

"As you may know, I have done extensive work at Hopeful Hill not far from the Native American burial mound of the same name. For some years the connection between my finds and the location of the mound did not interest me much. Why would there be a link between a twentieth-century event, and a Native American burial mound from thousands of years earlier? Then, suddenly, I became very interested indeed. I was reading about ley lines. I know those words may evoke in many of you some doubt, bringing to mind all kinds of dubious pseudo-scientific theories, but bear with me.

"Ley lines have been largely discredited by scientists, if by ley lines we're speaking of networks of energy that run across the surface of the earth. No such energy has been detected. But ley lines do have some validity if we're speaking of paths or trails peoples follow—and continue to follow. That is, traditional routes to particular places taken again and again over centuries. For example, the routes Egyptians took to the pyramids to inter the dead, or those which nomadic Native Americans followed seasonally. We can also understand ley lines as not lines at all, but as physical locations that historically have contained the same or similar structures, or have been the spot for the same kind of ritual or activity. For example, a spot where there was a church for centuries, where before there was a pagan temple in the same spot—the Middle East is famous for such things. It is even possible that if you connect certain such places with invisible lines and study the history of a region, you might find that peoples traditionally followed those lines from one location to another over centuries, even though the locations contained different structures, or people of different cultures or traditions walked those routes. This is where my work comes in, as archeology reveals much to us about what kinds of events happened in particular spaces, and which paths were walked over time.

"When I first started thinking about the philosophical implications of my Hopeful Hill discoveries, my initial quandary was time—how the past intrudes on the present. I was eager to understand the implications of archeology on how we understand and judge personal history. I did some research, wrote my book and some papers, then put the Hopeful Hill work aside and concentrated on other things. Until, that is, a few years ago I came across some articles on ley lines.

"Suddenly I was curious to know if there was a connection between the discoveries at Hopeful Hill and the Native American burial mound. Where we located human remains we also found artifacts which I analyzed in the context of my thesis. These were artifacts of a ceremonial nature, and there was nothing about them that seemed noteworthy beyond the confines of my study. When I started to look at them in connection with the Indian mound, however, things became more interesting.

"It seems that much of Hopeful Hill is not virgin soil. It is likely that ceremonial massacres have occurred in this area over centuries, possibly millennia. The remains of pre-Creek peoples have been found buried in the surrounding soils. What's more, it seems there might be a link between my now-infamous finds near the mound and the function of the mound itself as a burial and ceremonial spot—folklore supports this possibility. Furthermore, both spots were dots on an invisible line connecting the mound and woods to a peninsula off the nearby river—which is itself a place of modern significance: slaves escaping their bondage hid in a network of underground shelters on their way north. Today I'm going to tell you a bit more about those three places and how they might be connected, but first:

"It is my hypothesis that over time, people have engaged in ritual sacrifice at or near the spot of the Hopeful Hill discoveries, that hunted peoples have hidden on the peninsula, and that the Indian burial mound has been used for religious ceremonies. Just as Indian tribes have used the peninsula as a hiding place from enemy tribes, slaves hid from pursuing landowners. Just as natives used the burial mound for religious ceremonies—you might laugh at this—modern day youth engage in their own spiritual rituals by smoking marijuana in the same spot.

"I have the suspicion that history repeats itself in the same physical locations, as if the Earth has an energetic signature that attracts the same kind of event over and over again. I wonder, are we evolving, or repeating patterns which are as ingrained in our souls as they are on the natural world?"

The remainder of Dr. Jamison's lecture is focused on the archeology of his hypothesis; he leaves conjecture behind for some time as he elaborates on physical evidence and folklore. But I am stuck on his introduction.

We file out with the crowd. Sam gives Dr. Jamison a wave as we exit. He says they will meet again soon, for coffee and a chat before Jamison leaves town. Sam tells me he wants to tell Ben about his own experiences in some of the places mentioned in the lecture. They all took place in his hometown, of course. Sam tantalizes me with his emphasis on "experiences"—I know what kind of experiences Sam Hunter tends to have—but as I expect, he says nothing else about them now.

Sam and I seem to be heading somewhere specific—or at least Sam appears to know where we're going. We go past a group of girls smoking outside, away from the building toward a soccer field, moving quickly toward some unknown destination.

"What did you think?" he asks.

"Fascinating," I say. "A lot of the archeology I didn't quite grasp, but the beginning part was really interesting. Is that why you wanted to come? Something about ley lines and so on?"

"That's part of it. It's the notion that there are places on the earth where the same thing happens over and over again—that's the part that interests me. What happened to Lilya, Catherine, did you ever remember? She disappeared into thin air, didn't she?"

"Yes, she disappeared. I have remembered the entire scene. I can remember it all as clearly as if it happened to me just yesterday."

I tell him of my last vision: the meeting with Tilgar, the fateful walk to the hill, the fall, the odd sensations, and how I haven't remembered anything else about it since.

As I recount my experience I have few feelings of surprise and shock left; the story comes out matter-of-factly. Still, in remembering it, I go to some other place where I watch Lilya's life like a movie, from her perspective.

When I return and my surroundings come into focus again, I see we have stopped walking and that Sam has lost all color. I ask what is wrong, if I can do something. He does not respond but to say, "Just a minute." I am compelled to put my hand on his long, slender fingers, to transmit warmth. I realize that I trust this man implicitly, that I care about him, and I am once more grateful that we met.

"I am beginning to understand," he says, "what is happening here, and why I was intrigued by Ben's conjectures. It has to do with certain places where history repeats itself."

"What has to do with certain places?"

"Lilya disappeared in a particular place, didn't she?"

"What are you getting at?"

Sam seems to be considering his thoughts on the matter and is quiet. At last he murmurs, "If I explain it outright, you'll think I'm crazy."

"Possibly I already do."

"That's true, but just in case you'd like to preserve even an illusion of my sanity, I'll try to explain it step by step. Here. The package you had for Victor," he says as he pulls it out of his backpack. He takes a piece of paper from the package.

"Read this—from here," he points to the top of the page at the crease where the article is folded in half.

> Less mainstream religions are also enjoying a revival in the former Soviet states. Shamanism was widely practiced in Central Asia, for example, until Soviet suppression sent this tradition underground as well. Shamanism is considered by many academics to be the precursor to Islam in this region, and many people, some of Siberian, some of Mongol origin, still practice it today.
>
> No longer is association with shamans considered a political risk, and residents of the Altai region of Uzbekistan are not the only people to partake. In one small Altai village even Muslims and atheistic Russians visit the local shaman, Vladimir Aldar. They come seeking everything from a blessing for weddings and births to traditional medicines and spells. Vladimir Aldar is now a leader of the community whose authority is respected. Looking ancient beyond his sixty-five years, Aldar is not expected by his devotees to live much longer, and the search is on for his successor. Locals told this reporter that it is widely believed one of the community's most powerful shamans disappeared through a portal into another dimension in the 1940's. They say the long-gone shamaness has appeared to Aldar in his dreams and that he believes she will reappear one day and lead her people to a better world.

The paper is folded at the end of this paragraph and before I can unfold the paper Sam takes it from me. "And this," he says, pulling out another piece of paper from his pocket. It is a letter.

Dear Victor,

I admit defeat in this matter, or at least compromise. If, as you argue, reincarnation is an interpretation, not an explanation, then I can back off my metaphysical strictures and have a new perspective on recent events. I have interviewed two more villagers who claim they have had visions of the shamaness they call Tilgar having been transformed into a bear and returning to them. To interpret this story as their shamaness reincarnating to fulfill the prophecy does not really qualitatively alter the message they seem to be receiving: Tilgar's return.

Now, as for your promise that you will be sending this reincarnation my way, well, your sense of humor keeps me sane when things get hairy with the natives. I'll have to thank my brother for making you write to me. Here I thought he was a dope-smoking dropout, when all along he was looking for truth with a Native American philosopher. If he's not too stoned on peyote, ask him to write a few lines to his anthropologist brother in the wastelands of Central Asia. I may not be apprenticed to a master, but I am open to mystical experiences in this bar-less wilderness. I will let you know if the shamaness reappears as a bear, or as the young man you call the Dreamer. Meanwhile, to continue our discussion: Why do you suggest that viewing the prophecy as one of reincarnation will help me understand it better? I look forward to your reply, as always,

Yours,
Nelson

"It won't help you understand it better!" I cry out. "It just complicates things!"

"Catherine, listen, calm down. Don't you recognize the name?"

I take a deep breath. "Sorry. Tilgar. Of course. The shamaness."

"Not her. I mean Nelson."

"An anthropologist ... Nelson ... Fitzwilliam?" Of course! I'd seen him in person not long ago, had been seeing his name on articles for much longer.

"Yes!"

"But he's never written anything about Central Asia, as far as I know, and I've read everything he's written ... Wait, how do *you* know who he is—and why would you think *I'd* know?"

"I was there, at his lecture. I saw you there. Of course, I didn't know it was you at the time; only after we met did I recognize you."

"Why were you there, Sam? Okay, never mind. I guess for the same reason you're here at Jamison's lecture—looking for some answers. If I didn't already know you I'd think you were stalking me. What's going on? What exactly are you trying to find out?"

"The same thing you are, it seems."

I let that thought sink in against strenuous intellectual objection. We were not looking for the same answers, because my questions stemmed from curiosity—maybe even from desperation—and were very, very clear. His questions were the product of dreams, sought on the advice of medicine men, and were totally, completely, obscure.

"It's not just a coincidence anymore, is it?" Sam asks. He doesn't specify which coincidence he has in mind—attending the same lectures, meeting, running into each other, seemingly after the same information. I know that he means we are being brought together for a reason and that is not something I believe is possible. It smacks too much of destiny, and I tell him so.

"Are you saying all this is meant to be? Because I don't believe in that sort of thing." Then I laugh, because I must concede the obvious, "Let's call it an extraordinary series of coincidences."

"If it makes you feel better," Sam said.

"It does. But not that much better. I'm very confused," I admit, "because this is all completely atypical for me. From the moment I let you into my house, to this conversation, it's all out of character. I can't put my finger on it, but I admit, it's really odd, at least for me, that we keep meeting this way."

"It's kind of like a dream? Where nothing makes sense if held up against the real world, but in the dream itself there is some kind of internal logic?"

"Sort of, yes."

"It gets better," Sam says.

It has begun to rain, but we walk anyway, under the oversized umbrella I brought just in case.

"You believe that you are the reincarnation of Lilya, right?" he asks me.

"Yes." I have said as much to him before. "But that is neither here nor there. My experience confirms in my mind that I am reliving my past life. All I can say about that is that I know what is real and what isn't, and my experience has been very real. I have done some research, of course—" here Sam smiles, says, "Of course." which I interrupt—"and reincarnation is well-documented. Not just by religious or spiritual texts, because you know that sort of thing is not reliable, it's too metaphorical, mythical, unscientific. I mean hypnotherapy. Cases of people remembering their past lives in detail, and the details they remember being confirmed upon subsequent research. The details they remember explain quite well certain aspects of their present lives. So, I believe it's possible, and that I've experienced it. But, so what?"

"So what?"

"Yeah. What does it matter? It just raises more questions than it answers. Am I a soul that just keeps coming back, over and over again? Why? To reach enlightenment, as the Buddhists say? You see, I'm not sure what the point of my remembering it all is. I don't know what to do with the information. It's like what Dr. Jamison said about evolution; I'm not sure I'm evolving, just repeating a pattern. I don't know."

Sam looks thoughtful. I think if it were not raining I would not be walking so close to him. Our proximity makes this conversation—and the strange series of coincidences it evokes—all too real. I can't hear his shoes hit the wet concrete or see his bare arm out of the corner of my eye without thinking, "This is happening; we have met again; and *who are you?*"

Sam asks, "What about that letter from Fitzwilliam? The shamaness he referred to, in Central Asia?"

"Oh, yes, I suppose it must be the woman Lilya met—"

I stop and face Sam. We are chin to neck under the umbrella. I look up at him. "Spit it out. What is your conclusion?"

"I think I was the shamaness in your past life."

I feel a peculiar warmth spread over me, and then, there it is again, the feeling of familiarity with Sam. He is smiling at me. As if he's just told me a joke and is waiting for me to get the punch line.

"Am I supposed to laugh?" I ask.

"Is it funny?"

"No."

Who's to say he is wrong? That is why I cannot speak. Because he could be right. I've already embraced the far-fetched, so why not this? I suppose it would make sense, if we knew one another in a past life, that we'd meet again, and be comfortable in one another's company. How interesting—the idea has its appeal. A woman shaman, now become a male version of someone similar. I shiver as I remember how the shamaness fell on top of Lilya, how Lilya—I—fell and fell. We begin to walk again as I consider what it could mean.

I say, "It is possible, I suppose."

"You still don't believe in destiny?" Sam asks.

"Just because I believe in one kind of supernatural weirdness doesn't mean I've become a New Age junkie. Destiny is another matter entirely. I haven't yet decided if there is any rhyme or reason to this reincarnation business. I mean, did my wandering little soul want to be the granddaughter of my best friend, so that we'd meet again? Or was my soul simply attracted to her because of our familiarity, like a moth to the flame?"

"Likewise with me."

"What makes you think you were the shamaness?"

"Because of how you and I met, how we seem to know one another better than time can explain. Because of the letter. Because of everything. Because of Victor Tehusa."

"Victor?"

"In his letter, Fitzwilliam says that Victor promises that the shamaness will return to her people as the Dreamer." Now Sam stops, and I do, too. We are chin to neck again.

"I am the Dreamer, Catherine, remember?" He cannot conceal his excitement. "Even Victor called me that, in a dream. In the letter Victor wasn't just talking to Nelson, and Nelson wasn't just writing to Victor—they were communicating with me, too. *I'm* the one who should understand the link to reincarnation! I mean, Nelson should, too, but this letter was meant for me, too, all along. That's why Victor used your address: because I came to you. He knew I would, that I was supposed to."

"He knew he'd be dead by then?"

"Maybe he was already dead when he made these arrangements."

"Arrangements? This sounds ... do you know how this sounds?"

Sam smiles, confirming my intuition—he is thrilled to be onto something.

"My path is becoming clear, finally! Listen, I didn't know that Nelson Fitzwilliam was a friend of Victor's until I read this letter, but I went to his lecture because I dreamt of a man showing me a portal into another world. When I saw the flyer advertising the lecture I knew it was the man in the dream, and I didn't stop to think about it, I just went along. I saw you there, months before we met. And I would have seen you earlier if you'd answered the door the first and second times I knocked."

"I guess you were third time lucky," I laugh. "But what are you saying? What does it all mean? I know you are trying to tell me it was destiny, but why, Sam? I need more information."

"Catherine, the last thing you need is information!" He rolls his eyes. I can see he'd like to shake me by the shoulders, or at least it looks like he is sufficiently exasperated.

"Signs are everywhere. Sometimes you have to interpret life as if it were a dream. It is the interpretation that matters, which is what Victor is saying. The interpretation of the letter is helping me to see who I am, and what I must do next. I am the reincarnation of the shamaness! That is *our* connection. You were Lilya and I was Tilgar. Is it a coincidence that Victor had this article sent to you, not to him? He was bringing us together. That's why I dreamed of him as the butterfly man. We—you and I—are the butterflies. He's calling us together. This is my calling. I have to fulfill the prophecy of my people from my past life, and find that place where you, as Lilya, disappeared. Before the last war or … what did you say from your vision? The war that would end the world."

My spine tingles. "Victor told me years and years ago that he was the caller of butterflies," I say. "Do you really …?"

Sam takes my hand, squeezes it, lets it go.

"You see? You have been implicated in this all along."

"Why do you have to fulfill the prophecy? Assuming you were the shamaness in a past life … do your people still exist? Are the reasons still valid, for finding this portal? Is it too late? And how do you know it could save them? It might swallow them up and spit them back out. Lilya just came back as me, Sam. I'm hardly saved, just recycled. It seems rash, going off to find something because of obligations that …" I catch my breath. "This is a crazy conversation."

We have covered more impossible ground than I care to contemplate, and it has worn me out.

Sam says, "I can't answer your questions, because I don't know. I just know what I have to do next. But I know that I am going in the right direction, at least."

He has a look of contentment, self-satisfaction. And his eyes are lit up. He throws a glance my way and beams. I give him a weak smile. I am distracted.

I am not at all sure what is being asked of me, at which point I suddenly realize that something *is* being asked of me. I cannot comprehend why, how my life has got to this point, what the purpose of it is, but if one thing is clear, it is that, at least in Sam's eyes, I have a purpose. And it feels, uncanny as it seems, that I am being guided—whether by unseen forces or just by this Sam Hunter, I don't know. There is, however, no question that I am going down a path, and that Sam is nudging me along.

I am not smiling anymore, as I point out to Sam.

"What do you want?" I ask.

"You have to remember where it is, Catherine. You knew then, and you know now."

I want to protest, but I don't. I whisper, "I remember exactly where it was. I can draw you a picture, write down the description for you. I guess if there is such a thing as destiny, that's it. Now you can go there."

"There's more to it than that, Catherine. More to our meeting."

Why does he sound so certain? I feel that it is true, but cannot find words. Sam watches me for a response, any sign, I guess, that I comprehend what he's saying. Good luck to him—I must look a confused mess. I feel a sense of inevitability, a resigned acceptance to a fate I never could have imagined. And still I doubt everything he says, and fear it, all at the same time.

I cannot cope with any of it anymore.

"I have to go," I say. "I have to think about all this some more." I take a step back into the rain. Sam hands me my umbrella and as I take it I notice that my hand is trembling.

"Let me think this through," I say. "I'm sorry to be so rude."

"That's okay. Take your time. I know where you live." He smiles; I can't even smile back, I just walk away.

I don't know where I am now. I look around, trying to find something I recognize, to remember where I parked. There are two girls standing nearby, watching me. As I walk by one of them holds out a cigarette and asks me if I have a light. I say no. That's when I realize that Sam and I have made a giant loop around campus, and have ended where we began.

38

It takes me a week to work up the courage, but I have. I am here, in the garden. Between the nude vines of wisteria and the barren oak tree, next to the pond that used to be the home of koi and goldfish—I don't know if their lives could not withstand my neglect, or the location of their home.

Here I am, in the spot again. I have avoided it for a good, long while. After a few seconds of standing here, my skin crawls and a foggy light clouds my vision. When I move away, everything goes back to normal.

I force myself to remain until my eyes adjust and my body no longer registers the pins and needles. I have the feeling I'm not alone, and I see, from the periphery of my vision, that I am not.

"Hello Catherine!" a man waves at me over the hedge, as casually as you'd expect when supernatural things weren't happening. Only they are. It is Victor. At least it looks like Victor. The air seems to ripple in front of me, his image with it. I'm hallucinating. I must be.

"It's me. I'm real. Take a deep breath."

"Victor?" I ask. "Is it really you?"

I have a fleeting but insistent thought, the last vestige of my doggedly skeptical mind, its last bid for control: I have never actually seen Victor dead. I mean, if I have not actually seen a corpse, if I've just taken everyone's word for it, he could be alive. Right?

"Yes, it's me. Not in your world. I no longer exist in your world."

I can feel my insides quivering in nervousness and excitement. I wish there were something to hold onto, to give me balance. The oak tree is too far away. Still the air moves in my vision, the light is odd, as if the particles were charged and glowing. It's like seeing an undulating cloud of dust in the sunlight, with Victor in the center of it all.

"What am I supposed to say?" I call out. Victor disappears behind the hedge and appears on my side—but did he literally vanish and reappear? I can't say. He is coming closer to me. Now he is feet away. I can see the dark, unshaven hairs on his cheeks and neck. It is him, exactly the same as I remember him from when I was a child.

"Anything you want to say. Though really I should be doing the talking, seeing as you're all shaken up. It's okay, Catherine. This is perfectly normal."

"For whom?" I ask.

"For me, for you. You're actually really good at this sort of thing; you just haven't faced up to it yet."

Victor is looking for rain, I can tell by the way he sniffs and looks up. Such a normal thing to do when you're tending your garden, such an abnormal thing for a disembodied spirit to do. Isn't that what he is? Come to think of it, I'm not exactly sure what, or where, he is. What the hell am I supposed to do now?

"So," I venture, "I guess you're supposed to impart wisdom, right? Isn't that what happens when someone visits from the beyond?"

Victor laughs and I smile. Really, I think, this isn't happening, is it? It's too normal, too innocent.

"Yep, otherwise, what's the point of visiting other dimensions? Such a wasted effort."

He is humoring me.

"The light is funny here," I observe. "You're beginning to fade a bit."

"Not just yet. Focus. If you move away from that spot, I'll disappear. It's not the most powerful place around, so you can't go very far."

I focus on him. He looks fine again, substantial.

"Sam has said a few things about what is going on," I say. "I suppose you know all about it, seeing as, apparently, you brought us together. Do you have something to add?"

"Not really," he replies. He shrugs. "I think he's pretty much got it covered."

"So you appeared just to let me know he's on the right track?"

Victor holds up his shears. I hadn't noticed before he was carrying them—but of course, he must have been.

"No, I was just trimming my hedge when *you* appeared," he said. "If you don't mind, I'll get back to it. Take care of yourself, dear Catherine. Lovely to see you again."

He walks back around the hedge and continues to trim. I watch for a moment, content to stand there and do so, the air swirling around me, eddies of light dancing and rippling as the seconds tick by. I have no more questions. My curiosity has seemingly vanished, just like that.

A jumble of mens' voices bursts into sound around me. Suddenly, out of my peripheral line of vision a large group of men come walking by. Old men in uniforms, military uniforms, wearing army insignia and carrying helmets. I nearly jump out of my skin—have they appeared out of nowhere?—but I somehow manage to remain standing in the same spot. They come walking toward Victor, wave at him; he waves back; they walk past. They turn and walk toward me, twenty—thirty—forty—or more old men, laughing and talking, heading straight for me.

Just as the men reach me, when one particular man is just feet away, I take a step back. I see something written on his jacket sleeve. A numeral. A two and a one.

It's the men of the 21st Airborne. In my backyard.

I take another step backward and they and Victor Tehusa vanish.

39

Fact: Victor Tehusa and the men of the 21st Airborne just appeared in my backyard, then vanished. I feel lucid; I have my senses about me. When I pinch myself it definitely hurts. I walk over to Victor's backyard and inspect his hedge. The wisteria is bare, of course, at this time of year; there is no sign the branches have been freshly trimmed. Then I see a few green leaves on the ground. There are a few stems on the ground, too, and when I pick one up and look at it, I see that it is still clear and moist where it has been cut.

Conjecture: Victor did not say he had died, he said he no longer existed in my world. Therefore, the men of the 21st who were with him must also be in his world.

Maybe they've all died, and they are in the world, or dimension, where people go when you die.

Or maybe none of them have died, and instead have just stepped into another dimension. Which makes sense, because they've all aged.

Victor said the spot I stood in wasn't powerful enough for me to go far—there must be spots where I could go farther, into whatever dimension he was in.

Fact: When I stood on the hillside in Yugoslavia with Elisa when I was seventeen, I went farther; I went so far away I didn't know where I was, and I still don't know. I only know that the feeling I had was more powerful than anything I've ever experienced.

Instead of the one person I want to see from the beyond, from another dimension or whatever, I see my dead neighbor—a man I can hardly claim to have known very well—as well as an entire army unit of men completely unknown to me. I do not see my own mother.

She's probably partying with Yehudi Menuhin, having the time of her afterlife organizing some chorus of angels to be conducted by Mozart. Not a spare moment in eternity for her daughter.

It's been two weeks since I saw Sam, as many since I've seen Natasha. I haven't called her. I don't know how many days she met with Refat, or if she would want to see me again straightaway afterwards. She hadn't called me either, until this morning, and the first thing she says is, "Aren't you dying to know what Refat found out about Lilya?"

I can't very well tell her, "Gee, I've had this vision, this out-of-body experience, and consequently I know exactly what happened, thanks very much." So I tell her a different truth: "I was giving you time, Natasha. I didn't know when Refat was leaving, or when you'd be ready to see me again."

She's had enough time, she says, and tells me to come today. It is Thanksgiving Day, so I had hoped to see her today anyway, though neither of us had organized anything, maybe because it is our first Thanksgiving dinner alone.

Natasha says she's had enough of silly American traditions and prepares beef cutlets instead of turkey, and apple turnovers instead of pumpkin or pecan pie: traditional Russian fare, *kotletki* and *pirozhki*, with boiled potatoes. It's all the same to me. I never really liked Thanksgiving. For one thing, my mother used to make us all name one thing we were really thankful for. Natasha does not bring up this tradition, and neither do I—which, of course, I'm really thankful for. Actually, there are a few things I'm thankful for, but I'm not sentimental like my mother, so I won't say them out loud.

I'm thankful for knowing Natasha Aleksandrovna Matveeva, my grandmother. I watch her fuss at the table, lining up cutlets, setting out a bowl of potatoes. There is much too much food for the two of us. Natasha catches me watching her and asks, "What are you thinking?"

"Nothing."

I'm lying, of course.

Here we are, stuck together. We are our entire family. Once it was her and my grandfather, my mother and me. Our numbers have been reduced by half. I feel such a fierce loyalty toward Natasha at this moment. She has only me, and I have only her, and I know, with all the fullness of my heart, that this is as it should be, that we belong together.

"So," I ask her, "how did your visit with Refat go?"

"Oh, where to begin?" she asks me back, and gives me the most enigmatic wide-eyed stare, then giggles.

Her smile admits contentment, which is all I can gather. She's drawing it out, leading me on with enforced anticipation. She serves me a second helping of apple turnover despite my protestations, and we turn on the television to hear the football game. It's the aural wallpaper of Thanksgiving fare, homage to Andrew. We both know it without having to state it.

"Refat finished the story," Natasha says, between mouthfuls. "The very last chapter of Lilya's story, and my very last chapter with Refat Chobanov."

40

September 1996, Samarkand Region, Uzbekistan

Decades had passed since Refat and Natasha had parted ways, since Refat's wife-to-be had disappeared, and Refat's losses had of necessity been buried beneath the chores and routines of a new family, then the politics of repatriation, then the migration back to Crimea, then the Soviet Union's economic collapse. His losses were not so deeply interred as to be unfelt, though they lay gathering the dust of time, their pain forever relegated to another life, a life that hardly seemed to have ever existed.

Then on no particular day and for no particular reason, a vision swept Refat away from the present into his dust-covered past: Lilya appeared in his mind's eye not in the least bit obscured by the intervening years, looking exactly as he last recalled her. The vision did not recede and Lilya remained at the edge of his mind from then on. He found it difficult to focus on his present responsibilities and neglected them badly, going through the motions of physical life distracted by her presence. Over a period of months, Refat watched Lilya in his mind and thought about their past together more and more. Sometimes he heard a voice that sounded like hers or felt a hand brush against his arm. Finally, he had a single recurring thought that forced him to return his focus to the world again: what really happened to Lilya Bekirova?

Refat decided he had to find out. He had to make the effort he had not made when he realized Lilya would never return and again had had to build his life anew. He would go back to Uzbekistan, to the scene of Lilya's disappearance, to their place of exile. Perhaps there were people he could ask, contacts he could follow now that the Soviet Union had collapsed and official records of past events were more easily available. But there was one person in particular he wished to find first: an Uzbek woman called Sumai.

Refat had not contacted her after Lilya disappeared. He had not thought to, until now, until he had the motivation, and the courage, to confront Lilya's likely death.

In their early days of exile, Sumai had been Lilya's one friend in Uzbekistan, as far as Refat knew. They had spent many evenings together, and Lilya had often come home bearing the woman's meat pies or sweet biscuits. Lilya always seemed so dreamy when she returned—that's how he knew she had been with Sumai—no normal day at the factory could impart such a mood. He had been curious, a bit suspicious. So he insisted on meeting Sumai, claiming, as justification, that it was his right as her husband-to-be to know her friends. In truth, he would never have prevented her friendship with anyone. He just had to know the source of her contentment.

Sumai was odd. Outwardly, she was very conventional, for her people—married, with the usual daily chores and interests, but something about her was unusual. He never quite figured it out. He only met with her once. When she told him her husband was in a prison camp for possessing information on Islam, he had nothing more to say. It was as if she were telling him they were alike, she and Refat, her people and his, both Muslim, both persecuted. At the end of their visit, even though he could not in all honesty say he was happy that Lilya was friends with this strange woman, he felt sheepish for his curiosity. Why shouldn't Lilya have a good friend? Did he covet her contentment?

Perhaps his sheepishness had prevented him from seeing Sumai again after Lilya disappeared. Anyway, at the time it was a tragedy that immobilized him, so he accepted without question the authorities' conclusions (that Lilya had likely died in the desert after escaping the settlement regime). Later, Refat focused on moving on. Finally he had made it to his homeland, was settled in Crimea with his family, his work, his life, and now here he was going back into exile.

It was a risky endeavor. There was always the possibility the authorities would not allow him to enter Uzbekistan, and once there, to re-enter Crimea. He only had a Soviet passport; since he'd left for Crimea, Uzbekistan had become an independent state, as had Ukraine, only Ukraine was not yet granting Crimean Tatars citizenship. So Refat had lost his chance for Uzbek citizenship and, although registered as a resident in his local Crimean district, he officially had no Ukrainian citizenship either. He was without any valid passport whatsoever. Yet, somehow, the right people looked the other way for the right amount of cash, and when at last he arrived, all of his journey's bureaucratic difficulties faded fast. For there he was, as if some part of him had never left, not in Tashkent where he'd spent his adult life, but back in the dusty desert town where he'd worked the cotton fields and convinced Lilya to marry him. It had been forty years since he'd been in that place.

He thought he would pass out when he saw it—the old barracks, the market square, the apartment buildings and hills beyond. Too much nostalgia at once; he had to sit on a bench in the square and take very deep breaths. Then he took out a crumpled bit of paper from his pocket, with a number he'd written on it a decade ago and had stuffed into his phonebook; a bit of paper that had replaced its worn-out predecessor, and two before that. For some reason Sumai had given him her number those years ago; for some reason he'd always kept it. He went to a public pay phone facility to call her, queued at the cashier, trembling.

When Sumai picked up the receiver and exclaimed, "I'm listening!" the motion of his heart was suspended and, momentarily confused, he had the feeling that indeed this had been planned all along: Sumai had been waiting for his call, and Lilya was somewhere expecting that he make it. Abruptly he hung up the phone. In that blurred moment he was deluged with memories he had chosen not to recall, and a wave of guilt washed over him—that he had never been to see Lilya's only friend even to convey his condolences and accept hers, much less to make inquiries. His heart clenched again, he became hot, beads of perspiration coalesced in the hollow of his back, and he did not dare re-dial the number. He decided he would go see her directly, so that he couldn't back out.

Sumai could not have known Refat was coming, even if she had against all odds recognized his voice on the phone. He arrived unnoticed by neighbors and passersby and stood in the corridor inside her apartment building. She was evidently out, as there was no reply to his knock. She would not have moved out of this apartment if she'd answered the number he'd dialed, and indeed her surname was inscribed on the post box in the entranceway below. After Refat had been waiting in agitation for fifteen minutes, and having already informed a particularly obnoxious neighboring *babushka* that he was expected at number 410, Sumai trod up the steps beneath an armful of groceries. She did not notice him standing quietly in the shadows off of the stairwell until a tomato fell out of her sack and rolled nearly onto his foot, whereupon he picked it up and handed it to her.

She did not jump, rather froze, and seconds passed before she spoke. She stared at him, looked deeply into his eyes, her face showing surprise and also, he thought, disappointment. He had half expected her to drop her bags. But then, such a reaction would surely be unlike Sumai, who had come across, at their one previous meeting, as someone rarely ruffled by anything. Refat lowered his eyes to the floor, his heart pounding.

Sumai handed him her bags and opened her door. "Come in, Refat," she said, turning on the light in the living room. He entered and stood awkwardly in the doorway, holding the bags.

"Put them in the kitchen to your left," she instructed. He found a place on the kitchen counter to put the bags down, and looked around, thinking how little it had all changed over the years, but for the color of the wallpaper and a new refrigerator. His heart was still pounding frantically and it was all he could do to just stand there, his eyes gliding from one object to the next, from one detail to another. He did not know if he should leave or stay, and the moment seemed too long before Sumai spoke again.

"So what has taken you so long, Refat?" she asked him finally, reappearing from the living room and motioning him to a chair at the kitchen table. She sat across from him on the other side of the kitchen table and made no move to put the kettle on, nor offered him anything at all. He did not know how to respond. Had she been expecting him? He suspected from the surety of her manner that she had always known that, one day, he would try to piece together what had happened, that he would retrace Lilya's steps, and that included her friendship with Sumai. He had not, of course, known himself that such a day would come.

"You have not changed much, you know," Sumai said. His head was semi-bowed, and he stared at a spot on the table that was not far from where her hands lay clasped.

"You are not one to be so silent." Something in her tone—sadness, perhaps?—made him raise his eyes to her face, and he was surprised when she could not meet his glance. Did she suffer from private sorrows of which he knew nothing? Did he remind her of something? She reached into her shirt pocket and fished out a pack of cigarettes and matches. "Would you like one?" she asked as she slid the ashtray from against the wall to the center of the table.

"No, thank you," he responded, and so she slid it toward herself. She lit a cigarette and as she exhaled, blowing smoke at him, her eyes returned to his, appearing full of tears, though perhaps it was a trick of the light, or due to the smoke.

He was not sure how to continue. So many years had gone by and the little he knew of her life belonged to such a distant past. He cleared his throat, and spoke, "Nikolai Aleksandrovich still lives?"

"My husband died last year, at home. He had a heart attack."

Refat felt relief in knowing he had not died in a prison camp in Siberia, as had so many from that time. When had he been released? He wanted to know if they had had the precious chance to share very many years of their lives together as he had not with Lilya, as he never could have dreamed with Natasha. But he posed no further questions. He decided she must have come to terms with whatever had happened and did not need his intrusions. He took in a deep breath and exhaled just a little of his many years of yearning and not knowing, his anguish, loneliness, and finally his guilt.

"I have come to find Lilya," he said at last.

She made a small noise, a sort of gasp, which was almost—but he could not believe this—a giggle. "I know, Refat, and I have been expecting you for many years now." She took another long drag on her cigarette and sighed deeply. She lifted her free hand and swept it through the air in exasperation, her palm upright as if questioning him.

"There have been many times when I thought I saw you coming around the corner, or standing in the distance, watching and wondering. After you left, I thought many times over the course of the first year of your absence that any moment you would knock on my door and demand to know Lilya's whereabouts. And I would not have told you, as you would never have understood. I went over and over again in my mind how I would not tell you, how I would refuse, and would slam the door in your face. But you never came, and I thought perhaps you had met your fate, until I realized that you would never come—from fear of knowing, or ignorance that I could know, I've no idea. Then, nearly ten years ago, I began to expect you. I thought by now the wounds might have healed, and I heard bits and pieces of your doings and so on, and so I knew you had married, and I knew that you had a life for yourself now in Tashkent. I thought that the past would resurface for you, as it has done in my life, make you relive things you thought you had forgotten. I thought you would have to confront Lilya's disappearance for your own peace of mind, and that I could no longer hold to my intentions because Lilya would want you to know by now what she was doing before she disappeared." She tapped her cigarette in the ashtray, and took a last drag before putting it out. Refat sat silent again and could not think what to say. He could not allow his emotion to swell up, but it did, and he could not fight it back. He suddenly looked at her fiercely and pounded his fist on the table.

"I am already an old man, and do not have many years left on this earth," he gasped, then caught his breath. "I am going home, but I cannot go without knowing what past I have left behind."

"After all these years," she said and shook her head, neither asking nor exclaiming, just stating, as if commenting to herself. "All these years, and you want to know where she is." She pushed the ashtray away from her, and brought her hand to her eyes. Her eyes were red with tears, but just one trickled down her cheek and she wiped it away with her sleeve.

"I do not know, Refat," she shrugged. "I do not know where Lilya is now." She stopped herself at that and sighed, raising her eyes to the ceiling. "You know," she cleared her throat, "When Nikolai returned from the camps, I simply forgot it. Really. I just wanted it all put behind me ... we had only the desire to live out our days together in peace, and he did not wish to speak any longer of the past. But since you are here ...

"She went with the shamaness of my people. Wait"—Sumai put her hand up to stop Refat from interrupting. "If you want the truth you must hear it out, no matter how absurd it may sound to you. Yes, your suspicions were correct—they met through me. I know you did not entirely approve of our acquaintance, I accept it now as I did then. But, Refat, you must know that Lilya needed me. Her marriage was to be loveless, there were no children to look after, no family at all to spend time with."

"We were both looking for something," Refat said. "I hoped to find it with her, one day."

"You are a good man, and you were then, but you could not have given it to her. Don't give yourself a hard time. She was looking for something bigger than life, you see, and she could not possibly find it in another human being. The shamaness, Tilgar, asked me to bring Lilya to her; she saw into her soul and knew she needed guidance on the path. So I helped."

"The path? What path?"

"The path home, Refat. To discover her inner world. Some people seek it, others do not. Lilya had opened a channel in herself, I guess you could say. An idea, that there was more to life than *her* life, had become a longing—and where there exists desire, there exists magnetism. She drew truth toward her. Tilgar saw that a revelation was heading her way, and appointed herself guide."

"I don't understand."

"It doesn't matter. The one who needs to understand will understand."

"What do you mean by that?"

"I mean you will remember what I say, and tell someone one day who will know better what to do with my words. Just remember: desire for wisdom attracts wisdom. In this equation, space and time do not matter, for truth will find the way to the person who desires it. Don't fret over my words. What you need to know is simply that Lilya was restless, and wanted meaning in her life, and Tilgar asked me to help her. So we became friends, and I introduced her to Tilgar. They began to go for walks together."

"Lilya just trusted her, and you, just like that? It was that easy for her?"

"She was obviously comfortable."

Refat let that thought sink in. He was becoming more agitated because he could not comprehend what it was, exactly, Lilya had sought. He could only imagine it was like what he had sought in Natasha—the bliss of love for love's sake. Thinking of it made him uncomfortable. He hadn't thought of it in so long, he'd tried to forget it, had in many ways banished from his mind what had passed between him and Natasha, except in his dreams.

Of course, he had had those dreams. And what had Lilya had, but life?

"She wanted meaning," Refat said, to clarify.

"She found it, I suspect," Sumai responded.

"You're saying that she went away with Tilgar? Do you think she might still be alive?"

"I doubt it. Lilya disappeared into thin air. So the rumor went, so the truth went. My people found nothing."

Refat slammed his fist into the table.

"So no one saw anything! No one has heard anything! You don't know any more than me!"

"On the contrary, I know much more, because I do not count simply what people have seen and heard with their five senses."

Refat calmed down, looked guiltily at his fist. He rubbed his knuckles.

"What do you know, Sumai?"

"Before I tell you, may I ask you why you have come to me, after all this time, to find out?"

"I should have thought to ask you before, but I did not think you would know, or maybe I was afraid she had escaped the settlement somehow, as the authorities determined—that she had left me. I only recently began to think of Lilya again. She has been intruding into my thoughts. Sometimes it is as if she is standing behind me, and I turn around and of course she is not there, but I feel her. It is strange. Like being haunted. And I kept thinking of you, your face, your voice, and it is strange. I never thought you knew something, but I started to think, maybe you did.

"My life has changed much recently. I returned to Crimea with my wife four years ago. I am lucky to have cousins who returned immediately after the collapse, and they had bought a house when there were still houses to buy, before everyone returned and there was such a shortage—so we have a place to live with them. My children, who are grown and married, are moving to Crimea now. We went before them. We were more eager to return, I suppose. It is a hard life there for Crimean Tatars. Not much housing, no sympathy ... we have nothing there but a homeland. I have begun to work with a charity to help my people. It keeps me busy. My wife is busy growing vegetables in our garden, and making cakes—all to sell at the market for extra money. The charity I work for has funding from America, and I am going to New York soon to visit our sponsors and try to get more money. I know that when I return from New York I will work in Crimea until I die, and that I won't have another chance to come here, so I decided to come and put my mind to rest."

"You have not wasted your time. As I said, I have been expecting you. I have a feeling about things, too, and you have been intruding on my thoughts. I wish you well. Your people still have a hope to have a homeland in this world; the hope of my people is in another world.

"My people have always had legends about this other world, and always had premonitions about the destruction that would come to us if we stayed in this one. Much of it has come true, since the Bolsheviks. There was a prophecy that a shaman would lead us from this world to the other, and many expected Tilgar to do it. Many still do. When she disappeared, many said that she had left to go to that other world and prepare the way for us. No one, at that time, had any explanation for Lilya, whom we knew was Tilgar's companion that day.

"Only a few years ago was Lilya mentioned again. From time to time our shamans take foreigners as apprentices, not for long, and we tend not to pay them much notice. Lilya was not one of us, you see, so it was taken for granted that her whereabouts held no significance for us. Then our present-day shaman walked between worlds and found Tilgar and Lilya. They said they were sending someone called the Dreamer, a shaman to guide our people out."

Sumai got up to put the kettle on the stove as Refat sat, stunned. How could he possibly respond to this? It was the most preposterous story he had ever heard. Yet somehow, it was also compelling. Sumai was certainly serious; she went about making their pot of tea as if shamans and portals and other worlds were the most natural phenomena on Earth.

"So what does that mean about Lilya?" Refat asked.

"I was, once—at that time—apprenticed to Tilgar, and she told me that in the hills there existed a portal between worlds that one day her spirit animal would lead her to, and that she would journey to the other world and return to take her people back with her. I told no one that she felt close to finding that place, ever, as I had given her my word. Lilya went with Tilgar that day; that much I know, as I saw them leave together. When Tilgar and Lilya never came back, I suspected they had gone through the portal. Perhaps they stumbled upon it by accident.

Perhaps Lilya blindly followed Tilgar. Such things do not matter. When our shaman told us he had met them in his journey, I knew."

"You mean to say he went through the portal and came back?" Refat asked.

"No, he did so out of body. But our peoples' prophecy promises us the ultimate salvation—to leave this world in body. Tilgar and Lilya evidently took their bodies. I do not feel they will return, Refat, but I have hoped that in knowing where she is, you can have some peace."

Refat could formulate no more questions, and nothing else Sumai said that day helped clarify for him what might have happened to Lilya. In fact, the more he listened to Sumai, the weaker her spell grew, until at last Refat felt only that he had stumbled into a foolish fairy tale told by a foolish woman, that it was not to be believed by anyone, least of all himself. Never mind that Sumai's tale was adventurous, emotional, and therefore compelling in its own way, as fiction goes. He thanked her for her information and they parted on good, if enigmatic terms: she told him that he should not be shy in telling others of her peoples' prophecy, because even if he couldn't make sense of it, someone else would, and so it was meant to be.

To his mind the only preordained thing was to go home. Back to Crimea he went, his final journey home from the land of his exile. Lilya had probably stumbled and died in the hills, Refat decided, along with the shamaness. Acting at last on his curiosity and seeking out information had made a definitive answer unnecessary. It was not truth Refat sought, but closure.

First with Lilya, then with Natasha.

When he had learned he would spend several months in New York he knew he would have to find Natasha in person. He had tracked her down through a mutual acquaintance, a Russian woman he had met in Crimea.

He began his meeting with Natasha by recounting his visit with Sumai. He meant to break through the layers, familiar and passionate ones alike, that had grown between them over the years. To reach their hearts once again.

Because he had really come to Natasha to tell her something else.

First, that after decades together he did love his wife and was grateful to her for giving him children, a family—the roots which anchored him so strongly in his community and now his homeland. Second, that Natasha would always be an indelible part of his life, even if only in his memory. To sanctify his marriage and family life, he would remain a loyal husband and father until he took his very last breath. To sanctify his love for Natasha he would bare his soul aloud to her for the first time ever and tell her: I loved you then, I love you now, and I know in my heart that time will not change this fact—I will suffer our love for the rest of my days.

41

By the time Natasha finishes recounting Refat's story I am moved to tears.

"What did you say to Refat?" I ask her, wiping my eyes dry with my sleeve.

"I thanked him," she says. She is calm and dry-eyed. I can see that she is elsewhere, floating in her memories. I want to ask, "Do you still love him, too? Did you tell him so?"

But no, I don't want to ask. I'm satisfied to wonder because I could never voice such thoughts. I don't want Natasha to have to answer, because maybe—it is possible—she doesn't know the answer herself.

"Has he left?"

"Yes. He's gone. I don't imagine we'll meet again."

She is unexpressive. The football game is over. She flips the channel to some black and white movie.

"The prophecy!" I exclaim, as it has just hit me what Sumai told Refat. "I understand!"

"You what?" Natasha asks. I think I might have drawn her too abruptly out of the reverie of Refat's words.

"Why did you tell me about Lilya? Before you began you said you kept thinking you ought to tell me, but why? Because Refat was coming, and you had to share your story, you said, to relieve the weight of memory. But why me? And then you end up telling me what Refat said and what Sumai told him. She told him he might not understand it, but that her explanation would make sense to someone else. And she said that when there is a desire for truth, the desire is like a magnet that draws truth toward it, regardless of space or time. I'm sure Sam told me that too. Or maybe he just hinted at it …"

"Who?"

"Sam, a friend of mine."

"I didn't think you had friends. I'm glad I was wrong."

Natasha is fully back now, wearing a smirk.

"You weren't wrong. I just met him. Maybe I was meant to meet him, and I was meant to hear your story about Lilya, and Refat, and Sumai—I think I'm looking for truth, you see, and truth found me!"

"You've gone mad. Do you need a cigarette? I need one. It's all gone to your head. Why are you smiling like that, Catherine? Come here."

I go to sit next to Natasha, and she pulls me toward her, plants a big kiss on my forehead.

"You look happy, dear, that's all that matters," she says to me.

"Thank you, Natasha, for telling me all this. You have no idea what it's done for me."

"Thank you for listening. I don't know what you're going on about, but maybe you don't either. Never mind. When you figure it out you can tell your granddaughter. Or better, you can figure it out by telling your granddaughter."

Natasha seems to come into focus as I hear those words, as if before she'd been fuzzy and faded—or I had not been looking at her properly. Is that what telling her story has done for her? Helped her figure out her life, made sense of things? What, exactly, has she made sense of?

Natasha gets up and goes to her bedroom. I follow her, half-watching her, half-giddy with excitement about what happens to me next. I know what I will do now; I must go to Sam and tell him that it's true, about the prophecy.

"It's good to have ended things on these terms," she says. She takes a pack of cigarettes out of the drawer of her bedside table. "At last you've got a sparkle in your eye, my dear, for whatever reason."

I wonder how she feels now—is it as if the weight of her life is finally off her shoulders, is heavy in her hands like a novel worn with age and read and re-read—something she can put aside now for good?

I think that must be true. She looks very tired, but still there is a clearness about her that is not just due to my finally seeing her properly, her past and all. She exudes quiet, calm, equilibrium.

Natasha takes the picture of Andrew from her bedside table and clasps it to her chest. She gazes at it and runs her fingers over the surface. Then she puts it in its place, and she closes her eyes.

42

It has been a month now since my last vision of Lilya's life, when I learned how she disappeared. I still do not know where she went, if she survived, or what it was that actually happened to her. I would like to know—but I am not in a hurry. I no longer feel a need for some kind of self-completion via Lilya, not that I think I'm whole, but I feel more together than I can remember. My dearest possessions are still packed in the front closet, ready to go at the slightest sign of impending disaster. I don't expect disaster anymore, though. My nightmares have gone. I raided my cache of canned beans from the closet to make soup a week ago, and I have not replenished the supply yet.

On the other hand, I realize the extent to which I have lost control of my life. Okay, I know, at last, that I never had any control over it in the first place, that no one has control over life. This bit of wisdom may be obvious to the vast majority of the human race, and is therefore a pathetic revelation in my case, but at least it alleviates my urgency to know where Lilya went when she disappeared. I'll know when I know, if I ever know. In the meantime I plan to file away my research on the 21st Airborne, to clear my desk and put a potted plant where the papers have been piled up.

One other thing: like Lilya, I expect miracles. The unexpected and unexplained. I do not trust my day-to-day reality. At any moment it might shift and change, even disappear, and I might find myself God-knows-where, in an altered state of consciousness.

I have no idea what any of it means, whether there is a God, or if I have a soul, or a destiny, but life sure is a lot more interesting.

Sam appears on my doorstep, but this time I am expecting him. I slipped him my telephone number during Ben Jamison's lecture, and—surprise, surprise—he actually called me last night to confirm he could come by this morning. For once, I feel ready to meet. I have just had a shower and made coffee—and—this is fairly new—I am looking forward to the day.

"Coffee is ready," I tell him as I open the door. "I'm glad to see you, Sam."

I've drawn him a map of where Lilya and Tilgar disappeared. It is crude, the landmarks are almost fifty years old and derived from my memory-visions, but I believe it is accurate, and will help. I hand it to him with his coffee.

"Have you remembered? Where they went?" Sam asks me straightaway. I like that we don't have to engage in small talk, even if he doesn't ever come on lightly.

"No. But I have some confirmation of your theories."

I tell him what Natasha recounted to me about what Refat learned in Uzbekistan. I leave out the part when Sumai told Refat that truth always finds the way to the person who desires it, since I believe that Sumai was referring to me.

Sam becomes very excited, and says, "See! They *did* go to another world! Only, I'm not sure what that means—another planet, or dimension …"

"I suppose. But, Sam, don't you think it's curious that I can't remember what happened after Lilya got there? Perhaps she did die."

Sam is suddenly serious. "Maybe you're not supposed to remember."

"Who says?"

"That part of you that recalls your entire identity, not just Catherine in this life. I believe that our experience of reality in body is just a tiny part of who we really are, but it is as if in this dimension, in a physical body with a physical brain, we simply cannot contain our entire selves, so we experience part of it. But that other part is aware of *you*, and can guide you."

"Or withhold information? Really, Sam, let's just put aside for a moment the metaphysics of it all and assume that you're right, that there is a part of me that doesn't want me to remember what I experienced as Lilya. Why? Isn't *that* the important question?"

"In my experience, we only know as much as will help us at any point in time. Remember how I've told you that once I met another aspect of myself? Well it was actually my future self—"

"It was your future self?"

Sam smiles. "I know it sounds strange, but bear with me."

"Sorry. Go on."

"It was a part of my consciousness that, how do I put it, that sees me as its smallest, most ignorant envoy in this world we live in. It was—or at least appeared to be—an older version of me to guide me—"

I only have to give him a look for him to stop and say to me, "You should be getting used to strange things happening by now, Catherine, or should I call you Lilya?"

I give him a wan smile. True enough. "Yes, but," I remind him, "just because I believe **one** thing …"

"I know, you are very practical and logical, and that is a very good quality to have. I'm not asking you to believe me, just to listen and decide what you think. When I met this future me, call him what you will, he told me a few things about my journey in life. At the time he appeared I wasn't doing too bad. But I hadn't been doing so well earlier. I was not a particularly happy child and my teenage years in particular were not pleasant. Suffice to say, a lot of bad stuff had already happened when my future self appeared. You'd think I would have needed some guidance then, right, when I was really struggling? I mean, this future me has always existed, so why not come back when the bad stuff was happening? Then I realized that I wasn't ready earlier. I had to do a bit of living, first, a bit of processing, or else I wouldn't have been open to having any sort of guidance—I was too wrapped up in my own emotions, trapped in my head. Since then I've come to believe that I will only know as much as will be useful to me at any point in time, and I don't question why.

"Think about it, Catherine. You didn't remember Lilya's life until this year, yet some part of you has known it, and all of it, your entire life. Do you think there is a reason for that?"

"I see what you're saying," I say. I stand up, intending to have a moment to myself, to think about what he's said. "I'm going to make myself another coffee. Do you want one?"

"No thanks."

I notice Sam's eyes follow me, alert to my every movement. It is unnerving.

I purposefully linger, my back to Sam. For some reason I keep thinking of something Susan always said to me. "When you're ready you'll understand," she told me whenever I demanded an explanation for something she didn't believe I could comprehend. It irritated me. When I'm ready for what? Enlightenment? Actually, something not too dissimilar; in her words, "When you are ready to put yourself in someone else's place, and that requires emotional maturity." She said that after the one time she grounded me (I was fifteen and had stayed out with Elisa until three AM without calling—I'd forgotten). She also told me I'd understand when I'm ready when I asked her why she needed some kind of religious practice, and why, when I was sixteen, I shouldn't read *Anna Karenina*. I read it anyway, and was mildly entertained. I re-read it during my final year in college, and cried.

She had also told me I would understand when I'm ready why she could die so graciously. I'm not ready yet, I guess.

"Lots of things have happened this year," I tell Sam, "with my mother dying, me quitting my PhD, getting to know my grandmother, then Lilya, then you. I suppose you could say that this experience of remembering Lilya has come at a time when I am ready for something different in my life, some kind of change. A bit like your experience maybe."

Sam says maybe so. I return to my seat. I am buzzing from the caffeine, but I keep drinking coffee. Must be nerves.

"There's something I haven't mentioned yet," I preface my confession, "because up until lately I have been trying hard to ignore complications in my life. There is this spot in my backyard which is kind of ... weird. Anyway, I saw Victor there the other day. I spoke with him."

Sam's eyes widen to attention. "Just in that spot? Is that where you saw him before?"

"Yes. I've known the spot was there for some time, but I never had the courage to stand there very long before. I mean, long enough to wait and see what would happen."

"What did Victor say?" Sam asks. There is no pretense of surprise or wonderment, as if I always speak to dead people in my backyard.

"That you're on the right track."

"Good to know. And you?"

"What do you mean?"

"You know what I mean."

I choose not to respond. I'd like to be on the right track, if there is one.

Sam asks, "Has it happened to you before, finding a powerful point on a ley line?"

"You think it's a ley line?" It's not really a question, since I have suspected that is exactly what that spot is. "Yes," I admit. "It has. Once on a hill in Yugoslavia when I was seventeen. By accident. I had been avoiding the place all night but I was with a friend and we'd been drinking."

"What happened?"

It was similar to what Lilya experienced, I tell Sam. I've never really analyzed the experience before now.

"Exactly the same?" Sam asks.

"No, not exactly. In Yugoslavia I felt myself disappear. It was like I was passing out. I got weak in the knees and then—I was not *me* anymore ..."

"Who were you?"

"I was ... it sounds so weird. It doesn't make sense. I have never tried to put words to it before."

"Go on, try." He is trying not to smile, I can see that. He is excited, and why shouldn't he be? Of course it is fascinating for him, and exciting; this is his journey in life, after all. He could find the place where Lilya and Tilgar disappeared and have the same experience!

"I was everything. For a moment I was—everything."

Sam says nothing. I have never dared wonder what would have happened had I stayed there longer; at the time I feared I might simply cease to exist, and Lilya's memory does not give me reason to think otherwise.

"And then?" Sam asks.

"I got scared."

"Nothing else happened?"

"I tried to move away, and I almost couldn't, it was too hard."

I find myself tearing up. Thankfully Sam is a gentleman, he distracts himself with stirring the dregs at the bottom of his cup. After a moment he reaches out his hand, and looks like he's about to touch mine.

"Catherine," Sam looks me in the eye. "I don't suppose you'd come with me to Uzbekistan? To help me find the portal."

"You don't need me," I say. "You've got the map. You'll find it on your own. I don't want to be there, Sam, in my past. I've been there for many months now. I think I should have a break before my next big vision." I laugh. "Those are words I never thought I'd hear myself say. Anyway, I can't leave Natasha. I'm all she's got now. And I need her too. She's a good friend, the best friend I could have, isn't that funny? Lilya has changed everything in my life."

"But you need to do something with this gift you have," he says. "Finding places. Ley lines."

"Do you think it's a gift? I'm not sure what it is. I feel like I've just ended my life and am beginning another one. I don't know what the hell to do with it! Maybe it doesn't matter."

"Write down your dreams," Sam says.

"Write me," I tell him.

Then he says he has to go, to catch a bus.

We feel unfinished, like a half-eaten meal we're running out on, but I don't know what to do about it, and I guess, neither does he. I offer to help him plan his travel—he'll need a visa, money, an interpreter—but he doesn't seem concerned about all that. He says he'll manage it all and tells me to get on with my life. He says he's found work in Maine for the winter at a warehouse packing clothes for mail order catalogues, and that when he has money he'll leave for Uzbekistan, probably by the next spring. He leaves no contact details. He promises to write me, and makes me promise him that I'll write down my dreams, and visions.

43

I think I'm asleep, but I'm not sure. First I'm in my bed, at night. In my bedroom, where I've slept for the past two weeks now.

My eyes droop shut. I think of Lilya, of Tilgar, and remember the falling. Then there is a rush and I am enveloped in white light that swirls and closes around me and carries me until,

I land. I am within a column of light, and then, slowly

things come into focus:
a vast expanse of lawn, trees, a hedge with a border of flowers, a cottage—
still it is all fuzzy....

A woman walks toward me and helps me up. She is dressed in a mauve dress with peculiar braids hanging from her sleeves at the shoulder and a necklace I can see as she leads me to the porch at the cottage. A small yellow stone resting on her throat, a rosy-gold chain high on her neck. It is not a stone I know. It reflects the light like a prism, blinds me when the sun catches it.

She eases me onto a chaise lounge. I am confused; something is not quite right. I am having a hard time remembering what happened. I was on the rocks with Tilgar, and ran and fell.

"What happened?" I ask the woman. She is beautiful and reassuring. She takes my hand.

"You fell, my darling Faewyn. Rosalind will bring you a cup of farwood shortly. It's just a side effect of—"

Her face goes ashen and she brings out a fan and begins to fan her face.

"A side effect of what?" I ask. "Where am I?"

"Oh, dear," the woman says, and looks about to cry. "Rosalind! The brew!"

"Say it!" I command, thinking to myself, a side effect of falling?—I cannot remember falling now. I was with that old woman, going for a walk. Now where were we walking? I look around me. There is a lawn, flat and green, and faraway a hedge with purple flowers. There are no hills. Should there be hills, I wonder? I thought I had been walking in hills.

"I was going for a walk …" I begin. The woman takes my hand.

"Yes, dear, you were, and you simply passed out."

"I—I did?"

The memory is returning. I was coming back from the distillery behind the property, when I saw an old woman—who said something strange to me. No … that's not it.

I was carrying a flask back from the distillery, for our lunch, when everything began to swirl, and then there was a man—

I cannot make sense of it.

"Varsan found you," the woman says, "and helped you here."

"Who?"

"Oh, dear. It will come back in a moment."

The woman holding my hand now is called Nell. I know her.

"Something strange is happening," I tell Nell. "I seem to remember something else." I don't know what I remember. Running, an old woman, there were rocks, I'm sure of it.

I say, "I was where the hill is."

"Oh, Faewyn," Nell cries. "You must be remembering the hills of your childhood home. You must have had a vision when you passed out. How do you feel?"

I feel weak, numb. My joints ache. I ache all over.

"I'm sick, aren't I?" I ask, the realization dawning on me.

"Yes, darling."

"Is this a side effect? This forgetfulness?"

"Yes, of the medication, to take away the pain. The doser explained it to you after your treatment yesterday, but you were not fully conscious at the time."

"What else did he say? Do I have much time left?"

I have to know; suddenly there is an urgency about it. I have known for some time that I am dying, but a doser's opinion is practically law. He has been treating my condition for years. If he says how long I'll live, it is because his experience has proven it.

"He says you have some time," she says.

I won't press her. Less than a zodiacal cycle, more than a few moons is my guess; otherwise Nell would come across as either more optimistic or she would be behaving as if we were in a state of emergency. As it is she is calm, calming, merely sad.

Rosalind comes out with a tray bearing my farwood brew. I sit up to drink. I am fully restored to my senses. Even my mood is much better now. I love these women, these aunts who are my family. They will feed me lunch and we will while away the afternoon in the garden with the kittens Rosalind just brought home from market, and if the pain returns they will administer the potions and lay their hands on me.

The potions help the pain; it fools this disease that would otherwise cripple me. So my illness can spread without much more discomfort, even if the price is a tendency to pass out and a lingering forgetfulness.

Not much longer now.

Rosalind pins her waist-length hair back and sweeps it up into a cachement. She looks so pretty with her hair upswept, it sets off her cheekbones; I know that is how Jerind likes it best. She is meeting him later tonight. I predict they will be married by the time of my passing.

I have no husband, no children, no parents, so by rights, by the standards of this society, I should have no regrets about going Home. Still, this world holds much loveliness. It is hard to imagine how the next could be even better, but so the Shaman has promised me. He would know. He has walked between many different worlds, and come back to tell us of them.

I see him now, and call out, "Varsan! Thank you for helping me!"

It is not the first time he has found me when I have passed out during one of my walks. His workshop adjoins this property, so he is always in the vicinity.

Varsan has taken a special interest in my decline—he cannot make me better, but he eases my fears and teaches me to forgive my suffering. I am lucky. It is not often an Elder, much less a High Shaman, performs balms for a laywoman. He will help me cross over when I leave body.

"We have done it, my dear," he says, climbing the steps, kneeling by my side. "We have crossed into this world."

I do not know what he means. I assume my forgetfulness has gotten worse, and merely nod. It is a warm day and Varsan is perspiring. His long black hair is pulled back off his neck and his cape has slipped off his shoulders.

His triangle amulet glimmers in the light.

"Catherine!" a voice shouts. I turn. I open my eyes. I am in the garden. Who is that calling me?

"Catherine! I'm calling you back!" he shouts.

I know I am dreaming. I've never had this feeling before, lucidity within a dream. It is peculiar: I am unafraid, uncautious, calm, expectant, and I *know* things.

I know it is Victor's voice; I know he has something important to tell me; I know I will remember it when I wake up.

"You're right," he says. He is standing in front of me, cradling my cat like a baby. Pinky is unnaturally placid, legs splayed upward in Victor's arms. She is purring as he strokes her stomach and chest.

"About what?" I ask him.

"You were Lilya in a past life, and you were Faewyn."

"I was?"

"Actually, you *are*. And you are Catherine; you are all those people, all at once. Your consciousness, that is. It spans time and worlds. It is like a house with many rooms, and one day, you will remember what it is to inhabit the entire house at once. Right now you can only get your head around one room at a time."

"But that woman, who was dying, Faewyn—"

"She is in another world altogether."

"But—" I begin, "Another world? When, after Lilya disappeared?"

I have trouble grabbing hold of my thoughts; they are fleeting. I feel I should not ask questions, but I speak over the silent urging of my conscience. I speak so that I remain lucid.

"That woman—Faewyn. She lived only a few months, didn't she? And when she died did I become Catherine?"

"In a manner of speaking. Your notion of space and time is deeply flawed. Time only exists when you are focused in your life. Life only exists as separate when you are focused on your personality. You are in past and present lives all at once. You are connected to Lilya and Faewyn and many others. You, Catherine, are like a strand of a giant web. If this is true, and it is, can you say in all honesty that you are only a strand, and not the entire web?—because you are connected; you cannot be separate; therefore it is a matter of perspective. Right now, you have the perception that your consciousness is focused on Catherine. Faewyn and Lilya have the perception that their consciousness is focused on their lives, but it is only perception."

"So Faewyn is living her life now? Even if I'm not focused on her?"

"That's right."

"But Lilya is long gone ..."

"In time, she existed in what is your past, but outside of time, you all exist as once."

"But she went through the portal."

"And slipped into another room of your shared consciousness, into Faewyn. Via your memory of her you were slipping into the same room, and I have called you back."

"Did Lilya die?"

"You mean her body?"

"I don't know what I mean!"

I sound frustrated, and I am, as well as overexcited, intellectually. Physically (if one can refer to this state in a dream), I am calm, still. Victor Tehusa raises an eyebrow. He finds my frustration amusing, I can tell. Pinky jumps down and lands at his feet.

"Her body, like your body, is a product of her reality. When she left her reality and went through the portal to another reality, her body ceased to exist, because she had one in the other reality. She was—you are—Faewyn."

I stare at him, blankly. Pinky comes to stand by me. She sits on my feet and rubs her face into my calf.

I ask him, "You said you were calling me back. Why should it matter if you call me back, if we are all one anyway?"

"Are you asking about destiny?" Victor asks. He folds his arms at his chest and gives a great belly laugh.

"I'm asking what the point is!" I say, sounding a bit angry. I'm not; I'm just impatient and straining to comprehend. I don't really understand any of it. I understand his words, the concepts even, but not their meaning. I want to know, who am I in all of this? *Who am I?*

Victor is patient. He has read my thoughts. "You are vastly more than you think you are. It seems complex, but that is only because from where you stand you have a limited perspective. Don't worry about that now. Consider this instead: there are states of mind, or places, that blur the boundaries between lives and worlds. It might be a dream, or it might be a powerful ley line that can serve as a passageway and you, Catherine, can find those passageways and journey into other people and places. You do not have the discipline yet, but you will.

"I called you back for the simple reason that it is time to be back here as Catherine, in this particular dream. Because, yes, you have a destiny. You could fulfill it as Faewyn, but you'll fulfill it more quickly as Catherine."

"What is it?" I ask.

"I have a destiny!" I think. There is a point to it all. There is a reason I have remembered Lilya and met Sam, not to mention Faewyn.

Victor grins. He is making me wait for the answer. A few seconds feel like eternity. Pinky jumps into my arm and I almost stumble backwards. This dream is so real. Pinky is so warm. Victor's eyes really sparkle, he is so solid, his hair so black. I can see his pores if I look closely. I have all the patience in the world now. It is the ultimate question and the answer will repair whatever has been damaged in my life. It will seal my future; it will make sense of the past and the present. It will give my life meaning.

Victor puts a hand on my shoulder. It is heavy and hot. He licks my ear.

"Wake up!" he says.

Pinky is sitting on my shoulder and licking my ear, then my chin, my neck. Her hot, meaty breath does no one any good, especially me, especially at this time of the morning.

"Get off!" I snap, pushing her off the bed.

It was a dream?

Imagine that, my destiny is to wake up to Pinky cleaning my face with her smelly, prickly tongue. It should be amusing.

But I'm not laughing.

It was *not* just a dream.

Or did I wake from one into another?

The next morning I call directory assistance in Maine and ask for the number of any company that sells clothes mail order, so that I can find the warehouse where Sam is working. The operator chuckles at my vagueness and tells me to contact the Chamber of Commerce. After some research and more phone calls I locate a few warehouses.

None of them have heard of Sam Hunter. I guess I'll have to wait until he writes me, then I can tell him about my dream. If anyone has something helpful to say about it, I expect it will be the Dreamer.

Was it my own subconscious or Victor who told me to wake up, and was that—to wake up—the answer to my question?

44

That night, I go stand outside again. There is a full moon. The air is still. It is cold, and silent, and I feel truly alone. I stand in the spot. I have worn the grass down here, just a bit, or at least it feels like I've made a slight groove in which my feet fit perfectly. The ground is solid, so solid it takes me by surprise when I enter that strange space where light moves like dust, except it is dark now so only the shadows move as I sway, holding on to myself in the moonlight when dizziness takes me.

"So is it all fabulous there, mom, as fabulous as it was when you were alive?" I ask.

She doesn't have to be there, I suppose. Maybe there are many places one can go, as many dimensions as there are people to go there. Still, it doesn't seem quite fair, that I should see this in-between place, see the unfathomable, and not her.

"It's not that you didn't have any wisdom then," I tell her, if she's there, somewhere, listening. "It's just, I couldn't get to it through my anger. You weren't very good at dealing with hard things, and I guess I wasn't very good at having faith in good things. I'm better now. I'm going to try harder from now on, too. I'm going to be spontaneous, like you were. I'm going to Fiji for an entire month, to some resort with three swimming pools, one of which has an in-pool bar. Now that's pretty good for the daughter you knew, isn't it?"

My voice seems to echo, as if I'm not outside at all but in a room with tall ceilings. It just makes me feel more alone that my voice comes back to me. It has nowhere to go, because I'm not really here, standing in the backyard, looking toward the oak tree and the pond. I'm not really there, either, in that other dimension. I'm nowhere.

I don't really expect my mother to be here. I don't really feel that she is. I believe, though, that wherever she is, however her life is continuing, she hears me.

I say, just for the record, "I miss you, Mom."

978-0-595-42549-5
0-595-42549-6

Printed in the United States
85877LV00003B/232-234/A